THIS IS

My Church

ISBN: 978-1-7635380-3-0

Book Cover by Maria @ Steamy Designs

Edited by Kath @ Copy by Kath

NEWSLETTER

Subscribe to my newsletter via sashaavice.com for regular updates on WIPs, new releases, and thoughts on writing.

You'll receive two free novellas upon sign up.

Just want the books? No dramas: hit unsubscribe after you've downloaded them.

This one's for my Monster

1

♥

"**Y**OU'VE GOT A NEW friend," Cary said.

"Huh?" Lacy lifted his head from where he was bent over tying his shoe laces and followed Cary's gaze.

Thad—their new ruckman—was coming out of the showers; he'd paused on his way to his locker to listen to something Les was saying. His eyes were kind as he leaned down, something of the older brother in the way he addressed Les with a deep murmur, in the way he maintained a propriety and polite distance between them even though he was only twenty-three to Les' nineteen.

"Whaddyamean?" Lacy replied and returned to his shoes.

"You haven't noticed he sits wherever you sit? Like a little shadow," Cary said and sprayed his body in long bursts with heavy deodorant. Lacy had no idea how his wife put up with him, his smell announced his presence a mile before he entered a room and lingered for a month, he was sure of it.

Lacy kept tying his laces, but his eyes lifted to watch Thad chuckling at something Les was saying. At six foot ten inches, Thad was hardly little. But Lacy could agree Thad was around him. There was a reason for that.

"Yeah, 'cos Finn used to sit there," Lacy sat back. He ran both hands along the side of his head and decided to go see his barber. He had to get the mullet looking good for Finn and George's wedding.

"I don't recall Finn trailing around after you like a little lost puppy," Cary nudged Lacy's shoulder with his hip.

"I dunno know where you're gettin' 'little' from, he's built like a very tall tree," Lacy glanced up at Cary.

"Who's built like a tree?" Thad asked. He moved so quietly Lacy hadn't realised he was back at his locker on the other side of Lacy's, the locker Finn had vacated.

Lacy looked up the expanse of his torso. Droplets of perspiration burst around the divots of his abs and chest underneath the trickle of water from the shower. He had the body of an athlete, but not the sharp lines of Finn; defined but not cut. His brown eyes were crinkling at the corners as he looked down at Lacy, his expression warm.

"You are," Lacy said. He stood and knocked his bicep against Thad's pectoral muscle, the dampness leaving a mottled pattern on his sleeve.

Thad tilted his head to the side, smiled. "I guess I am."

Lacy laughed. "Alright, well, as stimulating as this conversation is," he looked between Thad and Cary, "I'm outta here, got shit to do."

"What're you up to?" Thad asked as he got busy drying his hair with the towel from around his neck. He rubbed his hair before dropping the towel on the bench and reaching for his necklace. He slipped it over his head, ran his fingers down the chain, turning the cross to face the right way below his throat. The white briefs with the Y-front were next. He had a habit of sliding them up his thighs and over his ass under the towel before reaching for his shorts, only letting the towel drop once the shorts were at his waist, his long fingers fastening them over the bulge of his underwear, the white disappearing under the navy shorts. Not everyone was as shameless with their nudity as Lacy was—he'd strip in front of his locker and walk naked to the showers, using only one towel as he came out to dry his hair, his body as bare as it could get given he was covered in tattoos on his torso, throat, back, arms and legs, only the skin of his ass and groin a shock of white skin, his cock hanging below his trimmed pubic hair. But even the shyest amongst them, like Les, dropped the towel and let their dick and ass see the room when they got dressed. Lacy knew it wasn't self-consciousness about his size that made Thad hide himself—Lacy had seen him in the shower and could attest the monster he'd seen in his training leggings was as thick and long as the outline promised. He wasn't checking him out, guys just noticed these things, and a size queen like Lacy could appreciate them like an art collector could covet a painting he'd never be able to afford to buy.

"Shopping," Lacy answered his question. He lifted his hand and began to count. "Lunch. Gonna see if the barber can fit me in. More shopping."

"You want some company?" Thad asked. He was focused on rearranging his cross under his shirt. Lacy felt Cary's eyes on him, he glanced over. Cary raised both eyebrows, his expression saying, *See, I told you*. Lacy shrugged.

"Course," he refocused on Thad. "But we're leaving right now."

"Oh, sorry, just let me—"

Lacy cracked up. "I'm joking, man, take your time."

Thad sat down and got his shoes on quickly, his big shoulders rolling with his deft movements, his breaths audible over the slamming of lockers, the conversations about the first week back at training, plans for the Christmas break, the loose plans being made to coordinate flights and share accommodation for Finn and George's wedding.

As they made their way out of the locker room, Lacy thought about what Cary had said. He felt Thad's presence at his back, looming over him but maintaining a polite distance.

"After you," Lacy said theatrically as he held the door open for him.

Thad thanked him, brown eyes warm over his smile.

Lunch, in Lacy's world, was a pub near the stadium. He told Thad to take a seat and went up to get them some beers.

"Orange juice is fine," Thad replied.

"No drinking during training? Fair enough," Lacy said with a nod.

He came back with their drinks and a menu, slid into his seat at the table they'd commandeered in a dark corner near the back of the place. The bar staff knew him, held the table for him. Lacy was all for talking to fans, but he preferred to eat in peace when he could.

Thad sipped his juice but didn't look at the menu. He was fidgeting with the corner of it.

"I don't drink," he said at the same time as Lacy said, "I always get the burger special with real fries."

"Sorry," Thad smiled. He was hunched down like he was trying to conceal his build. "You go."

"Whaddyamean you don't drink? Like, at all?" Lacy asked.

"No, never," Thad smiled apologetically, his soft hair was damp and hung in wavy curls around his face and neck.

"Why?"

Thad sat back, his smile turning surprised. "No one's ever asked like that."

"Like what?"

"Just come out and asked," Thad nodded approvingly. "I abstain," he said like that was a sufficient explanation. Lacy thought it explained absolutely nothing, but before he could ask, Thad said he would try the burger if Lacy recommended it and they moved on.

After lunch, Lacy said he needed to go clothes shopping. Thad readily agreed but then didn't select anything for himself. He seemed content to wait and comment as Lacy came in and out of the dressing room, trying various summer pants and shirt combinations to compliment his wardrobe for the Byron Bay trip. He had a suit for the wedding, but he wanted something stylish for the week when they'd inevitably go for lunches and dinners, for when he'd lose the guys for the night and go find what else he needed.

"You're not gonna buy anything?" he asked after Thad had confirmed Lacy looked good in the latest button-up he'd put on, a Hawaiian shirt with cat faces instead of flowers inside the leaves. The guy running the place said he could get it custom made with Lacy's own cat, but he didn't have a cat. His mum did though, so he was thinking about it.

"No, I don't really buy clothes," Thad replied with an easy shrug.

Lacy was looking himself up and down in the mirror, but he stopped and observed Thad in the reflection. Thad was fiddling with the hangers. He was dressed in a nice pair of navy shorts, a white polo shirt, his sunnies tucked in the collar, the silver of his chain visible under the popped top button. The outfit wasn't designer, just basic streetwear at least a few seasons old.

"You've obviously bought clothes at some point in your life," Lacy said.

Thad chuckled, his fingers flicking through the racks. "Yes, of course, I just mean, I don't buy anything unless I need it."

"Frugal," Lacy nodded. He certainly wasn't, but he was on a monster contract and Thad wasn't. 'Serviceable' was the word that got bandied around when they got Thad in a trade from the Gold Coast. A Tasmanian ruckman who went fifty-fourth in the second round of the draft when he was twenty-one; he got the job done, but he wasn't going to light the place up any time soon. But he was cheap and his addition to the side freed Cary up to play ruck-forward to Thad's ruck, allowed for future plans to spend on another Finn, another Lacy.

Thad met his eyes in the mirror like he'd just realised Lacy was looking at him. He reiterated that the black pants that hugged Lacy's ass and Hawaiian shirt looked good. His eyes lingered for a moment on Lacy's lower half before firmly returning to thumb through women's blouses. Lacy grinned obnoxiously to hide the jolt in his stomach. He headed over to the counter to see about getting the shirt with his mum's cat on it.

By the time they got to Lacy's barber—who was happy to fit him in—and Thad begged off getting a cut himself even though his hair was too long and not in the way of someone growing it out, Lacy had to offer.

"I can shout you if you want?"

"Oh, no, that's fine. It's not the money, I'll get it cut when I'm back home next."

Lacy shook the hair off the gown as he stood. "You headin' back to Tassie for Christmas? Reckon your barber's gonna have his work cut out for him."

Lacy could get onboard with only wanting to use your own barber, even though most of the guys, other than Finn, gave him shit about that; but like they understood anything, they all looked like shit in the hair and fashion department. But Thad didn't look like he was as particular about his hair as Lacy was, as Finn was.

"I feel like you've just been watching me do shit all afternoon. You didn't need anything?" Lacy asked as he went up to pay, Thad trailing alongside him with his hands in his pockets, smiling good naturedly. He had an easy-going manner that at first Lacy had assumed was the forced politeness you had to wear in a new place. But as the afternoon wore on, he realised Thad was simply that easy in his own skin.

He shrugged. "I'm good, just felt like hanging out, getting to know the city."

Lacy paid, agreed with his barber the cut was amazing and he'd be back in a month for another trim. He hit the street with Thad in tow.

"If you wanna get to know the city, you shoulda said. I could make it more interesting than this," Lacy winked.

Thad ducked his head like he'd heard the stories of how interesting Lacy could make the city. "This is great," he replied, rolling his shoulders and looking around the people bustling up and down the street, the glass shop fronts.

Lacy shook his head but couldn't help smiling up at him.

"Would you like to come over for dinner?" Thad asked as they made their way back to the training centre to get their cars. "I could cook to say thanks."

"Fucking, for real?" Lacy asked.

Thad raised both eyebrows. "Umm, yes?"

Lacy searched Thad's expression with a sidelong look. He couldn't find anything weird in the request; it wasn't a euphemism, Thad seemed to be genuinely asking him over for dinner. What a strange guy.

"Fuck, why not?"

Thad beamed, the most animated expression Lacy had seen on his face so far. "I've had the slow cooker on all day."

Lacy wasn't sure what a slow cooker was, but when Thad said to follow him when they got to their cars, he did.

Lacy's first hint something was different about Thad was all the religious shit adorning the walls of his house. As they walked into the pokey entryway and Thad flicked the light on—one of those old lights hanging down on a chord in the middle of the hallway—the first thing that greeted him was Jesus on the cross. He was hanging above a side table where Thad placed his keys in a crystal bowl, toed his shoes off and invited Lacy to do the same. They proceeded down the hallway in their socks—old floorboards that really needed a polish—and Lacy saw more of it. Glowing Jesus with his hands spread, people in robes looking up at him. Jesus as a baby in some kind of shed with his parents and some goats around. More crosses. He followed Thad, taking it in, and entered the kitchen to the most heavenly smell as Thad flicked another old light on, the static crackling as the light buzzed to life and lit up more religious shit everywhere. He'd seen the cross Thad wore. He guessed it wasn't a fashion statement.

Thad glanced over his shoulder, "Take a seat," he said with a warm smile, his head inclining to the dining room beyond the kitchen.

"So," Lacy began after they'd eaten a stew with crusty bread and a glass of cordial each—legit fucking cordial, artificially sweetened but still, who drinks fucking cordial?—and it had been an incredibly good meal, but Lacy had to ask, "you're into church?"

Thad smiled, nothing ashamed in it, and nodded. "Yes."

Lacy glanced around the walls of the dining room—Jesus having a meal with some other dudes, more crosses, baby Jesus in his mum's lap. "It's a lot of crosses."

"The crucifixion," Thad replied as he started to clear their plates. "It's good to have the reminder."

"Well," Lacy leaned back in his chair, "mission accomplished."

Thad laughed. "Would you like coffee? I have some sweets as well if you like?"

"Nah, might head out, thanks though."

"Oh, of course," Thad smiled pleasantly, but something was amiss.

Lacy could hear him in the kitchen rinsing their plates and wondered if he'd committed some kind of social faux pas. He grew up in Frankston—a place so notorious for producing shit-kickers, they'd even written a song about them, which they were all super proud about—and dinner usually came out of the freezer with a side of coke until he was fourteen and then it was a side of beer. He felt like a walking social faux pas most of the time and most of the time it didn't bother him.

"Actually," he said when Thad came back in. Thad smiled politely, a question in his eyes as he reached for the salt and pepper shakers.

"Coffee sounds lit."

Thad's mouth stretched into a real smile. "I'll put the kettle on."

He went back into the kitchen and Lacy heard the click of the stove like he was using a real fucking kettle. Lacy looked around again.

This place was old. He wondered if Thad had bought it. Thad had been given a three-year contract and while this area was hardly Toorak or Brighton, and this house was old and not in the charming way, it was still Brunswick and it would've come with a decent price tag. Lacy owned his place—a sweet converted factory in Fitzroy—and he'd bought his mum a nice place back in Frankston, but he was entering his tenth year in the league and making bank.

Thad returned with a plate of some kind of slice.

"I made these, dates for the sugar. Please don't feel obliged to eat it, but I don't know where my manners would be if I didn't put out dessert," he smiled, ducked his head and went back into the kitchen.

Lacy looked at the slice. Perfectly cut little squares with a golden tint to them like they'd been baked. Did Thad get up and fucking cook before training?

"Black no sugar?" Thad called from the kitchen.

"Yeah." He guessed Thad had seen him drinking the stuff at training.

"So," Lacy started as Thad placed the coffee in front of him, "did you buy this place?"

Thad took a seat and leaned back. "No, this our mainland house, my family's."

Lacy squinted. "So, like, you guys have a place in Melbourne for when you come to the mainland?"

"Yes," Thad replied, smiling fondly, "my nanna picked this one out and my grandfather bought it for her when she needed cancer treatment. That was 1983. Couldn't get what she needed in Tassie, so," Thad shrugged and looked around, "now we have this place."

"And your nanna?"

"She's gone now, grandad too, but we kept this place because there's stuff we just can't get in Tassie. Saves on accommodation," he glanced around. "And mum and dad were happy when I got the trade since now someone's living here all the time," he looked back at Lacy and smiled.

"So, who decorated?" Lacy asked.

Thad laughed, surprised. "It was a family affair. Most of our places look like this."

Lacy nodded and picked up his coffee. "Cool."

He wondered if Thad was going to start lecturing him on finding God.

But Thad picked up his coffee, took a sip, asked what Lacy thought about Adelaide's ruckman and Lacy relaxed. He'd been relaxed all afternoon.

Cary was right—he had made a new friend.

2

IT DAWNED ON LACY a few weeks into the season that he'd never had a friend like Thad before. Preseason had been the warm-up—a few more dinners, spotting each other in the gym, a lingering lunch before Thad flew back to Tassie for the break—normal stuff when you gravitated to a guy in the room. Lacy had flown up to Byron Bay for Finn and George's wedding. George's sincerity had found a whole new level now he was directing it at Finn, and Finn could be talking to Lacy, lift his head like he felt George's eyes on him, meet that gaze with a delighted smile in a way that made Lacy laugh and Finn say, 'What?', his grin fooling no one. The wedding was classy, but Lacy had to give them shit for the Vogue wedding spread.

But the week had been good, he got his fill with some of his favourite people in the footy world, got what he needed when he met a Swedish couple, tourists, in a club. The Swedes were happy to share him, taking turns on his ass and mouth until the sun rose over the ocean through the open curtains of their bungalow. They had no idea who he was, asking as he left if they could do it again once they travelled down to Sydney.

What he hadn't expected as he walked along the beach that morning, his body well-used by those two big dicks, was to be thinking about Thad. He wondered what he was up to back in Tassie. He thought about his concerned smile when he stood above Lacy to spot his bench presses in the gym, his deep voice rolling over Lacy's body as he asked if it was too much.

On the first morning back at training, Lacy looked up the second Thad walked into the room, his face stretching into a wide grin matched by Thad's own. At the end of the day, Thad asked, tentative, "Hey, we should exchange numbers? Maybe do lifts? You're in Fitzroy, right?"

Lacy had readily agreed.

Lacy had friends. Loads of friends. He was friends with every guy on the team. He had mates from back home he partied with when they came to Melbourne, the kind of friends he snuck into the Grand Final in his boot when he couldn't get them tickets after using his allocation on his mum and other mates. He had friends in Berlin and Amsterdam and London—the kind of friends who hooked him up when he came to town, knew what else he got up to, clapped him on the back and took their turn if they were feeling frisky for it. He had friends on other teams, like Finn and George, his mate Swanny he'd been drafted with and had beers with after they played each other.

But Thad was different. After that first day back, lifts together turned into running errands together, turned into dinner, turned into texting each other random shit over the weekend. During training, they ended up together—sitting side by side for video review, stretching together, their feet and thighs knocking, they stood next to each other on the oval to suck in pulls of air between quarters in games and drills in training, elbows touching.

It was a few weeks into the regular season when Lacy realised the only time they didn't make plans and Thad didn't respond to his messages immediately was Sunday mornings. It took Lacy two more games to realise why his invitation to brunch was always turned down.

"Oh!" he said as they got dressed in the locker room after they'd belted Western Sydney on a Saturday night. "You've got church, right?"

Thad ducked his head. "Yes."

"Why didn't you just say?" Lacy bumped him.

"I—" Thad broke off.

Lacy stopped buttoning his shirt and looked up at him.

Thad shrugged. "I don't know."

"I'm surprised you didn't invite me," Lacy said, faux-offended.

"Oh, sorry, would you like to come?" Thad asked.

Lacy cackled. "Nah, I'm kidding. I'm pretty sure the building would fall down if I walked in."

Thad smiled, his eyes lighting up; his head tilted down so his entire focus captured Lacy with it.

"The church would be lucky to have you," he said.

Lacy searched his eyes for the irony, found none, cracked up and bumped Thad to cover his embarrassment. It was a foreign feeling, he didn't feel inadequate because he was a heathen, he was proud of that, but maybe he wanted to believe he was as good as Thad thought he was.

But now that he knew he got Thad at all times except Sunday because that's when God or Jesus or whoever he was praying to got him, he could plan accordingly.

"Wanna try that new burger place we saw yesterday? After you're finished, I mean. And I reckon we might need to check out the shop next to it, there's a gap in one of my walls, a nice piece of art is in order," Lacy said as he waited for Thad to finish getting dressed.

"Sure, but I don't think voodoo knick knacks are actually considered art," Thad replied as he sat down to put his shoes on. He pushed his hair out of his face and looked up. "But I'm willing to be convinced."

"Yeah, you are," Lacy grinned. "C'mon, let's get dinner before we meet the boys."

"You want to go out or drop by my place?" Thad stood.

"Did you put the slow shit on?"

"Of course," Thad smiled.

"Your place it is."

George had begged off staying in Melbourne for the night to catch up since he had a recovery session in the morning and Finn was playing the next day in Sydney.

"Yeah, get a later flight. Swanny is," Lacy had said to him.

"Nah, better get home," George replied and leaned in for a hug, plenty of manly back slaps.

"You're so whipped," Lacy replied as they let go.

"Yep," George winked.

He'd catch up with both of them when they played in Sydney. Right now though, he had dinner with Thad and then some bars to shut down in Carlton.

"Les!" he shouted as they walked out.

Les startled at his locker and looked over, his big eyes wide; it looked hilarious on his body that was still too skinny.

"We'll meet you there." Lacy said. "Make sure my shots are waiting."

Les relaxed, smiled, "Yes, boss."

Thad always came out with the team, nursed a water, smiled amiably at everyone, joined the conversation when invited to do so, sat next to Lacy, kept his seat free when Lacy wandered off to do shots and talk shit up at the bar.

Thad got him into his car at the end of the night, drove him home, got him water and painkillers, got him into his bed with a friendly hand on his shoulder before he left.

That night, as Thad got him into bed, Lacy grinned up at him. "You're the fuckin' best, man," he slurred. "Like, legit, eh. The best."

Thad laughed and ducked his head. "Get some sleep. I'll pick you up after church."

"Yeah, yeah," Lacy grinned, "gotta do your altar boy duties."

"I'm far too old for that."

"But you were, right?" Lacy's eyes slipped closed. He could imagine it—little Thad in his white dress—he'd seen those kids on TV.

"Of course," Thad said and the last thing Lacy remembered was Thad's deep voice recounting his first time. He had to stay still for an hour, all eyes in the church on him as he held some cup, how it was difficult, but he felt so proud; he knew he was making his family proud and even when he was desperate to scratch an itch on his arm, where it got to the point it physically pained him not to do it, he stayed completely still and let the itch become a part of who he was. By the time the service was over, it was gone.

Since George's dramatic exit, coming out, wedding, and new job with Sydney, they got a new coach. Alanson was a scrawny, middle-aged ex-player and long-time assistant coach for Adelaide. It was clear from the first day of preseason training he was nothing like George. The differences were so stark and disorientating that all talk turned to him every time they went out.

Their team was infamous for playing the corridor—other teams even joked that they owned it. They ran all their plays down the centre of the field, dominating their forward lines and keeping an eye on their man, rather than the zone, so they rarely created turnovers that'd inevitably result in an opposition goal.

Alanson told them on the first day they were predictable and aside from the fact every other team had their number, they were also boring to watch. He delivered this line in such a bland tone, no one could decide whether or not be insulted.

The new style he designed for them was to push their charge to the wings, thus avoiding a turnover that'd easily turn into a goal if they got into trouble. It would become a throw in from the boundary—a play that relied on a solid ruckman and scrappy players who could get the ball out of a messy contest.

They also had to abandon playing man on man and protect the zone. And everyone was encouraged to fight for the ball with aggressive tackling.

It was a whole new style and it would take them a while to adapt; Lacy figured any reasonable coach would guide the change with a supportive and understanding hand.

Alanson regarded their fuck-ups with sarcasm. But the next day, he'd tell them they'd get there, it was still preseason. And the next, he'd ask them if they'd like to take a rest, hit the showers early? His tone so earnest that when Les took the bait, he'd scream at them to get their asses back on the field and do it again.

"Guy's like the fucking bible," Cary said under his breath after training one day, "impossible to read."

Everyone cracked up and the nickname was born.

Thad smiled, but his brow creased every time he heard it.

Lacy knocked his shoulder against Thad's arm after they left one day. "It's a joke, like, no one's actually ragging on the bible."

"Oh, I know, I get it, but I don't," he smiled helplessly at Lacy, "I don't get it."

"Well, you know," Lacy said as he held the door open, "'cos the bible's hard to read."

"No, I get what you're all saying, but it's not." Thad thanked him, went ahead, waited for Lacy to come alongside him before heading for his car.

"From what I hear, it like, really is," Lacy replied and got in the passenger's seat. "Full of virgins and guys with hundreds of kids and demons and shit."

Thad chuckled, put his seatbelt on. "You're talking about the Old Testament and it's not meant to be taken literally. Have you read it?"

"Fuck, no," Lacy replied, reconsidered. "I mean, sorry. Ah, no. No, I have not."

Thad started the car. "Well, you should give it a read, you'll see," he gave Lacy a quick smile as he reversed, "if you study a particular verse and apply yourself to pondering it for a day, see how it resonates with your life, you'll see that's how it's meant to be read."

Lacy thought about how he did that already with football. He'd think about a really good player, how when they made a snap decision, usually an unselfish play, a moment when a player broke free and got himself open for a split second, got the ball on his chest, it shifted the energy for the entire team.

"Sorry, of course you don't need to do that, I don't want you to think I think you should be reading—"

"Thad, man," Lacy cut him off, "I know you ain't tryin' to convert me or whatever, I was just thinking about what you said but like, with footy."

"Oh yeah?" Thad glanced at him as they stopped at a red light.

"Yeah, like," Lacy began and told him.

Thad blew out a breath. "I wish I could see the game like you. I know I shouldn't covet, but sometimes, between you and me?"

"Yeah?"

"I think it'd be pretty amazing to see it like you do."

"You're a solid player, you don't need to be like me," Lacy replied, vehement. He didn't know why, Thad wasn't and probably never would be a great player.

"No, I know," Thad smiled as he pulled into his driveway. "I just meant, I really admire you. I love seeing you when we're out there. Seeing what you do up close? Being on the same side? It's incredible."

"Biblical?" Lacy grinned.

"I'd say, almost." He clapped Lacy on the thigh, gave it a good shake. "Come on, I've got some cold cuts and fresh bread, let's have lunch and watch the Sydney game."

Thad took his hand back. Lacy felt the touch lingering on his skin, which was stupid. They touched all the time. Thad lifted him off his feet whenever Lacy kicked a goal and got mobbed by team-mates. They bumped shoulders, tapped each other on the ass when they were playing or training, sat close on the couch so their shoulders brushed.

As they got settled on Thad's couch, Lacy dissected Finn's play, but his mind was on the last time he got laid. He hadn't gotten fucked since those Swedes. Over two months. Unheard of. He'd head out tonight, get himself sorted. His play wasn't suffering for it, which was odd—normally if he didn't blow off steam with a combination of drugs, booze and sex at least once a month, he'd be a mess, too much footy and nowhere for his brain to relax from it.

When Thad asked if he'd like another beer before dinner, Lacy decided to call it.

"Actually, I gotta head out," he stood, patted down his pockets.

"Really?" Thad replied.

"Yeah, meetin' some boys from back home," he lied, glanced up, smiled quick, looked away, and headed for the door.

"Oh, of course, sounds good," Thad trailed along behind him. "You want me to give you a lift?"

"Nah," Lacy pulled out his phone and tapped for a car. "Got a ride."

"Are you sure? I can drop you—"

"No, I'm good," Lacy turned and gave him an exaggerated smile. "See you Monday."

"Okay," Thad replied slowly and of course he was confused—they always hung out on Sunday afternoons. But Lacy knew he'd be in no condition to see anyone tomorrow, so he lied again.

"Could be an all-nighter," well, that was true, "I'll be asleep all day," also probably true. So, not lying, just not entirely truthful about the why.

Thad smiled politely, frowning slightly.

"Well, have fun," he said as Lacy pulled the door open.

"Yep, later," he walked out, careful not to look back, even though he could tell Thad was watching him from the door.

3

THAD WAS DISTRACTED IN church the next morning. Nothing noticeable, he was sure of it, he spoke to the pastor and other church leaders after the service like always, chatted to the other members of the congregation out the front in the autumn sunshine, assured one of the men around his age that yes, he was still absolutely onboard with helping him start up a football league for troubled kids, and yes, he agreed with the young woman, Stacy, that he'd help out with the homeless, join her group to cruise the streets and set up coffee and meal stations just as soon as he had his head around his routine. The truth was, he had his head around his routine, but he spent all his free time with Lacy and, selfish as it was, he was really enjoying it.

He'd had close male friends before—the bond of brotherhood amongst male friends was important, imperative. In primary school he'd had Nathan, who'd also happened to be his closest friend at church. They remained friends, but when Nathan went to a boarding school in Melbourne, Thad became fast friends with Christian. He remained friends with him too. He hadn't made a close friend during his time on the Gold Coast, nor had he been particularly close to anyone when he played in Tasmania before he got drafted.

But Lacy was different. Thad knew who he was of course, had played against him, was already star-struck. And it was just chance that the seat next to Lacy was the one that was open in the locker room and on the bus and on the plane when Thad started because, as he put together later from the chatter in the room and from Lacy himself, Finn used to sit there. And before that Jack, who'd been traded to Fremantle. Anyone could sit next to a guy though, so that wasn't what made Lacy different. Thad felt drawn to his charisma—who wouldn't? He loved how at ease Lacy made him feel in conversation—but he had that effect on everyone, Thad was sure of it. So no, what was different was how he made Thad feel from their very first conversation.

Thad had walked in on that first day, sat down in the only available seat just before the new coach walked in. Lacy had looked over, smiled, stuck his hand out and said, "I'm Lacy. Well, Ridge Lacy is my full name, but I don't reckon I'll ever forgive my mum for that, so everyone just calls me Lacy."

Thad had taken his hand, a warmth blooming in his chest. "Thaddeus Clay, but everyone calls me Thad."

"I know who you are, Thaddeus Clay," Lacy replied with a grin. "Ruckman for the Gold Coast, went fifty-four in the second round of the draft three years ago at twenty-one 'cos you were already playin' some decent footy in Tassie. I don't reckon Gold Coast were using ya properly, pulling you in and out of the ruck, can't get your feet that way, can ya?"

"No, yes, that's right," Thad smiled, surprised, his hand warm in Lacy's grip.

Lacy had winked at him, let his hand go as their new coach walked in, and murmured, "But I reckon we're gonna use you just right."

And from that moment on the warmth hadn't left him. He knew a sign when he got one—Lacy was meant to be in his life.

And so far, their friendship had brought a light into his life that had bathed the last few months in a glow, had seen him rush back to Melbourne after the Christmas break in anticipation of the first day of training. Everything felt right when he was with Lacy.

Until last night. There was something off in Lacy's departure.

He excused himself from the conversation he was in and headed down the steps of the church to his car. He was sure Lacy was fine, but he couldn't shake the sense something was off. His faith had taught him to trust in his feelings, his instincts. This was the Holy Spirit communicating through him.

He sat in his car, drummed his fingers on the steering wheel and debated what to do. Lacy had said he'd see him on Monday. Thad understood he needed to sleep off his hangover, he'd seen it since they became friends. But Lacy always enjoyed a good meal on those days, and Thad figured it wouldn't hurt to drop around with some food, check in, make sure he was okay.

Decided, he started his car and headed for home, determined to collect some supplies and head to Lacy's place.

Halfway there, a steaming container of tomato noodle soup and a plate of date slice on the passenger's seat, he pulled over. A horn blared and Thad startled. What was he doing? Lacy said he'd see him on Monday and he needed to respect that boundary.

When he was in high school, his mum had told him gently that he needed to stop putting all his eggs in one basket. He didn't understand what she meant—Christian was his best friend, the person he felt best around in the world, of course he wanted all his energy in that basket. His dad had chimed in, explaining it wasn't healthy to invest so much of himself in one person, that he needed to have other people in his life so there wasn't so much pressure on that one relationship.

"Look at your mother and I," he'd said, "I have the brotherhood at the church, the boys at the club"—his footy club—"the other volunteers at the SES. It makes everything better with your mum since she doesn't have to meet all my needs."

Thad was perplexed—Christian wasn't his *wife*—and he was still bewildered by it now. But he got a feeling there was a point there and it was relevant with Lacy.

He put his indicator on, looked at oncoming traffic in the rearview mirror, pulled into a gap and made a U-turn at the lights.

Carol was the first to spot him when he walked into the function room behind the church. She smiled wide, all teeth, stood and pulled out a chair for him.

"You're back," she whispered, a smile in her voice. Thad thought she was a very nice young woman, around his age, but he'd had the urge to lean away from her since they'd met. It was the combination of the perfume and the teeth; the floral scent was heavy and her perfectly straight teeth dominated her face when she smiled. But she was gracious and kind and he felt judgemental for thinking that.

"Need to get the youth league started," he murmured and edged away while trying not to be obvious about it.

By the time he got home that night, he had solid plans to start the youth footy league for troubled kids on Tuesday nights, and Thursdays were booked to do a shift with Stacy and Glen with the homeless.

It was the right thing he was doing, the Christian thing. He threw out the container of soup since it'd gone bad sitting in his car all afternoon, put the slice back in the tin, served himself some dinner and ate it alone at his table and couldn't understand why he didn't feel good about it, the warmth in his chest dampened to a coal.

Lacy was already sitting in front of his locker when Thad walked in the following morning. He hadn't messaged for a lift and Thad had spent too much time opening and closing the message thread; he'd eventually left it because he figured the ball was in Lacy's court. Lacy never messaged.

But he was here now, alone given how early it was. He snapped his head up when the door clanged shut, broke into a grin.

Thad smiled back.

"Thaddeus," he said and stood, his bare torso unfurling as he stretched up. He had so many tattoos that even when he was naked, he looked like he was wearing painted clothes. The exception was his ass and groin, the white cheeks firmly muscled below the line of ink, his thick length at the front hung below a thatch of hair the same dark colour as his head. Thad tried not to look at him when he strolled around naked before and after a shower, but sometimes it was impossible not to pause in undressing or dressing and admire the perfection of the male form when it looked like Lacy.

"Lacy," he replied. "How was your weekend?"

"Eh," Lacy shrugged and took a few steps towards him.

Thad drank him in. He noted the dark smudges under his eyes, the faint tremor rippling along his skin. He'd never judge nor tell Lacy what to do, but he did worry about the cost of his lifestyle on his health.

Lacy reached up to clap him on the shoulder, grinning, his wide eyes lighting up as he looked up. He had interesting eyes—brown with whiskey-coloured flecks that changed. Today they were duller, more brown than whiskey.

"Feeling a bit rough now," Lacy said.

Thad patted him on the back gently and searched his expression—Lacy was fine, but when Thad looked closely, he could see a nervous energy running just below the surface.

"I was gonna come round yesterday," Thad stepped back, "bring you some food, but I thought maybe—"

"Fuck, man, wish you did," Lacy went back to his locker. "I coulda used a hug," he laughed like he was joking.

Thad stopped, his hand on his locker door. He glanced over. Lacy was getting his training jumper out, his deodorant, putting both back and reaching for his leggings.

"You should've messaged, I thought maybe you wanted some space."

Lacy snorted. He yanked his leggings on, snapped the elastic on his hips before running a hand through his hair. He looked up at

Thad, grinning. It was a sight with that front tooth missing, but he was an incredibly good-looking man in his own way. The charisma and liveliness combined with the intriguing-coloured eyes, wide-set against his olive skin. His cheekbones were high and defined, which made his full lips seem fuller. And his nose, which would've been straight and enviably proportioned in his face if it wasn't for the bump in the middle from being broken twice—the first knocking it sideways, the second straightening it back. But this seemed, like the missing tooth, not a blemish, but a character feature. Taken together, he was the epitome of a kind of pleasing manliness. Rough yet beautiful. Thad felt he could stare at him for hours and not lose interest, the way a painter fell in love with a subject.

"Nah, I was alright, eh," he said and Thad got the feeling he was downplaying it.

He made a decision.

"C'mere," he said and stepped into Lacy's space, his arms coming up to telegraph the play.

Lacy lost the smile. Thad thought he'd misread the situation, but before he could drop his arms Lacy slid between them, pressed his chest against Thad's, wrapped his arms around his back and gripped his shirt. Thad plastered his arms around him.

He wondered what this would look like if someone walked in—they were standing in the empty locker room, the birds barely up on a chilly Monday morning, caught up in a tight embrace. But it felt so unbearably good—Lacy's warmth, his bare chest pressing into the fabric of Thad's shirt—and he didn't really care. At five foot eight inches and lucky to be cracking eighty kilos, Lacy was a lightweight Thad could bundle up in his arms.

"Next time I'll come round," he murmured against the top of Lacy's head.

"Yeah," Lacy tightened his hold before loosening it, tapping Thad's back a few times. "Thanks."

"For what?" Thad asked, smiling and letting him go.

"For that, needed that," Lacy said quietly and it was so incongruous to his normal animation Thad feared something had happened, but before he could ask the door clanged open and Cary walked in, bitching about how early it was.

By the time training ended, Lacy was his normal self. They took showers next to each other and Lacy was talking non-stop about a play they'd just run—Thad tapping it to him out of a contest from the boundary line, "I'll be right there, I'll come out of the pocket, no one's gonna see it coming,"—and Thad nodded along, the steam billowing between them while they washed off perfunctorily when he saw it.

A mark on the side of Lacy's throat. The tattoos covered it if you weren't looking closely, but Thad was and he saw a mark between the black that shaded to grey; it was red with indents, it was red like it was going to bruise. A hot shame washed through him and rendered him speechless when he realised what it was—a hickey, a hickey with teeth marks in it.

"Yeah?" Lacy said like he'd said it a few times.

"Yes," Thad replied, unsure what he was agreeing to.

"Awesome," Lacy turned his shower off, shot Thad a grin as he grabbed his towel and started rubbing his head.

Did Lacy have a girlfriend? Thad got out and reached for one of his towels, wrapped it around his waist, grabbed another and dried his chest, his eyes on Lacy's bare ass as he padded out of the showers.

Of course it was fine if he did. It was just, why didn't Lacy tell him? And where was she when Lacy needed a hug?

They were back in front of their lockers, half dressed, Thad spiralling in these thoughts when Lacy bumped him.

"You alright, man?" he asked.

"Sure, sorry," he shook his head, "just thinking."

"Well, don't strain yourself. Still wanna get lunch?"

"Yes, of course," he sat down to put his shoes on. "Where do you want to go?"

Lacy didn't answer him. Thad glanced up.

"I thought we were goin' to yours," Lacy said. "Are you sure you're alright?"

"Of course. Sorry, distracted," his eyes darted to Lacy's throat and quickly away. He was blushing, he could feel it. Lacy was frowning down at him.

"Did you get a knock to the head?" Lacy asked after a strained moment. "'Cos concussion ain't no joke, you should see the doctor. Nance is in today, want me to get her?"

Thad stood, looked down at him, tried to smile. "No, no, I'm fine, just didn't sleep that well." In his state of confusion and shame, the last thing he wanted was to get grilled by the Team Chief of Sports Medicine—Dr Nancy Brewer. Nance looked like an inoffensive old lady, but she was shrewd; her eyes cataloguing the ability to maintain eye contact and seeing some deficiency confirmed if you couldn't.

"Are you ready?" he asked to change the subject.

"I was born ready, you wanna drive and I'll leave my car here? Pick me up tomorrow?"

"Of course," Thad replied before remembering his Tuesday night plans. "But I'll have to drop you straight home on Tuesday because I've got some stuff with the church."

"Oh, well, I can just drive then," Lacy grabbed his keys.

"Tuesdays and Thursdays," Thad announced. He didn't understand why this felt so awkward—it was a good thing; if Lacy had a girlfriend, this would open time for him to spend with her. Thad shoved his hands in his pockets, agitated.

"Church shit Tuesdays and Thursdays, got it," Lacy was smiling as he said it, but it was off.

"But I can still drive you, just drop you home straight after and then go."

"Nah, I can drive."

"It's really fine, my church thing doesn't start until six, so I can easily get you home and go straight there," Thad insisted.

"I don't want you skippin' dinner to ferry me around. I can drive."

"It's really fine—"

"Jesus, guys," Cary cut in and Thad winced. "Even me and the missus don't fuck around this much when making plans. It's like listening to a soap opera."

"Know a lot about soap operas, do ya' Cary?" Lacy quipped.

"Sorry," Thad apologised.

"Just because me and Thaddeus here are considerate doesn't make it some drama," Lacy said. "C'mon," he turned to Thad, "I'll follow you."

Thad wanted to get out of there if their captain was noticing how weirdly he was behaving. He couldn't explain it to himself, never mind anyone else. It was a good thing if Lacy had a girlfriend, she might take good care of him. Lacy was a functioning adult, but every man could do with a woman's hand in his life, keeping him from excess if he wasn't careful. Thad prided himself on being extra careful, so meeting a woman and getting married was the farthest thing from his mind. Obviously, he wanted to have sex at some point in his life—he was still a man and celibacy was no joke—but for now, for a while now, he was content to keep his own company. Especially when he had a good friend to keep that company with.

Only, he thought as he followed Lacy's car out of the parking lot, indicator blinking steadily, he wondered how long he'd have Lacy for if he had someone. He knew how this went—Christian and Nathan were both married and while they always made time for him, it wasn't the same. Once a man had a woman, the closeness went to her. As it should, he thought solemnly, his eyes on Lacy's head poking above his seat in the car ahead.

He just didn't understand why he felt so terrible about it when it came to Lacy. He needed to pray on it. Prayer would help his feelings unravel and dissipate. It always did.

4

L ACY ALREADY KNEW THAD was a weird guy. Not weird in some demented way, just different from most guys. He didn't drink or party or swear and he was so polite that on anyone else it would be annoying, but Thad did it with a sincerity that was disarming.

Nevertheless, in the week since Lacy didn't catch up with him on Sunday, he'd been acting weirder. Lacy had hooked up with a few guys he'd met at previous parties on the Saturday, gotten railed so deep and so good he felt it everywhere the next day. And he'd drunk too much, taken ecstasy, felt like killing himself on the come down the next day. But Thad didn't know that. Nobody knew about that—Lacy kept that shit anonymous for a reason, made sure to do it outside the football bubble, paid top dollar for masking agents, had never failed a piss test.

It was Sunday, and Lacy had rolled out of bed to let Thad in when the doorbell went, and here Thad was, once again darting his eyes around and stuttering through a greeting, asking Lacy where he'd like to go for lunch, peering down the hall as if he was waiting for someone to appear. Lacy never fucked people at his house, so Thad would be waiting a long time.

"I'm feelin' pancakes," Lacy said.

Thad scrunched his face up and for a moment the weirdness evaporated.

Lacy cackled. "Kidding! Probably just head down to St Kilda for a swim and some paninis if you want?"

"Yes," Thad replied with a relieved smile. Thad was all about keeping food as close to nature as possible.

"Such a weirdo," Lacy said fondly and left his door open as he went back inside to get dressed.

"Weird because I don't want pancakes?"

"Among other things," Lacy called over his shoulder. "Take a seat, I'll just get changed. Wanna swim first?" he shouted as he jogged up his stairs, "then I can skip the shower."

"Whatever you want," Thad called back.

They stripped down on the shore, tossed their clothes in a pile on top of the towels Lacy brought and Lacy bolted for the ocean—better to get it done in this weather. It wasn't winter-cold yet, but it was on its way. He could hear Thad's soft laughter behind him as he jogged to follow.

The water was cold, shocking him awake, and Lacy dove in, swam under water for a while. He breached the surface and spun around. Thad was nowhere in sight. He trod water and looked around.

Thad's body came into view next to him like a large white shark as he came up for air.

Lacy cackled. "Scared me for a second there."

"Huh?" Thad asked and stood. He was tall enough that the water slid down his throat and clavicles, lapped the top of his nipples. He had a great physique—tall with broad shoulders, his defined pectorals and flat stomach tapering to a distinct waist and muscled ass. He was lean, not bulky like some ruckmen, and his unblemished skin had a hint of a tan to it.

"I couldn't see you," Lacy smiled.

"I was right behind you," Thad smiled back.

"C'mon, let's get a workout outta this," Lacy said and started doing breaststroke parallel to the shore.

It made Thad laugh, like he hoped it would, and he swam alongside him on his back, his white jocks breaching the surface.

Lacy thought they were returning to normal, but when they got their paninis and sat on the wall facing the ocean, Thad bounced his leg restlessly.

"Alright," Lacy said, "out with it."

Thad froze. It took a moment, but Thad eventually asked neutrally, "Out with what?"

"Thad, man," Lacy said carefully, "you've been acting like a tweaker around me for a week. What's goin' on? Did I piss you off somehow? 'Cos if I did, you gotta tell me, alright? I never woulda done something intentional, ya' know?"

Thad squeezed his wrapped panini in his hands, eyes on it.

Lacy waited, tense now too.

"You didn't do anything," Thad said after a long moment. "It's just," he took a deep breath, "I guess I wondered why you didn't tell me you had a girlfriend."

Lacy was certain he misheard. "Did you just say girlfriend?"

"Yes," Thad nodded, eyes still fixed on the panini, "and I think that's great, but I was... confused because you never told me and maybe it's stupid, but it's been playing on my mind."

"Girlfriend," Lacy repeated, "you legit think I've got a girlfriend? What fucking girlfriend?"

Thad skittered his eyes up to Lacy's, gestured at Lacy's neck. "You've got a, you know."

Lacy touched his throat. One of the guys he fucked the other weekend put that there while he held Lacy down, thrust into him roughly, sucked on his skin and dug his teeth in as he came.

"It was a hook-up," he said.

"A hook-up?" Thad raised both eyebrows. "Like, casual sex?"

"Yeah, man. Sometimes I like to, you know, scratch the old itch," he shrugged and unwrapped his panini. "Girlfriend," he laughed and took a bite.

"So," Thad started carefully like he wasn't sure if he was allowed to go on.

Lacy, chewed and waved his hand.

"So, you won't see her again?"

Lacy wasn't going to correct the pronoun—he'd fucked girls, didn't do as much for him on account of them not having a dick and generally not being strong enough to hold him down and make him take it with said dick, and he was into dudes so he'd never tried the strap-on route, nor met a chick he was attracted to enough for all that, but as he looked at Thad's hesitant expression, he thought all that might be too much information.

He swallowed his mouthful and replied, "Wasn't planning on it."

"Oh, okay," Thad nodded, focused on unwrapping his food.

Lacy frowned. By the time he finished he'd put together what he wanted to ask.

"It bothered you I mighta had someone and not introduced you?"

Thad squinted at the horizon. "I guess it did. I thought maybe you were embarrassed."

Lacy scrunched his face up. "Embarrassed by the white trash hussy I was seeing to meet you?"

Thad laughed but Lacy could tell he was trying not to.

"C'mon, Lacy," he smiled at him, a real one again, "we both know you'd land a real nice girl if you wanted."

Lacy gaped at him. No one thought that. See? Weird bloody guy.

"But no, I meant embarrassed about me because I'm, well, you know," Thad smiled and focused back on the horizon.

"You're what?" Lacy shot back. "A top fucking bloke? Well mannered? Hot as fuck?"

"Lacy," Thad said and ducked his head, his body shaking with embarrassed laughter. "I meant because I'm into religion and I don't drink and stuff."

Lacy frowned. "So you're into God and his kid or whatever, ain't nothin' wrong with that and if I introduced you to someone who had a problem with it, I'd knock their fucking block off."

Thad smiled over at him and geez, he was a handsome guy. Not in an obvious way; it snuck up on you—the soft brown hair, the warm eyes, nicely proportioned features and a really fucking kind smile.

"Jesus," he said, "the kid is Jesus."

Lacy knocked their shoulders together. "Yeah, man, I know who Jesus is. Or, well, I do now."

Thad studied him. Lacy cracked up.

"You're joking," Thad grinned.

Lacy laughed harder. "Your face. Yeah, man, I know who Jesus is. I reckon it's pretty funny those signs outside the churches, but. You know the ones, 'Spreading the good news of Jesus.' Like, dude was born two thousand years ago, reckon we all heard about it by now."

Thad was laughing, Lacy could feel it against his side, but he was trying not to and Lacy reckoned it was his favourite Thad laugh.

5

♥

THAD WAS PROFOUNDLY RELIEVED Lacy didn't have a girl-friend, since it meant he got him all to himself for as long as it lasted. The season trudged along—winning some, losing more (Finn truly was irreplaceable). It was clear by the time they were in the backend they were going to struggle to make the final eight, even with Lacy playing out of his skin, so all talk at the club turned to 'rebuilding.' Thad's position was precarious in these discussions—if they traded for a better ruckman, he'd be relegated to their affiliated state league team and probably, eventually, delisted. He'd never expected to get drafted and therefore considered every game he got to play a bonus.

Lacy though, he wouldn't hear of it.

"What if you worked on your defensive game more?" he said one afternoon after they'd finished up with the ice baths. "If you make yourself invaluable in defence, you'd have another role on the team."

"You mean as a tagger?" Thad's lips curled up. It wasn't his build—tall and broad—it was the way his build dictated a slower pace. A lot of tall and broad, even lanky guys were a lot nimbler than him, but his body moved slowly, deliberately; his hand reaching up and tapping in the ruck was in a lot of ways his only perfect, quick move.

Tagging would mean chasing around and hassling athletes sprightlier than him.

"Yeah, maybe not. And not because you can't train some speed into this," Lacy grabbed Thad by the bicep and shook him. "But I don't reckon you could get in another player's head."

Thad leaned into the touch with a chuckle. Then he caught up to what Lacy said and ducked his head.

"Yep," Lacy bumped him as they got dressed. "You'd suck at telling some guy you'd seen his mother at a brothel the night before and now you got to thinkin' on it, the guy didn't look much like his dad, did he? Had he had that checked out? Done a paternity test?" Lacy tapped his chin thoughtfully. "Come to think of it, his kid don't look much like him either. Maybe the missus been gettin' it somewhere better too? 'Cos you'd also heard around the traps he weren't really packin' down there."

Thad was scarlet. And it wasn't funny—it was downright scandalous to even think this in another man's direction—but the way Lacy delivered it, rolling off the tongue like he'd been genuinely pondering it, was so funny, he had to hide his face in his hair to laugh.

"Was it a family trait to fail to deliver?"

Thad glanced over at his contemplative tone. Lacy met his eyes, expression so thoughtful you'd think he was really asking.

"To force those poor women to go elsewhere to get a good dicking?"

Thad sucked his cheeks in to keep from laughing.

"Poor old Shazza, gotta go on the prowl for dick 'cos she married a eunuch," Lacy finished seriously.

"Do you think they'd know what a eunuch is?" Thad asked.

"I reckon every man knows what a eunuch is," he leaned around Thad. "Les!"

Les startled and looked up from the shirt in his hands.

"What's a eunuch?" Lacy asked him.

Les darted his eyes to the side, then answered hesitantly. "Isn't it a man with no dick?"

Lacy grinned. "Close enough." He leaned back and looked up at Thad. "See?"

"Why're you asking me that?" Les called over.

"Vocabulary test," Lacy replied.

"Oh, okay," Les said and Thad watched him return to getting dressed, satisfied by that answer. He shook his head with a laugh.

"Point being," Lacy went on, "you can't do that."

"No," Thad said around his smile. "I'll be alright, no need to worry about me."

"I think we should work on your goal kicking then."

Thad shrugged. He shut his locker and waited for Lacy to finish getting dressed.

"We could practice. If you stay here and kick a hundred goals a day from different angles, it'll become like muscle memory. I'll teach ya."

Thad smiled at the top of Lacy's head as he sat to put his shoes on. He'd be happy watching paint dry with Lacy, so kicking some goals would be a real treat.

"Sure, we can do that, but I don't want to mess with your free time too much."

Lacy stood, grabbed his bicep over his jacket and squeezed. "You're my free time."

Thad smiled and nodded.

Well, he was most of Lacy's free time, he thought unhappily when Lacy begged off going out that Saturday after the game. He had some friends from back home in the city again. Thad knew that meant a bender, so he busied himself with cooking a hangover cure to bring to Lacy the next day.

He strolled up Lacy's driveway the following day just after noon, a canvas shopping bag full of containers over his shoulder. Lacy's place was beautiful and modern. A small factory that'd been converted to office spaces then converted into a house, it was square in architecture with tall hedges and trees flanking the front wall in a perfect square, a bird bath at the centre of a patch of lawn in front of the house. Inside, the second floor didn't extend over the bottom floor living area, so the front room stretched to the full height of the house and created a massive space for the long white couches in front of floor to ceiling windows. Out the back was a square of manicured lawn alongside a courtyard, a jacuzzi built against the side of the patio, everything immaculately maintained and cleaned. Lacy laughed when Thad said he was impressed by the upkeep. Lacy's mum had hired a gardener and cleaner when he bought the place. He'd never cleaned in his life nor had a garden, so wouldn't know where to begin.

The place was quiet now. A cool, concrete stillness stretching to the sky. Thad stepped up to the door and knocked softly. He waited a few minutes. Lacy was probably still asleep. He didn't want to wake him, but Lacy wished he'd come over last time and it was afternoon. He brought his hand up, hesitated, knocked hard a few times. He waited. Still nothing. He contemplated leaving everything on the doorstep and sending a message. But Lacy should be up by now. Unless something was wrong. He fished his phone out of his pocket and hit call.

Lacy answered just before it rang out.

"Thad?"

"Hi, I'm here," he glanced around. There was a bird on the edge of the bird bath, an Indian Myna taking a deep drink.

"Here? Here where?"

"Your place? Last time you said you wished I'd come, so this time I did," he replied, wavering at the end.

Lacy groaned and hung up.

Thad was uncomfortable. He shouldn't have come.

He heard Lacy's feet belting down the stairs. It was too late to turn around now. Thad stood stoically as the door swung open to reveal a shirtless, squinting Lacy.

"Sorry, I shouldn't have come. Here," Thad let the bag slide down his shoulder, gripped it and held it out, his gaze roaming over Lacy hunched in the doorway, face scrunched up against the sun.

"Nah, man, come in," Lacy yawned and shuffled back. "I could definitely eat in a bit."

Thad stepped inside, darted his eyes over Lacy surreptitiously. Lacy let the door fall closed behind him with a heavy thud, groaned and headed for his couch.

"I'm just gonna sleep some more, but make yourself at home," he faceplanted on his couch.

"I'll put this in the kitchen, and then," he looked at Lacy's bare back, the soft hair of his mullet stretching down his neck, the tight pull of his white tracksuit pants over his ass. "Right, kitchen."

He came back after he'd offloaded everything and debated what to do. His mission was accomplished. Lacy was breathing noisily, his face pressed into the cushion, but he wasn't asleep.

"Sit," Lacy said, muffled by the fabric.

"Okay," Thad replied automatically. He slipped his shoes off, crept into the living room and perched on the end of the couch near Lacy's feet.

He was debating what to do with himself when Lacy sat up, grabbed him by the shoulders and tugged him down. Lacy rolled onto his side, making a space for Thad behind him, then grabbed his arm and brought it around his chest.

"Hug," Lacy said.

"Oh, of course," Thad remembered. He pulled him closer so his chest was pressed against Lacy's back, his arm snug around his bare torso.

"That's better," Lacy murmured and wriggled back, his ass settling against Thad's groin. He slid his foot between Thad's. Thad felt self-conscious—this was unbearably intimate—but Lacy's breathing deepened, his body went lax, and Thad decided he could deal with it if it meant Lacy got more sleep. Besides, he liked the feel of it, being pressed against another body.

He just wasn't sure what he was going to do. He'd had his usual eight hours. And yet as he felt Lacy drift off in front of him, he couldn't bring himself to move.

That morning's church service was taken from the beginning of the Gospel according to Mark. Thad had found himself smothering a smile and ducking his head when the priest read from The Preaching of John the Baptist, 'This is the Good News about Jesus Christ, the Son of God.' It was certainly news then, so Thad didn't know why he was trying not to laugh. He regained his composure and focused, and thought about it again now—John preparing them for the coming of Jesus, baptising people in the Jordan River and urging them to turn away from their sins. He'd contemplated sin a lot in his life—his entire life had been structured around the binary of sinning and turning to God—and he pondered it again now, Lacy warm against his chest, the smell of his musky skin, like stale sweat, in Thad's nose.

Thad had concluded that it was impossible for a good man to sin, for even in error he would have meant well.

He woke up slowly, awareness drawn to his erection. It throbbed against something warm. It wasn't abnormal for him to wake up hard. He was a man; he woke up hard every morning, and always ignored it. But it was difficult to ignore now.

Thad groaned softly and rocked his hips forward. That felt even better. He did it again. He rarely gave into temptation, but sometimes he allowed himself to find release, consoled himself that he'd repent later, the familiar mixture of arousal and shame flowing through him whenever he did so. His dick flexed, strained against his pants. He rocked his hips forward, trying to get more.

The warmth answered him, rocking back to meet him with a low rumble from the chest Thad's hands were wrapped around.

The chest his hands were wrapped around—

Thad's eyes popped open to Lacy's silky brown hair, the sleeve of tattoos around his neck. Lacy pushed his ass back.

Thad needed to let go, he needed to get up. This was wrong.

"Lacy," he said, voice rough.

"Hmm," Lacy replied sleepily, "feels good."

Thad gripped him tighter. His hips worked against the warning in his head.

And Lacy met him. Rubbing his ass up and down Thad's erection. He groaned, adjusted his legs so Thad could get closer.

Thad humped him. The tingling in his groin spread to his stomach, his chest. His fingers gripped and released on Lacy's skin. He pulled him closer. A blind desire wiped out the warning in his head.

He gasped as he ejaculated, pressed his wet lips to Lacy's nape and mouthed at his skin. He remembered the hickey he'd seen and wanted to suck his own mark.

He kissed Lacy's throat as he caught his breath, became aware of his dick softening around the wetness in his pants.

He let go, wriggled back, hot shame and terror rushing through him.

"I'm so sorry," he whispered as he extricated himself and got to his feet.

"Mm," Lacy rolled onto his back, squinted up at him. "It's all good, it happens."

Thad's mouth dropped open. It happens? To who? To Lacy?

"I'm sorry," he said again. This didn't happen, it wasn't normal. On so many levels it wasn't normal or okay. Premarital, extramarital, deviant sex—homosexuality was deviant sex—were all sins. Shocking, abominable sins. The ways of a loose moral society. He'd been taught—and agreed wholeheartedly—that he must have discipline over his body in regards to sex. He was celibate. And he would remain that way until marriage. It wasn't a struggle for him. No woman had ever tempted him.

"Eh," Lacy shrugged and slipped his eyes closed again. "Wanna eat?"

Thad didn't understand what was happening. Was Lacy really okay with what had happened? Did Lacy do this with a lot of men? And if so, which men? Was he seeing other men? Not that he was 'seeing' Thad—

Thad gripped his head in his hands and tried to calm down. He'd never even kissed someone and now he'd gone and used another man's body to have an orgasm. He snuck a look at Lacy stretched on the couch—he was breathing evenly and he was... hard.

Thad's lips parted and he dropped his hands. He couldn't tear his eyes away. Lacy's penis was thick, it pointed up and flexed under the white material.

As Thad watched, Lacy reached down and squeezed himself.

Thad flicked his eyes up. Lacy was watching him with slitted eyes.

God help him, *he* wanted to squeeze Lacy's erection.

"I have to go," he said and spun to get his shoes.

"Go?" Lacy asked from behind him. "Go where?"

Thad fumbled to get his shoes on, decided to forget about the laces. He grabbed his keys from the side table.

"Thad, man," Lacy was saying from behind him—he was up, he was close.

Thad yanked the door open, pulled it closed behind him and power walked for his car. He struggled with the car door but managed to get it open and himself in, his fingers clumsy as he tried to put the key in the ignition. A knock on the window made him jump.

Lacy's face was pinched as he made the motion for Thad to roll the window down.

Thad did.

"Sorry," Thad rushed out, "I shouldn't have... I have to, I need to, I'm so sorry!"

Lacy didn't say anything, but his frown deepened.

"Thad, man," he said slowly, "I dunno what you're even apologising for, but I don't reckon you should be driving."

Thad gripped the steering wheel.

"C'mon, come back inside and have a glass of water. We'll pretend it never happened, alright?"

Pretend it never happened? How was he going to pretend it never happened?

Lacy opened the door. "C'mon, let's watch the Freo game."

Thad swung his shaky legs out of the car.

"I reckon they're gonna choke again, what do you think?" Lacy asked. Thad stood, shut the door, gripped his keys tightly in his palm.

"I think they've learned from their mistakes," he replied breathlessly.

Lacy laughed, bumped Thad's shoulder with his own to get him moving. "Always lookin' on the bright side, eh? Well, I like your optimism, but I reckon they're cursed."

"Curses aren't real," Thad said and followed Lacy back inside. He was shaking.

"Yeah? Tell that to a man and his goat and the Chicago Cubs," Lacy quipped and led Thad into his kitchen, told him to take a seat.

Thad watched him moving around. His tracksuit pants were so low on his hips, the crack at the top was visible above the swell of his ass. Thad swallowed. He'd rubbed off against that ass. Shame washed through him. And something else. Desire.

"Here," Lacy said and slid the water in front of him. "What'd you cook for me?"

"Soup," Thad replied on auto-pilot. "And I bought some—"

"Crusty bread!" Lacy grinned over at him from where he was un-packing the bag, his gap tooth smile on full display, his face lit up under the pallid skin and shadows flanking his eyes.

"Of course," Thad tried to smile. He drank his water.

His groin was wet. His face hot. He really should go.

But Lacy was pulling out bowls, slicing bread, shooting him reas-suring smiles like everything was fine, and Thad didn't know how to leave.

Nevertheless, he needed to do something about his pants.

"I'm just going to," he stood slowly, the stool scraping loudly on the tiles, making him wince as he waved towards the downstairs bath-room.

"No need to ask, man," Lacy grinned.

"Right," Thad smiled tightly, "of course. I'll just," he shuffled awk-wardly for the hall, trying to hide his groin from Lacy's sight. How was he going to sit through a game like this?

"You can borrow some trackies if you want."

Thad froze. He looked over his shoulder. Lacy was focused on cutting up the bread, speaking as if the conversation held little interest for him. Thad thought anew how good Lacy was at that—going by the media portrayal of Lacy, you'd think he was a feral party animal who barrelled through life with zero awareness of the feelings of his fellow men. But he wasn't like that at all. Quite the opposite.

"Shower's all yours too if you need it," he went on as he buttered the bread. "Trackies in the bottom drawer."

He gave Thad his back as he served up their soup.

"Thank you," Thad replied quietly.

He went up the stairs and stepped onto the landing of Lacy's bed-room. The king-sized bed was huge and yet the room was so large, it

fit with plenty of space around it. Black and white artistically
framed pictures adorned the walls—naked men, Olympians, dis-
cus, javelin, shot put, all posed in a way to conceal their genitals,
but showcase their back muscles, glutes, torso, their bodies shiny
in the matte grey finish. Thad stared at them.

There was a chest of drawers, lots of photos of Lacy with
various people on top of it—his mum, his drag queen date at
the Brownlow's, George and Finn at their wedding, lots of team
pictures, a black and white photo of an adolescent boy, the ghost
of a smile on his lips. Thad bent and opened the bottom drawer,
rummaged through the tracksuit pants for a darker pair, but they
were all whites and greys, and they were all going to be too small
and short in the leg for him. But it was better than free-balling it
in his jeans, so he took the grey ones and headed for the ensuite.

He deliberately turned his back to the mirror as he took his
pants off. His jocks were wet with so much come, he thought he'd
combust from embarrassment. He cupped the mess, shoved them
inside his jeans and rolled the whole lot into a ball. Pulling off his
jumper and shirt, he tried to calm down—he still couldn't believe
he'd done that. What on earth was wrong with him?

The shower was enormous with an equally large shower-
head—it was like standing in the rain. Thad washed himself
quickly with Lacy's fancy, eucalyptus-scented body wash. There
was a bag mounted to the wall, like a hot water bottle, with a long
tube coiled around the bracket, a nozzle on the end. It looked like
a piece of medical equipment. Thad had never seen anything like
it before.

By the time he came back downstairs in the too short, too tight
trackies, Lacy was on the couch, dipping his spoon in the soup and
taking small mouthfuls as he muttered at the TV. Thad's own food

was on the coffee table next to a glass of juice. It felt surreal in its domesticity and familiarity.

"Who's winning?" he forced himself to ask as he came over.

"Brisbane," Lacy replied and darted his eyes up. He cracked up.

"What?" Thad asked.

"Nothin', nothin', just, sometimes I forget how tall you are," Lacy looked at his feet. "Are your ankles cold?"

"No?" Thad replied and looked down at them. The pants came to mid-calf.

Lacy chuckled. "You can borrow some socks if you want?"

"I'm good," Thad replied with a small smile. He knew his face was embarrassingly red, his bundle of clothes under his arm a physical manifestation of that shame. "I'll just," he gestured to the kitchen, meaning, 'I'll just get a bag and stuff this somewhere out of sight, maybe set it on fire.'

"I got it," Lacy got up. Before Thad could protest, Lacy grabbed the bundle and slipped down his hallway. Thad heard the washing machine turn on. He was mortified.

"Aren't you gonna eat?" Lacy asked as he came back.

"Yes," Thad agreed and sat down. He made sure he was a good metre away—he didn't want Lacy to have to worry he'd get jumped again—and started eating.

"Still hot," Thad said.

"Waited 'til I heard the shower turn off," Lacy replied, eyes fixed on the screen. "Oh, come on, Hiller, you fucking clown!" he shouted. "Can you believe this guy? He's got Reaver wide open and he takes the shot himself."

"He does it all the time, but only to Reaver," Thad murmured, focused on eating.

"I know, it's fucking bullshit. Jack's a top fucking bloke, could be scoring way more for them, but Hiller, his fucking *teammate*," Lacy said, seething, "hangs him out to dry constantly."

"I wonder why," Thad said.

"Dunno, but it's fucked for Jack, really fucks him up," Lacy pushed his empty bowl away, sat back, eyes on the screen.

Thad knew they were ex-teammates, and it was hard to miss the news of Jack's request for the trade to go back home to Perth, but he didn't know they were that close.

"You're good friends with Jack?" he asked.

"Yeah, man, Jack's the best," Lacy replied. "It sucked when he left, but I got it too. I never had to leave Melbourne but I reckon if I did, it woulda been hard. I'm pretty close to my mum and all my mates. What about you? You miss Tassie?"

Thad set his bowl down. This all felt normal enough. He thought about it. "Not really," he answered honestly. "I did more when I was in Queensland, but not so much here."

"'Cos you're closer to home?" Lacy asked, peering at him.

"No," Thad shook his head. That wasn't it. The reason was Lacy. But he couldn't come out and say that after what he'd just done—geez, what would Lacy think of him? "Just a better fit here. With the team, I mean."

Lacy grinned. "Yeah, it is."

He focused back on the TV. "Oh, come on!"

On screen, Hiller was screaming at Jack. It was quite the sight between teammates and the commentators were having a field day. Jack snapped something and Hiller smirked.

"Maybe Jack did something to him?" Thad asked. "Because Hiller's normally really relaxed."

"I know, right?" Lacy said. "I said that to Jack but he was like, I never did anything! But he reckons it musta been something when they played against each other in high school. But Hiller should fucking tell him, not like Jack would ever do something on purpose."

"High school? That's a bit petty," Thad said.

"Right?" Lacy said and cleared their dishes. "That was fuckin' lit, man, thank you. I feel a thousand times better."

"Anytime," Thad replied, blushing.

Lacy came back and they watched Freo get thumped. By the time Thad left, back in his freshly washed and dried jeans and jocks, he felt marginally better. He'd never live this down in his own head, but he appreciated how much Lacy took it in his stride. It would never, ever happen again and they could continue to be good friends thanks to Lacy's graciousness.

6

♥

LACY CLOSED THE DOOR on Thad. He pressed his back against it, pushed his trackies down, grabbed his dick and jerked off frantically. He was wound up so fucking tight; he'd managed to keep his hands to himself for the entire, excruciating afternoon when all he wanted to do was beg Thad to take that big dick out, shove it up his ass, hold him down and fuck him until he couldn't breathe.

He'd still be loose enough from the guys he took at the party the night before—Thad could've slipped right in.

His hand was dry, and he was being rough, but he was already at the edge, teetering there, his whole body tingling. He was always horny with the lingering effects of the drugs. Having Thad rub off on him, fucking hold him, pant wetly at his neck—Lacy swore, panted, about to come.

As it hit him, he gasped with the fantasy—Thad in him, over him, crushing him as he fucked him, held him.

"Jesus," he whispered as he caught his breath.

He cupped his come in his hand and walked gingerly down the hall to the downstairs bathroom to get cleaned up. Thad had been so spooked, it'd hurt something in Lacy. Lacy didn't understand it—so he got off with a teammate, so what? They were young, horny guys. Shit happened.

He washed his hands, shoved his pants off, strolled naked down the hall and thought about Thad leaving. Lacy hated seeing Thad so cut up.

Well, he thought, as he flopped face first down on his bed, there was nothing for it but to let it go, to pretend it never happened.

He really didn't want to pretend it never happened. He wanted to do it again, but with more reciprocity next time. He huffed a laugh into the pillow. That was never, ever going to happen.

They had an early training session and then coach's video review the next day. Thad was stoic, just a hint of fear in his eyes when he met Lacy's in the car when he picked him up, but Lacy forced normal into the interaction and by the time they sat side by side for the review, Thad had relaxed, wasn't twitching whenever Lacy tapped him, bumped him or generally made any sudden movements in his vicinity.

The door clanged open as Alanson came in. Lacy couldn't shake 'The Bible' moniker, but felt weird saying it on account of Thad remaining perplexed.

"Right," he said as he stood in front of the room, clasping his hands together. "How many of you know I have three granddaughters?"

They exchanged glances, unsure where this was going.

"That wasn't rhetorical," he went on.

"I did not know that," Lacy offered.

"Anyone else?" Alanson asked, looking at everyone severely.

There was a chorus of "No," "No idea," and "Do we need to know that?" from Les.

"Well, I don't know if you need to know it, Les, but I think maybe you do," he rubbed his chin, "because my girls, at ages three, six, and nine, could've made a better showing with the football on Friday night than you lot. Fancy that? Little Grace can't even talk properly and yet, I'd venture she could handle a football better than you clowns."

"Fucking hell," Lacy said under his breath. "That's a bit of an exaggeration," he leaned over to whisper to Thad.

Thad twitched but didn't say anything.

"Lacy," Alanson zoned in on him.

"Yeah?"

Alanson stared at him.

Lacy waited.

"You were an exception."

The guys made scoffing noises and ribbed him. Lacy grinned. "Yeah, I was."

"Clay," Alanson snapped.

Lacy tensed.

"Yes?" Thad asked.

"Shocker. Absolute fucking shocker. Were you tryin' to tap to the opposition? Was that your aim on Saturday? Or are you simply colour blind?"

Thad didn't say anything, but he hunched further down in his seat even though Lacy could see he was trying not to.

"Well, can you see colour? Does black look like blue to you? Is that how colour blindness works?" he asked the room seriously.

"My cousin's colour blind," Les said. "But I've never asked him."

Alanson stared at him. Les shrank back in his seat.

"We're gonna watch this game," Alanson said after a long, painful minute, "and all of you, except Lacy, sucked ass out there. Clay, you especially."

"Steady on, for fuck's sake," Lacy said.

"What was that?" Alanson asked.

"I said, steady on, can't expect Thad to work a miracle when he's up against the best ruckman in the league," Lacy sat up. "He did his bloody job, what more do you want from him?"

"Lacy," Thad said quietly.

"No, let's be realistic," Lacy went on, "let's watch this fucking thing and I'll show you what I mean."

Alanson narrowed his eyes. "Are you looking for a suspension this week, Lacy? Feel like testing your skills in the State league?"

"So long as I get to play, I don't give a shit where," Lacy retorted. "But I ain't wrong about this. You're outta line."

"It's alright," Thad cut in, "I know I wasn't at my best." He spread his big palms wide in a peacemaking gesture.

"It's not alright," Lacy said. He turned to face Thad. Lacy searched his expression, swallowed down what he was going to say next and slumped back in his seat.

"Right," Alanson snapped, "Lacy, in my office after this. Clay, focus on how much you suck, I'll be givin' pointers."

Lacy tensed but before he could speak, Thad shot out his hand and gripped his wrist.

Thad nodded at Alanson. Lacy ground his teeth together.

It was a painful video review. It always was when they lost—watching themselves on screen making terrible decisions, fumbling, creating turnovers. Alanson was right in so far as Lacy was the exception—he kicked five goals and kept them from being a complete disaster, with

Cary shoring up some points. But he would still argue that Thad didn't do anything wrong; he was just outclassed.

"Sit," Alanson said when he had Lacy in his office after the video review.

"I'll stand," Lacy replied and shoved his hands behind his back, squared his shoulders.

"Suit yourself," Alanson remained standing behind the desk. "You wanna tell me why you think it's okay to question my assessment? Are you the coach, Lacy? Did someone forget to tell me?"

"I ain't the coach and I don't appreciate the sarcasm, but you're outta line when you say that shit to Thad. He was outclassed and we both know it. That ain't the same as havin' a bad game," Lacy said, voice steady. He knew he was right.

"And you think telling him to accept that and get a pat on the back, maybe even a participation award for the game, is the best way to improve his play, is that it?" Alanson smirked.

"Still not lovin' this sarcasm," Lacy said. "And what I'm sayin' is layin' into him isn't gonna change anything, is it? Singling him out."

Alanson continued to smirk and rub his chin thoughtfully. "I'm gonna run this team as I see fit and if you want to play on this team, you're gonna have to accept it. Even when it means I coach your boyfriend in a way you don't like."

He delivered the last line like he'd hit Lacy with a real zinger. Lacy scoffed, but his heart wasn't in it.

"Well, I reckon you're gonna be hearing from me then," Lacy quipped.

"And you'll be suspended this week for insubordination," Alanson sat down, picked up the phone. "You got a jumper or shall I get one sent down for you?"

Lacy hid his surprise. Of course he didn't have a jumper for their State league team—the reserve team—he'd never played a game there in his life. He'd gone number one and played his whole career in the league.

"You better get it sent down," Lacy smiled. "Make sure they use my number, and good luck this weekend."

He turned and headed for the door.

"Lacy?"

"Yep?" Lacy looked over his shoulder.

"I can respect sticking up for your mates," Alanson said seriously, "but I can't have this shit in my room, understand? Think about that if you wanna come back next week."

"I'll take it under advisement," Lacy replied and sauntered out the door.

"What happened?" Thad asked, standing as soon as Lacy walked into the empty locker room.

"Eh," Lacy shrugged. "You ready to go? I'm fuckin' starved."

Thad stepped forward. "Of course, but he didn't drop you, did he?"

Lacy turned for the door. "I reckon we should get a pub lunch, steak and salad, what do you think?"

"Whatever you like," Thad strolled quickly over to where Lacy held the door open. "I just don't want you risking your career for me. Alanson is right, I wasn't any good."

Lacy stopped dead. "Bullshit. Being outclassed is not the same as not playin' good. And gettin' hammered for it is not gonna help."

"Well, no, negative reinforcement has been proven ineffective," Thad said and Lacy snorted a laugh. "But I don't want you risking getting dropped for me. You're going to win the Brownlow this year."

Lacy rolled his eyes. "I don't give a shit about the Brownlow," he muttered. "C'mon, I'm starved."

They made it to Thad's car, Thad suspiciously quiet beside him. He had the key in the ignition but wasn't turning it. Lacy really wished he would—he'd plugged in his playlist that morning and while Thad's car was at least ten years old, a carefully maintained Toyota SUV, it had a decent sound system.

Thad looked at him. "You said you don't care about the Brownlow."

Lacy shrugged. "Well, I care as much as the next bloke."

"No, but," Thad shook his head. "Did you get suspended?"

Lacy sighed. "It's no big deal."

Thad's lips parted. "You got suspended."

"I reckon a trip is just what I need to rejuvenate, it's no big deal. It's not like a real suspension anyway. Just gonna lose some potential points," Lacy replied. "Can we go now? I'm seriously hungry, man."

Thad gripped the steering wheel and stared straight ahead.

"It's really no big deal. You woulda done the same for me," Lacy reiterated after they sat in uncomfortable silence for a minute.

"I would," Thad agreed readily. He turned to look at Lacy. "But I'm not half the player you are so it doesn't matter—"

"Stop—"

"No, listen to me," Thad implored. "Please don't do that again. Promise me you won't do that again."

"There's no way I'm makin' that promise," Lacy retorted and slumped in his seat. "The Bible's gotta learn that it ain't cool to shit all over you."

Thad frowned. "It's so confusing when you guys say that," he said, the comment taking him out of this conversation, which was Lacy's intention. But then he went on. "I don't take it to heart. So please, for me, promise you won't do that again."

"For fuck's sake," Lacy muttered. He sat up. "I can't promise my mouth won't run without my permission, but I'll do my best. It ain't right though, Thad. It ain't fuckin' right."

"Alright, well, a lot of things aren't right, but we have to accept them and you know..." Thad shrugged and turned the key, the old girl purring to life.

"You know what?" Lacy asked and cranked the volume. He fucking loved *The Prodigy*, started bopping his head to the beat.

Thad reversed, straightened the car and drove out of the empty carpark slowly.

"You know, trust in the higher good," Thad murmured.

"And sometimes the higher good needs a bit of a hand."

Thad shook his head. "Well, in this instance, he's got it covered, alright?"

Lacy rolled his eyes. "No promises except I'll do my best to trust this asshole to protect you, but if he fails to come in aces, I've got your back."

"Please don't call God an asshole," Thad said, trying not to smile.

"What if he's legit being an asshole?"

Thad was sucking his cheeks in to stop the laughter. Lacy always thought religious people would get all offended, but Thad seemed pretty secure in all that shit and took Lacy's mocking for what it was—a joke. He pulled into a spot right in front of the pub.

"He's never an asshole," Thad said, fumbling over the swear word. "He just works in mysterious ways sometimes."

"The Lord works in mysterious ways!" Lacy said in an imitation of a preacher.

Thad snickered. "It's true and that's when you've got to trust."

"Alright, well, maybe I'm part of the mysterious ways," Lacy unclipped his seatbelt. "You ever thought of that?"

Thad did laugh then, his eyes crinkling fondly. "I didn't, but, okay."

"Okay I can get into fights for you?"

"No, don't do that again, I'm serious," Thad said as they got out and meandered inside. He leaned down and continued softly near Lacy's ear. "But I'll accept you're a part of the big mystery working for the common good."

The proximity made Lacy shiver, the line made him laugh.

"Right, well," he shook it off, "better enjoy this before I have to dine on meat pies and choc milk down in the country."

Thad sighed, the fun evaporating from their conversation.

Lacy bumped him. "It's all good, man, seriously. Maybe this is part of your mysterious tapestry or whatever."

Thad shook his head, but he let it go when Lacy changed the subject to how good the hot chips were at this place and his theory they were cooking them in MSG.

"Like, in the oil," he finished as they took a seat.

And Thad looked like he didn't know whether to crack up laughing or take that seriously and ask the proprietor of this fine establishment if that was what they were doing. So, business as usual.

7

♥

T HAD WATCHED FROM HIS couch as Lacy had an absolute blinder in the State game that Saturday. Taking screamer after screamer out of the pocket, he'd launch himself on his defender's back with a knee for balance, mark the ball, crash-land to the ground, jump up to the sound of the thousands of people who'd come because they'd heard he was playing down there, all of them screaming and clapping as he lined up and belted perfect goal after perfect goal. He'd hold his hand up to his ear, grin madly as he ran along the boundary, his glossy mullet streaming behind him. It was so ridiculous even his defender was smiling at him by the end of it, clapping him on the back with a laugh when the final siren sounded.

The commentators had an absolute field day, asking if Alanson had lost his mind. Especially since they'd lost their game in an absolute shocker in the prime Friday night slot the night before.

But they asked the question like they'd been expecting it since Lacy was drafted and infamously turned up to the first day of preseason training so hungover he'd had to excuse himself during a media scrum to turn around and vomit. What nobody ever mentioned, and Thad knew like footy folklore, was Lacy had been the best on ground that day in the training.

And now they speculated knowingly, '*He'd miss his nine to fives eventually with his lifestyle,*' always with a grave intonation as if Lacy was sacrificing puppies on the weekend in some cult. Alanson refused to give an explanation beyond, 'Disciplinary action,' which Thad both appreciated and hated. He didn't want it known he was the reason Lacy got sent down, but he was physically repelled by the idea Lacy had behaved unprofessionally. He loved footy, he loved the team—he'd never disrespect the game or them like that.

That was incredible, he sent as soon as the game finished.

Showing em how it's done, baby!!!! Came back immediately and Thad laughed.

He was surprised to get the reply so promptly; Lacy would've only just gotten back to the change rooms.

When do you get back? he sent.

2moro morning. But could be later. Gonna celebrate.

Thad was happy because Lacy was happy, but the thought of Lacy celebrating, hungover, stretched out on his couch—it brought the memory roaring back. He'd firmly locked his indiscretion away, but save from having the memory surgically removed it was going to haunt him with reminders like this.

He'd prayed on it, which had gotten him nowhere. Never before had prayer coincided with feeling aroused. He'd focused instead on repenting. Why he'd done it would have to wait for the day when the memory didn't see him thickening up in his pants.

Gonna come right to yours.

Thad's stomach flipped.

See you then, he replied carefully.

He got back a series of emojis—party explosions, happy faces, an eggplant—and laughed.

Thad marched down the hallway when there was a knock on his door shortly after one the next day. He opened it to a smiling but tired-looking Lacy. He stepped forward and swept him into a big hug before he could think better of it.

"Oof," Lacy joked but gripped him back. "Miss me?"

Thad squeezed him, let go, stepped back, and ushered him inside. "Come in, come in. How was the drive?"

"Eh, you know, lots of paddocks and shit." Lacy stepped inside, grinning up at him. "You played well."

Thad scoffed, but he was smiling too much to pull off the derision. "I won't say I didn't do my job," he led Lacy down the hall, "but 'played well' might be stretching it. You though?" he looked over his shoulder. "You were amazing. I bet Alanson's wondering how to punish you if you enjoy it that much."

"He texted."

"Really?" Thad got busy serving the Sunday roast he'd cooked. "What did it say?"

"Good game," Lacy replied, smirking.

Thad cracked up. "Understatement."

Lacy shrugged. He cocked his hip on the kitchen bench and watched Thad's hands work, yawned. "Reckon I'm gonna eat and pass out."

"You can do that," Thad smiled.

"Here," he handed him a plate. "I'll bring your drink, coffee table's set-up."

"Man, I could legit fucking kiss you right now," Lacy beamed before wandering into the living room leaving Thad feeling winded.

It was a joke, of course it was a joke. He busied himself with pouring some cordial and bringing the glasses in. Lacy was sitting forward, waiting for Thad.

"No need to wait for me, eat." Thad was so glad he was back, it was ridiculous.

"I know you do some prayer shit every time we eat, man, don't lie," Lacy said as he picked up the remote and clicked on the TV.

Thad did, but he hadn't realised Lacy waited to pick up his knife and fork because he was waiting for him to finish. The only time he hadn't waited, Thad realised, was after his indiscretion—Lacy had been eating when he came down from the shower. Did he do it to make Thad feel normal?

He went and got his plate, set it down, sat, closed his eyes, recited a prayer quickly, then picked up his knife and fork. The Adelaide derby was about to start.

"What do you say when you do that?" Lacy asked. Thad felt like he'd never been away; he asked like he'd been sitting there on Thad's couch all day.

"You mean the prayer? You never said grace?" Thad asked.

"Nah, man, I get food put in front of me, I eat it. Wasn't always much of it when I was growin' up, reckon I was pretty thankful when it appeared. Does that count?"

"I think so, yes," Thad took a mouthful. The centre bounce was about to happen.

"So, what's the prayer? Say it out loud," Lacy said.

Thad looked at him. Lacy was watching him back, his expression friendly.

Thad swallowed. "Right now?"

"Yeah? Why not?"

Thad set his plate down and faced forward. He made a quick sign of the cross, clasped his hands and began: "Bless us Oh Lord for these thy gifts for what we are about to receive, may the Lord make us truly thankful. Through Christ our Lord, amen." He made another quick cross.

He picked up his fork and refocused on the TV.

"Huh," Lacy said. He resumed eating.

It was a sunny day in Adelaide; the grass on the TV bright green, the sky an expansive blue above the shitshow from the first bounce. Derbies were always a shitshow.

"Have you got a favourite prayer?" Lacy asked.

Thad jerked his attention away from the game. Lacy was sitting cross-legged on the couch, his food half-eaten, eyes on Thad.

"No one's ever asked me that," Thad said after a moment. "But I guess it'd be the Lord's Prayer, which is boring and predictable, I know. But it calms me, the cadence of it."

"Can you say that one?" Lacy asked and took a mouthful of roast potatoes. He swallowed. Pointed at his plate with his fork. "Fuck these are good? How do you do that?"

"I keep the drippings and cook in the fat. You really want me to recite another prayer?"

"Yeah, man, I like listening to you say it and do the fancy shit with your hands," Lacy replied. "And should we be eating stuff cooked in fat?"

"It's real fat," Thad said and set his plate on the coffee table. "And I'm making the sign of the cross," he did it slowly, said the words in English, then in Latin just to show off a bit even though their denomination never used the Latin.

Lacy whistled. "What'd you say?"

Thad laughed, shook his head, "Just 'In the name of the Father, and of the Son, and of the Holy Spirit, amen', but in Latin."

"Sounds lit. Are you gonna say the prayer?"

Thad ducked his head and huffed a laugh. But if Lacy wanted to hear it—he sat up, shrugged. "Alright." He made the sign of the cross, murmured the words, then began: "Our Father, who art in heaven, hallowed be Thy name. Thy kingdom come, Thy will be done; on earth as it is in heaven. Give us this day our daily bread, and forgive us our sins, as we forgive those who sin against us. Lead us not into temptation, but deliver us from all evil. For Thine is the kingdom, the power and the glory, for ever and ever. Amen."

Lacy clapped.

Thad shook his head and chuckled.

"You guys are real obsessed with sinning, eh?"

Thad tilted his head. "I think there's a lot of that in there, but it gets oversimplified. Like," he sat back, "people think it's about doing bad out in the world, right? About God judging and punishing out there. But if you read closer, it's not about that at all, it's about your relationship with God, your relationship with sin. It's about being a good man and that's between you and God."

"How do you know, but? If God reckons you're good?"

"That's the part that can't be explained, but you just do."

Lacy pointed at him with his fork. "And this is where you fall down."

Thad shrugged, smiled. "Can't really fall down if it's got nothing to do with anyone else, can you?"

Lacy didn't say anything. They watched the game.

"I guess not," Lacy said. Thad knew he was answering the earlier question, but didn't really know what to do with the reply.

"You want dessert?" he asked, clearing their plates.

"Is the Pope Catholic?" Lacy asked.

Thad laughed and went and got them dessert.

The end of the season was upon them too quickly. They managed to make the first preliminary final thanks to Lacy, but even playing out of his skin he got flooded by Adelaide's defence-orientated style. And with no one feeding him through the corridor, he had little to work with. The push to the wings collapsed, Thad struggling to get a clean tap in the crush of so many bodies. Lacy kicked four goals anyway, belting his chest at the rival supporters, cackling as they booed him, but it hurt to see his shoulders slump when the final siren sounded.

The flight home was quiet. The final meeting before they broke up for offseason similarly bleak. Thad wouldn't see Lacy until preseason training in three months.

"You're headed back to Tassie, yeah?" Lacy asked as they walked to his car.

"For a little bit, yes," Thad smiled down at him. "Then I'm off to Africa."

"Africa?" Lacy jerked and looked up at him. "What for like, a safari?"

Thad chuckled, shook his head. "No, it's with the church, we're building a school."

"Get outta here, for real?" Lacy bumped him.

"Yes?"

Lacy squinted up at him, the spring sunshine blinding. "That's awesome, man."

Once they were driving, Lacy spoke again suddenly. "Be careful there, alright?"

"I think it's pretty safe," Thad replied.

"No, but," Lacy turned in his seat, "sometimes it's not, it's really fucking not. I heard the medical navy ships train in Johannesburg to prepare for warzones."

"Well, I'm not going to Johannesburg, but I promise to be careful."

"Good."

Too soon, they were parked in Lacy's driveway. Thad wanted to come in, but Lacy had a flight to Amsterdam booked for that night.

"Have fun in Amsterdam," his voice felt tight and he didn't understand why.

"Yeah," Lacy looked out the window, head nodding. "C'mon, get out so I can hug you goodbye."

Thad did as he was told. Lacy came around to the front of the bonnet, and Thad took the two steps to meet him. Lacy's arms slipped around his waist, hands gripping the back of his shirt. Thad wrapped him up and held him tightly. His chest felt warm where Lacy pressed against him. He didn't want to not see Lacy for three months, but he couldn't say that. He rested his head against the top of Lacy's head, inhaled the smell of his shampoo, felt his glossy hair rub against his cheek.

Lacy loosened his grip, ran his palms up and down Thad's back.

"Okay," Lacy pulled back and Thad let him go. "Call me. Text me."

"Every day," Thad said without thinking, but Lacy lit up with a huge grin.

"Every day," Lacy agreed. He tucked his hands in his pockets and waited for Thad to get back in the car.

Thad reversed, looked back up the driveway. Lacy stood where he'd left him, smiling softly. He pulled a hand out of his pocket and waved. Thad lifted his hand off the steering wheel.

He straightened the tyres, hit the accelerator, and gave one last look. Lacy was still there; he'd been frowning, but he grinned when he caught Thad's eyes. Thad returned it. He wanted to drive back up the driveway, park, get out and ask if Lacy wanted some company in Amsterdam.

But of course, he couldn't do that. Offseason belonged to service, and that's just the way it was. Imagine his parents' faces if he said he was going to Europe for a holiday instead? His smile felt more real and he swore Lacy beamed when he saw it. Thad huffed a laugh, caught a car in his rear vision mirror and accelerated before he blocked traffic.

8

♥

*D*RINK PLENTY OF WATER.

Lacy blinked. He didn't know what time it was or where he was. He'd woken up, rolled over, opened his phone and scrolled through his texts with Thad from the day and night before. It was routine now.

He felt the bed move next to him and rolled over. There was a big dude sleeping next to him—naked, nice tribal tattoos on his arms, shaved head. Lacy couldn't remember him, but as he glanced around the room, he realised he must've been in his place. Somewhere in London. That's right, he was in London. In a small flat by the looks of it—he could see the pokey lounge beyond the open bedroom doors, imagined the tiny kitchen and dining room, probably a bathroom.

He glanced back at his texts.

Thad telling him about the kids. Thad asking if he was enjoying London, asking if he'd been to Hyde Park and urging him to check out some church. Lots of laughing emojis at Lacy's reply regarding where he preferred to worship—the bath house—and Thad's disbelieving, *good one.*

Lacy laughed under his breath. The messages always went awry once Lacy started drinking, but Thad seemed to keep pace with him, replying earnestly as Lacy's texts devolved into random questions—*where the fuck r the bathrooms in ths place?*—to unfocused photos, emojis, and the inevitable—embarrassing—series of, *I miss u. Wish u were here. Y didn't u come with me?*

He shook his head at himself, awash with the usual mix of humiliation and delight at Thad's careful replies, coming immediately, *I miss you too. I wish I was there too. I would have if you asked* and a winking face before the final series telling him to get some rest, to take care of himself and finally, to drink plenty of water.

His mouth was like a desert full of dry assholes. He remembered drinks. He remembered doing lines of coke. He remembered taking ecstasy. The last concrete thing he remembered was a dick up his ass and one in his mouth in the dark rooms at the bath house. The red lights in the hall. The sound of skin slapping on skin. Groaning. Soft swear words. Then, it all just blinked out. He'd read once that a blackout wasn't a failure to remember, but the brain not forming any memories at all—it stopped inputting data. He'd closed that bit of information down in a tab in his brain and tried not to think about it. Unfortunately, it was one of his first thoughts after a night out and another blackout and he wondered how in the fuck he got from there to wherever he was. Like right now. What had happened in those intervening hours? How was he still fucking alive?

The guy next to him shifted and Lacy scooted out of the bed. His bare foot landed on something slimy—a used condom. He shook it off and got up. He tiptoed around the room and found his clothes. He had a tremor, just a light thrum under the surface of his skin, an ache in his chest he knew would grow as the day wore on. He squinted, the daylight in the living area too bright for his eyes. He found the bathroom, drank some water with a cupped palm, washed his face, took stock of himself in the mirror. He looked like shit—black smudges under his bloodshot eyes, skin pasty-white, hair matted, caked and congealed. He stuck his head in the sink and rinsed it, used wet palms to wash the dried and flaking come off his stomach, between his ass cheeks and thighs.

Then he got dressed quickly, found his shoes and coat by the door and got the fuck out of there. His phone pinged as he stepped onto the landing before the small flight of stairs that'd take him to a street he didn't know.

Are you okay?

Lacy's heart clenched. Thad always sent this after Lacy went on a bender. He'd been in Europe for two months and he'd gotten this same message after these same nights every time.

Alive, he typed quickly, added a series of celebration emojis even though he felt the complete opposite, but he didn't want Thad to worry.

He stepped onto the street, glanced up and down the rows and rows of white buildings, the black iron fencing, the grey pavement. He had no idea where he was. He figured it out quickly with the share ride app, his hand shaking as he typed, sat down on the curb and waited for a guy named Ahmed to come and pick him up.

His phone pinged.

Hooray!!

Lacy snorted. Thad was typing. Lacy prepared himself—Thad always had a lot of questions about how Lacy's night had gone, only this time it was a simple question.

When do you get back?

Lacy had to think about it. He was pretty sure he had a flight out of Madrid in two weeks. Well, he knew he was leaving via Madrid, but he wasn't sure on the time. He opened up his emails. Fifteen days.

He replied.

Just in time for preseason, came back with a smiling face.

Then: *I'm back now.*

Lacy blinked. Typed. *Ur in Melbourne now?*

Yes.

Lacy's heart beat faster, he rolled his tongue in his mouth, trying to get his saliva working.

His car pulled up and he got in, said hello to Ahmed, sank into his seat and gripped his phone.

He opened up his flights and logged into their website. Searched flights from London to Melbourne. There was one leaving that night; it included a bitch of a layover in Doha—one hour in Doha was too long, so six was a real bitch—but he was paying the five-hundred-dollar charge to change his flights, even though he'd be downgraded to economy, and confirming his booking with relief.

Did you get some sleep? Was waiting for him when his phone came back on. He walked up the tunnel in Doha in search of a row of empty seats to lay down on. His skin was covered in a sheen of sweat and it wasn't from the oppressive heat he could see shimmering outside, the airport pleasantly air-conditioned. Hands shaking, he sent a thumbs up.

Hoisting his carry-on backpack up his shoulder, he stepped into the high-ceiling walkway, merged with the throng of people milling about doing god knows what. The place was always packed and there was nothing to do but shop. Not even a bar. At least, he'd never found one.

His phone pinged again. He clenched it in his hand and went to the wall of screens. He didn't even have a gate yet. He needed to lay down. Flying while coming down off a bender was a fresh hell he hoped to never live through again. But as his phone pinged again, he knew it'd be worth it to get to Thad's place, get a big hug, something to eat, stretch out on his old couch and listen to his calm voice telling him all about the kids in Africa.

He spotted three empty seats next to some women in full black hijabs, their eyes flicking up to him with disgust and apprehension as he collapsed next to them. They shuffled down and he wanted to assure them they were one hundred percent safe, not even a trace of interest even if they took off those black sheets.

He rolled onto his back and opened up the messages.

What're you up to today? Was the first message.

I'm thinking about starting a veggie patch was the second.

Lacy snorted. He typed and hit send—*Checking out Buckingham Palace*—which got an immediate laughing emoji.

Yeah? What're you gonna grow? Potatoes? Ur growin fucken potatoes aren't you?

That got another laughing emoji and Lacy settled in.

9

♥

T HAD WAS DETERMINED TO focus on digging the patch for his garden, lay the sleeper logs to mark the edges, and not obsess over the fact he hadn't heard from Lacy yet. He was probably asleep, which was good. The problem was, it was almost midnight London time and not a peep all day. And Lacy tended to drink too much, and he was alone; what if someone had taken advantage of him?

He shook his head at himself, focused on his shovel. It was hot for November, and he was already soaked through with sweat. Of course Lacy was fine. He was a grown man who'd managed so far without Thad or anyone else babysitting him. Thad pulled his phone out and headed inside for a drink.

It'd been twelve hours since their last message, Lacy's final—*I gotta hit the hay, talk later, plant eggplants* accompanied by a series of screaming laughing emojis. Thad's *sleep well, talk soon*, followed by, *You up yet? Let me know when you get up. You okay?* Thad would be embarrassed if he wasn't so worried. He wondered if Lacy would've contacted anyone else. He thought about contacting Cary. Finn was more likely, but he didn't have Finn's number. He was about to call Cary and ask for it when there was a knock at the front door.

He set his glass on the sink and wondered who'd be visiting. Probably Carol from the church group, but he didn't think he'd left anything after they reconvened at the church on arrival home from their trip.

He opened the door and his mouth dropped open.

"Thaddeus," Lacy grinned, "mind if I come in?"

Thad laughed in surprise. He swept Lacy off his feet. Lacy clutched him back with an answering laugh.

"What're you doing here?" Thad marvelled as he crushed him against his chest.

"Felt like comin' round," Lacy said against Thad's shoulder.

Thad squeezed him harder. "I missed you."

"I missed you too," Lacy replied and patted Thad's back. "Why're you all wet?"

"Been in the garden."

Thad let him go so he could look at his face again. He couldn't stop smiling.

"Come in, come in," he said and saw the suitcase and the small backpack at Lacy's feet. "You came from the airport?"

"What can I say? I missed your face," Lacy grinned and reached for his bags.

It was then Thad realised Lacy looked like he was about to fall over.

"Let me," he leaned past him and scooped up the backpack, reached for the suitcase, ushering Lacy inside. "You look like you're about to topple over, go and lay down, I'll bring you something to drink."

"Yeah, long flight," Lacy replied.

Thad kicked the door shut, set the luggage down. He flicked his eyes up to Lacy watching him, swaying on his feet, grinning a little manically.

"What?" Thad asked, his face breaking into an answering smile—it was just so damn good to see his friend.

"Nothin', just good to be home, I been imagining this for the last thirty hours," Lacy replied.

"That's why you didn't message," Thad placed a hand on the small of Lacy's back, gently herded him to the couch. "I was about to call Cary to get Finn's number."

Lacy shuffled along. "You reckon if my phone was on I'd be talkin' to Finn and not you?"

"Well, no, now that you mention it," Thad replied, but he was smiling so much it was getting ridiculous—he'd really missed his friend, of course he was smiling. And now he was here, not a million miles away; Thad could see him in all his corporeal reality and he felt high on it.

"Wanted to surprise you," Lacy said as he collapsed onto the couch. "Fuck, that's good. Fucking economy." He slumped down, stretched his legs out and spread them.

Thad stood at the end of the couch, his lips stretching into a smile that turned into an incredulous laugh.

"What?" Lacy asked; he was laughing back like it was infectious.

"Nothing," Thad shook his head. "Get comfortable, I'll be back."

He returned a moment later with a chilled glass of water and a cheese and salad sandwich. "Sorry," he said as he placed it on the coffee table, "I haven't got much, wasn't expecting you."

"You tellin' me you shop special for me?" Lacy asked as he sat up. "This looks fuckin' amazing. Best food I've had in months, I bet."

Thad rubbed the back of his neck. "I doubt my kitchen skills beat the chefs of Europe."

Lacy sculled the water, his Adam's apple bobbing, his tired eyes on Thad. He put the empty glass down and picked up the sandwich.

Thad went and re-filled his water, heard Lacy moaning from the other room.

"Fuckin', so good," Lacy said after a mouthful.

Thad placed the glass down. "Good." He stepped back. He was sticky with sweat and dirt. "I'm just going to change real quick, don't go anywhere."

Lacy swallowed audibly. "Where would I go?"

Thad grinned and went for his room across the hall. He grabbed a fresh shirt, rushed down to the bathroom, stripped off, washed himself with a flannel in the sink quickly, dried himself, sprayed on deodorant, yanked on the shirt, and ran a hand through his messy hair as he came back into the living room. Lacy was dozing, his hands folded in his lap. Thad smiled and went to clear the plates.

"Sit," Lacy said, eyes still closed.

Thad did as he was told.

Lacy grabbed his hand, cracked his eyes open as he tugged Thad down to stretch out behind him on the couch.

Thad wrapped him up in his arms and remembered the last time they were in this position. He wasn't going to lie to himself—he was a little frightened it would happen again—but having Lacy's back and ass pressed against his front, his legs tangling with Thad's, the feel of his ribcage expanding and releasing against Thad's biceps and forearms, he liked it so much he decided he could handle it.

"That's the ticket," Lacy murmured.

He was asleep in no time. Thad listened to him breathing and he wasn't tired, but he wasn't going anywhere right now, not for anything.

Lacy ended up staying with Thad for a few days. Thad basked in his company like he'd been living in months of winter, like those people in Antarctica, nothing but night for months on end and Lacy was the arrival of sunshine. Lacy helped him get his veggie patch set-up, including the reticulation, which Lacy marvelled at once Thad turned the tap on—"We can do it ourselves!" he cheered. Thad smiled, unsure what the big deal was. Lacy accompanied him to the shops and added a lot of junk food to the cart, cackling when Thad tried to stoically hide his reaction. Lacy got them up early for a run, pushing Thad further than he ever went on his own with his incredible speed and stamina. He helped him with the cooking and asked a lot of questions, hovering over Thad's shoulder as he stirred things, chopped, kneaded, his front plastered to Thad's back, his breath warm on Thad's shoulder. He made himself right at home in the spare room, and Thad wished Lacy was in here, in his room, with him. He wanted to keep on chatting, to hear Lacy's voice as he drifted off.

But Lacy had to go home eventually—unpack, get fresh clothes—even though Thad was more than happy to wash his clothes for him and keep him at his home. Fortunately, he stopped himself from saying that, which sounded like something a serial killer keeping a prisoner in their basement would say.

So, he dropped Lacy home, watched him strolling up his driveway with his suitcase and backpack in the early hours of Sunday morning before Thad went to church. He drummed his fingers on the steering wheel as Lacy disappeared around the hedges.

Thad sat in his usual spot near the front, flanked by Carol and the others from the Africa trip, the sunshine piercing the stain glass windows and flooding the space with refracted colours and a warm glow. The reading was from The Gospel according to Luke, 'The Need to Watch.'

"Be on your guard!" the pastor bellowed and Thad startled; he knew the man was one for theatrics, but that was loud even for him. He shuffled in his seat.

"Don't let yourselves become occupied with too much feasting and drinking and with worries of this life, or that day may suddenly catch you like a trap," he paused and took a deep breath as his eyes roved around the congregation.

"For it will come upon all people everywhere on earth. Be on the lookout and pray always that you will have the strength to go safely through all those things that will happen, and to stand before the Son of Man..."

He slammed the bible shut and gripped the edge of the pulpit. Taking a deep breath, he began to detail the dangers of temptation, of vices, of how indulging could lead to a lack of preparation for the day you die, where you must meet with the Lord, clean in spirit.

Thad didn't know if he agreed with the interpretation, and as it went on, he found his thoughts drifting. Wasn't the point to be a good man? To be good in your actions and intentions whatever they may be? Lacy enjoyed feasting and drinking and revelling in all the luxuries of this life, but he wouldn't harm anyone. He was kind and fun, supportive. And Thad believed his incredible talent—enhanced by a work ethic he didn't like too many people to see—was a gift from God, deigned to inspire mere mortals, not an indulgence as the church would call it—ego, narcissism.

"That was good, wasn't it?" Carol whispered in his ear.

Thad bowed his head to speak under his breath. "Yes, wonderful." He didn't want to have a detailed conversation about his points of disagreement. Maybe he'd talk to Lacy about it later.

"Can I ask you something?" he asked Lacy later that afternoon. They were at a bar in Fitzroy, a courtyard flanked with plants and picnic tables, Lacy sipping on a vodka and soda water, while Thad drank an orange juice.

"You can ask me anything," Lacy replied. He lowered his sunnies down his nose and winked.

Thad chuckled. "Okay, I was just wondering, well, this morning in church, the reading was from the Gospel according to Luke—"

"Who's Luke?" Lacy asked.

"An apostle," Thad replied. "Each of the apostles recounts their time with Jesus and those comprise the gospels of the bible, second testament."

"The apostles were those gay dudes roaming around in the desert with Jesus, right?" Lacy finished his drink in one go.

Thad tilted his head to the side, taken aback. "Gay? The apostles?"

"Yeah, man, bunch of dudes hanging out together for that long, like, weren't they in pairs? Like, couples. Gay couples," Lacy said and stood. "I'm gettin' another one. You want?"

"Uh, no, thank you," Thad smiled weakly—the apostles were gay? How did that square away with Leviticus 18:22—*You shall not lie with a male as with a woman; it is an abomination.* Unless Lacy dismissed it because it was in the Old Testament, which would be fortunate for the apostles since Leviticus also argues if man lies with a man as he does with a woman, he should be put to death. But then what about Mark and Jude in the New Testament?

Lacy was back pretty quickly, giving Thad a sheepish smile. "The pros of bein' a football superstar," he said as he placed two drinks on the table. He must've skipped the line and been bought another drink by someone.

"I don't think the apostles were gay," Thad said.

"Probably bi," Lacy shrugged.

Thad didn't know what to do with this information. "I don't think they had sex at all."

Lacy laughed. "You put a bunch of dudes together in the desert with nothin' but each other for company and some dicks are gettin' sucked, that's all I'm saying. Look at the army."

"What about the army?"

"They're all gay, man. All of them," Lacy said like it was obvious.

Thad looked at Lacy for a moment, speechless. Maybe this was an entire world Thad wasn't aware of? He'd certainly never heard anything about it. Regardless, the points in the bible regarding homosexuality weren't at issue in this conversation. Nor was the army.

"Well, anyway," he cleared his throat, "at church this morning, it was all about feasting and drinking and it got me thinking about you and I just wondered what you get out of it. Drinking, I mean, partying, why do you do it?" he asked.

Lacy frowned, but Thad got the impression it wasn't at the question. He was thinking.

"I guess 'cos I always have," Lacy said. "Like, I started drinking when I was fourteen and I haven't really stopped. It's how I unwind, switch off."

"But," Thad sat forward and tried to put his thoughts into words, "you don't seem that highly strung to begin with."

Lacy snorted a soft laugh. "Thanks, bud." He sat back, ran a hand through his hair and glanced around. "You're right, I'm not, not really. To be totally honest?" he looked back at Thad. "I reckon I'm bored. Like, footy's always been where I come alive. Other than that, I never really felt like there was much here for me, it's just goin' through the motions, you know? So, I go on a bender to break that up, switch off."

Thad thought about that. He didn't understand it personally, but he got the sentiment.

"And now I reckon it's just routine," Lacy said. "Why? You wanna reform me?"

"No, never," Thad replied.

Lacy was smiling at him like he knew it too. "I'm kidding, man. I know you don't. I like it, how you keep your shit separate from us."

"And you keep that world separate from me too," Thad said and didn't know where the words came from. It was true, but did it need to be said?

But Lacy laughed. "Believe me, that is for the best. You don't wanna see me in that state."

"There's no state you could be in, in which I wouldn't accept you," Thad replied.

Lacy stopped laughing and stared at him. Thad could only see his own reflection in the sunglasses, but the mood shifted.

Lacy cleared his throat, chuckled softly. "Well, let's not test that theory, eh?" He finished his drink. "Wanna get out of here? This music sucks ass."

"Of course," Thad finished his juice and stood while Lacy sculled his second drink in one go.

10

PRESEASON TRAINING DIDN'T OFFICIALLY start until the new year, but the first to fourth years were required at a two-week training block in early December. Other players were welcome to attend, but didn't have to. Lacy always attended. Thad would be there, which was a bonus.

Lacy smashed all of his personal bests in the morning session and took the head shakes from Kurt and Todd in the cool down, both men giving him fondly paternal looks as he stretched.

Les was across the room with the new rookie, Darren McDonald, who Lacy had decided to call Donald rather than Mac, looking troubled.

"Les!" Lacy shouted after he lifted his head off his knees.

Les jumped and looked over. "Yeah?"

"What's up? Ya look like you're about to cry. It wasn't that bad," Lacy spread his legs open and started twisting his body from side to side.

Les chuckled. "It was awful," he said, smiling, "but nah, me and Donald just talking about offseason."

"Yeah? What'd you boys get up to? Head to training camp in Bali?" Lacy joked. Some of the players actually did that and Les looked down.

"You did!" Lacy laughed. He bumped Thad next to him. "Can you believe these kids, Thaddeus? Meant to be takin' a break and they be training."

"It was good," Les defended. Donald nodded along next to him. Thad huffed a laugh, bent his head to his knee. Lacy got distracted looking at his back for a second—man was looking good from the rear.

"So what're you crying about?" he refocused on Les.

"Nothin'," Les murmured.

"He's got a girlfriend," Donald rushed out. He was red, which was obvious in his pale complexion against his frizzy red hair, and his eyes darted around like he was talking to a superior and not sure how much he could say.

"Les!!" Lacy shouted. "Good for you, man. What's her name? How did you convince her to go out with you?"

Les smiled, toothy and shy. "Katie. And I had to buy her a few drinks."

Lacy cackled. "Good job, buddy."

"So, what's the problem?" Thad asked. He was smiling warmly at Les. He was different around the team, especially the younger guys; a quietly commanding cadence entered his deep voice, and he seemed older. Combined with his height and seniority to them—twenty-four was senior to eighteen, to twenty, in this room—he was like a charming and reassuring older brother.

"Ah, nothin', you know," Les mumbled.

"He thinks she's gonna break up with him when she realises he's stupid," Donald said quickly.

Lacy's eyebrows flew up. "You're not stupid."

He felt Thad nodding next to him. "Who said you were stupid?"

"Guys," Les shook his head, twisted his lips to the side, "I am, but."

"No, you're not," Lacy retorted sharply. "You just take everything literally."

Thad was nodding again. "You're earnest. Nothing wrong with that. And I don't think she's the right woman for you if she doesn't like you for being earnest."

Now Lacy was nodding. "Yeah, what he said. Fuck that hussy if she says that."

"She's not a hussy," Les said, but he was smiling.

"I reckon we better meet her," Lacy looked to Thad. "You busy tonight?"

"Guys, no, c'mon," Les pleaded.

"I'm not busy," Thad smiled.

"Good," Lacy looked back to Les. "We're comin' round. Tell her to be there. We'll suss this chick out for you."

Les was laughing. "Please, no, I'm just being paranoid."

"Better get the party pies and sausage rolls outta the freezer, Les, we'll be there at seven," Lacy jumped to his feet, took Thad's hand when he reached up and yanked him up to stand beside him.

They could hear Les pleading and laughing from behind them as they jogged down the tunnel for lunch before the afternoon session.

"We really going to head over?" Thad asked.

"Yep," Lacy grinned up at him.

Thad laughed. "Okay then."

Katie turned out to be a very nice girl, if a little too quiet and shy for Lacy's tastes. Add the tiny woman part, and she did nothing for him. She was perfect for Les though. Les, who looked at her with open adoration when she opened her mouth to speak, giggle or breathe.

"I think he's got nothing to worry about," Thad said as they made their way down Les' driveway for Thad's car, the space between them widening as they went for their respective sides.

"Yep, but it's fun freaking him out a little bit," Lacy replied with a grin that referred to Les' shock when he opened the door to them and stammered out a question about what they were doing there.

Fortunately, he did have frozen meals and he rushed around serving everyone dinner, constantly checking if everything was alright with Katie, to which Lacy and Thad had to keep hiding their laughter. Katie didn't seem to notice.

"She's as guileless as he is," Thad said as he got in and started the car.

Lacy cracked up. "Yeah," he shook his head. "Good for him, eh? Seems like the type who'll do better with a partner. Fuck, I'm feeling that session today, how about you?"

"Yes," Thad agreed. "You want to head home, or?"

"Nah, I'll come round."

Thad smiled, drummed his fingers on the steering wheel as they drove.

"You ever think you'd do better with a partner?" Thad asked.

Lacy tore his eyes away from the suburban street whipping by. "Are you legit asking me that? Me?"

Thad glanced at him. "Yes?"

"Fuck, no," Lacy shook his head. "Can you imagine anyone wantin' to put up with all this?" he waved a hand up and down his body.

Thad frowned. "All of what?"

Lacy stared at his profile, lit up intermittently with an orange glow from the street lights as they zipped along. Nothing about his calm face said he'd been joking.

Lacy shook his head and snorted. "But no, in answer to your question. I definitely don't reckon I'd do better with a partner. What about you?" he asked and regretted it because after it left his mouth, he realised he didn't want to know. Of course Thad would get married one day and have a bunch of church babies because that's what religious people did. Lacy didn't actually get why—he assumed it was to re-populate the world with fellow religious nutcases, or in Thad's case, just super religious because he seemed pretty sane otherwise—but he did know it's what they did.

"Umm," Thad shot him a weird smile. "Yes and no?"

"What does that mean? Maybe you'd do better?" Lacy pushed.

"I, umm," Thad glanced at him, a hesitancy in his eyes. "Well, it's always been the plan. Marriage, kids. But I," he cleared his throat awkwardly, fixed his gaze on the road. "Well, I'm quite happy with the way things are for the time being."

Lacy jerked his chin in acknowledgement. He'd supposed correctly then—marriage and kids were on the cards—and he didn't like it. He didn't hate marriage and kids when other people did it—he was happy for George and Finn when they got married. But he didn't want Thad doing it—how could they hang out like they did if Thad had a wife?

"Are you happy?" Thad asked as they pulled into his driveway. Lacy realised he hadn't said anything to Thad's confession. "I mean, with the way things are."

"Yeah, man, course," Lacy replied, forced himself to smile.

"Good," Thad replied.

"You got any food? That pre-made shit at Les' sucked ass," Lacy unclipped his seatbelt.

Thad grinned. "Have I got food? Are you asking *me* that?"

Lacy huffed a laugh, smiled at him over the console. "Stupid question. Lead the way."

Lacy waved goodbye to Thad, meandered up his driveway, hands stuffed in his pockets, a small smile playing on his lips. He was so distracted he almost missed the thick, white envelope sitting on his doorstep. It was propped against the door like someone had placed it there carefully. His name was embossed in gold calligraphy on the front.

Nerves and desire zipped up and down his limbs. He clutched it in his hand and let himself inside.

Once he was in the kitchen, he looked at it on the counter, drummed his fingers next to it.

"What am I doing?" he muttered. He picked it up and slid his index finger under the seal, ripped it open.

The party was in two weeks, coinciding with the end of preseason training for the first to fourth years, nothing but days off afterward until he was back for regular preseason training in January. It was Christmas-themed. He snorted and tapped the thick card on the bench and blew out a breath. He was horny just thinking about it. He reached down to squeeze his dick.

Thad's question floated through his mind, "*You ever think you'd do better with a partner?*"

He released his dick, shook his head. This right here was one of the many reasons he'd never be doing better with a partner.

11

BY THE TIME PRESEASON was done, Thad had stopped turning the unsettling conversation over in his mind. It's not like he was getting married anytime soon. He wasn't blind—he saw the interest from Carol at his church group. It did nothing for him. One day he'd meet a woman and she'd hold his attention, he was sure of it. But for right now, he was, as he'd said to Lacy, happy as he was. His parents asked too often, but so long as he was in Melbourne and they were in Tassie, he could get away with being a bachelor for a little bit longer. He'd be twenty-five in August, he was hardly old. Most of the guys from his church were married with kids by twenty-two; but Thad had footy, and his dad, at least, backed off when he used that as an excuse.

It was Saturday night and Thad wasn't really sure what to do with himself. He could head down to the church social he supposed, Carol and the others invited him every week and it's not like he had a game.

Yes, he thought firmly, Lacy was busy with 'mates from back home' and it was unwise to expect Lacy to be his only form of entertainment.

He selected a nice pair of pants and his best button-up; he wasn't planning to date anyone, but his parents had impressed upon him the need to dress nicely—he was representing them, they'd say, he was showing his respect to the church.

He wondered what Lacy would say about that? He snorted a laugh as he went for the bathroom, the old floorboards creaking, the light bulb hanging from the chord dim in the hallway, the musty smell and emptiness of the place impossible to ignore. It was better when Lacy was here, he livened the place up, made it feel less like it had one foot in the grave and the other in a bygone era.

Showered and dressed with a hint of his best cologne on, he was about to leave when he noticed Lacy's summer jacket hanging beside his own. It was warming up, but it was still cool at night. Lacy was probably going to need it. He grabbed it and headed out.

"Thad?" Lacy asked when he opened his door. "What're you doin' here?"

"You left your jacket at my place," Thad replied and tried to smile, but Lacy's tone put him on guard. "Sorry, just thought you might need it."

Lacy took it, looked at it. "Thanks, man, I was gonna wear another one but this is my favourite."

"I know," Thad tucked his hands in his pockets. He needed to turn around, get back in his car and go, but with Lacy in front of him, he had the urge to ask to accompany him out. Lacy never invited him to go out with his friends, and Thad respected the boundary, but it was hard when coming face to face with Lacy made him feel better than the prospect of the church social.

"Well, I better," he jerked his chin behind him.

Lacy gave him a once over. "Are you going out?"

"Yeah," Thad shrugged. "Figured I should get out of the house as well."

"Hot date?" Lacy asked. He smiled, but there was something fake in it.

Thad shook his head. "Church social."

"Oh," Lacy seemed surprised. "What's that, like a dance?"

Thad pictured the people from his church dancing—they really got into it, but they were terrible at it. "No, it's like," he pulled a hand out of his pocket and waved it around, "where unattached people meet and mingle, that kind of thing. There's families there too, kids, but it's more for young people I guess, socialising."

Lacy frowned, but turned that into a bright smile quickly. "Sounds lit."

Before Thad could respond how not "lit" it was, Lacy's phone pinged and headlights washed over them from the driveway.

"Well, that's me," Lacy stepped outside, shut the door, his body right up in Thad's space. He smelled good—freshly showered with his eucalyptus soap, sprayed lightly with his deodorant—and his hair bounced, shiny and clean, as he pulled the jacket on. Thad stepped back.

"You meeting everyone there?" He fell into step with Lacy as they moved down the driveway.

"Yeah," Lacy rubbed his neck. He looked up at Thad, a part of his usually expressive face closed off.

"Well, have fun," Thad said as he stopped at his car door.

Lacy lifted his hand over his head but didn't look back. "Yeah, you too."

Thad got in his car and waited for the car Lacy was in to reverse, the closed-off look on Lacy's face seared in his brain.

He didn't know what made him do it, but as he reversed out after them, he followed the car. He was careful not to be obvious about it once they were on the main roads, keeping a car between them, and his heart was absolutely pounding, but something like curiosity and concern made him follow.

They ended up in one of the flashiest suburbs in Melbourne—houses didn't line the streets, estates with mansions did. Thad parked a few spaces away once he saw Lacy get out and head up the driveway of an enormous place, his pace quick, purposeful, like he'd been here before.

Thad rubbed his hand over his mouth as he watched him disappear around some hedges. This was not a night on the town with mates. But why would Lacy lie to him? Thad's first thought was a cult. He snorted. As if. He should leave him to it; it was obviously a party, based on the number of other men arriving and leaving their cars to meander up the driveway, dressed sharply in suits.

The more Thad watched, the more he noticed it was only men. Was it some kind of meeting? Some kind of exclusive men's club?

He was getting out of his car, locking it and striding up the street before he could second-guess himself.

The driveway was long and winding, flanked with shiny, glowing lights alongside pristinely maintained hedges and sweeps of manicured lawns. Thad had his hands firmly planted in his pockets and he tried to imbue his gait with a sense of belonging as he approached the wide entrance and fell into line behind a few other men. They were older, dressed in suits, maybe forties and fifties, and they were telling a large, hulking man in a black suit with a black t-shirt their names. The man checked their names off a list on the clipboard he was holding before allowing them to pass.

Thad swallowed. He was in front of the man.

The guy looked at him expectantly, not smiling, but not indifferent either, just waiting.

"I'm with Lacy," Thad blurted out.

The guy raised both eyebrows in surprise, glanced down at his clipboard. "Lacy didn't mention bringing a guest," he said, his voice gravelly.

"It was a bit last minute. I was, ah, parking the car and he went ahead," Thad said.

The guy looked him up and down. "Your name's not on here," he shook his head, exasperated. "Bloody Lacy. Right, here," he leaned back and pulled out another clipboard with a wad of paperwork attached to it, "fill this in and tell Lacy next time he's bringing a teammate to get this done beforehand."

Right, because while Thad was not as famous as Lacy, he was on TV every weekend, he was recognisable.

"Will do," he replied as he clutched the paperwork.

The guy handed him a pen. "You got your driver's license? I'll get a copy done here. Give us your credit card as well, we can charge it."

Thad tucked the clipboard under his arm and fumbled for his wallet, handed both over without question even though he had a lot of them. The guy radioed for someone to come and make copies, jerked his chin for Thad to step aside to let the line of men pass him.

He focused on the paperwork. Name, address, phone number—seemed normal enough—he filled it in. He flicked over to the next page.

It was a series of questions with options for him to tick. Indicate your preference: top, bottom, switch, watch. Thad frowned—what did that mean?

The next page was optional. Thad scanned it, utterly confused—watersports? Did they have a pool? He decided to skip it.

He flicked to the next page. It was a non-disclosure agree-ment—pages and pages swearing him to secrecy, and the legal conse-quences if he broke that.

He was beginning to think this was a cult. Men were strolling past him, laughing with each other, greeting the guy on the door with familiarity and the odd handshake.

Thad refocused on the documents. He gripped the pen tightly and signed everything. The secrecy part wasn't a problem, but the first questionnaire was. He decided to tick the first option—top—then frowned because he didn't want to end up doing something he wasn't sure about. So, he crossed that out and ticked watch. Watching was safest. He waited for the guy in front of him to go in, his thick cologne heavy in the air, and then handed the paperwork back.

The guy took it, tapped the pen while he checked it all, flicked to page two, smirked and leaned behind him to grab something. He handed over two wrist bands.

"Here, in case you change your mind," he winked.

Thad stared at them in his palm. "Thanks."

"Here," the guy handed back his license and credit card, "and tell Lacy to give us a head's up next time."

And then he was dealing with Thad's paperwork and Thad as-sumed he could go in. He clenched the bands in his palm and pro-ceeded inside.

The lobby was enormous, a winding staircase at its heart under chandeliers. Men in suits milled around the black and white tiled landing with champagne flutes being served by—Thad did a double take, they were being served by men in tiny shorts, bow ties and nothing else. Thad stumbled and went for the stairs, the murmured voices and soft laughter loud behind him. He wasn't sure what he was planning to do—check Lacy was okay and then leave?

He arrived on the next landing and went left at the sound of voices and music. He shrugged the bands onto his wrist like he'd seen the other men doing. A very young man in hot pants sauntered up to him with a tray full of bottled beer. He smiled, gave Thad an obvious once-over and asked, "Beer?"

"Thank you," Thad replied on auto-pilot and took one. He noticed the guy's wrist bands—he had several—none the same colour as Thad's.

"Hopefully see you later," the guy winked and moved on.

Thad clutched the beer bottle and made his feet move. He'd never had a drink in his life, but as he entered a room full of men in small groups, saw a lounger with a younger man in the lap of an older guy, the pair kissing passionately, he was tempted to down the whole bottle in one go to take the edge off his shock. He left the room quickly and found himself in another room. He almost fainted when he saw a man on a couch with his pants open, a guy between his legs. The one sitting held the base of his penis while the other man fellated him. Other men were in the room, some giving the pair a glance, some rubbing their crotches. These men reeked of money in their perfectly tailored suits, in the way they held themselves—upright, arrogant—and under the bright lights, against the exquisite furnishings, the openly sexual behaviour they were exhibiting seemed obscene. A display of decadence that belonged in the Book of Revelations.

Thad moved on.

The place was a labyrinth—sitting rooms, a library, a ballroom, a dining hall—and each one contained men in various stages of undress and sex acts while other men watched.

But he was sure Lacy wasn't doing *this*. This, this... public group sex. Lacy probably came for the party aspect—the alcohol was flowing and Thad had been offered pills, some kind of powder, and colourful little bottles called "poppers" by more than one of the waiters. Thad knew Lacy was into that. Knew it in a vague, rumoured way, not from Lacy himself. But this is why Lacy came. For the drugs.

He'd been there for at least an hour when he found him. His brain short-circuited. He could not believe it was Lacy sitting slumped on an elegant white couch, head tipped back, eyes closed as a man in a suit pressed up alongside him, his hand inside Lacy's open pants as he kissed his throat while another man on his other side opened his shirt, kissed the other side of his neck, pinched his nipple causing Lacy to arch and gasp.

Thad gripped his bottle of warm beer so tight he thought it was going to break in his hand. He took a step backward until he was behind a large fern. Not that it would matter—if Lacy opened his eyes and looked in his direction, there's no way he'd miss him. Except when Lacy's eyes did pop open, his gaze was unfocused. Thad had seen that look before, or close to it, perhaps not this bad—Lacy was completely out of it.

"Room," Lacy said as one of the men slipped to the ground in front of him and tugged his pants off.

Thad's heart pounded as the guy pulled Lacy to the edge of the couch, spread his ass cheeks with his thumbs. He licked him there. Lacy groaned and rolled his hips down, gasped out, "Room."

Thad swallowed. Lacy said it again. Through the fog of incomprehensibility, Thad realised what Lacy was asking for—he wanted them to move this to one of the bedrooms, he didn't want them to perform these sex acts on him in a public room where other men were watching him and another couple engaged in fellatio. Thad did another double take when he recognised the man between an older guy's legs—he was an actor from a soapie.

"Room," Lacy begged and Thad gripped the bottle tighter. Why weren't they listening to him?

The guy between his legs pulled back. "He's ready," he said to the guy on the couch.

Thad froze when the man stood and undid his pants. The man beside Lacy rearranged him so Lacy was stretched out, his ass pointing up while his head hovered over the man sitting down, poised so close to his crotch the man's knuckles brushed his face as he undid his pants.

It seemed to happen fast and yet, as Thad watched the one behind Lacy roll a condom on, get in position, the one in front rub the head of his erection over Lacy's panting lips, it felt agonisingly slow.

"Room," Lacy said again, his voice reedy. It was the last thing he said. A hand on the back of his head pushed him down onto the man's penis. Lacy instantly began to suck, to moan.

The man behind him placed one knee on the couch, pushed himself against Lacy and slid inside him forcefully.

Thad held his breath. He wanted to go over there and stop them, yell at them for not doing as Lacy asked. But he couldn't move. He finally understood those people who didn't intervene when a crime happened in front of them—a similar fear rendered him immobile.

But this wasn't a crime. Lacy's back was arched, he sucked the man in his mouth and he rocked his ass back to meet the guy thrusting into him. His own penis was hard as it slapped audibly against his flat stomach with every rough thrust.

All Thad could do was watch. And, to his absolute mortification, get an erection. This was turning him on—what was wrong with him? The guy having sex with Lacy still had his pants on, his erect penis entering Lacy with a dull sound as the material slapped against Lacy's naked flank. This noise mixed with Lacy's mouth sucking wetly on the other man, his moans mingling with the grunts of the men. Thad's brain struggled to put the scene into words—two men were holding Lacy firmly, the one having sex with him gripped him by the hip and shoulder and yanked him onto himself, while the other one had Lacy's hair in a fist, shoved his head down as he thrust up. For a hysterical moment, Thad wondered why they were bothering with the show of force—Lacy was welcoming the guy inside with his back arched, accepting the one in his mouth with suction.

"Fuck, he always feels good," the guy penetrating him said as he grunted.

"Best fucking cocksucker too," the guy in his mouth replied and shoved Lacy's head down, held him there.

Thad could see Lacy struggling to breathe and he was going to move now, stop this. But the guy rocked into Lacy's mouth in short bursts and as Thad looked closer, he saw Lacy's throat working. He almost dropped the bottle. Lacy's erection slapped against his stomach as the guy behind him really went for it, and Thad realised he was going to come too. Of course he was, but for some reason it brought Thad up short. He felt irrational relief that the man wouldn't be able to come inside Lacy. An absurd thought and the least of the concerns here. The wastage of semen in self-gratification was obviously a concern. One must not, as written in the Book of Genesis, allow 'his seed to fall on the ground'—semen belonged inside a woman for procreation, all else was a sin. But what troubled him most, to his horror and shame, was the men touching Lacy as if they had free reign to do so.

Thad could tell the man was ejaculating when he stilled, tugged Lacy back against him with a rough grip and a groan. The three of them stilled, breathing loudly. But as soon as Lacy's mouth was free, he gasped out, "Room," his scratchy voice breaking the stillness.

The guy behind him chuckled, breathless, and slapped Lacy's ass as he pulled out. He stepped back and pulled the condom off. Thad was frozen in fear as he saw him turning to where he was standing, but the guy was focused on tying the condom off, throwing it in a small bin, and walking out of the room as he did up his pants.

"Thanks, champ," the guy Lacy had fellated said and pushed Lacy back as he got up too. He put his softening penis back in his pants and ran a hand through his hair, went over to where the actor was now straddling another man, having sex with him.

Lacy rolled onto his back. Thad got an absolute eyeful of how hard he was. Lacy's hand went around himself. He planted his feet on the couch and masturbated into his fist, his body covered in a sheen of sweat visible over his tattoos. Thad was struck by how beautiful he was—his wiry, muscular body so much smaller than Thad's own, than those men who'd had sex with him, the thick patterns of tattoos that covered every inch of him except his groin and his feet—he was like an erotic painting come to life. His eyes were squeezed closed, his long eyelashes fanned his cheeks as he moaned, his lips shiny and wet so they looked even redder. Thad understood why those men wanted him. It was wrong, a sin of the highest order, but he could do nothing to stop the traitorous feelings as he watched him masturbating on the upholstered couch under the chandelier-drenched room.

Before Thad could move, a burly guy went over to Lacy and stopped his hand.

"Room," Lacy said again.

"Yeah, let's get you to a room," the guy said softly. Thad would have thought he was nicer than the other two, but he was rubbing his erection over his pants and smiling frighteningly.

"Get his clothes," he said to another guy. Thad watched in horror as he scooped Lacy off the couch bridal-style and strolled out of the room.

Thad didn't think, he just followed. They wound into a wide hallway, passed dark rooms with open doors, the sounds of sex ricocheting through his brain, pushing against his last tendrils of incomprehensibility.

The man holding Lacy entered a room, the guy behind him holding his clothes in a clenched fist, and Thad stopped before he was at the doorway. He heard the sound of bed springs creaking, the soft murmuring of the guy's voice, and then Lacy's reedy voice, "Need to come."

Both men laughed. Thad clenched his fists. How dare they. He made his feet move and paused on the threshold. The room was dark and it took a moment for him to make out more beyond the shapes of three men on the bed. Lacy was on his back, writhing around, while the burly guy moved his hand between Lacy's legs, stroked himself with his other hand. He was naked. The other guy was on the other side of Lacy, his fingers in Lacy's mouth as he pumped them in and out.

"I'm gonna enjoy this," the bigger one said and Thad made out the sound of a condom wrapper opening, saw the guy rolling it on before he lifted Lacy so both his legs were up, his ankles resting on the guy's shoulders.

The other man straddled Lacy's face, pointed his erect penis at Lacy's mouth.

They thrust inside him at both ends, Lacy's words once again silenced. Lacy's erection was still evident, slapping anew against his stomach, and as Thad watched the man pumping into him so hard the bed knocked against the wall, he felt indignant that neither of them touched Lacy, pleasured him, they just let his penis, which must have been painfully hard, slap against his belly as they trapped him between them and used his body.

"You just gonna watch?" the one in his mouth panted.

Thad felt his heart stop when he realised the comment was directed at him. He jerked his chin because he didn't know what else to do.

The guy had his head tilted down, his gaze focused on Thad in the doorway. His erection slid in and out of Lacy's mouth and he held Lacy's hair in a fist to move his head up and down.

Lacy made a muffled, high-pitched sound and the moment broke, the guy refocusing on him.

"You're gettin' him good," the guy in his mouth said around breathless laughter as he sped up.

"God, he's such a slut," the guy in his ass laughed and rammed into Lacy with quick jabs of his hips, his hands going tight on Lacy's thighs. "Fuck, I'm gonna."

"Same," the other guy replied and they sped up.

Thad was ashamed of his erection; it throbbed as he watched both men use Lacy's body so roughly.

"Fuckin' swallow it," the man in his mouth ground out as he shoved Lacy's face right into his crotch, humping his face.

The guy in his ass stilled, his glutes clenching and releasing.

Thad didn't know what to do with himself as he watched them pull out, share breathless laughter, thank Lacy as they gathered up their clothes, tugged on pants and came to where Thad was hovering in the door.

The one who'd used Lacy's mouth clapped him on the shoulder. Thad had the urge to hit him. He was around mid-thirties with a broad, flat nose, and oily skin beneath his sweat.

"He's all yours," he chuckled.

And then Thad was left alone with Lacy.

"Please," Lacy said, his voice rough.

Thad moved into the room. He didn't know what he was doing.

Lacy was looking at the ceiling, but Thad could tell he wasn't really seeing anything.

"Please, need to come," he whispered and he sounded like he was about to cry.

Thad swallowed and placed his beer on the bedside table, one knee automatically going onto the bed.

Lacy had a hand around himself, stroking his penis ineptly, his usually pristine coordination gone. He rolled his head to the movement of Thad beside him.

Maybe Thad could just touch him, help him come, then take him home so no one else could touch him.

His hand shook as he reached for him. Lacy rolled onto his side, his free hand coming up to grab Thad's hand, but he missed and clasped Thad by the forearm. Thad lost his balance and fell forward, pushing Lacy onto his back. He scrambled to get up but Lacy wrapped himself around him, rubbed his erection against Thad's shirt.

Thad didn't know what to do—his heart was pounding, his penis was hard, his breathing was laboured, and he was scared. Lacy's hand reached between them and squeezed him over his pants. Thad bucked into the touch.

"Please," Lacy whispered against his throat, his wet lips brushing Thad's skin.

Thad inched back and made out Lacy's face in the dark; his eyes held a sheen like he might cry, but his hand gripped Thad's erection painfully. He released the tightness before squeezing again—the movement was hurried, desperate, and it felt unbearably good.

Lacy spread his legs and all thought left Thad's mind, there was only the urgency in his groin. He undid his pants with trembling hands, got himself free as he breathed shakily. His whole body was shaking, but as Lacy rolled his hips up, latched his lips onto Thad's throat and sucked, rubbed his erection against Thad's skin under his shirt, Thad thrust forward.

His penis slid beside Lacy's and the feeling of their flesh meeting was like getting struck by an electric current. He gasped, pulled back, shook his head. He could not have sex with his best friend without consent. He shook his head again—that should be the secondary concern! He could not have sex outside of marriage. He could not have sex with a *man*. And in someone else's home no less.

Lacy's lips released his throat. He rubbed his face up to Thad's chin and his breath felt wet on Thad's cheek as he made these high-pitched sounds, like he was in pain. Thad pulled his face back a fraction. He watched Lacy's tongue wetting his lips. He tilted his head down and brushed Lacy's lips with his own.

And if he thought their penises touching was electric, this was next level. He did it again. Pressed his lips softly against Lacy's and his whole body lit up. Lacy slid his tongue into his mouth, those little sounds getting lost as he tangled his tongue with Thad's.

Thad groaned. He cradled Lacy's head in his hands and kissed him deeply. He'd never kissed anyone before. He'd always feared it—the mechanics had worried him; he'd look at a woman's lips and wonder how he was supposed to move his lips against hers, how he'd make her feel good with just the touch of skin on skin.

He wasn't worried now. He held Lacy's head in his palms, moved his lips against his, met his tongue with a brush of his own. He groaned and Lacy's legs wrapped around his waist in response, lifting his ass off the bed. Thad rolled his hips back, his erection gliding alongside Lacy's. He pulled back further until the tip of his penis caressed Lacy's testicles. He knew if he slid down further, he would slip inside him.

This is wrong.

But his body was following a path his mind could not comprehend.

He reached between them, wrapped his hand around himself and pushed his penis down until he felt the tip brush against Lacy's entrance. The ring of muscles was loosened by the men who'd come before him and God help him, that made him want it even more. He pushed inside, half of himself encased in warm heat. He broke the kiss, his lips hovering over Lacy's, the skin brushing as they shared air.

"Please," Lacy whispered, his lips touching Thad's around the word.

Thad rocked forward, his gaze roving over Lacy's face to see how it made him feel. The whiskey and brown of Lacy's eyes were consumed by the pupil, the black saucers glazed like he wasn't seeing, only feeling. And if he was feeling what Thad was, he was getting a taste of heaven.

He inched out, kissed Lacy gently and rocked inside. Lacy's hands gripped his bare ass, the tips of his fingers sliding under the material of his pants bunched around the clenched muscles. He pressed down, urging Thad to move.

Thad stayed buried inside, his strokes small jerks of his hips dictated by Lacy's hands. Lacy rocked up to meet him, his erection trapped between Thad's shirt and abdomen; it was hot and it seeped warm liquid onto Thad's skin.

Thad could not stop kissing him. Even as his hips worked faster into him, his tongue danced with Lacy's like it knew the moves, even though Thad had no idea how.

Lacy broke the kiss and arched. He pressed his head against the pillow, pushed his ass into Thad's thrusts, his breaths stuttering in time with Thad's hips.

Thad tightened his hands against his scalp, kissed his throat.

"Need to come," Lacy begged.

Thad increased his pace. He was gripped by those punched-out sounds. He pressed Lacy harder into the mattress, increasing the friction for his erection between them and used his glutes to get as deep inside as he could.

Lacy groaned and Thad felt his semen coating his stomach, seeping into his shirt. He hovered above him, watched Lacy's eyes squeeze shut, his lips part around his harsh breathing, his body jostling as Thad continued to work in and out of him. Thad stroked his high cheekbones with his thumbs, leant down to kiss him even though he could not seal their lips together against their breathing.

It began in his testicles, a tightening. Warmth spread through his groin. His penis throbbed and he ejaculated inside someone for the first time. He groaned, burying the sound in Lacy's neck. He mouthed at his skin as he clenched and released inside of him. Lacy's insides felt warmer, wetter.

Lacy's hand stroked his nape, his body lax against the bed, crushed under Thad's weight.

And as the height of his orgasm receded, Thad's first instinct was to pull out and run away.

Lacy kissed his temple. It was a sloppy kiss, a sated, wasted kiss. Thad's heart clenched in his chest. He was horrified and yet he felt content. Encased in Lacy's arms, inhaling his smell—the musk of sex mingling with his sweat, his designer deodorant—he thought, I could die here and it would be enough.

"You done?" came from close beside them.

Thad reared back.

A man in a suit was standing over them.

Thad wanted to crush Lacy to his chest and tell him to go away.

Lacy squirmed in his hold.

"His mouth then," the guy said. He shrugged his broad shoulders as he undid his pants and pulled his penis, floppy and thick, out of his pants. He kneeled on the bed, the mattress sinking beside them, and positioned himself at Lacy's head. He was so close to Thad's face he could smell his musty skin, feel the heat from his groin.

He gripped his semi-erect penis and pointed it at Lacy's mouth. "C'mon, slut, I know you haven't had enough tonight." He slapped the flesh against Lacy's lips with a fond chuckle.

Lacy wrapped his lips around the tip, moaned as he sucked on the head. The guy huffed, satisfied. He tipped his head back and pushed into Lacy's mouth.

Thad pushed up onto his elbows. He was still inside Lacy. He'd gone soft but the pressure continued to squeeze him in an exquisite dance of pain and pleasure. It was heightened as they were jostled by the man thrusting into Lacy's mouth.

Another man walked in, a dark figure against the dim lighting of the hallway.

"Here he is," the new man said as he came closer. "Been looking for that ass. You done?" he directed at Thad.

Thad didn't know what to say, but damn his ingrained politeness because he was pushing himself up onto his hands. He paused. His penis was lodged inside Lacy's body, Lacy's thighs spread wide around his waist. Thad marvelled at how they looked together. Lacy's penis had slipped out from under Thad's shirt when he moved up and it was soft now, lolling to the side. His testicles sat neatly below, not a low hung set nor a tight pair, but perfectly in between. Thad had the urge to take them into his mouth. The bed dipped behind him.

Thad glanced over his shoulder and jerked at the sight of the man's pants off, his erection pointing up while he stroked it.

"My turn," he said and Thad could hear the smile in his voice as he pressed closer.

The fear of the man touching him propelled him to slide out of Lacy's body and move to the side. He pulled his pants up and fastened them quickly. His breaths were sharp and panicky. He watched from the corner of his eye as he fumbled with his top button. The other man yanked Lacy's leg up onto his bicep, lined up and pushed inside at an angle.

Thad scooted close to Lacy's side. He felt a confusing mix of shame, fear, and arousal as he watched Lacy move with the man's thrusts, his moaning muffled by yet another penis in his mouth.

"Ah fuck," the one inside him groaned as he slid out, looked down at himself and then shoved back in hard. "You fucked him bare?"

Thad realised the question was pointed at him. He stared up at the man, eyes wide.

The guy shoved in and out of Lacy, his voice rough. "Fuck, he's so wet."

Thad understood. He didn't use a condom.

"Gonna have to report it," the guy said even as he started to slam into Lacy harder, guttural sounds punching out of him as he went so hard Thad felt like he was trying to punish him.

But, report it? Thad panicked. If this man reported him for something then Lacy would be informed. Lacy would know. If Lacy didn't know already—Thad glanced up at him, his mouth stretched, making those little sounds that hit Thad in the solar plexus on repeat, went straight to his groin, and he wasn't sure how much Lacy would remember.

He would tell him, of course he would, but not like this, not coming from some stranger.

"He's my boyfriend," Thad said. He rested his hand on Lacy's hip, stroked his skin. His voice was quiet, but firmer than he thought it would be; he knew the men heard him when they both groaned and, for some bizarre reason, started to slam into Lacy even harder.

"Fuck, that's hot," the one in his mouth said. He had one hand on Lacy's chin, holding his head up while he watched himself pump in and out of his mouth.

The guy inside him pushed Lacy's leg back so it was up in the air and he too could watch himself plunging in and out. His voice was rough and breathless when he spoke. "God, knew he'd end up with a guy who got off on sharing him. Such a slut."

Thad frowned, but it was a lot to try and think about as he was jostled on the bed with Lacy and these men hammering into him so fiercely. He could just make out their faces twisted in pleasure, but with the room so dark it was the smell of them—foreign deodorant, sweat, a male musk tainted with sex—and the sound of their skin smacking against Lacy's, the sound of Lacy's wet throat, that overwhelmed him.

He watched both men come, his hand clenching and releasing on Lacy's hip as he felt his own penis thickening. The man who had finished inside him told Thad he needed to tell Lacy to update his paperwork. Thad was bewildered.

Once they were gone, Thad looked up at Lacy; he was asleep, his breaths quiet, his body boneless against the mattress.

Thad squeezed his hip, relaxed his grip, repeated the motion and listened to Lacy breathe softly beside him. He tucked Lacy closer against his side, felt his ribcage expanding and contracting against his chest, and tried to think. At least with Lacy asleep, they could get a reprieve and Thad could decide what to do. He wanted to leave. He wanted to bundle Lacy up and leave.

Another man strolled through the door. He was shorter and stouter than the men who'd come before. Thad held his breath as he came over to the bed and grabbed Lacy by the wrist like he was allowed to just touch him. He dropped Lacy's limp wrist and to Thad's horror, started to undo his pants.

"He's asleep," Thad made his voice work.

"I know," the guy said.

"You're not," Thad stumbled for the word, "doing anything while he's asleep."

"He likes it," the guy grabbed Lacy's hand and lifted it again. "See."

Thad saw the bands on Lacy's wrist, but he had no idea what any of that meant.

The man dropped his hand again, shoved his pants down and was about to get onto the bed when Thad sat up.

"Not tonight," he said and was surprised by his tone—blisteringly cold. It made the other man pause.

"What not tonight? He loves it," the guy said.

"No," Thad scooted around Lacy and got off the bed. The man was forced to step back.

Thad towered over him. He'd never thought of himself as particularly intimidating, but the thought of someone having sex with Lacy while he was unconscious made him furious.

The guy put his hands up in a placating gesture. "Alright, alright, geez, but he's going to be pissed off when he finds out you stopped me."

Thad snorted, it was a new feeling, but his anger made him bold. "No, he won't. I know him."

The guy's belt jangled as he fastened it, his head shaking. "Yeah?" he looked up, blew his hair out of his face. "So does every other guy in this place and I'm telling you, he's going to be pissed. Who are you anyway? Get yourself a taste of that and get all possessive? Bless."

Thad clenched his fists, but he stood his ground and didn't say anything.

The guy laughed meanly, but he left. Thad let his shoulders drop. He was flooded with adrenaline. He needed to get out of there. He needed to get them both out of there. He scooped up Lacy's clothes and turned to him stretched out on the bed.

Thad moved quickly to get Lacy's boxers out of his pants, worked them over his ankles gently and pulled them up to his thighs. Lacy didn't even stir. Thad got the pants on and slipped them with the boxers up to Lacy's thighs. He grabbed his shirt and jacket, knee walked up the bed until he was hovering over him, his hands in the waistband of Lacy's pants. He pulled them up, lifting Lacy's ass off the bed easily.

Lacy still didn't move or acknowledge what was being done to him. Thad seethed—and that guy was going to have sex with him like this?

He sat Lacy up, resting his body against his chest, and got the shirt and jacket on, lay him down again gently so he could do up his buttons. He found his shoes and socks, got those on. He zipped up his own jacket to hide the semen all over his shirt. He should've been disgusted, but it sent a thrill through him.

Shaking himself, he crouched down, slid his arms under Lacy's back and knees and lifted him up. Lacy's head bounced on his shoulder and Thad used his grip to jostle him until his head was cradled against his chest.

It felt unexpectedly nice to hold him like this. He looked down at his face, his features slack with sleep, his full lips parted around short puffs of air. He wasn't conventionally handsome, in fact, the bump in his twice-broken nose seemed more pronounced under the light spilling from the hallway. His lips were really too big and they looked plumper now, wet, but next to his angular jawline and sharp cheekbones, his flawless olive skin and shiny, clean hair falling over Thad's arm, he looked beautiful. Debauched and beautiful.

A couple of guys appeared in the doorway.

"Moving this party to the ballroom?" one of them asked as the other one snickered. They sounded drunk, full of bravado.

Thad didn't reply as he walked towards them, holding Lacy close—he was a ball of wiry muscle and he felt light under the strength Thad felt to get him away from these men.

"Nice," the guy said as he stepped back and let Thad pass.

When he made to follow, Thad turned back to him. The pair of them were in tailored suits, the shirts untucked, hair dishevelled, younger than the other men Thad had seen so far, maybe late twenties. Something about their eyes, saucers like Lacy's, told Thad they were on more than alcohol.

"Don't follow me," he said.

The guy in front laughed. "This is a gangbang, mate. You can't just steal the best lay here."

Thad scowled. "He's had enough."

The other guy cackled and to Thad's horror, they started coming towards him. "It's barely midnight, he's not even close to what he can handle."

Thad held Lacy closer and the lie was coming out again. "He's my boyfriend and I say when he's had enough."

Bizarrely, both men stopped; they looked surprised, but that quickly disappeared and they grinned at Thad.

"Fucking nice, man," one said.

The other one nodded along. "That's awesome, you gonna share him at the next party too?"

Thad was perplexed, but he just wanted to get out of there so he said, "Yes," and turned to go.

"Fucking sweet," he heard from behind him.

"Only thing hotter than a man whore is a man whore with a pimp," he heard around cackling laughter and he flinched.

But he just needed to get them out of there, so he tugged Lacy close and made his way through the labyrinth of halls and rooms, didn't meet anyone's eyes, just focused on Lacy warm and snug in his arms, his breaths fanning across Thad's throat as he slept.

Thad felt his chest burst with joy when he found the grand staircase that'd take him out of the place.

He strolled by the guy who'd let him in.

"Already heading out?" the guy asked.

Thad jerked his chin and walked faster.

"Don't forget to tell him to update us next time he's bringing someone," he called after them.

Thad ignored that because he was hoping to God there wasn't going to be a next time. He was all for letting other people live their lives, but Lacy was his best friend and that there was not safe. Lacy could get hurt; those men didn't care about him, it was only a matter of time before something went wrong.

He got Lacy in the passenger's seat, wound the seat back and strapped his seatbelt on. Lacy rolled his head to the side and his eyes popped open. Thad froze. Lacy was staring right up at him, his black pupils fixed firmly on Thad's, trapping him.

"Thaddeus," he said and his face broke into the softest smile before his eyes slipped closed again.

Thad exhaled. His heart was pounding. How was he going to explain this to Lacy? What had he done?

He got in and drove Lacy home. He'd get him cleaned up, into his bed and deal with all that tomorrow.

12

Lacy groaned and rolled over. Why was he awake? There was a noise blaring. It was near his head. He smacked his hand around, trying to reach the bedside table. The noise stopped. He let his hand drop.

The noise started up again. It was his phone. Who the fuck was calling him this early on a Sunday? He hurled himself closer, reached for it blindly and saw Thad's name on the screen. He felt the irritation evaporate and then felt annoyed at himself—anyone else he'd ignore them and then bitch them out next time he saw them, but Thad? He was too soft for the big idiot.

"Thaddeus, you do know what time it is, right?"

"I'm here," Thad said. Lacy was still half-cut, but he was pretty sure that was a strangled sound in his voice.

"Here where?" Lacy asked and yawned, rolled onto his back. He was wearing tracksuit pants. He cracked his eyes open and looked down his chest—he was clean. Did he shower when he got home?

"Here at your house," Thad said. "Can I come in?" His voice unbearably unsure.

"Did we have plans?" Lacy rolled to sit up. "Also, how do you know I'm alone?" He asked just to be a dick.

"Aren't you?" Thad asked sharply. And that was a bit much.

Lacy rolled his eyes, snorted and got up. "Course I'm alone. Who would be here? Hang on."

Thad was standing in his doorway, his broad shoulders up around his ears, his eyes searching Lacy's desperately. Lacy squinted up at him and woké right up.

"Thad, man, you alright?" he stepped back. "Come in, come in. What is it, bud? Did something happen?"

Thad laughed but it wasn't a funny laugh, it was hysterical. But he dutifully stepped inside, his arm brushing Lacy's chest as he passed. The smell of his deodorant layered over a scent like Lacy's soap. It was disorientating yet familiar. Lacy knew he got fucked last night, but he was out of it after the guys on the couch. He was drunk when he took the ecstasy and even though he'd done a line of coke, it never really straightened him out, just made it harder to come. Except as Thad went by him, he felt the impression of one of those guys kissing him. Lacy shook his head. No one at those parties kissed him.

He shut the door. Thad stood in his entryway, hands jammed in his pockets, eyes darting everywhere but at Lacy, his fists clenching and releasing beneath the material.

"Jesus, Thad, what happened?"

Thad flinched.

"Sorry, didn't mean to take the kid's name in vain or whatever."

Thad cracked up, but his eyes skittered to Lacy's and the laughter died.

Lacy stepped closer and gripped Thad's biceps. He looked up at him. "Talk to me, man, what's going on?"

Thad searched his eyes like he was looking for something, desperately looking for something. Lacy saw the moment he didn't find it in the way a flicker of disappointment crossed his face.

"Nothing, sorry, I, sorry," he dropped his gaze.

Lacy squeezed his arms and waited. Thad shuddered, his breath was shaky around the touch.

"I missed church," Thad said.

Lacy had to suck his cheeks in to stop from laughing. He did his best to sound like a concerned friend. "And you're freaking out because the big man is gonna be mad at you?"

Thad laughed, another hysterical sound, but he met Lacy's eyes briefly as he said, "Yes." He looked over Lacy's shoulder.

"I reckon he'll forgive you for one mistake. Everyone's gotta have sickies, yeah?" Lacy said as seriously as he could.

Thad sobered, eyes on the wall. "You really think mistakes are forgivable? I mean, if in everything else, well, most everything else, it's perfect, so it's just one mistake, you think," he pinned Lacy with that terrified look again, "you really think one mistake can be forgiven?"

Lacy wondered what they were bashing into their skulls in this religious fuckery if Thad was this worked up over missing a day of church. But he dutifully answered with the truth. "Absolutely, man. Everyone fucks up. To err is human, am I right?"

Thad smiled but it didn't touch his eyes—they looked inexplicably hurt.

"C'mere," Lacy tugged Thad against him, wrapped him up in a big hug. Thad sagged into his arms. He was a big man, twice as big as Lacy, but in that moment, in the way he sank into Lacy's arms like he needed to be held, he felt small, fragile.

Lacy tightened his hold and Thad gripped him back.

"I'm so sorry," Thad whispered against the top of his head.

Lacy hid his eye roll. "I'm sure the Lord will forgive you or what-ever."

Thad breathed roughly. It fanned over the top of Lacy's head.

"Isn't that your whole thing, anyways?" Lacy said against the material of Thad's jumper; he rubbed his face there. "Sin, say sorry, get let off, sin again and repeat?"

Thad huffed a small laugh. "Kind of, though that's more the Catholics than us."

Lacy squeezed and pulled back. Thad let him go.

"Well, kind of is not nothin'. I'm sure you're all squared away too. C'mon, if you're gonna haul my ass outta bed this early, you can make me a coffee." He headed for the stairs. He needed to get a shirt on. And probably some boxers. If Thad was going to get all handsy, he needed more material between his dick and Thad's body.

"Of course," Thad said and when Lacy glanced at him over his shoulder, he caught Thad watching his back, but he looked away quickly.

"Why'd you miss church anyways?" Lacy asked. They were sitting outside by the jacuzzi. Lacy had his legs dangling in the water, soaking in the sunshine before it got too hot, while Thad sat stiffly on one of his patio chairs. Lacy remembered Thad had gone to that stupid church dance. He knew what that was about—it was the church equivalent of a hook-up joint, only they would be trying to marry Thad off to the classiest hussy in the bunch. He'd felt a sting of jealousy so painful when Thad said where he was going last night, he'd had to talk himself down the whole way to the party, do three shots of vodka on arrival to calm down.

"Did one of those church ladies give you a hard time?" he asked when Thad didn't answer immediately.

Thad frowned at him. "Church ladies?"

"At the church dance," Lacy said.

Thad tilted his head to the side, eyes fixed on the patch of lawn. Lacy saw when he got it. "Oh, no. No, they were... fine."

Lacy frowned. Thad had calmed down, but he was still skittish as fuck.

"'Cos I'll go down there and smack them around if they bothered you," Lacy said.

Thad cracked up like he couldn't help himself. "You can't hit a woman."

"It was a metaphor, I'll metaphorically smack them around."

"I think you mean figurative. You'll figuratively smack them around," Thad replied, he glanced at Lacy with a quick smile before darting his eyes back to the lawn.

Lacy appreciated the smile, but he didn't like Thad being so worked up over some woman he missed church.

"Yeah, that, I'll figuratively smack them around if they made you miss church."

Thad shook his head. "I missed church because I wanted to come see you," he said quietly.

Lacy was relieved, charmed.

"Aww, thanks, bud," he kicked his legs in the water. "Sinning for me, I'm touched."

Thad gripped the side of the chair, his forearms bunching.

"I'm kidding," Lacy said. "I'd never want you to like, break your vows for me or whatever."

Thad kept his eyes fixed on the grass. "I need to tell you something."

And that sounded bad.

"Shit, what is it?" Lacy asked.

"I, well," Thad cleared his throat, shook his head.

Lacy got up, went to him and clapped him on the shoulder. Thad jerked at the touch. Lacy let him go but Thad grabbed his hand.

"You can tell me anything, I ain't in the business of judging anyone," he smiled with teeth and Thad glanced up at him. Lacy was taken aback by the haunted look in his eyes. Jesus, what in the fuck happened?

"I know," Thad said, sad eyes on Lacy. "You're such a good man."

Lacy snorted. He squeezed Thad's hand. "I dunno about that, but I'm always here for my mates. You killed someone? I'll help you bury the body, man, for real. Just gotta let me know and I'll get my shovel out."

"You have a shovel?" Thad asked, a desperate attempt at normal in his voice.

"I don't actually know," Lacy looked around his courtyard, the little square of lawn and the vines growing up the orange brick walls. It was well maintained by his gardening bloke. "Probably?"

Thad blew out a breath. He asked if Lacy wanted another coffee, and Lacy did, and the conversation died. Thad was still off—Lacy kept catching these looks, like he wanted to say something, but then he'd dart his eyes away—and as the day wore on and Lacy's comedown worsened, he found this terrible certainty that Thad had met someone at the church fling. Thad was going to start seeing someone. Thad needed to tell Lacy they couldn't hang out as much anymore. Because what else could it be?

Only the thing was, as they wound down to Christmas, Thad kept coming around; they hung out every day and nothing changed. Thad was twitchier than usual, wouldn't hold eye contact, but he was calming down in increments and Lacy didn't want to pry. Because if Thad had a girl, the only time he was seeing her was for the hour at church on Sundays and at those church things he did on Tuesdays and Thursdays.

Lacy was at Thad's the night before Thad flew back to Tasmania for Christmas and Thad was antsy.

"You're going home for Christmas?" Thad asked as they lazed on the couch and watched *Die Hard*. Thad had asked him several times.

Lacy rolled his eyes. "Yeah, man, I told you. Mum always does a big lunch, big piss up for the old crew, same shit every year. Why do you keep asking?"

"I just wasn't sure if maybe you'd, I don't know," Thad glanced at him, skittered his eyes away. "Changed your mind."

"Well, I can safely say that as long as the old hag is alive, I'll be spending Chrissie in Frankston." His mum was hardly a hag—she was a classy-looking lady. When Lacy got his ten-year deal, he paid for the plastic surgery she wanted, just some nip and tuck stuff, Botox, got her boobs done, nothing too outrageous, but she liked to look good, and she did.

"That's good," Thad nodded.

On screen, Bruce Willis was picking his way through shattered glass with bare feet, saying something to a cop on a radio. Lacy had all of them lined up and *Bad Santa* and he planned to keep Thad there until he absolutely had to leave or risk missing his flight.

Lacy sipped his beer and got lost in the movie. He could recite it at this point.

"When are you back?" Thad asked.

"Ah, I'll come back before New Year's," Lacy replied. He'd already told Thad this too, but if he wanted to hear Lacy's schedule a million times, Lacy would tell him. He had a special party to go to on New Year's and he knew Thad would ask, again, what his plans—

"And for New Year's?"

Lacy huffed a laugh. "Thad, man."

Thad shook his head. "Sorry, I just like to know what you're up to," he waved his hands around and slumped back on the couch.

Lacy scooted over and rested his head on Thad's shoulder. Thad tensed, then relaxed into it. He'd been doing this every time Lacy touched him since the freak-out after the church dance.

Lacy pushed aside the splinter of hurt and carried on the conversation.

"It's all good, I like knowing what you're doing too. Church Christmas Eve, church Christmas morning, then lunch, then more church, am I right?"

Thad chuckled and it vibrated through Lacy's body. "I guess it's just what we do, but I'll be back on the third."

"And I'll pick you up from the airport," Lacy reiterated.

"And you'll pick me up from the airport."

Thad was quiet again. They watched Bruce Willis fighting Alan Rickman.

"Where's the party?" Thad asked and Lacy could tell he was trying to be casual and failing miserably. He'd already asked plenty of times and Lacy had told him it was at a nightclub in Fitzroy, told him he'd be able to stagger home at dawn on foot. It was a lie of course, but he wasn't going to tell him the truth.

"Fitzroy," he murmured.

He got the feeling Thad knew he was lying. As bad as Lacy felt about that, this was one secret he was taking to the grave. He knew Thad loved him, but knowing about that would be a strain on any friendship—all the guys knew he got up to some shit, but only George and Finn knew he fucked around with guys, and even then, he reckoned only Finn, because he was such a hippy, would be cool with exactly what he did with those guys. And cool was a stretch, but accepting.

Thad though? Thad would have a heart attack and probably have to quit football so he could spend all his time repenting for Lacy's soul.

"Hmm," was all Thad said, and Lacy let it drop.

It was early the next morning when Thad had to go. They'd stayed up all night watching their movies, Lacy getting steadily drunk, Thad finally relaxing, smiling at his slurred commentary as the night turned to dawn.

"You're gonna miss your flight, if you keep checking your suitcase," Lacy slurred from beside him.

Thad ran a hand through his hair and smiled self-deprecatingly down at Lacy, his tired eyes crinkling.

"C'mere," Lacy reached for him.

He was taken aback when Thad wrapped him up so tightly, it took the wind out of him.

"Oof," Lacy laughed.

"Take care of yourself, okay?" Thad said against his hair.

"Always, man, I can handle my shit," Lacy replied.

Thad squeezed him harder. His voice was a whisper when he went on. "I don't want to go."

"Then don't," Lacy replied. "Come to Mum's lunch."

Thad held him but didn't reply. They stood like that for a while and Lacy guessed at this rate, he was coming to his mum's because he was sure as shit going to miss his flight.

Lacy slapped him on the back a few times. "C'mon, man, get it together. Your parents will be pissed if you don't show."

Thad squeezed him one more time before letting go. Lacy let him. He met Thad's eyes boring into his.

"You're going to be careful at your party?" he asked.

"Mate, I'm the definition of careful."

Thad flicked his eyes away, a hesitation before he spoke. "I better go."

"No shit," Lacy replied. "Go on, I'm gonna crash in your bed and then I'll lock up and head home."

"Okay," Thad nodded. "Stay as long as you like, there's plenty of food in the freezer—"

"Thad, man, you gotta go."

"Okay." He gripped Lacy's shoulder, squeezed. "See you when I get back."

"With bells on."

Thad smiled, let his hand drop, grabbed his case, gave Lacy one last look before he finally went out the door.

Lacy exhaled roughly. He didn't want Thad to go either. He went into Thad's room and collapsed face-first down on the bed. It smelled like Thad. He inhaled deeply and passed out.

13

♥

THAD KNEW IF HIS parents had to repeat themselves one more time, they'd sit him down and want to talk.

"Sorry, mum, I missed that."

"I said, can you pass the beans," she smiled, exasperated.

He passed the beans.

It was just the three of them in their big old house on an acreage outside Launceston. His parents had wanted more kids, loads of them, but he'd pieced together from his grandparents, aunts, and the people at church that his mum had a lot of miscarriages, even a stillborn, before she'd managed to have him. She was going to keep trying after him, but the doctors said absolutely not, she'd die, she needed to get a hysterectomy. Apparently, this was all decided while she was under general anaesthetic as they cut Thad out of her. They told his dad he needed to authorise it; he refused on account of the church, but he made her a ward of the state and handed authority to Thad's Aunt Celia, his mum's sister, the only person in the family who'd left the church. Celia authorised it over the phone then flew down from Cairns so she could slap his dad across the face. Thad wasn't sure if that was true or not, and he rarely saw Celia, but she was always really nice to him when he did, pretty cold to his dad, so maybe she did.

As Thad looked at his mum now, he thought these stories painted her as such a sickly woman, but she was so vibrant. He got his features from her, nothing remarkable, but those same twinkling brown eyes and warm smile. And she was always busy—with the chickens and the goats and her vast veggie patch, her orchards and canola crop, with the cooking, the house, the church group. But he guessed women's bodies were a mystery.

In any event, they had Thad and he bore the brunt of their love and expectations.

"How do you think Lacy will go this season?" his dad asked from the head of the table.

Thad got butterflies at the mention of Lacy's name—which was constantly when he was at home. Lacy was a celebrity in any foot-ball-loving crowd, and the fact Thad played on the same team meant Lacy was pretty much all people asked about. But the butterflies were chased away by gnawing guilt and overwhelming fear. He knew Lacy was going to another party. And Thad couldn't be there to protect him.

Nevertheless, Lacy remained a topic he could always talk about.

"Lacy is Lacy," Thad smiled. "He's going to have an epic season."

His dad began peppering him with thoughts on how they'd be better off letting Lacy come out of the forward pocket more. Thad thought about it, watched his dad get more animated as he talked. Thad got his height and build from his dad, but that's where the similarities ended—his dad was handsome, with dark hair and dark eyes, a chiselled face. Thad knew he looked alright, but he was hardly turning heads. Not like his dad must've when he was younger, not like Lacy did, which brought him back to Lacy under him, their lips meeting, bodies joining. Hot shame twisted inside him, made him feel like he was going to throw up all over Christmas lunch.

"Well, we're all looking forward to meeting him when you play down here next year," his mum said.

Thad ducked his head and nodded. He was looking forward to them meeting Lacy as well, only he didn't know how it would all go since he'd—he couldn't even think the word. He was sitting there at the Christmas lunch carefully prepared by his mum after they'd attended two church services, and tonight they'd go to a church dinner, and he was haunted by the fact he was no longer a virgin and he'd forfeited that vow in the most heinous way; with a *man*, unable to give consent. He was a monster.

"Thaddeus," his mum said.

"Sorry, what was that?" he asked.

"Are you feeling alright?" she went to stand. "I'll get the thermometer, maybe you've got that flu."

"No, Mum, I'm fine, really, just distracted with the season around the corner," he smiled reassuringly.

She sat down again, her smile relieved but not wholly convinced.

"Right, well, there's a time and place for games," his dad said, voice gruff, but he could not hide his approving smile. His dad might be one of the most religious men in the district, but he was a footy nut and he'd had to work very hard to conceal his pride at Thad playing in the league.

Thad managed to get through the rest of lunch with passable conversation, but he escaped to his room after he'd done the dishes.

His phone was pinging with messages on his bedside table. He went over to it, saw the messages from Lacy and couldn't stop his smile even if it was accosted by the familiar guilt.

It was a stack of photos from Lacy's Christmas lunch. He was in a backyard—presumably his mum's—at a long table full of food, a gaggle of guys with tattoos and mullets, women with as many tattoos next to them, Lacy's mum a regal figure at the head of the table with bleached blonde hair, everyone beaming at the camera. As he clicked through the photos—Lacy's face crammed in the corner with a bunch of selfies, grinning his gap-tooth smile—Thad couldn't stop grinning in response.

Merry Xmas from Frankston!!!

Thad chuckled.

Merry Christmas from Launceston, he typed and hit send.

Pics or it didn't happen!! Came back immediately.

Thad didn't know what to photograph—his parents wouldn't be interested in him doing a selfie with them in the background. He held his phone up, smiled, clicked and sent without overthinking it.

Fark!!!! Appeared in response.

Then: *Rocking that fucken suit, Thaddeus!!!!*

Thad laughed. He wanted to be there so badly. But being around Lacy hurt now in ways he didn't think he'd get over. He'd repented but it felt hollow. Without Lacy's forgiveness, it would remain hollow. Begging for forgiveness for forfeiting his chastity, for committing homosexuality still felt terrible, but God could work with that, he could work with that with God—he wasn't taking it to the church leaders even though he knew he was supposed to. But this other thing?

"Thaddeus," his mum asked from outside his door. "Ready to go?"

He quickly silenced his phone and put it back on the bedside table.

"Coming," he replied and left the room as she opened the door.

He could hear it vibrating as he followed her out. He clenched and released his fists, he hated leaving Lacy hanging until he got back later that night, but his mum would have a coronary if Thad brought his phone to church, never mind spent the evening texting.

The days following Christmas were much the same. Church functions. Helping his mum in the veggie patch, feeding the chickens and the goats, collecting eggs, picking fruit. Accompanying his dad to the hardware store and helping him build a new woodfire potbelly for a young family at the church, going over to their place and installing it.

The New Year's Eve party was like a timer in the background, ticking down ominously, making it difficult for him to concentrate, to sleep.

On the evening of the thirtieth, he went to bed, eyes wide open on the ceiling. His penis swelled like it had every night since he'd been with Lacy. The guilt was horrendous—the size and weight of it a force he'd never get over—but almost as bad was the desire to be with Lacy like that again.

The memory of being inside him, kissing him, the feel of his breath against Thad's lips, his hands on Thad's ass—it came alive for him in high definition every night, his erection throbbing, heart pounding. He buried his hands under his back to stop himself from masturbating. And he told himself again and again that Lacy knew what he was doing at those parties, was in fact safer if Thad wasn't there to take advantage of him.

He knew that's where Lacy was going. He knew when Lacy was lying—he answered dismissively, rushed over the words like it was no big deal, "Just a party in a club in Fitzroy, down the road." Quick smile and subject change.

Thad swallowed. The sound of the farm was familiar around him—the rustle of the trees in the light breeze, the hum of the tawny frogmouths that held the territory and preferred the big tree right outside his window, the brush of its branches against the tin roof above him, a scraping sound he was well acquainted with and fond of.

Sweat beaded on his forehead. He couldn't go on like this. He needed to tell Lacy. It might damn the friendship to hell, but he could not keep this secret and remain his friend. He also couldn't allow him to go to that party—it wasn't safe. It was only a matter of time before something went horribly wrong.

Decided, he kicked off his sheet, sat up and grabbed for his phone. He hit Lacy's contact. His thumb hovered over the call button. What was he going to say? He inhaled sharply and stood, gripped his phone tightly. He'd just tell him—*I know where you're going, please don't.*

No, he couldn't say that. Who was he to tell another man what to do?

He'd just say, or ask Lacy to skip the festivities this year because it was too dangerous with that flu going around.

He almost laughed at the thought of Lacy's face at that one—his eyes would widen, then he'd squint up at Thad like he was ascertaining how serious he was, before reassuring him that he'd be fine, he had the constitution of an ox.

His phone buzzed in his hand and he almost dropped it.

The screen lit up with the beginnings of a message from Lacy.

Henny reckons there's no way u could swim from Melbourne to Tassie...

Thad opened the message. Henny was one of Lacy's best friends from back home and Thad knew they always got into it when they were together—drunken arguments that would go in circles for hours before Henny would ask Lacy if he wanted to take it outside, to which

Lacy would always laugh and ask if Henny was insane, he wasn't fighting him, he'd lose for sure. Henny was a big man, good with his fists, and one punch would knock Lacy out cold. Thad had been aghast until Lacy told him not to worry, if they ever really went at it, Lacy would bring a weapon. Thad didn't know if that was reassuring or not, but thankfully they never seemed to get that far; apparently, this had been going on since kindergarten and while they went at it physically until high school, they'd managed to 'mature and keep it to dialogue' according to Lacy since they became adults.

Tell him he's wrong, the message continued once Thad saw the whole thing.

Thad cracked a smile. He ran a hand through his hair, sat down on his bed and typed his reply.

Well, I don't know if anyone's done it, but it'd be pretty dangerous. Never say never though.

Exactly!

The reply was instant and Thad read the messages flying in—Lacy was clearly researching Bass Strait and hunkering down in his argument—and as Thad typed his replies, he calmed down.

He couldn't tell Lacy not to go. He couldn't tell him what had happened. He couldn't lose this. He had to learn to live with it.

Thad's mum wanted him to help her with the shopping the next morning—she needed a few things to finalise the New Year's Eve dinner—and he was in his room, doing the buttons up on his shirt, his hair still damp from the shower, a trickle of water running down the back of his neck, when he was seized with a feeling of certainty. His body, his soul, and his mind clicked into sync and he knew what he was about to do.

He'd had this feeling before, when he'd decided to enter the draft, and he knew it was his relationship with God. Everything would align and he knew—even if he was terrified—what he had to do. Sometimes, he could pray and pray on something and yet, all would remain out of order, a decision would elude him. And then, this.

He pulled his case out from under his bed and started shoving everything into it. When he had a calling like this, it didn't matter what other people said or how they'd react—he just knew what he had to do.

With the wind of God at his back, he packed his stuff, finished getting dressed, went out and found his mum.

"I need you to take me to the airport," he said.

She looked up from where she'd been looking in a cupboard, her eyebrows raised.

"Sorry? Now?" she shut the cupboard. "Has something happened?"

Thad squared his shoulders, cleared his throat. "I need to go to Melbourne. Now, yes, right now."

"But we've got the dinner," she came over to him and craned her neck back to search his eyes.

"I'm sorry, but I have to go. Can you please take me to the airport?" his voice dropped to a plea.

The tap dripped once into the silence of their old kitchen; the morning light caught the motes and the air felt full with the bustling energy that permeated the wood of the floors and the walls of the room. She studied him, a stillness to her in front of him.

"Alright," she replied quietly and turned away, her hands making quick work of her apron at her waist. "Just let me get the keys."

"Thank you," he said on an exhale. He pulled out his phone and searched for a flight.

He panicked when he saw the mid-morning flight fully booked, but a seat was available for the afternoon. He booked it and ignored the price.

His heart was pounding as he got in the passenger's seat of her little Cortina, but she was calm, if filled with questions he could tell she was choosing not to ask, and it helped him settle.

"We'll just tell your father one of your friends needed you," she said as she reversed.

"Thank you," he replied and looked out the window, the farm familiar and sunny around them.

They didn't speak on the drive, the music and chatter from the Christian radio station filling the quiet between them as Thad did his best not to fidget, to hide how he was about to burst out of his skin at the thought of the conversation ahead of him.

His mum parked in one of the drop-off bays. She got out and waited on the curb as he got his case out.

"Thaddeus," she said calmly but firmly.

He set the case down and straightened, met her eyes. Those deep, warm brown eyes—a mirror of his own—looked up at him, full of curiosity and concern, but as she reached for his arm and held him, she simply smiled.

"I know you have your own world there," she squeezed his arm. "But we're your world too," she smiled, eyes shining, "you're our son, we love hearing about your life. You can talk to us. About anything."

He wasn't so sure about that and he had to swallow a few times before he could reply. But she was looking at him like she really meant it. He decided to believe her.

"I know. Thank you," he leaned down. She brought her arms around him, gave him a tight hug.

He kissed her cheek, stepped back, told her to apologise to his dad for him and headed inside before he could change his mind.

14

♥

LACY POPPED AN ECSTASY tablet, drained his vodka and soda water, dropped the glass in the sink, and headed for the door. He was giddy—these parties were always baller, but something about the last one left him more keyed up for it than usual. He didn't know what it was, but he felt so fucking horny for it, he was buzzing.

His phone beeped, notifying him of his car's arrival. He slipped the phone into his back pocket and stepped outside. He jogged to the car idling on his street to burn off a bit of this feeling.

Address confirmed with his driver, they were off, Lacy's mouth going a mile a minute to do something with his energy. He thought of Thad as he talked, wondered how his New Year's was going. He rolled his phone in his hands and wondered why Thad hadn't messaged him back. Lacy wouldn't be able to text again for a while since he was about to roll. An ugly feeling twisted in his gut at the thought of Thad at another one of those church socials. Thad never said, but Lacy got the feeling his parents would want Thad to settle down. Hell, for all Lacy knew, they already had a girl lined up for him.

"Thanks, mate," Lacy said as the driver pulled up a few mansions down from the address of the party. Lacy always gave this address just in case, though it was probably a foolish hope—if he got caught, he got caught and that'd be the end of it. He wasn't ashamed of what he did. Well, he was—a man didn't take cock at a gangbang like a pro and want to fucking talk about it with other men, never mind the whole country—but he was addicted to it, he loved it, and he didn't think anyone would understand that. He almost scoffed, of course no one would understand it!

As he jogged up the street, he saw guys in suits ahead of him, was about to jog past the enormous hedges through the gates when someone stepped right in front of him.

"Jesus, watch it—"

The words died on his tongue. Thad stood in front of him, his bulk blocking Lacy from proceeding.

Lacy's world stopped spinning. He took a step back to make sure he was seeing properly. He was. That was definitely Thad looming in front of him, his mouth a tight line, his eyes searching Lacy's like he was scared.

"Thad, man, what are you, what?" Lacy tried.

A couple of guys in suits went by them; one of them met Lacy's eyes and Lacy could see the moment he was about to speak. He grabbed Thad's arm and yanked him down the driveway, around the hedge, and kept walking until they were on the far side of the compound under a streetlight.

He let Thad go and stepped back so he could look up at him.

"I need to tell you something," Thad said quickly before Lacy could ask what the hell he was doing there.

"Now?" Lacy asked. "Shit, man, what are you? How do you know about this place?"

Thad looked at his feet. He was dressed nicely—tailored black pants, a fitted mint green button-up open at his throat, tight on his broad shoulders, his hair wavy at his temples like he'd washed it and it'd dried in the sun. Lacy shook himself, actually physically shook his body like a dog to make sure he wasn't hallucinating.

"I," Thad said, voice soft. "I need to tell you, I..."

Lacy's heart pounded but as he watched Thad, really took stock of how petrified he was, he grew more alarmed.

"Shit, Thad, what is it?" he reached for him and Thad leapt back.

All the life drained from him. Did Thad know what he did here? Was he coming here to end their friendship because of it?

"I don't want you to touch me because once you know, you won't want to," Thad said with difficulty. He flicked his eyes up and Lacy saw the shine there.

Lacy was about to reach for him again when Thad spoke.

"I raped you," Thad whispered.

Lacy froze.

"What?"

"I raped you," Thad said again, louder this time, his voice cracking.

Lacy frowned up at him. Was this about what happened on the couch? Was Thad still carrying that around? More importantly, what the fuck were they learning in church for Thad to think that?

"Thad, man," Lacy said gently but didn't step closer—Thad looked like he might shatter if Lacy touched him, "that wasn't rape, that was just, you know, getting off. It happens."

Thad met his eyes, incredulous and hurt. "I had sex with you without you knowing. I, I," he dropped his gaze again. "I raped you."

"Well, it was hardly sex-sex," Lacy reasoned. He rubbed his head. He was starting to feel it, but he needed to stay here in this conversation, reassure Thad, get him to leave so he could get inside before he was completely under. He reckoned he had about twenty minutes.

But Thad didn't look reassured, if anything, he looked angry, which was so incongruous it sobered Lacy right up, like when he was drunk and he needed to sharpen up because he was about to get in a fight.

"I penetrated you," Thad said, fumbling over the word. "I had sex with you."

Now Lacy was really confused.

"When?" he asked because he was pretty fucking sure he'd remember that.

Thad glanced to the side. The mansion was glowing beside them, every window lit up, the muted sounds of music filtering out to them on the street. Lacy followed his gaze, then looked back and squinted up at him. Thad didn't say anything, but he folded his arms over his chest like he was trying to hold himself together.

"Oh," Lacy said, voice faint. Someone had kissed him, he had a flash of it in the haze of a blackout, someone kissing him. But that drifted by him now and evaporated under a series of other pretty fucking important questions like, 'What were you doing here? You saw me like that?'

Oh God, Thad saw him like that.

But Thad looked like he was about to pass out—he was white under the street light, his eyes glassy, and he was holding himself so tightly he looked like he was in pain.

"I'm so sorry," he said. "I don't know what came over me, I just, I lost control and I, I, oh, God."

Lacy stepped forward and grabbed him by the biceps. "Thad, man, listen to me. You didn't rape me. In there?" he jerked his chin to the side, swallowed. "I'm willing."

But Thad was shaking his head. "I penetrated you and you didn't know."

Lacy's heart fluttered, but he squeezed Thad's arms. "It's kinda the point? I, you know," he released his grip and patted Thad's arms, "I like it. Like that."

"But it was me," Thad said weakly.

Lacy didn't know what to make of that; he felt pained by Thad's tone—was he hurt because Lacy didn't remember?

He couldn't deal with much more right now since he needed to get inside.

"Look, we'll talk about this later, okay? But, Thad, man, seriously, you didn't rape me. I'm sure I woulda loved it and all that, alright?" he stepped back. "Now, you need to get going 'cos I gotta, yeah."

"You're not going in there," Thad said and dropped his arms.

Oh, hell no. "Ah, yeah, I am."

"It's dangerous," Thad replied.

The anger vanished—so Thad wasn't having a go at him, he was worried?

"It's really not, they got all these safety protocols and—"

"I fucked you bare!" Thad stepped into his space and Lacy had to step back. He'd never heard Thad swear.

"Those other guys, they didn't listen to you! You wanted some privacy, a room and they ignored you. It's not safe," he said firmly.

Lacy was beginning to feel like he needed a defibrillator to get through this conversation—Thad saw all of that?

"It's kinda the point," he repeated because he didn't know what else to say and he didn't have much more time. "It's really fine, just go home, we'll talk tomorrow, okay?"

Thad grabbed his arm. "If you're going in there, I'm coming with you."

Thad had already seen it all apparently, so Lacy didn't know why he was so against him coming in again. But he was so repelled by the idea, of Thad fucking someone else—everyone did at these things—he just needed him gone. Then another thought hit him—who else did Thad fuck when he was here last time? It made his voice cold.

"Go home, I can handle this. Just," he went to turn away and Thad grabbed him again.

"No," Thad tightened his hold. "I'm coming with you."

Lacy felt a surge of anger. "Go home," he snapped. "I don't want you here."

Thad let him go like Lacy had struck him.

Lacy charged up the street, half expecting Thad to follow him. He didn't.

Lacy had a vodka and soda water in a high ball glass clutched tightly in his hand, the conversation of the three guys around him swimming past his head. The ecstasy was rising in his system like a tidal wave that was about to hit him from behind and take him under, but he was holding it at bay while he panicked.

Thad had been here. Thad had fucked him. He didn't know which one of those points was fucking him up more—Thad had seen all of that. What did he think of Lacy now? Thad had fucked him. Did he like it?

"Oh, man, you're already out of it," the guy next to him said with a low chuckle. Simon, his name was Simon. He was a rich prick, forty-odd, had a gut but his big dick made up for it. He was smirking down at Lacy now, the soft lighting in the room casting him in a glow.

"Not yet," Lacy said and cast about for a waiter. He needed another drink. He was about as far from relaxed as he could get in this state.

He wondered how the fuck he was going to talk to Thad after this.

A glass appeared in his hand.

"Thank you—"

Thad leaned down and kissed his throat, fumbling like a kid who'd seen it done and was trying it on.

"Sorry I'm late," Thad said to Lacy, to the men around them. "Traffic."

"You'd think everyone would be ensconced in their place by now, being New Year's..." Simon started prattling while Lacy stared up at Thad.

Thad. Who was here. Pressed against his side, his hand resting loosely on Lacy's waist, fingers clutching and releasing on his hip.

"Excuse us for a second," Lacy said. He grabbed Thad by the hand and tugged him into the hallway.

He spun back and Thad loomed over him.

"What are you doing here?" Lacy hissed. A warmth flooded his limbs, his body was losing its edges and he was about to drop into the pool of it, drift away where he had no boundaries. But he needed to hold on, needed to get Thad to leave.

"I told you," Thad replied calmly enough, but Lacy did not miss the scared shitless tone. "This isn't safe. If you're doing this, I'm going to take care of you."

Lacy closed his eyes, opened them, blinked a few times. He was so warm, he was dissolving. But his voice was sharp when he spoke, "If you want to join in you can just say."

Thad winced.

"Sorry," he said and tucked his hands in his pockets, shrunk in on himself. "I thought if it wasn't, you know," he brought his hands out and made air quotes. Lacy got it, 'rape.' "You'd want," he took a shaky breath, "me. Again."

"Hold up," he said, his voice felt funny, but he got the words to work, "do you mean take care of me or *take care of me*?"

Thad blushed. "Both."

"No one else?" Lacy asked, his tone acid.

"God, no," Thad glanced up and did the sign of the cross quickly. Lacy snickered—even in the midst of an impending gangbang, he was apologising for taking the Lord's name in vain. "I'd never," he met Lacy's eyes, "with anyone else!"

Lacy slipped his hand down and tangled his fingers with Thad's.

"Let's go then," he said and then it crashed over him, warmth flooding him everywhere.

Thad's arm came around his waist and held him together, moved him.

He was in a room. It was dark. And Thad was everywhere. Sliding his shirt off his shoulders, kissing his shoulder. Thad's hands were unbuttoning his pants. He heard his own voice begging, felt Thad's fingers tremble as they pushed the material away and off. Thad's lips brushed his hip. Thad's naked skin pressed against his own. Thad's lips caressed his while his fingers moved inside him. Thad's eyes shone as they met Lacy's and his dick pushed in.

"Thad, Thaddeus," Lacy chanted, the pleasure in his core spilling out everywhere and washing over both of them.

All he could feel was Thad rocking inside him, Thad holding him, Thad kissing him, Thad whispering, "Is this okay?"

15

IT WAS DIFFERENT, THAD thought as he held Lacy. He had his arms under his back, Lacy's head cradled in his hands. He stroked his cheekbones with his thumbs as he pushed inside, catalogued Lacy's lips parting around a sharp inhale. He felt the presence of another man beside them, and yet he ignored him, made this just them.

He kissed Lacy softly, sharing more air than touch. He did it because he couldn't not. He did it so no one else could have his mouth. Not yet.

"Is this okay?" he whispered, his body trembling.

Lacy arched. "Thaddeus," he gasped. His legs wound around Thad's waist and his hands ran up and down Thad's back, his fingertips sweeping the top of Thad's ass, making him shiver.

He was uncoordinated and inexperienced, but he felt so incredibly good, he couldn't care too much that he was already about to come.

He rubbed his nose alongside Lacy's, felt Lacy's hot breath on his cheek. His throat was tight with emotion. He couldn't speak, he could only roll his hips into Lacy in tight thrusts, pant against Lacy's lips.

Lacy was erect between them, rubbing up against Thad's abs. It sent Thad over the edge; he was accosted by a longing for it—he wanted Lacy's hard length in his hand, in his mouth. He was scandalised at himself, but he couldn't stop it. His balls tightened, his hips pressed forward erratically. He made a deep noise against Lacy's throat as he pulsed inside him.

"Alright, that was sweet, but you've had your fun," came from beside them.

Thad jolted, slanting his head to the side. The guy was shirtless, his penis poking out of his dress pants as he stroked himself.

"Need to come," Lacy said against Thad's cheek.

The guy laughed. "You'll come when we say you come."

Thad bristled. He slid out of Lacy's body, gasped embarrassingly, got it together and moved down.

He could feel the other guy moving to get between Lacy's legs, but Thad crowded around Lacy's groin, brought his arms under Lacy's thighs to hold him open. He gripped Lacy's erection with an uncertain hand, ignored his panicked thoughts and kissed the crown.

Lacy arched up, his length pulsing in Thad's hand. Thad licked at the head, curled his tongue around until he could suck the crown between his lips. Lacy's hands dropped into his hair and he groaned as he started to rock into Thad's mouth, his fingers sliding through the strands and scratching his scalp.

Thad took a deep breath through his nose and slid further down, licked around the skin. He inhaled Lacy's scent, the muskiness mixed with a light sweat.

Lacy's moan was muffled. Thad flicked his eyes up and saw the other man pushing into his mouth. Lacy was arching to get more of it, pushing his hips up to get more of himself into Thad's mouth, his fingers tightening in his hair.

And God help him, it turned Thad on even more. He increased his pace, groaned around Lacy's length in his mouth. He brought his other hand into play and rolled Lacy's testicles in his palm.

The man in Lacy's mouth thrust in and out roughly, Lacy rocking his hips up to get the same rhythm going. Thad responded, sucking up and down his length in faster bursts. The man pulled out, held Lacy with a tight grip in his hair and stoked himself. He started to come on Lacy's tongue.

Thad's heart pounded. He redoubled his efforts. The man stepped back and Lacy arched away, pressing his head back into the pillow as he gripped Thad's hair. His breath hitched as he pumped his hips against Thad's face.

Come flooded Thad's mouth, shocking him. But the noises Lacy made, hitching breaths, matched the pulses of semen shooting into Thad's mouth. It aroused him and he began to swallow eagerly.

He was vibrating by the time Lacy slumped back onto the bed.

The sound of a belt unbuckling drew Thad's eye. This man was tall, older, at least forty, and he was moving to the end of the bed, ready to position himself where Thad was still crouched between Lacy's thighs.

Lacy's legs dropped open, and Thad moved up the bed beside him. He slid his arm over Lacy's waist and tugged his side against his chest. As the guy settled between Lacy's thighs, bent him at the waist, Lacy's hip rubbed against Thad's abs.

Thad was still catching his breath. He stroked his hand over Lacy's torso as he watched the man push his condom wrapped penis inside. Lacy was soft, but he spread himself to allow the man to penetrate him deeper.

Thad looked up. Lacy's face was turned to look at Thad as he was jolted against the bed, those punched out breaths slipping from his parted lips as he took it.

Thad leaned over to kiss him. He tasted the other man and it was weird, but Lacy slid his tongue into his mouth, scrabbled clumsily at

Thad's head to pull him closer. Thad caressed his rib cage, brushed his thumb over his nipple, stroked up his throat, touched his jaw, his cheek, the shell of his ear.

A slap rang out in the room and Lacy broke the kiss to gasp.

The man in him was shoving in hard and fast, Lacy bent in half on the bed, his ass up as the man slapped his cheek. He was wheezing.

Thad pressed closer, kissed Lacy under the ear, wrapped his arm securely around his torso. He watched Lacy's face under the on-slaught—his eyes were closed, lips parted, punched-out sounds came out of them, and his forehead creased like he wasn't sure if he was in pleasure or pain. There was something beautiful about that pain meeting pleasure etched on his face.

"Oh, fuck, yeah, fuck, fuck, fuck," the man said and Thad glanced down to see him, his glutes clenching as he came.

Lacy's breath fanned over Thad's cheek as he took it.

Thad's heart pounded into the pause when it was over. The man breathed heavily. Lacy was restless beside him. The man slapped Lacy's ass and laughed, breathless. Thad tensed. The man pulled out, his hand around the base to hold the condom in place. He was shuffling back, pulling it off, tying it. Thad looked back to Lacy. Lacy was already watching him—his eyes weren't quite tracking as he licked his lips and pressed closer.

Thad pushed up to kiss him.

Thad remembered every man who came into that room in high definition. Old, young, fit, fat, the way they moved Lacy like he was a doll—onto his hands and knees, flat on his stomach, on his side—how they used him, how they groaned and called him names, how their skin slapped against Lacy's, how they gripped his hips and hair so tightly it'd leave a mark if Lacy weren't covered in colours.

But what burned into Thad's brain was Lacy's gasps, the way he let it happen, his body open and willing for them, the impatient twitch of his hands, the crease between his eyes, the perfection of his sinewy muscles as he was stretched and manhandled. Thad was overcome with this feeling of awe, with feeling so turned on it hurt.

He took Lacy again once more that night. Three men had just left and Lacy rolled from his stomach to his side to push his back against Thad's chest. Thad hauled him in, kissing desperately up his throat, down to his shoulder. He crushed him against his body as he rutted against his lower back. Lacy craned his head back and Thad stretched up to kiss him as he fumbled to line himself up. He pushed Lacy's thigh up, held him there with a hand on his hip as he manoeuvred inside with his other hand. Once he was in, he wrapped both arms around Lacy's torso and held him close. He heard himself making these broken sounds as he pumped his hips, slid in and out of that wet, loose heat. His eyes were squeezed tightly shut and he could feel Lacy's hand bumping against his arm. He opened his eyes to watch. Lacy's body was straining, the definition of his muscles bunching and releasing in his abdomen, his mouth open as he sucked in air.

"Does it feel good?" Thad panted against his ear.

Lacy made a high-pitched sound, like he was choking.

Thad watched him come, felt it too in the way he clenched around him. Thad responded with an embarrassing sound as he came. He was the only one doing it without a condom.

It was almost light out when Lacy dozed beside him and Thad told a young man who came in Lacy was done. The guy was handsome, blonde, lithe like a cyclist, his eyes betraying how high he was, but he wandered back out without argument and Thad hugged Lacy close.

16

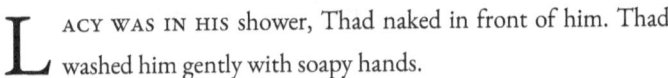

Lacy was in his shower, Thad naked in front of him. Thad washed him gently with soapy hands.

"Did you do this last time?" Lacy croaked.

Thad met his eyes, a flash of guilt crossing his expression. He nodded and dropped his eyes.

Lacy realised it was the first lucid sentence he'd said in a while. He hadn't drunk as much as usual, so the night wasn't a black out. But he was rolling and the memories felt like snapshots from a dream. Thad was a warm presence in every frame.

"I tried to keep it professional," Thad said to the tiles as he ran his hands up Lacy's back.

"But you couldn't?" Lacy stepped into Thad's space, forcing him to lift his gaze.

Thad looked so guilty, but his hands moved down Lacy's flank to tease his ass.

"I'm sorry," Thad whispered.

Lacy groaned and kissed him. Fuck, but that was hot. Thad losing control. Thad touching him because he couldn't not.

Thad made a surprised sound into his mouth, but quickly kissed him back, quickly took over the kiss as he crowded Lacy back against the wall and kissed him with tongue, with harsh shots of air from his nose brushing Lacy's cheek. Lacy rested his hands on Thad's ass and held him there.

Thad broke the kiss but stayed close. Lacy watched him, the water dripping into his eyes from the hair plastered over his forehead, his lips parted as if he was searching for something to say.

"I'm not," Lacy said when Thad did nothing more than stare at him and breathe noisily.

Thad swallowed. His lips lifted in the ghost of a smile before he huffed a little laugh.

"What?" Lacy asked, his hands rubbing Thad's ass—it was a great fucking ass, firm with those dips on the side from how taut the muscles were.

"Nothing, just, Happy New Year," Thad said.

Lacy snickered.

He knew this wasn't the end of it. He knew Thad was probably going to freak out, same way he knew that remark was meant to try and reach him on the ground Lacy had dragged him to.

But he needed to pass out and sleep before they got to all that.

"C'mon," he said and grabbed Thad's hand as he turned the taps off with the other. He let him go while they dried off, took his hand again once they were in his room and tugged until Thad got the message and got into his bed.

Thad curled around him from behind. The feel of him layered with the memories of him doing it at the party, something caught between reality and a dream. But the feel of his strong arms, his soft breath on Lacy's nape, the brush of his lips on Lacy's shoulder was very real.

It was dark when Lacy woke up. He knew he was alone. He blinked a few times. He'd slept all day. Thad had probably gone home. Thad had fucked him last night. Thad had fucked him before last night.

Lacy rolled onto his back and felt so fucking turned on, he had to reach down and squeeze his dick.

If Thad was gone now, maybe he'd messaged since he left.

He sat up too quickly, his head spinning. Bracing himself on the edge of the bed, he took stock for a second—he was naked; he was clean; he was lightheaded; his mouth was dry; and he was coming down and killing himself might not be a bad idea if only to get away from the bleakness settling in his chest.

But it'd pass, it always did.

He patted his bedside table, found his phone and tapped it to light up the screen.

There were a lot of messages. He scrolled through them and felt the desolation in his chest sink deeper. Nothing from Thad.

Fuck, what had Lacy dragged him into?

There was a glass of water on the bedside table and it made his heart ache. Even freaking out, Thad had got him sorted.

He drained it, hit the lamp, got up and rifled through his drawer for some trackies.

He needed to eat something, he knew it would be difficult. He knew from past experience bread, pasta, meat, basically anything in the not-liquid menu would be like trying to eat cardboard. Thad always brought him soup. How did he know to bring soup?

He walked into his kitchen and stopped.

Thad looked up.

"You're up," he smiled, relief flitting over his features.

"You're here," Lacy replied, equally relieved.

Thad glanced away. He had a mug next to his hand, a bowl in front of him, the newspaper spread out under it and now Lacy inhaled, he could smell it—soup.

"You cooked?" Lacy asked and went to the stove.

"You didn't have much..." Thad trailed off and Lacy heard the chair scraping on the tiles.

Everything felt unbearably awkward; he was focused on lifting the lid, but his awareness was on Thad simply standing and doing nothing more.

"So I went and got some stuff," Thad finished.

"And the paper," Lacy shot Thad a smirk over his shoulder; it felt strained, but he was in it and needed to keep going. "You can read all that shit on your phone and you got the paper."

"It's good to have a record of New Year's Day," Thad replied and Lacy could hear the smile in his voice.

Lacy got busy getting himself a bowl of soup, thanking Thad for making it, his eyes darting everywhere but at Thad. He needed to say something, but when he felt like this, it was too difficult to find a groove.

He sat down and Thad resumed his seat across from him. He startled when Thad got up again with jerky movements.

"I'll get you something to drink. Coffee?" Thad moved away.

"I can do it—"

"No, no, eat," Thad said and Lacy listened to him moving around behind him, the rattle of the shelves as he pulled out the water jug, flicked the kettle on. Thad moved around like he knew the place as well as Lacy did. Because he did.

A glass of water appeared in front of him.

"Thanks, man," Lacy said and took a mouthful of soup. It was the tomato noodle one and it was incredible. "Fuck, this is good."

"The fruit and veg place was open, I thought maybe I'd have to make do with a supermarket since it's a public holiday, but the guy said they're always open..."

Lacy nodded along, his ears picking up every chord in Thad's voice trying to get them back to normal.

Thad set his coffee down.

"Thanks, shit, but I feel like I owe you, this is amazing," Lacy took a sip before washing it down with the water.

Thad didn't say anything. It was a loaded silence. Lacy rewound that sentence and hoped there wasn't an innuendo he'd missed, but he was too far in the mess of his comedown to figure that out, so he finished eating and listened to Thad doing the dishes. Lacy had a dishwasher, but Thad never used it.

Lacy drained his coffee and stood. He needed to lie down on the couch and stare at the TV; he hoped Thad would join him, but he had a feeling that even if he did, it'd be painfully awkward and Lacy needed to pass some hours to get rid of this feeling before he could deal with it.

He slipped behind Thad and dropped his dishes in the sink, his hand brushed Thad's hip like he always did.

"I can do those—"

He cut off at Thad's sharp inhale.

Lacy froze. He looked up. Thad glanced down, his eyes flicking to Lacy's lips.

Goddamn it, he was trying to be normal, and now here he was, heart pounding, dick rising up as if it'd been extended an invite to the world's most awkward morning after. Night. Whatever.

Thad leaned down and kissed him so suddenly, Lacy took a split second to respond. Thad pulled back. Lacy grabbed him by the head to drag him back down. Thad met him, his hands coming out of the sink with a slosh of noise, grabbing at Lacy's hips, wetting his bare torso before slipping lower, hauling him in and lifting him up, placing him on the kitchen bench. Lacy wrapped his legs around his waist, yanked him down so they could keep kissing.

Thad broke away, but stayed close. "Sorry, is this okay?"

"Shit yeah," Lacy breathed and kissed him again.

He was so fucking horny, all Thad had to do was kiss him and he was dialled up beyond his control. They were kissing frantically, no in between, just nothing and then warp speed to desperation.

Thad gripped his ass and pulled him flush against him. Lacy's dick pressed against his flat stomach. Lacy started grinding on him, his breath hitching in Thad's mouth, those strong fingers flexing and releasing on his ass.

Lacy broke the kiss. "Fuck me," he said against Thad's lips.

Thad groaned. "I can't make it to the bed."

"Here," Lacy said and pushed on his shoulders. Thad got the message and moved back an inch, his grip loosening.

Lacy hopped down and spun in the hold, pressed his chest flat to the bench and worked his pants off.

"Oh…" Thad trailed off. His hands caressed Lacy's bare ass. "I haven't got lubricant," he said, he sounded so apologetic.

"I can handle it." Lacy rocked back against Thad's hard dick. Lacy moaned; it was embarrassing, but with the lingering effects of the night before he was aching for it.

He pressed his forehead into the granite. Thad's knuckles bumped his ass as he undid his pants. Lacy panted, arched his back. Thad's dick slid against his bare skin.

"C'mon, c'mon," Lacy whispered.

Thad slid his palm down Lacy's back and let it rest on his lower back, he pushed the head of his dick against Lacy's entrance.

"I can't," Thad started.

"You can—"

"Make it as good."

Lacy inhaled sharply. "It's always good, it's you."

"Oh," punched out of Thad and he pushed inside.

It burned; even with however many dicks Lacy took the night before, he was feeling this. Thad had a big dick and he was dry. He wasn't stopping though, and Lacy was grateful for it as he pushed all the way in, nothing but his rough breathing filling the air as he seated himself, pulled out a fraction, rocked back in.

Oh God, it was a lot, but Lacy knew if Thad kept going, picked up the pace, it would hit him just right.

Thad didn't do that. Instead, in between his erratic thrusting, he plastered himself to Lacy's back, buried his face in the crook of Lacy's neck and sucked on his skin, reached under him and wrapped his hand around Lacy's dick, stroked him in his palm.

Lacy felt held, enveloped in Thad. He was everywhere—fucking him, holding him, stroking him, giving him the world's biggest hickey by the feel of it and it started to feel good, better than good.

"I'm going to come," he panted.

Thad tightened his hold, stroked him faster, punched into him with tight rolls of his hips.

Lacy was coming before he was even aware he was doing it. Every part of him was tingling—his throat, his chest, his balls, his dick, he was so fucking horny.

Thad moved his lips over Lacy's neck, his breath hot as he started to come.

Lacy could feel it—the wetness of Thad's come inside him; he'd never fucked without a condom before.

"You didn't use a condom," he said, Thad's breath still harsh in his ear.

Thad tensed.

Lacy reached back and patted his flank. "No, I mean, you never used a condom with me," he said as he caught his breath. Thad had told him that too, last night. "Even the first time?"

Thad pulled back and pressed his forehead between Lacy's shoulder blades. "No," he said, his own breathing rough. "I should have, I don't know why I—"

"Fuck, that's hot," Lacy said into the bench, rocking his hips back.

"Yeah?" Thad asked weakly; Lacy felt the lightest kiss on the top nob of his spine and it was doing things to him.

"Yeah," he breathed out, very aware of Thad still inside him, of his come inside him. He swallowed down what he wanted to say—because it was you, Thad, *you*. But he wasn't sure what this meant to Thad. He wasn't entirely sure what it meant to himself, but he had a feeling it meant something.

Thad kissed his spine, ran a hand down Lacy's side, pulled back achingly slowly. Lacy groaned as he pulled out and he felt the come leaking out of him. God, why was that really doing it for him? He knew he was into some kinky shit, but this was a new one.

Thad tugged Lacy's tracksuit pants up, slipped them gently over his groin and adjusted his dick. Lacy rubbed his face against the bench—that was fucking hot too. He listened to Thad doing up his pants, listened to them both breathing.

"Wanna watch that glass blowers show?" he asked against the granite, his voice muffled. Thad was right into it, some contest with people blowing glass to make shit.

Thad laughed, like it'd been stunned out of him, but said, "Okay," and Lacy straightened up.

He turned and caught Thad's soft smile. It was an unguarded smile that rapidly morphed into a blush and Lacy leaned up and kissed him. Thad hauled him in and kissed him back.

"Glass blowers it is," Lacy said against his lips with a grin.

He grabbed Thad's hand and dragged him into the living room.

17

♥

T HAD LET HIMSELF INSIDE the old house, flicked the light
on—it was one of those old switches, cumbersome and black
with the thick rectangular knob sticking out of it, igniting the light
that hung on a chord in the hallway and started with a buzz. One
of these days, he thought as he worked his shoes off, his dad needed
to come to the mainland and together they could do a re-wire of the
place. Lacy's place had the latest electrics—flat pads with dimmers for
switches, lights seamlessly built into the ceiling creating a haloed glow,
rows of two at every point throughout the place, casting the clean
white walls in soft light.

He made the rounds of his house on autopilot—flicking on lights,
checking the locks, peering out at the dark backyard, the foreboding
presence of the enormous mulberry tree—and knew he couldn't put
it off forever.

His phone was against his ear and ringing before he could talk
himself out of it.

"Hello?" his dad's voice asked from across Bass Strait, gruff yet
warm down the home line.

"Dad, hi," Thad said and paced around the living room. "Sorry, I
haven't had a chance to call until—"

"Thaddeus," his dad breathed out, the phone moving away, "Maria, it's Thaddeus," he called out. His voice came back on the line with a shuffle of the phone. "You alright, son? Everything alright with your friend? You had us right worried when we didn't hear from you."

And that was excessive for them; their family lived in a serene trance, secure in the knowledge their faith would take care of everything, even when things were rocky. But Thad guessed he'd never done anything like this before; left abruptly and been radio silent for three days.

"Sorry, yes, everything's fine, we, he," he flailed around for reassuring words, "he needed a fair bit of help," he finished awkwardly and blushed, his mind flashing with images of the help he'd provided Lacy.

"He's lucky to have you," his dad said warmly and Thad felt even worse. "Here, your mum wants to say hi."

The phone rustled with the change of hands and his mum came on the line. "Thaddeus?"

"Hi, Mum," he said and started pacing again. "Sorry again for all this. How was the lunch?"

"You were missed," she said but Thad could hear her smiling. "And there's no need to apologise, if your friend needed you, you did the right thing."

Thad winced. He wasn't sure if Lacy needed him or it was the other way around. And if so, what Thad needed was an abomination. He had no idea how he was going to sit at their table again; he'd be a mumbling, fumbling, red-faced mess. He'd be petrified they could see right through him, see everything he'd done. Once was a mistake, but twice?

He managed to get off the phone quickly after that—reassuring them that his friend really was fine, that he looked forward to seeing them when they played in Tassie, and that of course he'd call every week like he always did.

The phone felt heavy in his hand as he stood in the quiet of his house.

His room was the same when he went in and flicked on the lamp. He plugged his phone into the charger and went over to the shrine he kept on the other side of the bed. His battered copy of the bible, a framed image of Jesus in white robes, palms spread wide just as he'd left him, as if he weren't a whole other person who'd done a terrible thing. Another terrible thing, he corrected himself.

He kneeled down, made the sign of the cross, clasped his hands, closed his eyes and began to repent. He prayed for forgiveness, begged for the courage not to do it again, made promises to reform.

"They're looking at a ruckman from Perth," Nick, his agent, said over the phone.

Thad blinked a few times. With everything going on with Lacy, he'd forgotten his precarious position on the team.

"I don't reckon they'll drop you, necessarily, but I thought you should know they're looking," Nick went on.

Thad blew out a breath. "And if they drop me? I'm still in contract."

He could practically see Nick nodding along—Nick was an Italian Australian, around mid-thirties, and he handled at least forty league players all over Melbourne, Sydney, and Brisbane.

"They'll drop you to the state team. It's not a big contract, they'll keep paying it, but more important—they could afford to break it, which'll put you up for free agency in October. From there, well, could be delisted, you know how these things go," Nick said.

Thad would be lucky to get picked up. And if he got picked up by anyone outside of Victoria, he wasn't sure he'd want to go. Even though he probably should go. It would certainly remove the temptation.

"Look, none of this is really gonna matter this season, they can't do anything except possibly drop you back and forth. But I know they've got scouts out and that's what they're looking for. So..."

So, Thad needed to have a brilliant season.

"Alright, thanks for letting me know," he said.

"Course, it's my job," Nick replied and Thad could hear the grin. "Don't worry about your contract, I got you and it's rock solid, but if you got something else in the tank, well..."

Well, now was the time to use it.

"I'll do my best," he said.

They exchanged goodbyes and Thad spun his phone in his hands. He'd woken up to a message from Lacy asking if he wanted to hang out, which had given Thad butterflies, which led him to recall his resolution from the night before: it was not happening again. They couldn't be intimate. A mistake he'd owned and repented over was one thing, but to continue doing it? Lacy had, miraculously, forgiven the first indiscretion. Now Thad needed to hold the line with his faith and return to his celibacy.

But of course he'd messaged in the affirmative, suggested mini-golf, lunch at The Union, public activities where he couldn't give in to temptation. But now he needed to go and train.

He typed a new message, tossed his phone on the coffee table and went and got into his training gear.

When he got home that night, he realised it might all be for nought. Kurt, their fitness expert, had agreed to work with him and they'd done a good session, but Thad had limits. Kurt had said he'd talk to Todd about working on plays with him, but Thad knew it wasn't going to matter.

He went into his room and kneeled at his shrine, made the sign of the cross and asked for a sign. Was it worth it? Was he kidding himself? Should he let it play out, get delisted, head back to Tassie and work with his dad?

But. Lacy. It was Lacy. Lacy was the reason this news hit him so hard. He couldn't bear the thought of leaving him. He could rationalise a million reasons why this would be a good thing, but his heart wouldn't hear even one.

There was a knock on the front door.

Thad got up, stomach doing somersaults because he knew it could only be one person.

He opened the door to Lacy, a nervous smile on his face, mouth in motion immediately.

"I know you said you're busy, but I just wanted to come round and reassure you I'm not gonna be like, doin' anythin' or..."

Lacy trailed off. Thad was smiling down at him, his first real smile in twenty-four hours.

"What're you smiling about?" Lacy asked.

"Nothing, just good to see you, come in," Thad stepped back.

"So you really were busy?" Lacy asked as he came in. "It wasn't because..."

Thad shook his head. Lacy's hair was shiny, like he'd just washed it, and he smelled like himself, the faint traces of his soap and shampoo, the musk of his skin. He looked good too, even though he was wearing a matching tracksuit and jumper combo, white and purple with some logo obscenely bright against Thad's drab hallway.

"No, I decided to do some training," he replied, and ushered Lacy down the hall.

Lacy took a seat at the kitchen bench. "Training? Already? Why?"

"Do you want something to drink?" Thad asked, and got the water jug out.

He couldn't meet Lacy's eyes as he got them a glass of water each, slid Lacy's over and stepped back. He leaned against the bench, crossed his ankles and held the water in front of his chest.

Lacy tapped the side of his glass. "I'd-a been up for training," he said, eyes on his hand.

Thad's heart clenched. How was he supposed to stop wanting this?

"Well, I'm going in again tomorrow," he replied.

"Yeah? Alright," Lacy smiled, but his look was unsure. "What brought all this on?"

"They're looking at a ruckman from Perth."

Lacy's mouth stayed open.

"They won't trade me this season, they can't," Thad said, setting his glass down and tapping his fingers on the bench. "But they could drop me, eventually delist, and you know," he shrugged.

"No," Lacy said.

"No?"

"No fucking way," Lacy said, head shaking. "I'll train with you."

Thad shook his head, smiled briefly. "No matter how hard I train, I'm never going to be you or Cary or Finn or Scotty, I'm just," he shrugged, "I'm just me."

Lacy pointed at him. "Trust me, I can get you there. Fucking trade you," he muttered and drank his water. "What'd you do today?"

"Ah, laps, weights, sprints."

Lacy was already shaking his head. "No, we're not doing that. You got a pen, paper?"

"Um, yes," Thad went and got a notebook and a pen.

Lacy thanked him and started writing furiously. Once he was finished, he slid it over, tapped the top. "This is what we're gonna do."

Thad looked at it. It was the days of the week, criss-crossed into blocks, each square containing scribbled activities. Skills. Interval. Beach. Video. Scotty.

"Scotty?" Thad looked up.

"Yeah, I'll tell him to fly his lard-ass down here and he can work with us."

"We really don't have to—"

"Yeah, we do," Lacy replied. "It's not your body, plenty o' guys are built, big, cumbersome."

"Cumbersome?" Thad smiled and cocked his hip against the bench.

"Well, not always," Lacy flashed him a grin and it went straight to Thad's groin, which was very bad. He took a sip of his water, focused on the notebook.

"But they come in real handy when they use that size in the forward, see," he was pulling out his phone and searching for something.

The tinny sound of a game came on and Thad leaned down to watch it. It was their team, but an old game, maybe five or so years ago.

"Watch Scotty," Lacy said and then proceeded to break down the play as they watched—Scotty getting a beautiful tap out of the centre, George catching it and kicking to Jack on the breakaway. Jack hesitated like he was about to take a kick to the forward line when Scotty belted past him—Jack made the quick decision to handball it off and Scotty shrugged off defenders, running down the middle, he snapped it to Lacy waiting in the pocket. Lacy turned, kicked the goal.

"You guys were so good," Thad said.

"Never mind about that," Lacy said and paused it. "See how Scotty used his size to his advantage, he never lingers in the centre or falls back to half back, unless we were put on the defence. He comes forward 'cos he knows he's a big body, hard to take down. Here, look."

He pulled up another video, and another one. Thad thought it was little wonder they were a consistently top-four team in those years, that they won a Grand Final and the core group won a bunch of awards amongst them; though it was still a travesty Lacy hadn't been recognised beyond the club's best player and the best according to the players' association. He deserved the Brownlow, he deserved the trifecta.

Still, Thad didn't see himself developing Scotty's power, his confidence to tear down the middle and shake off opposition players like they were children. And with Alanson's style of play, he'd have to learn to do it on the wings where there was every chance he'd knock it out or create a huddled mass of bodies, a continuous stoppage of play, which went against the free-flowing attack they were going for. He said as much.

"I reckon you can," Lacy grabbed him by the bicep and shook him, "you got the body for it, just need to work the plays 'til it becomes muscle memory, then convince your head you can do it. We'll start in the middle, get your confidence up, then work the wings."

"Okay," Thad agreed, attention on that hand. He couldn't meet Lacy's eyes because if he did, he'd lean down and kiss him.

"Right, well," Lacy let him go and got up. "We better get a good night's sleep since we're gonna be boot-camping this shit up."

"But," Thad straightened, moving to follow Lacy as he went to the sink, "your offseason, we still got two weeks. I don't wanna mess up your break."

Lacy snorted. He turned and looked at Thad, but not directly, his gaze darted around as he moved to get past him to leave the kitchen.

"I was just gonna hang with you anyway," he replied.

Thad reached for him as he went by, his hand brushing Lacy's chest. Lacy stuttered a step and finally met his eyes.

"Thank you," Thad said, though his words were an afterthought as his hand paused on Lacy's stomach, slid more firmly against the silky material.

Thad didn't think he'd ever seen this look on Lacy's face and it took him a moment to parse the lack of a smile, the hesitation in his eyes—he was nervous.

"Thad, man," Lacy started but Thad was leaning down to kiss him.

It was just a brush of lips, Lacy's shallow breaths ghosting over Thad's. Thad pressed in again, his lips caressing Lacy's before he broke away but stayed close. He did it again. The clock ticked on the wall but the room was otherwise quiet except for the sound of their mouths meeting.

Thad knew it was wrong, but he couldn't help it. He slid his hand around Lacy's waist, pulled him against his chest and deepened the kiss. Lacy went with it, his arms coming around Thad's back as they moved together.

Lacy broke the kiss but stayed close. "Shit," he whispered against Thad's lips.

"What is it?" Thad whispered back.

"I've never done this sober," Lacy said.

Thad pulled back but kept Lacy in his arms. "You were sober the night after, when we..."

Lacy shook his head. "No, I was still half-cut, ya know? Not stone-cold sober."

"Oh," Thad ran a hand up his back. "I don't have any alcohol."

Lacy snickered and dropped his head on Thad's chest. His voice was muffled. "I don't wanna drink, I'm just sayin', I might suck at this. I feel..."

Thad scratched a hand through his hair. "You feel?"

"Nervous," Lacy mumbled.

Thad had to laugh. "I always feel nervous." He blushed. As wrong as this was, he felt a foreign pride rising in himself—he actually wanted to be a good lover for Lacy, but admitting to being nervous when Lacy was so experienced was not a turn on. And besides, how could Lacy be nervous around him? "And it's just me, no need to be nervous around *me*."

Lacy looked up, his chin digging into Thad's sternum. "Who else would I get nervous around?"

Thad's stomach swooped.

Lacy stretched up to kiss him. The kiss was rougher this time, going somewhere. Thad felt a flicker of guilt over his resolve crumbling like it'd barely been a resolve at all. But he'd pray on it after, it'd be fine.

He managed to shuffle them down the hallway, stopping to push Lacy against the wall and deepen the kiss. Lacy ground his dick against Thad's thigh, hips hitching like he couldn't stop himself. Thad felt a thrill at Lacy's hard length rubbing off on him. He pulled him in, moved them down the hall towards his bedroom. He stumbled as he kept trying to shift him up and down his thigh as they moved. Once his bed was behind them, he pulled Lacy down on top of him.

His hands were clumsy as he tried to push Lacy's pants down. Lacy pushed up and shoved at Thad's waistband, his panting breaths ghosting over Thad's chin. Thad kissed his throat, shoved urgently at the material until it was bunched under Lacy's ass. He lifted his hips and Lacy shoved his pants down, his erection springing up and slapping against his stomach.

He rolled Lacy under him, shoved his jumper and shirt up so he could splay his hands over his rib cage, take in the dip of his stomach.

It was one of the most erotic things he'd ever seen, Lacy's body, and no amount of prayer could stop him from feeling that way when he looked at him. Lacy's wiry build, taut and hard with not a scrap of fat, made Thad lose his breath.

Lacy clasped their erections together in his hand, his eyes flicking up to meet Thad's, hesitant, a question. Thad groaned in answer, rolled his hips into Lacy's fist. It was dry and it felt rushed. And it should've been disgusting—his penis was rubbing off against another penis in another man's hand—but it wasn't. Disgust was the farthest thing he was feeling. He couldn't stop running his hands over Lacy's chest, his dark nipples. He dipped down to kiss him as his hips pumped faster.

Thad felt the orgasm coming on and quickened his hips. Lacy read the play and tightened his grip. Thad came and Lacy caught the liquid in his hand. Thad watched, panting, as Lacy smeared Thad's come all over his erection and stroked himself quickly. Thad kissed the corner of his mouth, his cheek, felt Lacy's harsh breaths against the side of his face.

Lacy stretched back with a gasp as the white liquid shot up his chest, hitting Thad's chest and nipple. His eyes were closed as he sucked in pulls of air, made these little sounds that hit Thad in the solar plexus. His throat was a taut line, the ink rolling and moving with his breathing. Thad kissed his Adam's apple, traced the skin of his throat with his lips.

He groaned and rolled onto his side, his hands automatically dragging Lacy with him, wrapping him up. Lacy curled around him.

"We're disgusting," Lacy mumbled.

Shame rushed in and Thad went to pull back.

"No," Lacy said and yanked him closer. "We can sit in it for a bit."

Thad huffed a surprised laugh; Lacy meant the physical mess, not the abomination mess. Thad pressed a firm kiss to the top of his head, breathed in the scent of his shampoo.

After a while, Lacy made noises about getting up and going home.

"Or you could stay?"

Lacy's sleepy eyes met his. Thad kissed his forehead gently.

Lacy burrowed back against his chest and Thad held him.

He'd repent tomorrow.

18

♥

"**L**OOK AT THIS FUCKING shit-cunt," Lacy said. Scotty was strolling across the oval, the only other figure on the ground besides Lacy and Thad at the centre.

They'd been training at the Paddock, the ground open to the public, for a week. Word had obviously gotten out on the first day, a crowd steadily building since late that afternoon. A ripple went through the people pressed up against the fence when they realised who was walking towards them.

Scotty was grinning, his mad hair longer and even more unkempt than it used to be. He was wearing big sunnies, a pair of black tracksuit pants and a white shirt.

"You should not be wearing white with your figure," Lacy said as Scotty arrived in front of him and grabbed him in a headlock, rubbed his head with his fist.

"Ah, you missed me, eh?" Scotty said as Lacy tried to break free, laughing and flailing.

"Let me go before I get stuck in your folds," Lacy huffed into his generous gut.

Scotty laughed, kept him there and extended his hand out to Thad. "Nice to meet you, Thaddeus Clay."

"Scotty," Thad said. Lacy heard the respectful awe in his tone, but it was distracted. He was probably worried his best friend was about to be suffocated.

Lacy couldn't stop laughing as Scotty released him and pulled him in for a big Scotty-hug. He wasn't really fat; he was a huge man, and since he'd stopped training, his once muscled body had turned to soft padding.

Scotty released him, beamed down at him. "You're lookin' good. Maybe finally stop bein' a bridesmaid this year."

Lacy gave his bicep a friendly punch. "Yeah, I don't give a shit, you know that." Everyone cared more than he did about winning the Brownlow, but he'd suffered through being the 'favourite' every year only to come second or third and had to listen to it. He cared on some level—it was the Brownlow, crowning achievement of the best and fairest player in the league—but he didn't care in the way people thought he should.

"Course you don't," Scotty smiled. "Right, well, you got me down here, what's the training emergency?"

"Emergency?" Thad asked.

"Yeah, it's an emergency," Lacy stepped close to Thad and slung an arm up around his shoulders. "My man, Thad here, needs some pointers."

Scotty pushed his sunnies up and rubbed his jaw, lips quirked. "Yeah, I been watching. You got the body, but you ain't got the power. Alright," he nodded like it was all decided, "let me get warmed up, then we're gonna practice knocking Lacy over."

Thad's eyebrows went up comically. "I don't want to risk injury."

Scotty cracked up. "Believe me, little princess here can take it."

"Alright, fatty, do your laps. You reckon you'll make one? We ain't got an ambulance on stand-by," Lacy looked around, made sure to ham up the concerned look.

"Can you believe the appreciation I get?" Scotty said to Thad as he jogged backwards.

Thad smiled, he didn't appear to know what to say. Scotty didn't seem to notice or care, just turned and started running the perimeter, stopping every few metres to sign stuff for little kids.

"Some warm-up," Lacy chuckled. He sat down and started a stretch routine—he knew what Scotty was planning and he needed to be loose when he hit the ground.

Thad was still quiet beside him as he stretched his hamstrings, his thigh muscles bunching and releasing as Lacy looked up at him. He thought about touching him, how he'd managed to get his hands on every inch of Thad's skin so far this week. They'd been fucking every night and it was incredible. He'd decided to let Thad take the lead because he knew if he was in charge, he'd be climbing into Thad's lap every time Thad sat down.

He hadn't expected much, but every night they'd go about their usual business, except Thad would glance at his mouth, or his hand would brush Lacy's hip, and then it was on.

As Thad stretched his arm over his chest, stretched his groin at the same time, one knee bent as the other leg stretched long, Lacy followed the movement, dragged his eyes up the flat planes of Thad's stomach, his chest, his nipples brushing the fabric of his singlet, the thickness of his neck, nothing brutish about it, just the solid build of a gorgeous, big man. He arrived at Thad's eyes and found him watching him back.

Lacy felt a wave of desire go through him and it rocked him, sitting there on the grass, the sound of people talking in the distance, the hum of traffic and trams behind them, the kick-up of the breeze rustling the trees before it settled again, the sunshine in a clear sky making the green of the oval and the blue of the sky sharper around them.

"It was really nice of Scotty to come down," Thad said like he didn't think he was worthy of it.

Lacy snorted. "Yeah, a nice break from drinking beer and fishing."

"I thought he worked a farm up there?"

Lacy went to get to his feet and Thad's hand appeared. He took it and Thad tugged him up. Before Thad could let go, Lacy squeezed his hand, ran his fingers over his knuckles. It was a quick touch, but Thad's voice was gravelly when he spoke.

"A station?" he asked.

Lacy let his hand go and laughed, breathless. "Scotty? Wrangling cows?"

Scotty appeared in front of them, panting. "Not cows," he winked. "Alright, Thaddeus, you get down in the forward pocket. I'm gonna charge for the goals, we'll just pretend I already won the tap, kicked it off, kept on running forward and received another pass. Lacy's gonna try to intercept me. Try being the operative word," he rubbed Lacy on the head.

Lacy took it and rolled his eyes.

"And if you get it to me, I'll kick the goal," Thad nodded, squinted against the sunshine and rubbed the back of his neck.

"Thad can kick a beauty. How many times did we practice last year?"

Thad huffed a laugh and seemed to loosen up. "Too many to count."

"Right," Lacy gripped his bicep, gave it a good shake.

Thad dropped his eyes to the ground, his lips curling up and it killed Lacy, it really did; this big, gorgeous man, and he was shy? How dare he. Lacy laughed at the thought and let go. He felt Scotty looking at the side of his head as Thad jogged away.

"Well, well," Scotty said, grinning, "emergency training session, eh?"

Lacy huffed a soft laugh, his eyes on Thad running, the sheen of sweat already covering his body from the heat in the day and the warm-up. His tan shoulders against his white singlet looked fucking incredible, glistening in the sunshine like a Roman gladiator.

Scotty tossed the football in the air and caught it a few times. "So, are we gonna actually do this or just perve on your boyfriend?"

Oh man, imagine if Thad was his boyfriend? Like they'd actually talked about it and it was all squared away. He grinned, bright, as Thad turned around and bounced on his feet fifty metres away.

"What's taking you so long?" Lacy asked Scotty, and looked up at him.

Scotty shook his head, gave him a sly grin. "Okay," he threw the ball up, caught it, "that's me, catching the kick off a feed outta the centre bounce..." and then he was running, bouncing the ball as he raced down the centre of the oval, the ground thundering with his heavy tread.

Lacy took off after him like a shot. Not that he needed to, Scotty was hardly known for his speed. He launched himself at Scotty's back to take him down, and with a barely perceptible movement of his shoulder, Scotty swatted him off. It had the power Lacy knew it would and he stumbled back, landed on his ass. Scotty's feet thudded in the grass as he took the clear run and kicked straight to Thad's chest.

Thad marked it with a happy 'Oof' in the distance, turned and executed a perfect kick straight through middle. Lacy snickered as Scotty mobbed him and the pair of them danced around, the crowd watching, cheering and laughing.

Lacy had spent more time on his ass by the time Scotty got through his demonstration than he had in a long while, but it was Thad's turn and he was amped.

Scotty was down in the pocket, chatting to some guys on the edge of the fence.

"You okay to keep going?" Thad asked.

"Yeah, man, course," Lacy wiped at the grass stains on his ass. "You were watchin' how Scotty did it, yeah? It's not a hit, nothin' that'll draw the umpire's eye, it's comin' from your core," he pressed his hand to the centre of Thad's stomach, felt the rise and fall with Thad's breaths.

"I'll do my best," Thad replied, sinking into the touch.

Lacy removed his hand. "Maybe sometime this week?"

Thad shook his head, lips curling up, but he turned and ran, bouncing the ball as he headed for the goal.

Lacy took off after him and jumped on his back. He felt Thad try to shake him off at first, but then he fumbled the ball, let it dribble away so he could reach around for Lacy, pull him under his arm and brace Lacy's fall as they both crashed to the ground.

He could hear Scotty laughing in the distance as Thad rolled onto his back and brought Lacy with him. "You okay?"

"Okay," Lacy replied, doing his best not get distracted by the way they were tangled together, his hand planted in the grass near Thad's head, "that was terrible. You don't help the defender."

Thad squinted up at him. He was smiling, his nose and cheeks pink, but his eyes were dancing. "But if the defender's you..."

"Well," Lacy pushed himself up, a little breathless, "it's never gonna be me, so just pretend I'm like, Carter or someone."

Thad scrunched his face up. Even we're-all-God's-creatures-Thaddeus knew Carter was a private school, world-class dick.

They got up and re-set, ran the play again.

As the afternoon wore on, Lacy had to concede Thad was never going to go at him like Scotty did, but he felt the shift in his movements, the way he was getting it into his muscle memory.

"Buy me a beer?" Scotty asked as they packed up for the day.

"Of course, thank you—"

"I reckon you should buy us beer and dinner," Lacy cut in. "We probably helped you lose a few kilos today."

Scotty grabbed him in another headlock and Lacy cackled.

Dinner with Scotty was great. Thad sneakily paid the whole bill, so Lacy informed Scotty they'd be going to a more expensive place the following week, on Scotty, which got him a roaring laugh and "Sure, buddy," like Scotty wouldn't be opening his wallet for anyone.

"He's such a cheapskate," Lacy said as Thad followed him into his house. "You know he's got a real popular podcast about football and sheep or some shit? Got cash. Hey," he looked up at Thad as they toed their shoes off, "let me know what it cost and I'll go halves."

Thad smiled fondly down at him. "I'm happy to pay, you guys are using your time off to help me."

"Yeah, but, me and Scotty drink a lot and that's like, three quarters of the bill, hardly seems fair compared to your two orange juices," he went through to the kitchen, unlocked the sliding doors and stepped outside. "You comin'?"

He could hear Thad behind him, his tread was soft given his size, but Lacy reckoned he'd be able to feel his presence anywhere. He flicked the lights on, turned on the jacuzzi and got the cover off.

Lacy got naked and slid into the water. He groaned. He could take a pounding, no problem, but that didn't mean he didn't feel it afterwards. Thad was standing in front of him, playing with the collar of his shirt.

"I promise I'll stay on my side," Lacy said in an effort to tease. Thad's nerves fed his own, and he'd felt nervous every night since they'd started fucking.

But Thad just huffed. "I don't know if I can make that promise." He was blushing as he pulled his shirt over his head.

Lacy swallowed and watched the show. Thad's dick was thickening already and Lacy thought about the four times he'd sucked it so far—between Thad's legs while Thad was on his couch; in Lacy's bed; at the kitchen table at Thad's place; and in the entrance to Lacy's place. Thad patted his head so gently every time, his hands running through Lacy's hair, and Lacy could feel how hard he was trying not to fuck Lacy's mouth while he trembled and babbled compliments. It was romantic as shit and Lacy wanted to do it again right now.

The water spilled up to the edge as Thad got in and sat across from him. He slid his foot over to rub against Lacy's.

"Feels good, eh?" Lacy asked.

"It really does," Thad smiled, but then he drew his foot back. "Can I ask you something?"

"Anything, you know that," Lacy said. He felt the energy shift from impending sexy times to seriousness and braced himself.

"Does Scotty know, we're," Thad stopped, but Lacy got it, since he hadn't missed Scotty loudly telling them they made a beautiful couple at dinner. Scotty was joking, but who knew what that old maniac really knew and didn't know? One thing was for sure, if he did, it wouldn't matter; Scotty was rock solid.

But Lacy got the feeling that wasn't exactly what Thad was asking. So he answered the real question.

"I haven't told anyone about it," he said.

"Okay," Thad breathed out, relieved.

Lacy concealed his reaction to that. He didn't want to be George and Finn, out and married, but he wasn't ashamed of what he was doing with Thad.

"I'd never tell anyone anything unless I asked you first," he said instead of saying that.

Thad gave him another relieved smile, which should've annoyed him, but it was so sincere it did Lacy in, it really did.

"I know you wouldn't. I thought maybe... I don't know what I thought," Thad said and looked at the water.

Lacy wanted to say more on the subject, but Thad's foot slid against his and that progressed to kissing, to finding himself in Thad's lap, making out hungrily until the need to come became too much. He dragged Thad up to his room and sucked him off from the luxury of his bed. Thad hit him back and the sight of him down there, watching Lacy's reactions with more concentration than he was bringing to the football drills, was one of the most erotic things Lacy had ever seen.

Lacy took great pleasure in the twitch in Alanson's eye when they got back to regular training later that month and Thad was fucking rock solid. He won every tap and then made himself available in the forward line, shaking off Les and Lesley like they were nothing. Sure, he wasn't Scotty, but no one could say he wasn't solid.

And he made some good defensive smothers when the ball went to the opposition end, like they'd practiced with Scotty the second time. It's not like Alanson could've missed they'd been training with Scotty—they were all over the papers and social media because of the crowds they'd drawn practicing at the Paddock like that—but Lacy wasn't above acknowledging, if only to himself, that'd been his point.

Let the old prick see and shut his fucking mouth. Thad had the work ethic to get them there and he'd proved it today, first day back and a statement had been made. Fuck you very much, Alanson.

"Okay, but please don't say that," Thad said to him as he sucked in pulls of air back in the locker room while Lacy muttered all of the above.

Lacy made the sign of the cross. "You have my word."

Thad gave him the side-eye, then snickered around his breathing, his brown eyes dancing. His hair was falling in his face and Lacy wanted to reach up, drag his fingers through the sweat on his forehead and push his hair back.

The door clanged open and Alanson walked in, flanked by Todd and Kurt.

He didn't say anything for a while, just looked around the room with a blank expression.

"Cary?" he asked finally and Cary looked up from where he was sitting on the bench on Lacy's other side. "You wanna have a word?"

Cary was still their captain, even though he said to Lacy all the time that Lacy was basically the captain, which was probably true. Lacy talked to everyone, ran all the plays on the field, maintained morale. Cary glanced at him now before he stood.

"I like what I'm seeing. Speed, stamina, I reckon we could be real contenders this year if we keep up this intensity..."

Lacy listened and nodded along, but he always felt—and no shade on Cary, he loved the dude like a brother—these speeches lacked the specifics, they felt like vague pump ups. Once Alanson left, Lacy would mention to each player what they were doing well, what they could work on.

"Hmm," Alanson said once Cary sat back down. "Right, we've got a new rule this season. Drinking ban," he jerked his chin and Kurt came forward and started handing out pieces of paper. "No drinking if we've got a six-day break. No drinking if you're out injured. And of course, no drinking if we've got a game. Now," he took a deep breath, "I know these rules have been around for years, but we've never enforced them. We are now. If you're found in breach, you'll be suspended."

Lacy didn't react outwardly to this news. He hated this fucking puritan culture. If a man could still play, who gave a flying fuck what he did on his off time? He loved footy, but over the years, he'd gotten sick of how much the clubs felt they owned them as players, owned their bodies outside of work. The rules had been league-wide for years, but never enforced here. Not drinking? Fuck that noise, he'd be worse if he didn't drink. He'd be fine though, he used a top-notch masking agent.

"And if you're thinking of trying to cheat the piss test, fair warning, we've got new technology that'll find anything," he looked at Lacy. "Anything."

And then he left. Guys let their shoulders come down, the evidence they were hunched appearing only once they let them drop. A few shot Lacy quick glances, acted as if they hadn't, before turning back to getting their stuff for the shower, undressing. Lacy breathed in steadily. The mixture of wet grass, stale sweat and Deep Heat filled his lungs with a familiarity he knew better than his own home.

Alanson wasn't a bad coach per se, Lacy could concede his new approach had started to come to fruition in the second half of the last season, allowing them to squeak into the preliminary final. Although it had collapsed on the big stage, it would only get better this season if the element of surprise continued in their favour. But he was also an asshole who'd get it in for players and ride them for a season. He'd done it to Thad. Now he was doing it to Lacy.

"Right," Kurt said to the room, gesturing at the piece of paper they all had. He sounded embarrassed. "You all know the league rules. Cocaine, two-year suspension if you're using for performance enhancing, otherwise illicit substances will be a two-week club ban if you're using for ah, other reasons I guess."

Lacy snickered, he couldn't help it. He could imagine Kurt doing a line of cocaine and taking ecstasy the same way he imagined a cat using a toilet—you could kind of picture it, they're smart enough to do it, but it'd be something to see.

Kurt shot him a weak smile and carried on.

"What're you going to do?" Thad asked once they were getting into his car.

"I'm gonna find out about these new tests," Lacy said and strapped his seatbelt on. "Feel like taking a drive?"

"Sure," Thad said. "Where to?"

"Frankston," Lacy replied.

Thad raised his eyebrows, but he followed Lacy's directions, one hand tapping on the steering wheel, the other one reaching over to pat Lacy's thigh.

Colton Baisley had been in Lacy's year at school. They'd been stoner buddies in high school and remained good friends even though Colton never came into the city. Lacy wasn't even sure if he left his house anymore. He'd started a little business in the heart of Frankston with his mum's portion of his grandad's inheritance, shortly after they'd left school. He sold bongs, pipes, all the smoking paraphernalia, posters, shirts, the usual stoner shit. He also sold great pot under the counter, masking agents, and was the general go-to guy for what was happening with testing, the law, that kind of thing. He'd gone out of business when that part of Frankston got gentrified and they hiked the rent up on him. Lacy wasn't sure if he'd gone out of business exactly, or simply didn't want to pay the rent on principle. Colton had chuckled when Lacy had said that, but hadn't elaborated, which was pretty much his style. Now he was selling everything from home and online.

His mum, Jenny, let Lacy and Thad in with a hug and big smile, told him Colton was out the back—he lived in the granny flat once occupied by his grandad.

Colton blinked up at them when Lacy knocked on the sliding door and opened it. He looked like he was just waking up, but he always looked like that. He was sitting on the edge of a futon, knobbly knees pointing out like a V, his hands rolling a joint between his long fingers like the paper was a part of him.

"Colton, my man," Lacy said as he stepped into the dark space.

"Lacy?" Colton asked but didn't get up. Lacy couldn't make out his face in the dark, but he sounded like he was smiling; he always sounded like he was low-key smiling.

"Yeah, dude, how's it going?" he replied and tapped Thad on the back. "This is Thad. Thad, Colton."

"Thad," Colton said and a lighter flickered, casting his face in the glow. He inhaled deeply, spoke around the exhale. "You boys want somethin' to drink? Think Mum stocked it last night."

"Yeah, I'll have a beer, you want?" Lacy asked, and got himself a beer, one for Colton, and found a water for Thad.

They sat on the sunken couch across from the futon. Terry, Colton's cat, cracked an eye open to look at them from where he was taking up the other end of the couch. He was black and the couch was black, but he cast off a blackhole vibe so no one ever sat on him.

"The club's talkin' about using new piss tests. Ya know anythin' about that?" Lacy asked, because there was no point in small talk with Colton—he'd look at you like he was confused, smiling yet baffled.

Colton smoked, rubbed his chin. He was shirtless, his long black hair spilling over his shoulders onto his tan skin; objectively, he was a striking guy, but he'd always given a non-sexual vibe. He'd never had a girl, or a guy, as far as Lacy knew. Lacy had always thought of him as both beautiful and untouchable.

"I been hearin' chatter, yeah," he stubbed out the joint and rose like a cat. "I got a maskin' agent for it if you want."

"Is the Pope Catholic?" Lacy asked. Colton made a sound that could pass as a laugh, while Thad actually laughed. Lacy bumped his shoulder.

Colton rummaged around in a box, one of many lining the walls of the place. "I dunno if it's a hundred percent guarantee, but. Probably, but like, they take a step, we take a step. Not much chatter online. Think everyone's waitin'."

He handed Lacy a bottle. Lacy studied the orange plastic with white writing while Colton stayed in front of them. He stretched, scratched his chest. His bare torso was thin, a tuft of black hair visible above the shorts just managing to stay on his hips.

"Been gettin' a lotta orders from guys doin' FIFO up in Queensland, I'll ask if it worked," he relaxed and moved away.

"But," Thad started and Lacy looked at him. If he was affected at all by Colton's ethereal, masculine beauty, Lacy couldn't see it on his face. Thad was leaning close, trying to read the bottle; he barely seemed aware of Colton rolling another joint next to his coffee table.

"How do you know when to use it?" Thad asked.

"I got my girl in the office, she always gives me a heads-up," Lacy realised he'd never told Thad that. In fact, the more he thought about it, the more he realised he'd never talked to Thad about his drug use at all. And Thad, for his part, had never asked, never seemed to want to get up in his business about it.

Thad tilted his head, a question.

"Good old Sandra," Lacy said.

Colton snorted, a soft huff of breath.

"We went to school together," Lacy went on, "got her a job in the office when I got out of my entry level contract and took the ten-year deal. She does admin or something. Anyway, I got her the job, she gives me a heads up. Part of her job is putting in the order."

"That's handy," Thad said.

The crackle of another joint being lit and Colton's inhale as he spoke drifted over them, "That's Frankston," he said, voice tight around the smoke. "A deal's a deal."

Lacy nodded. "I scratch your back, you scratch mine. Capisce?"

"Bit like the church," Thad mused.

Lacy smiled and bumped him again. Colton gave Thad a quizzical smile.

"I mean," Thad rubbed the back of his neck, "we help each other out, if someone new joins the congregation or refugees come in, we make sure they have everything they need."

"And then they make sure you have everything you need?" Colton asked.

"Well, not really, no, we've got everything we need. But if we were ever in need, then yes, they'd probably help."

"You'd expect it?" Colton sat down again. He lifted his beer, sliding the joint to the side of the bottle.

"No, never. Giving is its own reward."

"Then it's not like Frankston," Colton said and took a sip, his sleepy black eyes on Thad.

"A deal's a deal," Lacy added. "But we're all friendly about it, does that count?"

Colton made a soft scoffing sound.

"I think so," Thad smiled. Lacy rubbed their shoulders together, a friendly jostle that lingered for a second as he watched the warmth of Thad's eyes watching him back.

"Right, give me a box. What do I owe you?" Lacy asked Colton.

Colton got him sorted and they left shortly after.

Back in the car, Lacy told Thad they needed to go see his mum.

"Jenny's gonna tell her I was round and if I don't drop in she's gonna know Jenny saw me and she didn't," Lacy explained. Jenny would give his mum a smug smile, like she'd seen Lacy but his mum hadn't, and with that smile a whole lot of power dynamics would be at play. He'd never do that to his mum.

"Ridge Dylan Lacy," his mum said as she hugged him, leaned back, assessed him. "This is a surprise."

Lacy winced at the use of his full-name—he'd never forgive her for her love of *The Bold and the Beautiful*, and now Thad heard the damn middle name as well. Screw *Beverly Hills 90210*.

She looked at Thad behind him without moving her head, it was a shift of the eyes, a sharpening of the gaze.

"And you must be Thaddeus Clay," she said, her tone changing to nice if you didn't know what to listen for—it was fake, the niceness, not necessarily in a mean way, but it was a guard she brought up.

"Mrs Lacy, so nice to meet you," Thad said, his own tone disarmingly genuine.

She ushered them inside. "It's Mrs Parker, but Cherry will do since Mr Parker was an asshole and I ain't too fond of Miss Lacy, makes me sound like some housekeeper," she smiled, rote. "If I'd known you were coming, I'd have gotten dressed and ordered something for tea." She led them down the hall to the dining area. It was a nice place and she looked pretty well-dressed in it—tight jeans and a tight, floral singlet. But he knew she meant she'd get dressed—the whole nine yards—and order platters from the deli counter.

"I wanted to surprise you," Lacy said and followed her outside to the patio, took a seat.

She gave him a look.

"I had to see Colton," he said.

"Ah, I see," she nodded. "Good boy. I'll get you something to drink. As for food, I'm afraid I've only got frozen, but I think there's a McCain's pizza in there. Hawaiian."

"My favourite," Lacy grinned at her.

"I know," she went back inside.

"Your mum knows what Colton does?" Thad whispered.

"Yeah, but that's not what she meant," Lacy turned to him, keeping his own voice low. "She knows I woulda seen Jenny, so I had to come here to prevent World War Three."

Thad frowned. Lacy didn't have time to explain the intricate social rituals of mothers in Frankston, so he just said he'd explain later, and Thad nodded and leaned back.

It was a nice evening, his mum was polite with Thad, although Lacy could see she was studying him under the friendly smiles and easy, "Are you sure you don't want some more?"

As they were leaving, Lacy came into the living room after taking a quick piss and found Thad looking at all the family photos on top of the buffet cabinet. Lacy's school pictures, footy pictures, and the ones of Lacy with his brother, lots of his brother on his own. Lacy didn't like coming into this room so he herded Thad out of there and hoped he wouldn't ask.

They were catching their breath in Thad's bed later that night—Lacy had asked if Thad wanted to drop him home "or…", to which Thad glanced at him quickly, not smiling, but not-not smiling, focused back on the road as he asked, "Come over?"

They were kissing before the door was fully shut, shuffling down the hallway, Thad's big hands running up and down Lacy's back, making him feel held, wanted, so fucking desirable.

Lacy was surprised they were too keyed up to do more than get their pants bunched up under their asses, dicks out, rutting together as they made out on Thad's bed.

And now, after, Thad rolled his head to the side and Lacy responded by doing the same and meeting his gaze, the overly starched material of the pillow crunching under his head. He smiled, sated, come cooling on his stomach. Thad smiled back, hesitant at first, but then relieved as if some camaraderie had been established between them and what they'd just done.

"You know how you and Colton were saying about giving, about it being like an exchange," Thad said, his eyes never leaving Lacy's. His voice was soft but Lacy knew this tone—Thad had been pondering it and wanted Lacy's opinion.

"Yeah," Lacy replied.

"Did you just get Sandra the job so she'd do that for you?" he asked.

"Nah," Lacy smiled and Thad smiled back like he already knew that. "It's more like, if something came up, she'd have my back."

"I think," Thad rolled his head back to the pillow and stared at the ceiling. "I think some people at the church only do stuff for others to get something back. They believe in the principle of it, service, but I don't think that's why they do it anymore."

"Not surprising," Lacy said and touched Thad's hip. Thad tensed then relaxed, he tended to do that sometimes—he was jumpy, but then in the next breath, he'd lean into it like he'd been waiting for it; like now, he was bringing his hand up and sliding his fingers between Lacy's on his hip.

"Not surprising?" Thad asked.

"Yeah, I mean, they're still people, aren't they?"

He watched Thad take that in, eyes fixed on the ceiling, his chest rising and falling with the tail end of catching his breath. In a moment, it'd dawn on both of them that they had their dicks out, all their clothes on, including their shoes, and they probably needed to do something about that. But for now, they were in that blissful moment just before reality resumed.

"Yeah," Thad breathed out. "It's just disappointing, I guess."

Lacy had a series of canned responses to that—'Yeah, well, welcome to the world of people' or something similarly dismissive he'd heard growing up. The words wouldn't take shape though and they didn't feel right because Thad was right, it *was* disappointing.

"I'm sorry," he said.

Thad looked back at him, a soft surprised look on his face, a smile that said Lacy never had to be sorry for anything, ever.

"What're you sorry for?" he asked quietly.

Lacy slid his hand up, Thad following with his hold on it. The room was poorly lit because Thad's electrics were from the nineteenth century—probably—but it did give the room a soft glow, the walls and space beyond the bed dark. It was intimate and it made the dips and rises in Thad's muscles stand out like he was lit up on a photo shoot.

"I'm sorry people suck." That was woefully inadequate but he wasn't sure how much he should say. He wondered if he would've said it before they started fucking. He hoped Thad felt the same way as him, that this was more than just fucking. And that hope made him guarded, like he wanted to be good enough for Thad.

Thad huffed a laugh, slipped his fingers under Lacy's so he could bring his hand up to rest over his chest. He closed his eyes and Lacy watched him. He needed to get cleaned up, get undressed, either get into Thad's bed or go home.

He'd just take one more minute to stay like this, watch Thad's profile as he breathed, the shadows his eyelashes made on his cheeks, the smell of him, clean with the residue of the standard issue soap they used at the stadium.

19

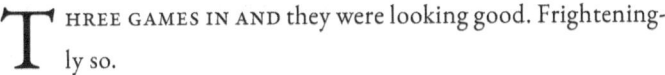

THREE GAMES IN AND they were looking good. Frighteningly so.

"What's frightening about it?" Lacy asked when Thad said that
after an easy win—too easy—over Brisbane.

"It just feels like a bubble set to burst," Thad replied. They were at
Lacy's, having a late dinner, watching the highlights from the game,
freshly changed into tracksuit pants and t-shirts. And Thad knew neither of them were wearing underwear. His mind snagged on this detail
whenever they settled in at the end of the day. They had a routine.
At least in the evenings. The kissing, oral sex, and actual sex they did
all over Lacy's house and his own place at random points during the
day, ignited with a look or a passing touch, were unpredictable and,
Thad felt, out of control. He wasn't sure which he liked more. He
loved them equally. He felt hot shame and guilt over both equally.
Spent as much time on his knees praying about it as he did with Lacy's
erection in his mouth—worshipping it too. He had a balance—have
sex, repent, pray for help to stop it, beg for forgiveness, plan to change
his ways and repeat. In a way, it was working. He knew it couldn't
last. And he ached for Lacy as much as he ached over that unknowable

point in the future when this would become his past. A time when he was truly happy.

For right now though, he knew they'd watch the TV, eat, knock their knees together until he didn't draw away. His hand would come up tentatively to rest on Lacy's thigh, drag slowly back and forth. He'd turn towards Lacy, lean forward and his lips would hover over Lacy's as his hand slipped inside his pants.

Lacy shook his head at Thad's remark, eyes on the TV where the highlight showed Cary handballing to Thad breaking away from the centre huddle. "I never really go in for all that abstract shit, what matters is how long until they figure out what you're doin' now," he jerked his chin at the play on screen, "and what they're gonna do to shut it down, what're you gonna do to be one step ahead of it."

"Hmm," Thad replied and let his knee rest against Lacy's.

Lacy slid his plate onto the coffee table and leaned back. He murmured about mixing it up by heading for the centre again on some plays, mixing up the corridor with the wings, but then Thad would need to work on marking.

Thad dropped his hand onto Lacy's thigh. Lacy slumped into the couch, let his legs fall wide. Thad's hand rubbed Lacy's muscle over the material, his thumb drifting inside the crease. Lacy was watching him when Thad looked away from the TV.

He leaned in and Lacy quirked his lips in the sexiest little smile. Thad had to kiss him. He wondered if he'd ever stop being surprised by how much he wanted it, how much that scared him.

Lacy's phone rang. Thad sat back as Lacy sat up and reached for it; the moment broken but the desire lingering as Lacy's face lit up.

"Finnegan Flynn, you callin' to congratulate me on a fuckin' baller game?" he said.

Thad heard laughter through the screen and got up to clear their plates.

"*George says I shouldn't encourage you,*" Finn's voice came through the phone.

Lacy grabbed Thad's hand and tangled their fingers together, eyes flicking up as he grinned.

He focused back on the screen and scoffed. "I know you're my number one fan, don't front."

Thad squeezed his hand, smiled, inclined his head at the plates and Lacy let him go with a wink. He was sprawled on the couch with his legs wide and Thad's eyes were inevitably drawn to the thickness resting against his thigh under the white material. Thad got busy with the plates, Lacy's laughter following him into the kitchen.

Finn must've had some news because Lacy shifted to a series of "Fuck, really? That's fucking awesome, man. George must be stoked. Is he stoked?"

Thad cleaned the kitchen and got their stuff ready for tomorrow—a recovery session at the beach—and tuned out the conversation. His arousal simmered, but it had an edge of panic at being interrupted.

"Good news?" he asked when Lacy found him in the kitchen.

"They're having a kid," Lacy replied.

Thad stopped refilling water bottles. "How?"

"Surrogate, donor egg, Finn's sperm, then they'll do George," Lacy replied like this was a completely normal way to have a child. "Finn's so fucking happy and I can just imagine George," he cackled, "he's gonna be on cloud nine but tryin' to act chill. I wish he was here just so I could make fun of him."

Thad tried to smile. He was having regular sex with a man and yet, his contemplations of homosexuality remained limited. The church said it was wrong and that's about as far as he'd gotten. The idea of men having children felt so foreign, incomprehensible, he wasn't sure what to do with it.

But Lacy was happy. And Finn was his friend. And that's all that mattered, that's all he was really required to think about here.

"I'm glad they're happy," he said. "And you're happy."

Lacy's smile turned sly as he sidled up to Thad. "I could be happier."

Thad choked on a laugh, blushed, slid his hand around Lacy's waist. He met Lacy's eyes and the arousal rushed back in, overwhelming him as he kissed Lacy, but Lacy met him with the same hunger and he felt less embarrassed about how eager he was.

He slid his hands over Lacy's ass, between his thighs so he could hoist him up and carry him back to the couch, Lacy's huff of laughter when Thad lifted him lost between their kisses.

Later that night, after he'd sucked Lacy on the couch, mapping the sounds he made, watching intently for what he really liked, wanting to be better than those other men, but also weirdly turned on by the thought of their shadows in the room, after Lacy had dragged them to his bed and returned the favour with expertise that shocked and electrified Thad and took him hurtling over the edge embarrassingly fast, he hugged Lacy against his chest in bed. He kissed his nape, savoured the skin on skin, and thought about the boy in the photos at his mum's place.

Lacy never mentioned a brother, but everything about that kid looked like a brother. Not in looks, that kid was taller in the later pictures, a lot taller, and his shaved head would've been blonde, based on the younger photos, the head stockier where Lacy was angular, but their eyes were the exact same whiskey-brown combination like their mother's. And they were pictured with arms around each other in little school uniforms, and later, with beers in hand.

Why wouldn't Lacy mention him? Why hadn't any football news cycle mentioned a brother—another potentially great player? Not all siblings played, but usually discussion of one of the great ones would mention a brother if he played too. And one of those photos was early teens, both boys in football jerseys.

He couldn't come out and ask about him because it felt like a closed door. Lacy, he'd realised in the year they'd become best friends, gave the appearance of being chill, up for anything, an open book. And he was all those things, it wasn't a lie. But there were closed chapters too. The men. The parties. The sex. And now this. The former he could understand—no amount of spin would soothe the football world if it came out one of their biggest stars enjoyed countless, nameless men having sex with him. The gay part was manageable, as attested by Finn and George. It wasn't wholly accepted, Thad's parents and church stoically didn't talk about it, gave it a knowing look as if they knew where that was going to end up—hell. But that was a committed relationship; Lacy was different. What he got up to was something out of the pages of the apocalypse no bible scribe could've dreamed up.

But a brother? Maybe?

"Hey," Lacy asked sleepily. "You okay?"

"Yes," Thad replied and pulled him closer.

"You're so awake," Lacy murmured.

"Sorry."

"Wanna talk about it?" Lacy asked and snuggled back.

Thad kissed behind his ear, stroked his hands up his torso.

"No, it's nothing, just pondering," Thad whispered.

"Here if you wanna talk," Lacy said softly and Thad could tell he was drifting off.

He was caught again by how nice this felt—to hold Lacy, to be close to him like this. He was awake for a long time, allowing himself to fully enjoy it, to memorise it. The compartment of guilt and shame closed for the night.

The week before they were set to play down in Tasmania, Lacy stopped on his doorstep so suddenly, Thad bumped into his back.

He gripped his hips from behind to steady them both. "Sorry."

Lacy wasn't moving. Thad peered over his shoulder.

There was a white envelope embossed with gold calligraphy on Lacy's doorstep.

Lacy moved as suddenly as he'd stopped and scooped it up, let them into his house without a word. Thad swallowed around his nerves; he didn't know why he was nervous, but the energy felt charged. He took his shoes off while Lacy went into his kitchen.

Thad took a deep breath and followed him.

"I don't have to go," Lacy said when Thad rounded the corner.

He was tapping the envelope on the counter. He looked up when Thad came closer. His face was hard to read—his usual ease was gone and there was something in his eyes, like he was checking in with Thad, like he wanted Thad to have an opinion on this.

Thad reached for the envelope and Lacy let him take it.

The party was that weekend. Saturday night. They played a day game. Sunday off, recovery session Monday and a random drug test scheduled.

"The test," Thad trailed off.

Lacy squinted up at him like he didn't understand what he was saying.

"I'm not worried about the piss test," he said after a moment.

Thad slid his hand around Lacy's waist, fingers sliding under his shirt and trailing up to his ribs and back again. He was getting hard.

Lacy gave him a surprised look.

"You want to go?" he asked.

"I'm worried about the test," Thad said, breathless. He couldn't say it, was ashamed of it, but taking care of Lacy, seeing him like that—writhing in pleasure as Thad watched, as he held ultimate control over what those men did, if they were allowed to do anything at all, knowing he could stop them or permit them and Lacy wanted him to.

He groaned and crushed Lacy against his chest, burying his face in Lacy's throat, mouthing at his skin.

"I'm really worried about the test," he murmured again.

Lacy laughed, breathless too, but surprised. "Shit, this really turns you on?"

Thad groaned again and rubbed his hard dick against Lacy's hip. "Sorry, yes, I don't know what's wrong with me."

Lacy drew Thad's face out from where it was buried in his shoulder, hovered his lips over Thad's as he spoke. "There's nothing wrong with you."

Thad pulled him in with restless hands. He stripped Lacy out of his shirt so he could get to that perfect skin, stroke his nipples, kiss his throat, rub off against his abs.

Lacy undid Thad's pants and pulled him out, stroked him with firm pressure, like he knew that's exactly what Thad needed. They were pressed close and Thad felt Lacy pull himself out with his other hand.

Thad gasped and came. The tingling, blinding pleasure was accompanied by mortification as he watched his semen trickle over the black and green ink of Lacy's torso.

"I'm sorry," he panted.

Lacy stroked him through it, lips pressing softly onto Thad's pecs.

"Fuck that was hot," Lacy said, awed.

Thad buried his groan into the hair on top of Lacy's head. "Embarrassing," he mumbled.

"Hot," Lacy looked up and Thad was forced to pull back, meet Lacy's eyes. He couldn't help himself from sliding his hands into Lacy's hair, cupping the back of his head as he looked down at him.

"Sexy, it was so fucking sexy. Did you know you were sexy?" Lacy grinned, sly. But Thad knew he was telling the truth, it was in the vulnerability in his eyes.

"Sexy?" Thad blushed. He was never going to be sexy. Lacy though? Lacy was the reason Thad understood what that word meant. "Here, let me," he rubbed his hand over Lacy's bulge.

He loved touching Lacy there. He loved everything about it—the weight of it, the feel of the soft skin and the way it hardened in his hand or mouth, the way the foreskin pulled back when Lacy got hard, the smell, the taste of his muskiness under the foreskin. Thinking about it, he sank to his knees.

"Thad, you don't need to—"

"Please," Thad asked and felt self-conscious at the pleading note in his voice.

But it was hard to feel too bad when it propelled Lacy into motion, his hand moving into Thad's hair, the other one guiding his erection into Thad's mouth.

Thad opened for him, slid his tongue along the soft skin as he sucked. Lacy groaned, let go of the base and put both hands on Thad's head. He ran his fingers through the strands, caressing him. It was such a soothing, gentle touch, while he rocked his hips politely into Thad's mouth at the same time.

He could've stayed down there for hours with how much he loved it, but Lacy warned him like he always did and Thad brought his hands up to his ass to bring him closer. He sucked and waited with excitement and trepidation for the first jet to hit his tongue. When it did, he felt the hot flush of shock, then the blinding, filthy desire as he swallowed. Lacy stroked his head the whole time, chanting his name.

"Okay, so I reckon you're into the party," Lacy said later. They'd cleaned up, collapsed together on the couch, watched the light outside change the tree lined street from bright greens and blues to a darker blue.

Thad rubbed his face. "I'm into the parties with you, but I am worried about this test. So close to a game..."

"Yeah, but don't worry about that, alright? The masking agent is gonna be solid, enough of the guys up on the mines have had no trouble, so, it'll be fine." Lacy sounded so sure of it, Thad knew it probably would be fine.

"Maybe we skip this party so you're less," Thad rolled his head to look at Lacy. Lacy was already watching him. "Potent," he finished.

Lacy smiled lazily at him. "I'm already potent, baby."

Thad chuckled.

"I'm fucked either way, party or no, 'cos of the booze, the coke," he shrugged, his shoulders rolling against the couch. "The smart thing to do would be to quit and not have this worry, not be dragging you into this worry—"

"I don't mind."

"I know you don't," Lacy smiled, "but it'd be easier on us, you, if I just quit. But I gotta unwind. If I don't cut loose, my play is fucked."

"I know," Thad reached for his hand.

Lacy watched him; he looked like he wanted to say something, but then didn't. He'd done this a few times since they'd started having sex. Lacy was always in Thad's space and carefree with his words and his affection. But this was new. Thad didn't like it, but he was terrified of what Lacy was choosing not to say. So he gripped Lacy's hand in his, squeezed, and didn't press.

"Wanna go up the street for dinner?" Lacy asked.

"Yes," Thad smiled. "Do you mind if we drop by the fresh market after?"

Lacy grinned. "No, I do not mind if we drop by the fresh market after."

20

L ACY STRETCHED AS HE came awake, unsure what time it was, where he was, where he was supposed to be. Palms were spread on his chest, big arms held him and pulled him back against naked skin.

"You okay?" Thad asked, his voice rough as it vibrated on the back of Lacy's neck.

Lacy relaxed. "Yeah."

The party was flashes of memory, like flickers from a movie with some scenes opening up and spilling out longer than others. Thad was, once again, in every frame. Holding him. Ordering the other men around, a note of fragility behind the firmness he was injecting into his tone.

"Yeah," he said again and sighed.

Tomorrow he'd get up and sit in front of his locker after training and wait for Sandra to call his name off the 'random' piss test in a bored voice. His heart thumped; it was a spike of fear brought on by the comedown and nothing more.

Thad's hand caressed his pectoral muscle right over his heart. His breath ghosted over Lacy's ear when he spoke, "You're okay, I got you."

He'd said that last night. A lot. Lacy shivered, a searing ache shot from his chest up his throat, his heart exploding with feelings. It was the comedown, making everything pronounced. But comedown or not, the feelings behind it were real.

He sucked in a shaky breath.

"I'll get you some coffee," Thad said sounding more awake. "Water, maybe a Gatorade."

"No," Lacy gripped his arms and held him still.

"I'll come right back," Thad said, a smile in his voice.

"Do it in a minute," Lacy replied.

Thad hesitated. Lacy tried to breathe. Thad settled back down behind him. Lacy exhaled in relief and Thad pulled him tighter against his chest, his breath a warm, soft tickle on Lacy's nape.

"Lacy," Sandra said, the empty specimen cup with a yellow lid held out while her eyes tracked her list. She sounded bored.

"Les," she said as Lacy took the cup from her and headed for the bathrooms.

Lacy went down the corridor with Kurt behind him. The door whooshed open to reveal Thad standing near the sink. He jumped nervously before moving towards Lacy, wiping his hands briskly on his pants.

"I'd use the first one if I was you," Thad said, he sounded like he'd been practicing the line, his face twisting into an exaggerated grimace before he dropped his gaze and pulled his phone out, the door sweeping closed with a double clang as he left.

Lacy went into the first stall. His phone pinged.

"Make it quick, Lace," Kurt said, trying to come off bored, but he was clearly nervous. Lacy knew there'd be chatter behind the scenes—why was Alanson deliberately trying to get their best player a serious suspension? Why not just leave him be? He can bloody well play, who gives a shit what he does in his spare time. He was hardly getting arrested for beating up taxi drivers and starting pub brawls.

Lacy checked his phone.

Behind the toilet.

Lacy frowned. His heart ticked up as he crouched down. A specimen cup with a yellow lid: it was full. He reached for it, the plastic warm against his hand. Nerves shot through him, gratitude mixed with fear and surprise. He stood, placed it on top of the toilet and opened the cup in his hand.

He fumbled his dick out and started to piss, stopped mid-stream, angled it at the cup so as to make the noise of urine hitting plastic, then aimed back into the toilet and poured it out. He gave himself a good shake, tucked the empty container into the back of his jocks. He hoped Kurt wasn't paying close attention because there was no way that wasn't bulging. He wondered why Thad didn't give him a heads up so he could've put a hoodie on. But he knew. He would've told Thad no—this wasn't Thad's problem, he wasn't going to make him complicit in it.

Except now he was. Lacy tucked himself away, picked up the container with Thad's light-yellow urine and went out.

"Here you go, boss," he said to Kurt and hoped he didn't notice how he struggled over the usual joke.

Kurt was clearly up in his head because he simply took it, muttered his thanks, his eyes briefly meeting Lacy's with an apologetic look as he left. Lacy slipped through the door behind him before it clanged shut.

"You ready to go?" Thad asked too brightly when Lacy reappeared beside him.

The rest of the guys were shooting him worried looks and trying to pretend they weren't, but Lacy was focused on Thad. He knew he had a part to play here and he could throttle Thad once they were in private.

"Hold your horses, Romeo, gotta get my shoes on," he said and sat down.

"I could really go for a burger for lunch. What do you think? Feel like a walk?" Thad asked.

Lacy craned his head back as he tied his shoes and met Thad's eyes. *No*, he wanted to say, *I do not feel like a fucking burger and a fucking walk. I feel like getting you somewhere private and asking what the fuck you were thinking.*

"Actually, I got some steaks out at my place," he refocused on his shoes, he couldn't keep looking at Thad's strained, happy face. "Better use 'em before they go off."

"We could have them for dinner?" Thad asked. "I'm really feeling it for those burgers."

Lacy stood, met his eyes. Thad was never really 'feeling it' for anything. He was avoiding the conversation. Lacy knew everyone could hear them, they probably thought Thad was being a good friend, trying to take Lacy's mind off an impending suspension. He wondered at their collective lack of faith in him, but he was more preoccupied with Thad trying to hide his nerves in front of him.

"Okay," he said.

Thad sagged.

"But it's raining, so we'll drive."

Thad tensed, but Lacy knew there was no way he could argue with that.

Lacy waited until they'd driven out of the parking lot.

"Thad, what the fuck, man, you could—"

"You're *not* getting suspended," Thad cut him off.

"I know, that's why I used the masking agent. You could get in so much fucking trouble. Like, fucking legal trouble, Thad, do you get that?"

"I don't care," Thad replied, his voice firm but Lacy didn't miss the tremulous note under it. "You'd do the same for me."

And that sounded practiced too. It was difficult to argue with—Lacy would do anything for him—but Thad would never put him in this position, which is why Lacy didn't want Thad to help like this. He chose this, he'd wear it if it came to that. He knew some of his teammates secretly felt perplexed and possibly even resentful, wondering why he didn't just quit the partying if the noose was tightening, quit for the team. But he also knew the guys who'd known him longest knew the answer to that too. 'Lacy's gonna be Lacy and he wouldn't be the player he is if he's not allowed to let off steam,' he remembered George telling a media scrum after pictures of him hammered at a party were plastered all over every paper and website when he was a rookie. It'd set a tone that'd protected him in the locker room. He hated the feeling of that shield cracking.

But he hated the thought of Thad putting his own career, his livelihood and reputation, in danger more.

"You'd never put me in this position," he said quietly when Thad stopped at a red light.

Thad gripped the steering wheel and didn't look at him, his jaw was clenched. The light blinked green.

"I'm not saying I don't appreciate it," he went on. "I mean, fuck, I don't reckon anyone's ever done something so nice for me."

It was the truth, but he meant it as a joke too, something to break the tension, but Thad didn't laugh.

They were on Lacy's street, Thad's car sliding slowly down the tree-lined road crowded with parked cars, the sweep of jacarandas lining the median strip. He pulled into Lacy's driveway. They'd both known the burger place was a play for time on Thad's part and there was no point maintaining the charade.

"Thad, man," Lacy said helplessly, "I know that must've been hard and I really appreciate it, I do, like, thank you so fucking much, dude, but you can't—"

Thad turned suddenly. "Stop thanking me, you're my best friend, of course I'm gonna protect you."

Best friend. It stung, made Lacy's stomach drop. But they were best friends. Except—

Except he couldn't even finish the thought.

"Yeah," he said once he'd recovered, his breathing felt too loud in the confined space. "And that's why I'm tryin' to protect you too."

Thad shook his head. He made no move to get out of the car.

"Don't do it again," Lacy said firmly.

Thad gripped the steering wheel. "You know I will," he murmured.

"Then I'm not gonna tell you about it, you won't know," he replied and it hurt to say it.

Thad shot him a betrayed look.

"It's for your own good," Lacy replied and hated that he sounded like his mother.

Thad looked out the windshield but didn't say anything. His whole bearing radiated defeat and Lacy didn't know what to do. He was doing the right thing, but it pained him to hurt Thad like this.

"Do you really have steaks?" Thad asked.

"No," Lacy replied.

Thad huffed a laugh, finally looked at him with a soft, happy look. Lacy exhaled in relief.

"I didn't think so," Thad said and unclipped his seatbelt, "since I do all your shopping."

Lacy unclipped his seatbelt, but gripped Thad's hand before he could get out. Thad looked back at him.

"Thank you," he said.

Thad shook his head. "It was nothing." He squeezed Lacy's hand and let go, opened the door and got out of the car.

It wasn't nothing and they both knew it.

"My parents want to have you over for dinner after the game if you want to?" Thad asked. They were heading to an early morning beach session and they were almost there. Thad sounded nervous. Lacy wondered if he'd been waiting to ask.

"Yeah, course. Sounds lit. I can't wait to meet your parents," Lacy grinned over at him.

Thad smiled at him, relieved and grateful. Lacy's stomach fluttered and he wondered if Thad knew anything about his feelings at all; of course he wanted to meet his parents.

He pulled out his phone as Thad drove and booked an appointment with his dentist for Thursday afternoon.

When Thad picked him up to meet the bus to the airport, Lacy grinned and Thad's eyes widened.

"You got your tooth fixed," he said and leaned forward.

"Eh, it was about time," Lacy shrugged.

Thad's face was close. Lacy smiled. Thad huffed a laugh and kissed him, a deep kiss with tongue.

Thad pulled back with a chuckle. "Feels different."

"Different better?"

Thad started the car, rolled his shoulders. "A different kind of good."

"I'll take that," Lacy replied and rested his hand on Thad's thigh.

He caught sight of Alanson coming down the aisle on the plane in his periphery and flicked his eyes up. Alanson didn't look at him; he'd been a consummate professional since he'd walked into the locker room on Thursday, gaze landing on Lacy with an expression somewhere between stern and curious, and Lacy knew he'd just gotten the news about the clean test. Sandra had messaged him the night before. Obviously it was no surprise to him—the lab technician probably got the shock of his life when he saw angels singing in the liquid through the lens—but it'd be a surprise to Alanson. One he no doubt shook off and pondered how Lacy had done it. When Alanson's gaze shifted from Lacy to Thad beside him in the locker room, Thad busy snapping his leggings at his waist, eyes down, hair wavy and falling over his face to barely conceal the amused smile he was wearing listening to Lacy talk shit, Lacy felt seized with panic, even though he'd managed to keep talking. There was no way Alanson knew. No fucking way. He'd watched his inscrutable gaze move on and reassured himself there was just no way.

"Thanks for coming to dinner, Dad's excited," Thad nudged him now, oblivious to Alanson and the rest of the coaching staff, trainers, medical staff, and office personnel boarding around them.

"Free meal from the source? There's no universe in which I'm turning that down," Lacy replied with a grin.

Thad chuckled. "You might not think I'm any good after you've had her cooking."

"Impossible," Lacy nudged him and let his arm stay resting against Thad's the entire short hop down to Launceston.

The game was the next day at 2pm under the high sunshine stretching across the vastness of the cool, blue sky of Launceston. The air was crisp and cold and Lacy thought it was odd that an island felt vaster, more spacious than the mainland. But when he'd said this to Thad in their room the night before, Thad had replied it was because Lacy was talking about Melbourne, the denseness and business of the city, and all cities felt like that, but if they went out to the desert or even up to the mountains, it'd probably feel like Launceston. That had reminded Lacy of the trip he'd been planning, to go antiquing in the Blue Mountains. Thad agreed to go with him easily before lying down on his bed and watching the Friday night game. Lacy had thought they'd sleep together—they slept together every night—but this was their first away game since all that started and Thad didn't make any move to get into bed with him. Lacy felt awkward making the first move. He didn't want to get into it the night before a game in front of Thad's home crowd, so he let it be. They were staying back the extra night to see Thad's parents; they'd probably fool around after.

"Got a few friends here," Cary said as he jogged up to where Thad was behind Lacy, about to run his turn on the goal kicking drill to get warmed up.

"Home town," Thad replied. It sounded rehearsed.

Lacy belted a kick straight through the middle and charged the fence line, holding his ear up to the crowd. People cheered, clapped, the flags waving in his face and he grinned as he streaked past them.

Halfway through the first and they were up two goals, no thanks to Thad. He was off in the centre bounces, reacting a fraction of a second too late. Lacy jogged to the centre to regroup after kicking the latest goal, Thad jogging in front of him. He got alongside him, tapped his ass.

"Get your shit together," he said around his panting breaths. "You're twice the ruckman this guy is."

Thad shot him a look. Embarrassed, tense. It was a packed crowd, but half the numbers they played against in Melbourne. Except of course Thad had family and friends in this crowd. Lacy played in front of his people all the time—it energised him, showing off for them. But maybe it was different for Thad.

"And it's another sunny day in Melbourne!" Lacy shouted at Thad just before they parted, Lacy to fall back again, Thad to take the centre.

Thad glanced at him.

"Which means it'll probably be raining by this afternoon!" Lacy finished and winked, jogging backwards.

Thad smiled and his shoulders loosened the tiniest bit.

He was hardly a superstar for the second half of the first, but he was winning the tap at least, getting it to Cary handily, if not charging down the centre with the confidence he'd shown in the first few games back in Melbourne, surprising the opposition like Lacy knew it would.

"Home crowd jitters?" Cary asked Thad as they made their way to the huddle for the first break.

"I guess," Thad shrugged. Lacy was on his other side. He bumped him.

"But it's such a nice day today," Lacy mused. "Who woulda thought Melbourne would turn it on for us?"

Thad dropped his head and chuckled.

Cary gave him a questioning look.

"Maybe the Greens got all cars except electric banned," he looked up at the sky as they stopped. "Maybe I should start voting for them instead of the Liberals."

Thad laughed. "You do not vote for the Liberals." He was still breathing heavily, his brow sweaty, and his fond eyes were shining down at Lacy, the tension receding. He had Lacy's number—there's no way he'd vote conservative. If he ever voted.

"Well, actually, that's true," Lacy replied. "I've never voted. I always forget."

"Three-goal lead is not enough," Alanson said and Lacy focused on him, hands on his hips as he got his breathing back. Alanson had Kurt next to him with a whiteboard, breaking down plays, listing everywhere they were falling short.

Lacy missed George. He'd missed him all of last year as well. He wasn't one to really pay all that much attention to his coach's suggestions either way, he knew what he was doing out there, but the energy they brought mattered. He'd been blessed with men who were focused on building confidence in his high school days, and on honing skills in the junior league. It wasn't that he disliked Alanson—apart from the guy's blinding hard-on to get him suspended for, Lacy guessed, embarrassing him last year—he could see his angle, see he was actually a good coach for a certain type of player. The Cary's and the Lesley's (not the Les') of the world—the guys who were sure of who they were, settled men, married men. But he was terrible for the younger guys, incapable of bringing out the best in them, and he had a clear problem with anyone who 'disrespected the club', which to his mind meant anyone who didn't behave like a robot 24/7, 365 days a year in service of the club's image of discipline and focus.

Suffice to say, Lacy ignored him until he heard Thad's name.

"Clay, get your head out of your ass and into the game," Alanson tapped the whiteboard. "They got a second-rate ruckman out there and you let him win two centre bounces, which makes you third rate. You wanna play down in the country, be my guest."

Lacy ground his teeth together. Thad shifted subtly, his arm brushing Lacy's; it'd look like he'd just sucked in a deep pull of air and released it with his arms swinging closer by accident. But Lacy knew he was telling him to let it go.

Thad nodded.

The siren went and they fanned out.

"Don't listen to that fucking wanker," Lacy said softly. "You fucking got this."

Thad ducked his head, his smile crooked, his eyes lightening, and it disarmed Lacy. "I know. We're in Melbourne, right?"

Lacy beamed. "Yeah, we are. Gonna get wasted at Harlow's after this."

Thad chuckled. "Then I'll carry you home."

Lacy tapped him on the ass before they had to part ways. "You better."

"Always," Thad shot him a smile over his shoulder before taking his position in the centre. Lacy knew he'd put more into the ruse for his sake, to get him to calm down, but if it got him playing the way Lacy knew he could play then so be it. Lacy wanted to punch Alanson anyway—a fight that could honestly go either way. Alanson had a good six inches and forty kilos on him and he was fit, but Lacy knew if he was angry enough, he'd kill anyone in a fight.

In the end they won it easily and Thad was loose enough in the second half to start playing the way they'd practiced, the home crowd on their feet and waving flags when he scored a goal in the fourth. His first in the league.

Lacy saw Thad talking to a group of people on the boundary, the men dressed in suit pants and collared shirts, nice jackets, hair neatly combed, while the women wore their hair long, faces plain, their bodies encased in skirts and blouses or long dresses, long coats over the top. None of them wore team gear. They were all smiling, looking up at Thad, the tallest man out front speaking when he caught Lacy's eyes over Thad's shoulder and said something. Thad turned and waved for him to come over. Nerves hit Lacy with a force that surprised him.

He jogged over, clocked Thad's nervous smile meeting his as he got closer. And it was Thad's nerves that made Lacy determined he wasn't going to fuck this up.

"Lacy, this is my father, Kevin," Thad said once Lacy was beside him.

The man reached his hand out, smile gruff, but his face was a little red and his voice wavered faintly as he spoke. "Lacy, it's so nice to meet you. Incredible game, son. Just incredible."

Lacy shook his hand and grinned his public image grin. "Thank you. It's so nice to meet you," his smile turned more genuine as he glanced up at Thad. "Thad talks about you a lot, so it's great to finally meet."

Thad gave him a grateful look, before he introduced his mother. And Lacy saw immediately where Thad got his looks. The build was all on the dad's side, but the face, the warm brown eyes, the unblemished skin, it all came from his mum.

"So nice to meet you, Lacy," she said, her soft voice radiating calmness. "Thad talks about you all the time," she parroted back at him, but it was friendly. "So it *is* good to finally meet."

Thad rubbed the back of his neck. They were both sweaty and puffing from the game, bodies still in the restless motion that took a while to settle, so his movement was easily dismissed as part of that energy. But Thad's nerves fed Lacy's and he really didn't want to fuck this up.

Meeting everyone else was a blur, relatives, people from the church—they were all polite, a little awed, quiet for a football crowd, and none of them asked for an autograph or a selfie.

"We'll meet you near the ticket booth," Thad said as they said goodbye to everyone.

"Wow, your parents are like, super fuckin' nice," Lacy said as they walked back to the visitor's locker room.

Thad snorted, rubbed his neck again. "I guess."

"I won't swear tonight," Lacy said.

Thad gave him an odd look. "I know you won't."

"Good," Lacy breathed out.

About halfway through the dinner, Lacy realised the difference in Thad around his parents wasn't simply down to his presence. He'd thought at first the semi-formal way he spoke, the rigid way he moved, the polite way he said grace before the meal with none of the usual fanfare with his hands—he still made the sign of the cross, but whenever he did it back home, he was dramatic about it and he did it in Latin, smiled at Lacy, but here it was in English, subdued—was all because he was anxious about Lacy's presence. About how close they were. About how much they were fucking. That was probably part of it—Lacy didn't expect to be announced as Thad's boyfriend anytime soon—but it was also who he was here. Contained. A gentleman in a straitjacket.

Lacy couldn't fault his parents though. His dad—'Kevin, please call me Kevin, Mr Clay is for the workshop,' he'd said around a smile, breathless with a pink tint to his cheeks—was clearly a fan and trying to contain his exuberance for the game, for Lacy as a player in particular. It was evident this wasn't simply because Lacy was sitting at his table, but also in general if the slightly admonishing looks Thad's mum, Mrs Clay, who hadn't asked to be called by her first name, gave him.

The save, in Lacy's opinion, was the food. Woman could cook. He moaned around a mouthful of mashed potato and apologised immediately. Thad laughed at him, loosening. "I told you." He focused on his mum across from them. "Lacy has been looking forward to your cooking."

She smiled, gracious and kind. "Thaddeus is very good too, I taught him well."

"You sure did," Lacy replied. He was about to bump Thad but held back, the phantom movement there in the air between them in the way Thad stiffened.

"Lacy's favourite is anything out of the slow cooker," Thad said, spine straight, voice warm but a little awkward.

"The electric," Mrs Clay scrunched her face up playfully and Thad shrugged, smiling.

"Can't leave an open flame on when I'm out all day," he dutifully replied.

"Yes, we can see all the training paying off," his dad said from the head of the table. "Alanson's got you doing more down the centre?"

"Lacy," Thad glanced at him, flashed a quick smile. "Lacy and Scotty worked with me over the break."

"Alanson doesn't know what's hit him," Lacy laughed. Thad's dad raised his eyebrows, smiling with a question, and Lacy explained the summer training program they used, Scotty coming down. He glanced up at Thad in question before mentioning the scouts in Perth looking for another ruckman.

"I needed to improve," Thad said to his parents.

So, they didn't know.

"Well, mission accomplished," his dad smiled winningly at him, but a part of his attention darted to his wife as if he were biting it back. It was strange, it was like this big man was brimming with joy and pride for his boy, wanted to get up and lift him out of his seat and spin him around with how proud he was, but it was so restrained it was visible. Lacy didn't get it. He'd never met his dad, his mum had told him variations of, 'Coulda been a few of them,' regarding the boys she was hooking up with in high school. The boyfriends she'd had over the years were somewhere between going-nowhere deadbeats and assholes, one man she'd married so briefly Lacy was too young to remember him at all, though he sounded harmless enough. But he looked at Thad's dad, at that love and thought, if he'd ever wanted a dad, it'd be one like that.

"Dessert?" Thad's mum asked, and Thad stood when she did to help her prepare it.

As they left the room, Lacy felt the energy shift between him and Kevin and wondered for a panicked moment if he was going to ask what was really going on between him and Thad.

He leaned forward. "I have to ask," he said, voice lowered. Lacy's heart thumped against his breast bone. "What was it like in that Grand Final with Creed? Some people say the other side was simply worse, but I never believed that. Creed was on fire, wasn't he?"

Lacy almost laughed. He didn't, he nodded, smiled wide, more from relief than remembering the game—though it'd been a great game—and Kevin returned the smile, giddy, taking it for confirmation, thrilled at getting the inside scoop.

"You're right," Lacy nodded. "George, Creed, he was so amped in the locker room. He was dragging us to the win whether we turned up or not."

He detailed the highlights he knew a footy fan would get off on and Kevin hung on every word until noise from the kitchen led them to both sit back.

"So Thad tells me you've helped him put in the veggie patch," Kevin said in a normal voice when Thad and his mum placed the fruit cake and ice-cream on the table.

Lacy had to laugh and Thad broke his mask for a moment, a real smile for Lacy as he leaned over him to place his dessert in front of him, his hand coming to Lacy's shoulder to give him a squeeze.

"A great help," Thad said and shook him before stepping away and taking a seat.

The conversation turned to gardening, Thad's mum peppering him with questions and suggestions, Thad replying easily, the conversation between them like a dance they'd performed a thousand times. Lacy saw in it how close they were, in their own way; he could almost see Thad trailing around after her as a kid as she taught him to cook and clean and garden and read.

She was far from warm, at least with Lacy, but she clearly loved her son. And expected things from him if her next question for Lacy was any indication.

"So, Lacy," she smiled at him, "Thad doesn't tell us much about the other parishioners, is there someone special?"

Lacy tilted his head to look at Thad in question, though he had a sinking feeling that even if he didn't know what parishioners meant, he got the gist of the question. He had no idea. His first thought was, of course not. How could there be someone else when Thad was with him? But his second thought was, of course there will be one day, and possibly could be someone of interest now.

"Lacy doesn't come to the church, Mum," Thad said and Lacy was struck with how awful that answer was.

Was there someone special at his church?

"It would be good if there was," she went on, oblivious to what her words were doing to Lacy's perception of the world. "You're almost twenty-five. Your father had a five-year-old at your age."

Lacy glanced at Thad. He smiled politely at her, shrugged. Lacy didn't feel like that was a conclusive answer.

Back in their room after Thad's mum dropped them off, Thad acted completely normal. No, relieved. His shoulders loosened, he smiled gratefully at Lacy as he got changed into his trackies and a t-shirt before he went to use the bathroom.

Lacy stood in the middle of the room and didn't know what to say when Thad came back out. Before the trip he'd been preoccupied with whether or not they'd fuck while they were in hotel rooms. Now he was wondering about the women at Thad's church. Thad had mentioned Carol from the trip, and Lacy wanted to ask about her, ask if Thad liked her, what she looked like, what happened on the trip.

"You okay?" Thad asked as he came out of the bathroom and saw Lacy standing where he'd left him. "I know my dad probably grilled you on the glory days," he smiled wryly.

"Glory days are yet to come," Lacy quipped and hoped Thad missed how breathless he sounded. He didn't, given the frown Thad gave him.

"Excuse me," Lacy said and Thad raised both eyebrows. Yes, it was strange for Lacy to use manners like that, but he needed to hide in the bathroom for a minute.

He shut the door firmly behind himself, braced his hands on the counter and looked at his face. His eyes looked more whisky-coloured than brown under the sharp fluorescent light over the mirror; he peered into them, tried to really look into himself for a moment, to see what the fuck he thought he was doing. He looked at his lips and thought about the number of guys who'd fucked his mouth and gotten really worked up over it, groaning stupidly, losing control. His lips were big, full, but the bump in his nose, the stubble on his fine jaw line, the high cheekbones that looked sharp if he didn't balance his eating well enough with the coke he snorted, all that made him look unmistakably like a man. His hair, recently shaved on the sides but left long in the middle to start the season with a mullet, the tattoos that stretched up his throat, all of it combined into an aggressive masculinity. He resented it suddenly.

Lacy had never hated himself. He'd never been consumed with the introspective self-loathing he suspected George had been. He'd refused to do much introspection at all. But right then, as he looked at his face, studied the sad cast to his eyes, a look that belonged on a stranger's face, he didn't like what he saw.

There was a soft knock on the door.

"Lacy? You okay?" Thad asked.

"Yeah," he bit out, sharper than he intended.

Thad didn't reply. Lacy could feel him on the other side of the door. He wanted him to go away. He wanted to open the door and pull him close. He was scared of Thad pulling away if he did.

"They're showing the highlights after these ads if you want to watch," Thad said after a while.

"Yep," he said and turned on the tap, washed his face.

When he went out, Thad looked up at him immediately, face creased with concern, his long body stretched out on his bed, ankles crossed, but there was a careful smile below the frown, like he was checking in.

"They keep showing your mark in the second," he said.

Lacy snorted, it felt forced and he knew Thad knew it, but he didn't say anything, let his gaze return to the TV.

He got changed, made all the right comments, felt a semblance of normal returning. He paused when he was about to get into bed. Since this thing started, he got into bed with Thad. Now he didn't know what to do. He saw Thad shifting in his periphery like he was waiting for what Lacy would do. And Lacy swore he tensed, if only subtly.

Lacy sat down on his own bed, trying to make the movement seem natural so it seemed anything but, and scooted back to the headboard, mirrored Thad's position.

They half-heartedly commented on the highlights, the swell of everything they weren't saying putting pressure under the words.

It was Lacy who got under his blankets, flicked his lamp off and said he needed to get some sleep first, his voice all forced friendliness.

He felt Thad's surprise behind him—he'd rolled onto his side, giving Thad his back.

"Of course," Thad said apologetically and turned everything off.

The room plunged into darkness, the sound of Thad's blankets rustling as he got in. Lacy stared at the wall waiting for his eyes to adjust.

"Goodnight," Thad said softly.

"Night," Lacy grunted.

Neither of them slept for a long time. He could feel their wide-awake energy like it was permeating the walls, but he didn't know what to say. He didn't know what to do with this unnameable feeling rattling around under his skin. He needed a fucking drink, that's what he needed. Maybe a fight. Or an anonymous fuck. Anything to help him process a feeling like he'd lost something before he'd really had it.

21

W HEN THEY GOT BACK to the stadium to collect their gear
and drive home, Lacy asked Thad to drop him home, said he
needed to get some shit done, his smile friendly and normal enough,
but Thad didn't miss all the things he was concealing with it. He
hadn't missed it since the night before.

"Of course," he replied though, returned the smile with a tremulous one of his own, which would've been embarrassing except Lacy
wasn't looking at him, he was staring out the passenger's window, the
back of his shiny brown hair looking back at Thad.

Thad wanted to reach out, drag his fingers through the strands until
Lacy turned into the touch. But he gripped the steering wheel instead,
drove Lacy home and forced himself to reverse once Lacy disappeared
behind the wall enclosing his house.

The whole drive home, the embarrassment and inadequacy that'd
welled up inside him last night spilled out further. He knew what his
family and the people from his church looked like next to the rest of
society. It wasn't overt, but there was a conservativeness to their dress
and manner that people picked up on during an acquaintance. They
might not be able to name it, but they knew there was something.
They weren't the Catholics or the Anglicans who passed as regular

people until they were actually in a church, who, according to his church, weren't even really into it, they were just 'hedging their bets'.

He didn't know why he'd thought Lacy wouldn't care, wouldn't be like everyone else. But he had. He hadn't even been all that worried about it. But what else would explain the sudden withdrawal, the—no doubt—disgust he felt for Thad? As if everything that'd come before was now tainted with this image of him. And Lacy was repulsed by it.

Truthfully, he'd been relieved when Lacy hadn't touched him at first back in the hotel room; he wasn't sure he could do that so close to his family and church, so close to the smell of his home and his mum's hug goodbye lingering on his skin. But when Lacy had come out of the bathroom and changed and Thad saw his bare ass, the taut muscles of that one part of un-inked skin, the flash of his gorgeous dick before he covered himself, the desire was so intense it rocked him where he sat.

But Lacy got into his own bed. Lacy didn't want that.

Thad went inside the empty house in Brunswick, threw his keys in the bowl on the side table, dropped his bag, ran a hand through his hair and tried to convince himself this was a good development. He went about his routine for the house, reminding himself how good this was, and when it came time to pray that night, he didn't feel relieved when he had nothing to ask forgiveness for that day. He felt empty.

He wasn't sure what the plan was for the following morning. They always went to training together.

Pick you up at 7am. He typed and hit send, his heart pounding, his limbs tingling.

The reply was swift.

U better.

Thad laughed with tremendous relief. He made a breakfast toasty and wrapped it carefully, got his bag and headed to Lacy's.

Lacy was already waiting on the driveway, eyes hidden under his sunglasses.

"Hey, man," Lacy said easily when he got in.

"Hi, morning," Thad replied. He handed him the sandwich to distract himself.

"No way," Lacy grinned. Thad could see himself reflected back in the lenses. "Thad, man, you're the fuckin' shit. Thank you," he said with more enthusiasm than normal, but Thad was too grateful to acknowledge why. They were okay, they were still best friends, everything was going to be okay.

As they drove, Lacy told him about his 'boring ass day' yesterday, ate, wondered what 'fresh hell' Alanson had planned for them, and asked Thad if he wanted to get dinner that night.

Thad knew his smile was too full of feeling when he breathed out, "Yes."

But Lacy punched him playfully on the bicep and they headed inside.

They had dinner at Lacy's and it was good, normal enough, and Thad decided to head home before he did something stupid like wrap his arms around Lacy's waist. Lacy was standing at his kitchen bench, snapping lids on take-out containers. Thad wanted to press his face into Lacy's hair, kiss the shell of his ear.

"Right," he said too loudly. "I better go. Pick you up at seven again?"

Lacy stacked the containers and turned. "Okay, sounds good," he flashed Thad a grin. It didn't touch his eyes.

"Thank you for dinner."

Lacy rolled his eyes. He was putting the containers in the fridge, his face in profile, but Thad caught it.

"Reckon it's about time, eh?" he winked as he slammed his fridge shut. "I'll walk you out."

Thad got his shoes on and Lacy leaned on the wall beside him with his arms crossed over his chest. It was excruciating. Before, Thad would've hugged him. But if he hugged him now, he wouldn't be able to just hug him.

"Thanks again," he said as he straightened, ran a hand through his hair and smiled down at him.

"Yeah," Lacy replied, distracted.

Thad shoved his hands in his pockets. "Okay, well, bye."

"Yep," Lacy said and looked past Thad at the door. His arms were tight across his chest and his smile was rigid.

Thad gripped the door knob clumsily, opened it and fled onto the street.

A week later after a thrilling win over Sydney that ended in Lacy going out with Finn and George for drinks, and even though he'd invited Thad to join them, insisted even, Thad had begged off. He didn't think he could handle being around inebriated Lacy at the moment. What if Lacy touched him? Thad would break and push him against the nearest wall and kiss him. Worse, what if Lacy talked? Told him in his loose, drunken ramble the reason he couldn't touch Thad anymore was because he was a religious freak with a fanboy for a dad. Thad couldn't bear either scenario.

So he went home, worried like he usually did when Lacy went out without him. But Lacy was fine on the Monday morning, waiting on his driveway for Thad to pick him up.

"Sandra texted," he said once they were on their way.

Thad shot him a nervous look. "And?" His heart pounded. He'd left the sample and he would absolutely do it again, he didn't care what Lacy said on this, he would protect him, but that didn't mean it hadn't been the most nerve-wracking moment of his life. He was surprised he was able to get his urine in the cup, his hands had been shaking so badly. He'd used a wad of toilet paper wiping the edge of the container.

"Hey, it's all good," Lacy said. "Sorry, I shouldn't have started out like that, like some crime drama, but you'd normally be right next to me and 'cos you weren't I had to think how to tell you all night."

Thad got caught back at Lacy mentioning he'd normally be there and almost missed what he said as he went on.

"... so, yeah, Sandra said Kurt and Todd told Alanson to leave it alone 'cos WADA got their sample now, I'm clean, why keep pushing it, you know? Jim's backed them up."

"So no more tests?" Thad asked. Just because the governing body got their sample, doesn't mean the club couldn't go after him. But if Jim—the club's President—supported that decision, Alanson might have to leave it alone.

"Well, I wouldn't put it past him to do it again for his own reasons, but yeah, for now, sounds like Kurt and Todd have got him to back off. And I dunno if he'd cross Jim."

"What a relief," Thad breathed out.

"Yep," Lacy said and looked out the window. "Might just be the regular ones."

It wasn't until the end of the day that Thad wondered how much of a relief it really was. Because if another party happened, or Lacy had a big night and did some coke, where would Thad be in that picture? The thought of Lacy going to a party without him was unbearable.

He walked into his empty house and realised he didn't mind seeing Lacy with other men if he was there. 'Didn't mind' was a stretch. He didn't like those men touching Lacy, and yet watching how aroused he was made something in Thad crazy for him. But the thought of him doing something with another man if Thad wasn't there? It was intolerable. In fact, Thad was so hurt and angry at the thought of it, he had to grip the side table for a moment.

His mind forced him to contemplate the future that following his mother's expectations would lead to. One day, he'd have a wife. Kids. He'd be back in Tasmania. And in that picture, Lacy would be in Melbourne, having sex with nameless men without him. Worse, he might meet someone himself. Look at George and Finn? It wasn't impossible. Lacy could have a boyfriend if he wanted to.

He stumbled into his room, got to his knees and clasped his hands together and prayed. He prayed for forgiveness for wanting the man Lacy chose to be him. For not wanting a wife and kids and a plot of land outside Launceston, but a house with Lacy in Melbourne, a townhouse maybe, like the flashy places in Prahran, with a long pool built into the side like Cary's place. The place didn't matter much beyond what he knew Lacy would like. He'd like that. The clean lines, white walls adorned with his artwork, carefully selected antiques strategically placed in the minimalist space with indoor plants. Lacy was in every frame of the fantasy—laughing, kissing him good morning from between their white sheets, swimming naked in the pool, his ass white against the blue, slinking up the steps and straddling Thad where he watched from the lounger.

"Forgive me Father, for I have sinned," he whispered desperately, willing his erection to go down.

He had a horrible night, felt cranky when he picked Lacy up the next day, which for him meant subdued and struggling to meet Lacy's eyes.

Lacy watched him curiously during training, but looked away quickly whenever Thad caught him at it.

Thad sighed from where he was standing on the oval, waiting his turn to run a kicking drill.

"You all good?" Cary asked from behind him.

Thad glanced back at him. "Yes, sorry," he wasn't sure what he was apologising for.

Cary snorted though. Thad liked Cary, liked his wife too, their kids. The team BBQs at their house were a paragon of the settled footballer's life.

"Good work outta the centre the last few games," Cary said. "Lacy's got such a good head for the game, footballer's brain. It's good, keep it up."

Thad's heart fluttered, but he made his voice steady and deep as he replied. "He does. I'm very grateful."

"How come you missed drinks with George and Finn? Lacy was about as much fun as a funeral director without you there," Cary said.

Thad glanced over his shoulder. Cary was squinting against the sun, panting lightly from the workout, nothing but friendliness in the question.

"Oh, sorry, I was busy," he fumbled out.

Cary grabbed his shoulder and gave him a good shake. "Well, try not to make a habit of it, eh? Julie and I don't mind driving his sad ass home, but it's kinda depressing when he just stares out the window and doesn't speak. You're good for each other."

Thad turned to look at him.

"You're up," Cary smiled and nudged him forward.

Thad ran out and managed to mark the ball on his chest, run down the centre and kick through the middle, but his mind was stuck back there—Lacy didn't have a big night? He was unhappy? Thad was relieved the image of some guy having sex with Lacy that night hadn't occurred. But Lacy not the life of the party? Unheard of.

"So, I was thinking," Thad started as they walked to his car under the late afternoon sun.

Lacy nodded like he was listening, eyes on the ground.

"I was thinking, we should do something fun," he finished.

"Fun?" Lacy asked, glancing up at him. "Like, get shitfaced?"

Thad huffed a nervous laugh. "No, more like, go out fun. Luna Park maybe?"

"You wanna go on that death trap they call a roller coaster?" Lacy asked as he swung his bag on the backseat and hopped in the passenger's seat. "Have you looked at the poles on that thing? It's gonna collapse."

"I'd say the odds are in our favour that it won't while we're on it if it hasn't yet," Thad replied and started the car. "But something like that? If you want? I've never really done anything like that."

"Been on a roller coaster?" Lacy asked.

"No," Thad smiled at him. It was difficult to maintain the eye contact and yet he did it. "I meant more, done the stuff people come to Melbourne to do."

"If people are comin' to Melbourne to ride the world's smallest and shittiest roller coaster, I feel sorry for them. But," Lacy tapped his hand on the console, his smile more open than it had been in a while. "I take your essential point."

"My essential point?" Thad grinned at him.

"Yeah, you wanna do Melbourne fun shit," Lacy nodded to himself.

"Maybe on Friday night?" Thad asked. He felt like he was asking for a date.

"Friday night it is," Lacy replied. "Give me some time to plan."

Thad huffed a laugh. "Don't go to too much trouble."

Lacy looked like he was about to say something, swallowed it down and said, "I'll go to just the right amount."

"Good," Thad smiled as he focused on the road.

It was a date, he thought daringly.

Before Friday, he had another order of business to take care of. He rarely went up to the labyrinth of offices, spending most of his time below in the bowels of the facility, but a receptionist greeted him and directed him to the back of the open plan office space readily enough, telling him he'd find Chelsea from payroll and she could help him.

He didn't want to speak to Chelsea from payroll, but he spotted the bleached blonde head of Sandra pretty quickly and strolled over to her desk. She glanced up.

"Can I help you?" she asked.

"Have you got a moment? Sorry," he stuck out his hand, "I'm Thaddeus Clay, Lacy's friend."

She shook it. Her grip was tight, a deliberate crunch of his bones.

"I'm not sure I do have a *moment*." Her expression was derisive and suspicious. Thad supposed she was attractive in a quintessential way—big eyes, small nose, brightly painted lips—but she had the rough edges too, the shirt too tight, skirt too short, nails too long and painted black.

Thad realised the suspicion was for Lacy and tried a different tact.

He dropped his voice. "He's my best friend. I want to help him."

She let his hand go and sat back, crossing her arms over her chest. It drew the eye to the middle button about to pop around her cleavage. He averted his gaze back to her face. She was smirking like she was very used to men staring at her breasts.

"Meet me in the downstairs break room in twenty," she said.

"Not there," Thad rushed out. Lacy could wander in there. "Haven't you got a tea room up here?"

She scoffed. "No, we do not have a *tea room*," her sigh was long suffering. "There's an alcove with vending machines down thataway a bit, I'll be there in ten."

She sat up and refocused on her computer screen. Thad took the dismissal and went to see Chelsea in payroll so if anyone asked, not that anyone would, but if they did, she would confirm he was there to see her. She was a nice older woman, plump and efficient, but she seemed baffled when he asked if he needed to update his Tax File Number.

"Did you get a new one?" she asked like this was absurd because it was: you got one until you died.

"Oh, no," he replied. "I thought maybe it needed updating annually."

"The same number needs updating?"

He hadn't thought this through at all.

He forced a laugh. "Now I say it, it sounds stupid."

She smiled warmly at him—the dim athlete, good for looking at and playing sport and not much more—and he excused himself.

Sandra was waiting. As Thad explained what he wanted from her and why, her scowl turned down a notch and she dutifully took out her phone, added his number and said she'd text.

"Thank you," he said on a relieved breath. That was easier than he expected. "I didn't think you'd agree so, well, easily." He held his breath—he'd managed to do this painlessly and now he was going to mess it up.

She shrugged though, her face indifferent. "Colton said you were alright, said you were with Lacy."

Colton, the handsome friend from Frankston who smoked a lot of marijuana and sold masking agents. Thad had wondered at the time if Lacy and Colton had slept together, if they would've if he wasn't there. But other than that errant thought, he'd found him pleasing to be around, calming, beautiful in an androgynous way. He was nothing on Lacy, but Thad could see he was an appealing guy.

"Colton, yes, we visited."

"Duh, I know," she replied and walked off without saying goodbye.

"Where've you been?" Lacy asked when Thad came down the hallway. "Thought you'd left without me."

"Never," Thad replied, giddy with adrenaline after successfully completing his mission. "I had to see Chelsea from payroll."

"Is something wrong with your pay?" Lacy asked as he fell into step with him. "There shouldn't be, the contract gets paid as a fortnightly disbursement."

Thad shot him a smile at the formal language. "No, I thought I needed to update my tax file number." That sounded even worse the second time round.

"You thought you needed to update your tax file number?" Lacy asked incredulously. "That's it until you die."

Thad laughed. "I know."

Lacy bumped him and Thad bumped him back, his hands tucked in his pockets, smile sheepish as he looked down at him.

22

I T KILLED LACY, IT really did, when Thad looked at him like that. Head tilted down so his brown hair fell in his eyes, his smile shy yet cheeky, a boyish charm in that masculine face. It was a look Lacy felt was only ever pointed in his direction, which made it worse.

The last few weeks had been killing him. He'd decided after the Tassie trip to leave it alone. But the thought of Thad kissing him, touching him, fucking him, kept him up at night until he was jerking off desperately. So he'd decided to change course and leave the ball in Thad's court. If Thad was backing off because he was taking his mum's push to get married seriously—which led Lacy down a hole of depression so deep it affected his ability to drink, he got too morose—but if he was getting on that path, he wouldn't hook-up with Lacy anymore would he?

Lacy was willing and available if Thad did want that. But Thad had to make the first move.

Thad left after they shared dinner and Lacy leaned against his door, rubbed his dick over the material of his pants and pondered whether to jerk off here or in his bed.

Friday night rolled around and Lacy shaved, used his favourite cologne, dressed nicely and drove to Thad's with a nervous flutter in his stomach and chest.

Thad was also dressed nicely, smelled good, his face clean-shaven, hair artfully tousled, and his smile was shy when he got in the car.

"Hi," he said, his voice excited.

Lacy couldn't help his nervous snort. "Why're we so nervous?" he asked without thinking.

Thad chuckled breathlessly. "I don't know."

"So, where are we going?" Thad asked once Lacy got them onto Sydney Road.

"Luna Park," Lacy turned to look at him. Thad always drove, even though Lacy had this perfectly nice Audi SUV, and it was weird to turn his head to look at him and then remember he had to look back at the road. He'd gotten used to watching Thad unimpeded.

Thad looked surprised.

"I know, I know, it's cheesy as fuck," Lacy said and gunned it around a car that was going too slow, swung across an intersection and forgot to give way to the tram so he had to floor it. "But if you haven't been, you gotta go. Plus I made reservations for after. It's one of the best Italian restaurants in Melbourne apparently, so we can eat there and then I was thinking a walk?"

When he glanced over, Thad was holding the handle above his window, eyes darting from the road to Lacy.

"We can do something else if you want?" He'd looked up 'cool shit to do in Melbourne' and seen a footy game at the MCG was top of the list, but for obvious reasons that was out, as was the tennis, racing, and Grand Prix because it wasn't the season. Art galleries, theatre shows, stand-up all sounded dull as shit to him. And then he asked Cary where he'd take someone who was visiting Melbourne for a good night on the town, but Cary had blithely replied, "You're asking me that? You?" Cary was from Adelaide, had moved to Melbourne for high school and footy, which wasn't even the point—Lacy had mapped every inch of this city in his booze-fuelled benders, snorted coke in the classiest and shittiest bathrooms, fucked guys in them too, and in fancy hotel rooms overlooking the Yarra, thrown up drunk in the streets from St Kilda to Fitzroy and everywhere in between.

But none of that was Thad's scene. And while Thad happily followed him on those adventures, he wanted to do something Thad might like.

"No, I think that sounds amazing, it's just..."

Lacy looked at him. He was staring at the road, eyes darting to Lacy's when he realised he was looking at him.

"Have you ever driven before?" he asked.

"Yeah, course," Lacy replied and glanced back at the road. A white BMW SUV plodded along in front of them, traffic moving steadily by on his right. "How fuckin' slow can you go," he muttered and put his indicator on and moved into the oncoming traffic. A horn blared from behind him as he accelerated. "If you're that pissed about it, slam into me."

"I like driving," he said to Thad. "I just don't do it much anymore 'cos you drive me everywhere. But I used to drive before you came."

Thad nodded, shot Lacy a nervous smile, his hand gripping the hand rail.

"Luna Park and dinner and a walk sounds perfect," he said once they were stopped at a red light.

"Phew!" Lacy said. "I was about to do a uey at this light and take us somewhere else. There's some nice parks back thataway. And an old boat house."

"What would we do in a park at night?" Thad asked.

"Buy a six pack, sit on a bench, drink it," Lacy replied. The light turned green and he raced through the intersection, narrowly missing another tram.

"I think you're meant to give way to them, not get in front of them," Thad said with disbelieving laughter.

"Then they need to go faster."

Thad laughed again, relaxing a fraction, though he didn't let go of the hand rail.

Luna Park was cheesy as fuck, but as they meandered around, went on the roller coaster, Thad looked so charmed by it, Lacy thought maybe cheesy was alright. He got stopped for selfies and dragged Thad into them, took a selfie of his own with Thad's smiling face pressed against his, his cheek warm. Lacy pulled away quickly and asked if Thad minded if he posted it on his socials. Thad smiled when he said yes, and Lacy focused on his phone so he didn't lean up and kiss him. He didn't post much, but he liked to give the people something. It was a good photo too, he made it his screensaver before he pocketed his phone.

The restaurant was louder and busier than Lacy anticipated—he'd imagined low lighting and murmured conversation—but it was bustling, waitresses moving between the tables steadily, the other tables occupied with tourists in casual clothes. Lacy apologised to Thad, but Thad tilted his head to the side, a question in his eyes as he looked up from the menu.

"I thought it'd be, you know, classier," Lacy explained.

"It's really nice," Thad said.

Lacy glanced around at the black walls, the bartenders mixing drinks, the waitresses queued and waiting for them, the steady hum of people walking up and down the street outside, the whole place brightly lit and noisy.

Next time he'd ask Finn where George took him—Finn had said George took him to nice restaurants, did the whole gustation thing under dim lighting, spent time looking them up and making reservations.

"Next time," he said and he focused on the menu. "I'll find something better."

"This is really, really nice," Thad insisted and kicked his foot under the table.

He left it there and Lacy relaxed.

The food was incredible, so that must've been the reason it was so popular. After, as they strolled around St Kilda, down to the beach, shoulders bumping as they walked and talked about the game on Sunday, about Les' angst over finding his girlfriend the perfect birthday present, about Cary's renovation, Lacy thought it was one of the best nights he'd ever had. He'd had one vodka and soda water with dinner, so he was sober, and he was having fun. He didn't think that'd ever happened before—being out on the town, not getting shitfaced, and having one of the best nights of his life.

"Wanna come round?" he asked once they got back in the car.

"Definitely," Thad replied. "Thank you, that was incredible."

Lacy snorted. "Dunno about incredible. The restaurant coulda been nicer and Luna Park is hardly Disneyland."

"I've never wanted to go to Disneyland. Too many lines," Thad replied, smiling. "And that food was something else. The Italians must learn to cook from knee high, it's all so passed on, the food is so grounded."

Lacy thought the food wasn't as good as Thad's, but he didn't say that, just peppered him with questions about what the hell 'grounded' meant as he drove them back to his place.

They kicked their shoes off in Lacy's entryway. Lacy needed to offer Thad a drink—he had the juice he liked in the fridge—and he needed to ask him if he wanted to watch the replay of the game from that night, Adelaide versus Fremantle in Adelaide. He looked at Thad's socked feet, breathed in shakily and met his eyes.

Thad was already watching him back. His lips parted slightly but not like he was about to speak; he wet his lips and his eyes searched Lacy's nervously.

"Fuck this," Lacy leaned forward.

Thad reeled him in, kissed him and pushed him back against the wall. The kiss was aggressive, going from nothing to a hundred instantly.

Thad's hands unbuttoned Lacy's shirt quickly, his hands running over skin as soon as the material parted. Those big palms splayed on his rib cage, ran up and down his sides, over his chest, stroked his nipples.

Thad slid his hands out of his shirt, around the outside of Lacy's thighs and hauled him up, their lips parting.

"Fuck it's hot when you do that," Lacy breathed out.

Thad kissed him, held him against his chest as he went to carry him up the stairs. Lacy might've been smaller than Thad, but this was a disaster waiting to happen. He wriggled back until Thad let him slide down his body.

He met Thad's eyes as he took his hand and tugged him up the stairs. Thad crowded behind him, kissing his nape, running his hands under his shirt as they stumbled for Lacy's room.

They fell onto the bed in a tangle of limbs and Lacy laughed with a wheezing breath as Thad crushed him.

Thad pulled back. "Is this okay?"

"More than," Lacy replied and kissed him.

By the time they fumbled their clothes off and Thad was pushing inside, their foreheads resting together, everything had slowed down.

Thad fucked him with slow rolls of his hips. He cradled Lacy's face and swept his thumbs up and down his cheeks. His lips touched Lacy's lightly, his breath a puff of exhalation each time he rocked in.

Thad groaned as he started to come. Lacy gripped his ass possessively as he felt the muscles bunch and release while he emptied himself.

Lacy was desperate to come, but in the pause, he savoured Thad losing it.

Thad snapped into action, slid a hand between them and gripped Lacy's cock, stroked him off until Lacy was panting into his mouth with punched out sounds. He came with a groan, felt it spread over Thad's hand, their stomachs and chests.

They stayed tangled together, kissing slowly, and Lacy had never had sex quite like it—it felt like something that had been building was released and something else was settled on the other side of it.

It would be just over a year later when Lacy would think of this night again, think about the way they held each other, kissing slowly as they stroked each other's skin, their eyes meeting and holding. Lacy had thought everything that needed to be said was said with those looks. But he would think of this night in a year, the new beginning it had marked, and realise this was the moment they should have talked. And if they had, if they'd said what they both thought this meant, which wasn't the same, then the inevitable, terrible conclusion could've been avoided. Sure, they would've had to end it there and then. And Lacy wondered in those excruciatingly painful months that followed if he would've given up the blissful year they shared if he'd known that.

A part of him knew he wouldn't, even though it meant he'd been ruined forever. But like he said to Finn in those drunken calls, filled with bitter tears after it all went to shit, "All of this is just like, speculation though, isn't it?"

And Finn replied, "I'm sorry, Lace." Because what else was there to say?

23

THE MORNING AFTER THEIR trip to Luna Park, Thad knew Lacy was already awake because he could feel him shuffling around like he was thinking about getting up. Thad pulled him against his chest. Lacy huffed.

"Where are you going?" Thad asked sleepily.

"Was gonna make coffee," Lacy whispered back. He sounded nervous. It woke Thad right up—he wondered if he'd done something wrong.

"Are you..." he loosened his arms.

Lacy turned in his hold but stayed gratifyingly close. Thad ran his hand up his side, swept it back down again, met Lacy's eyes.

"Am I?" Lacy prompted, voice still quiet.

Thad let his hand rest on the swell of Lacy's ass cheek, danced his fingertips lightly along the skin.

"Alright?" Thad finished.

"Yeah, course." Lacy smiled, something almost shy in it; it was disarming. "Are you?"

"I'm great," Thad answered too quickly, too honestly. Because he was. He knew the shame would come later, but he'd gotten good at compartmentalising it, saving it for evening prayers, and he was too relieved, too grateful, too enamoured with having Lacy in his arms again to really care about all that just yet.

Lacy's smile widened. He dropped his head to Thad's chest. Thad's hand came up automatically to cup his skull and hold him close.

The season shifted from the beginning, which was always full of naïve hope and energy, to the long middle, which was marked by the reality of their capabilities and injuries. Cary was playing with a back injury and regular cortisol injections, Lesley had broken a finger, Les shook off a concussion, Thad twinged a muscle in his groin but could mostly ignore it, and to everyone else, Lacy seemed completely fine.

"He's like a machine," Cary told Thad. "He's never been injured, not a thing."

But Thad knew that wasn't entirely true. Lacy hadn't sustained anything career-threatening or anything that'd put him out of a game, but he did hide things. Not from the trainers behind closed doors; there he'd get a muscle in his back brutally worked for an hour, a pain in his shoulder shot up with cortisol, a pain in his wrist manipulated.

"Nothing major," he reassured Thad with a grin when they got home. They alternated between their houses, but Thad secretly preferred Lacy's place. For obvious reasons—it was modern, open and light, and imbued with Lacy's impeccable flair for design. Plus the bed was bigger and didn't groan like it was in pain when they had sex on it.

For less obvious reasons, the simple absence of reminders every-where. Thad didn't have to catch a glimpse of Jesus' face while Lacy fellated him in his entryway if they went to Lacy's place.

And they had sex every day. Most mornings. Sometimes in the middle of the day if they had the day off. At night when they got under the covers. It wasn't always penetrative sex either. Thad had discovered there was so much you could do to bring another person pleasure. Fellatio, certainly, but also hands, grinding, penetration with the tongue. He didn't think he loved anything as much as he loved watching Lacy panting, writhing, struggling to keep his eyes open as Thad licked at him, drove in with his tongue, his fingers clenching and releasing on Lacy's thighs as he held him open. Or the sight of him blinking water out of his eyes as Thad kneeled before him in the shower and worshipped his erection, sucked lovingly on the head, inhaled the musky scent of his groin as he sank down. And holding him. On the couch as the sun sank earlier and earlier as winter descended, his hand running up and down Lacy's chest after they'd wrung pleasure out of one another, the soft murmur of Lacy's voice commenting on the game they were watching as Thad pressed soft kisses behind his ear, down his throat. Absentminded kisses, natural kisses.

At Lacy's he said evening prayers in his head in the downstairs toilet before they went to sleep. Lacy knew he said prayers at his shrine at home and always left him to it. When he asked what he did when he was at Lacy's, Thad shrugged and mumbled about doing it before they went to bed. Lacy realised he was doing it in secret in the toilet and insisted he set-up a "shrine or whatever" in his spare room. Thad said it was no problem, but was touched when Lacy opened the door one night and waved a hand at the little table he'd set up—complete with a candle, Jesus on the cross, and a brand-new bible.

"You bought a bible?" he asked because he was too affected to say anything else.

"Yep, the lady gave me a weird look but I was like, 'Whatever, shouldn't you be not judging me right now?'" Lacy replied. He was blushing.

Thad laughed. He crushed Lacy in a hug because he didn't know what else to do with the giddy energy racing under his skin.

Lacy closed the door firmly on the room when they went back downstairs, which made Thad feel like Lacy wanted him to know it was his space and no one else was going in there. Thad was grateful for that closed door for more reasons than privacy; closing the door kept the reminders in there, made the compartment in his mind a tangible space he entered only when he needed to.

They clinched their spot in the finals a few weeks before the season was over and while everyone was jubilant in the locker room, it was marred by the knowledge they couldn't win it. Depending on how the bottom of the eight panned out in the final games, they'd be facing Adelaide or Fremantle. They could beat Fremantle, the absence of Hiller after his offseason accident and the poor season Reaver was having meant anyone could. It was a miracle they'd managed to stay on top of the table for most of the season. But they'd never beaten Adelaide and probably wouldn't. They'd become their hoodoo team and no one could see a path through them—even with Alanson berating them on how to get it done, to which Lacy always muttered, "Maybe he should jump on the field and see how he goes with that plan."

But finals footy was finals footy and they were going out to celebrate.

They'd gone out during the season, though not to another party. Thad was surprised that didn't bring him any relief. He wasn't sure if there'd been an invite and Lacy decided not to go, or if there hadn't been one. He couldn't bring himself to ask. But they still went out and Lacy drank too much and did coke in the bathrooms and Thad carried him home where they had frantic sex until Lacy passed out. Thad wasn't sure which he preferred more—Lacy sober and focused, occasionally shy, or out of it and completely abandoning himself to Thad's touch. He was certainly chattier when he was wasted. Thad lived for all the words he'd say—"God, you're hot," "More, give me more, Thaddeus, please," and, "God, I love you, I love you, I love you," as Thad pounded into him, driving him to orgasm.

It was drunk talk and Thad couldn't even be mad at how much he took the Lord's name in vain when his heart sang at the drunken declarations. But that's all it was, drunken ramblings. He'd once seen Lacy at a bar in Northcote get into a heated drunken argument with some 'fuckin' hippies.' They didn't look like hippies to Thad—they were dressed in oversized shirts, the girls in short skirts, the guys in torn jeans, some of them in those horn-rimmed glasses, the girl's hair long under their arms and on the legs. He and Lacy had been drinking at the bar and watching a game after checking out all the thrift shops from Fitzroy to Northcote for a 'piece' Lacy wanted to put in his bathroom. He hadn't found it and was telling Thad, while they sat at the bar and Thad sipped his orange juice and Lacy downed his fourth vodka and soda water, that they really needed to take that trip up to the Blue Mountains.

Someone in the other group recognised them, but politely pretended not to. Thad appreciated it, but as the afternoon wore on, one of the guys came over, drunk, and began by stating who they were, cackling like he'd come up on a dare. He leaned too close to Lacy and started drunkenly lecturing them on how just because the league had some out players, it didn't mean it wasn't homophobic. Thad saw Lacy tense, but he nodded, interjected a few remarks like, "Yeah, it's gettin' there," and "Give it another ten years."

He'd ordered another drink, agitated, when one of the girls came up and joined the conversation. She told him it was players like him, with their "insufferable hyper-masculinity" that made it unsafe.

"I mean, imagine if a trans player wanted to play?" she said, her friend nodding enthusiastically. "The league won't even comment on where they stand on it."

Lacy drained his drink, held it up for the bartender before spinning to face her. "Whaddya think the fucking WAFL is for?"

He proceeded to go on a tirade about the women's league, which was for *women*, and if some woman who wanted to be a dude wanted to try out for the men's league, "She was fucking welcome to try but there's just no way she's gettin' a fuckin' game."

It spiralled out of control when the girl told Lacy he couldn't call 'him' a 'she' and Lacy looked bewildered for a moment before he went on another tirade about who has a dick? Who has a pussy?

"Come on," Thad had said and stood. He stepped to Lacy's side, hand at his elbow. "We got to get to that dinner, remember?"

Lacy looked up at him blearily.

"The sponsor dinner, remember?" he looked at the group, who'd all come over to join the conversation. "Nice to meet you," he said in a tone that conveyed it really wasn't.

Lacy stood, shouted a few insults as they left and then asked Thad what dinner did they have to go to?

"Oh, none, I just thought it was time to leave," Thad replied as he pulled the keys out and unlocked the car. "They weren't very nice."

"Fuckin' hippies."

The next morning, Thad had told Lacy he wasn't aware he was so passionate about the transgender issue.

Lacy raised both eyebrows. "I'm not."

"But last night..."

Lacy grinned, quick and sharp. "Just drunk talk, wanted to rile them up," he shrugged. "I could give a shit who plays if they can play. And I'll be respectin' whatever someone wants to be called. You know how I run my mouth when I'm pissed. Could be sayin' anything."

Thad smiled weakly. Drunk talk, of course. Like the stuff he said when they were in bed. A good development, Thad reassured himself because he'd felt worse praying for forgiveness after Lacy had said he loved him. But if it wasn't real, it was fine.

"Some of the guys are gonna meet us there," Lacy said. He was dressed and ready to meet the team at a bar with a private room booked in Prahran, busy texting on his phone. It pinged in his hand. He snorted. "Or probably the casino after," he glanced up.

Thad was looking at himself from side to side in the bathroom mirror, doing the final check. Lacy leaned in the doorway behind him. He met Lacy's eyes. Lacy's grin shifted to something softer.

"You look great, ya know that, right?" he said.

Thad ducked his head and smiled. "Thanks. You too."

He turned. "Your friends from back home?" he asked to change the subject.

"Yeah, but they'll meet us after," Lacy stepped back as Thad stepped by him, his hand stroking Lacy's waist as he passed and they moved downstairs together. "'Fuck Prahran' was the direct quote."

Lacy laughed and Thad joined him. He wouldn't admit it, but he wasn't a big fan of the venue either. They'd been there before for team functions and it was always full of men who seemed overdressed even though they were wearing pants and button-ups, same as Thad, but they wore it in a way that seemed shinier, excessive. And the women were rail thin with big hair, their large breasts swelling beneath bony chests, and they talked about their kids and their latest ventures selling candles or lifestyle plans and how "leveraging their social presence meant even if the venture failed, they'd make it up in endorsements." Thad had no idea what they meant, and he didn't like standing too close to them because they smelled like too much—their deodorant and perfume. Combined with the darkness of the room under strategically placed lightbulbs, the cacophony of voices, the clink of glasses and bottles against the backdrop of music that had no end, just a single beat—Thad wanted to leave as soon as he arrived.

But he smiled and didn't tell Lacy any of that. Lacy, who seemed as effortless there as he did at a dive bar in the Western suburbs.

"You cool to meet up with them after?" Lacy asked as they headed for Thad's car.

"Of course," Thad smiled. "They're good guys."

"I wouldn't go that far," Lacy grinned. "Bunch of shit-cunts, but ya know, ya can't choose your family."

Thankfully, Lacy's phone was blowing up in his pocket all night and they got to leave after a couple of hours.

His friends were at a bar in the casino and there were hugs, back slaps, a lot of in-jokes and insults passed around as Lacy and Thad settled into the group. Lacy always included Thad in every conversation, drunkenly explaining who each person was as the stories flowed, and Thad relaxed.

It was getting near the time where Thad would ask Lacy if he was ready to go when Tommy, Lacy's 'mate from school' leaned in. They were all 'mates from school' but what distinguished Tommy was a closeness. Thad couldn't put his finger on what it was, but there was something in the way Tommy studied Lacy a moment longer whenever they met up, the way he paid attention to Lacy's answers, the easy way they hugged hello and goodbye where the others did complicated handshakes or focused on the back slap.

"You didn't come," Tommy addressed Lacy.

Lacy tensed. "Yeah, had some shit on, ya know."

"You didn't come last year either," Tommy went on. He was drunk, they all were, his voice loose with the booze. "You gotta turn up. It ain't right when you don't."

"Yeah, I know," Lacy looked down at his drink. "But I had some shit on, so."

"Shit more important than that? You didn't have a game and it was a Sunday," Tommy replied sarcastically.

Thad had no idea what they were talking about, but Lacy hunched in on himself; he seemed smaller. Lacy was a small guy, but he was always the largest presence in any room. Thad had never seen him so minimised.

"I think it's time we headed out," Thad said, bumping Lacy gently.

Lacy reanimated, picked up his drink, drained it and stood. There was a chorus of boos from his other friends but as he went to shuffle out of the booth, Tommy grabbed his wrist.

"You'll be there next year?" Tommy said. It didn't sound like a question.

"Yep," Lacy replied shortly, eyes on the table.

"Good," Tommy let him go.

Lacy was subdued the whole ride home and Thad didn't know what to say about it, so he talked about some couple at the first party telling him about their business. They were importing coffee beans from somewhere in South America and selling 'authentic coffee from the Aztecs.' And they'd told him about their 'platform' and the importance of preserving cultures by preserving their heritage through their authentic products.

"But I kept thinking," Thad told Lacy as they wound into Fitzroy, "aren't they just selling coffee? Can't we already get coffee?"

Lacy laughed, his head turning on the seat to look up at Thad. "Fuckin' authentic coffee beans. What're the other ones then?"

"That's what I thought!" Thad grinned over at him, relieved to see Lacy smiling. He looked tired, washed out; Thad knew he was getting worked over more by the physios for the pain in his shoulder, and he was going harder than usual in training for finals, but that wasn't it. There was always a light in Lacy's eyes, but now it was dimmed.

Thad wasn't a violent man, not even close, but in that moment, he had a vicious urge to go and shove Tommy, tell him not to ask Lacy vague questions that made him feel bad.

It was in the second last game of the regular season when Thad had another violent impulse. This time to shove Lacy against a wall. And not in a sexy way. The game was pointless—they were in the finals and Gold Coast weren't. This was Thad's old team and while he was friendly enough with the guys, he wasn't close to anyone. He was playing on Carter, the ruckman they'd traded in when he was traded out, but it was Jacobson who was all over him from the first bounce. Shoving him, trash talking against his ear whenever he got close enough to do so—nothing Thad hadn't heard before and found himself even more impervious to since he'd been hanging out with Lacy.

The homophobic insults were a little harder to bear since he was now, well, engaged in a sexual relationship with a man, but he could compartmentalise that too. He was getting very good at it.

The siren was about to sound at the end of the third. He was jogging back to the centre after Lacy had kicked a goal, Lacy beside him as they smiled at each other. Jacobson ran alongside him.

"Ya still praying after every game?" Jacobson asked loudly.

Thad ignored him, but he felt Lacy zone in on him.

"Still fuckin' deluded, eh?" Jacobson gave him a hard knock on the shoulder. Thad felt slightly winded, but he was used to it. "Ya reckon God's gonna forgive you for bein' a cocksucking fag?"

Thad continued to ignore him—he'd been listening to it all game and he knew where Jacobson was drawing his ammunition. Back when he'd played on the same team, he'd seen Jacobson watching him when Thad zoned out on a naked teammate in the locker room for too long; Thad had blushed, dropped his eyes, and Jacobson had given him a look Thad had never understood. He'd just been appreciating their form, but in the looks Jacobson gave him he felt like he'd been doing something wrong.

So, the insults weren't a surprise.

Lacy should've dropped back by now, but he hadn't. He was looking over at Jacobson with uncharacteristic seriousness.

"Two minutes," Thad said to Lacy.

"Tell me, Clay," Jacobson said, "how many cocks ya reckon ya gotta suck before they won't let you into heaven?"

It happened so fast, Thad had to replay it in his mind afterwards to be sure it'd happened. Lacy flew at him and cracked his skull against Jacobson's. Jacobson's head snapped back. Lacy lunged for him, but Thad grabbed him around the waist and hauled him back as a whistle blew and referees and other players were flying at them.

"What are you doing?" Thad asked hysterically because all he could think was what this meant.

And what it meant played out in the tribunal that Monday. Suspended. He'd been the Brownlow favourite and now he was out of contention.

24

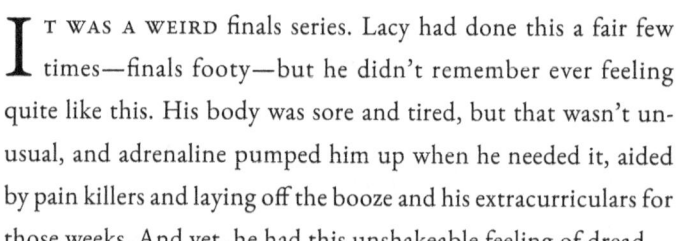

I T WAS A WEIRD finals series. Lacy had done this a fair few times—finals footy—but he didn't remember ever feeling quite like this. His body was sore and tired, but that wasn't unusual, and adrenaline pumped him up when he needed it, aided by pain killers and laying off the booze and his extracurriculars for those weeks. And yet, he had this unshakeable feeling of dread.

He'd messaged Sandra to see what was happening on that front. Maybe that was his problem. She'd told him all was quiet on the Western Front and he'd laughed (they'd been made to read it at school, so Lacy downloaded the film and kept falling asleep; but his mates had managed to watch it so he used their notes to write the essay on it). When he saw her later, she said she'd heard from Alanson's assistant that he wanted to do some drug tests before finals, beyond the mandated WADA ones, but Kurt and Todd had shot him down, calling it a "pointless witch hunt." The WADA ones were standard and he was already prepared for them.

He was less prepared for Thad pressing a cup of warm urine into his hand near their lockers before the collection.

Lacy was surprised, but he shouldn't have been. Thad wouldn't meet his eyes, busying himself with another specimen jar and handing it over with a polite smile when it was their turn.

"You shouldn't have done that," he murmured at Thad once the woman had left.

Thad shrugged, eyes on tidying his pristine locker. He wasn't unaffected by the criminal behaviour he was engaging in—his hands were shaking—but when he finally met Lacy's gaze, his brown eyes were unflinching. He didn't say anything, but then, he didn't need to.

So, it wasn't that behind the feeling of impending disaster either. And it wasn't the games. They beat Fremantle in Perth pretty easily, the flight home jubilant with a naïve hope they could take Adelaide. Maybe go all the way. Win the flag. Lacy knew it was a pipe dream, but for that week of training, he indulged in the fantasy too. You had to at this level, had to believe the impossible was possible or you wouldn't be at this level.

Of course Adelaide tore through them and they were done.

On the Monday night before the Grand Final, dressed in a colourful, vintage Jean Paul Gaultier suit, he sat with his 'date'—the girlfriend of his mate from back home, Jordie, who'd 'always wanted to go to the Brownlow's'—Thad on his other side with his date—Carol from his church, who looked stunning in a white gown and whose presence had pissed Lacy off before he'd even seen her, even though Thad said she's 'just a friend.' Lacy wondered if this was the cause of his uneasiness. As the count went on and it was clear he'd win it based on numbers but couldn't win it because of the suspension, he wondered if this is what he'd been dreading.

But as Riley from Adelaide won it and Lacy clapped, he realised he didn't care. Thad had been angry with him, but Lacy would do it again in a heartbeat. Thad took that shit seriously and it wasn't right to bring it onto the footy field. Turned out, some things were actually sacred.

They were provided good seats and access to a box for the Grand Final, the usual invite arriving as an emailed ticket with the standard spiel about the dress code—suits—and behaviour—don't get shitfaced being the gist of it.

Thad had a flight booked for the Monday after—he was heading to the Philippines to work in an orphanage—and Lacy had a flight to Rome the next day—he was checking out a bath house. He'd head to Spain after to continue his sex tour of Europe. Spain had a great scene, and he remembered his excitement from years ago when he'd heard about it. He didn't feel excited now. He felt that dread.

He looked up at Thad coming down his hallway, dressed in his suit, hair falling in his eyes, smile soft, and the dread intensified into an ache. He leaned in once Thad was right in front of him and Thad met him, natural as breathing. Lacy pressed him back against the wall, his kisses turning rough and Thad hauled him in, those big palms splayed on his ass.

They didn't make it to the Grand Final.

When they resurfaced on the Monday morning, the dread returned. Lacy finally got it as he watched Thad run a hand through his hair and he tried to smile.

"I better go," he said.

"Yep," Lacy replied. "You got everything?"

"I think so," Thad patted his pockets aimlessly. His suitcase was sitting at the door, his carry-on backpack on top of it.

"Don't wanna miss your flight," Lacy murmured.

"No," Thad said and didn't move. "You'll text every day?" he asked, a fragile note in his voice.

"Every day," Lacy agreed.

"And you'll be careful?" Thad asked—his face was serious and he always looked so mature when he was serious, but his eyes betrayed his trepidation.

"I'm always careful," Lacy quipped, but it came out faint.

He was about to tell Thad they better get going when Thad grabbed him, hugged him like they were both going off to war. Lacy sagged into it.

"I'm going to miss you," Thad whispered against the top of his head.

"Me too."

But as much as Lacy wanted to stay that way forever, they couldn't.

The drive to the airport was punctuated with strained small talk, the unnameable dread morphing into longing.

He pulled over at the drop off lane because Thad had insisted he just drop him off, the church group would meet him, and Lacy saw the back of Carol rolling her case behind her as she went into the departure terminal. He clenched his jaw.

"Thanks for the lift," Thad said.

Lacy looked over at him. He lunged without thinking and kissed him hard and fast. The miracle was, Thad kissed him back like he didn't care either.

"Okay," Lacy said as he pulled himself back just as quickly. "Text me when you get there."

"I will," Thad replied, breathless. He opened his door and Lacy heard his shoes hitting the asphalt.

"Bye, Lacy," he said.

"Later, Thaddeus," Lacy replied, eyes fixed on the windshield. He couldn't look at him again, he was worried if he did, he'd yank him back into the car, climb into his lap and fuck him right there where other people from the church group were probably milling around.

The door clicked shut softly as Thad got out, removed his bags from the back, the hatch closing just as gently.

Lacy glanced at the sidewalk. Thad lifted his hand and waved. Lacy waved back and then got the hell out of there.

25

THE PHILIPPINES WERE HUMID. The church group was a hive of activity that arrived in a village three hours outside of Manila to the startled eyes of the children. Surprise quickly turned to glee when the toys and candy came out and it became clear they weren't leaving. Thad knew he should be enjoying the work—the men were helping to build an expansion, while the women were helping in the school. He knew he should feel good about finally doing service after a year of pursuing his own glory in the league.

"Are you okay, Thaddeus?" Carol asked a few days into the trip. They were sitting in the dining area—an open space with a thatched roof. The jungle murmured around them, the kids chattered and squealed in the courtyard. He met her eyes.

"Great, thank you."

She glanced down at his phone. He'd been rolling it in his hands.

"You seem," she tilted her head to the side, her smile warm, "distracted?"

"I'm all here," he returned the smile.

He wasn't. Since he'd gotten Lacy's text, affirming he'd arrived in Rome in one piece, he'd been beside himself wondering who Lacy was with. He was accosted with images of Lacy fellating other men,

Lacy being penetrated by other men. Worst of all, Lacy kissing other men. He was blinded by jealousy and worry. An ache that left him so distracted he could barely function. Lacy didn't know those men, he never knew the men, and he drank too much, took too many drugs. Something could happen and Thad wouldn't be there to stop it. He was barely passing as normal with how much it was consuming him, and he was surprised it'd taken Carol three days to ask how he was doing.

"Well, I'm here if you ever want to talk," Carol said smoothly. She reached over and touched his hand. "I know it's difficult for you, making the adjustment from the football world back to ours."

He wanted her hand off him but didn't know how to remove it without looking crazy.

"It is," he agreed, but of course it wasn't that. He was fine blending service and football.

He slid his hand back and stood. "I better check Matthew isn't making a mess of the cabinets."

She smiled up at him, her long chestnut hair catching the sun, her brown eyes and porcelain skin vibrant against the vivid greens and shimmering humidity. He felt nothing for her beyond friendship.

Matthew was making a mess of the cabinets and Thad was glad for the distraction. He huffed, amused, at the incorrect measurements.

"Here, let me," he said and bumped Matthew aside.

Matthew watched, murmuring about how he wondered why they weren't fitting, and Thad focused on explaining the job.

He tried, surreptitiously, to ask Lacy about it when they messaged, to see something in his face when they spoke over video call. But Lacy sent vague answers about churches and the Colosseum, looked away, shrugged and changed the subject. If Thad wasn't so consumed with roaring concern, he might've thought about how withdrawn Lacy seemed. As it was, he noticed, but put it down to Lacy not wanting to share what he was doing with Thad. And that made it so much worse.

A week into this pattern, Thad woke up gasping. He was covered in sweat, the sheet twisted around him, his erection throbbing against his stomach. He'd been dreaming of Lacy. He had a man above him, the man's hands in his hair and he was plunging into Lacy's mouth, stretching those plump lips taut around his thick length. He was going too fast, uncaring of the tears streaming down Lacy's face. Lacy was looking up at him, his whiskey eyes beseeching, his moaning like a cry. There was another man behind him, inside him. His bare penis violently assaulted Lacy's entrance, his hand slapped the spread cheeks, leaving painful red imprints, a smacking sound drowning out Lacy's noises.

He'd woken when he saw himself enter the dream. He slid his hand over Lacy's back, curled his palm under his chest. He stroked him gently while whispering in his ear. Lacy tried to say something.

He got himself out of the sheet and stumbled to his feet. He adjusted himself in his jocks and reached for his pants. His body was wet with the sweat and his hand slipped on his phone as he grabbed for it and yanked it out of the charger. Hopping around the room, he got his

pants on one handed, tripped as he got his feet moving to get outside
and away from Matthew sleeping soundly in the other bed.

The moon lit up the courtyard in a blue hue and the jungle was
loud around him—insects, a constant rustling, the rush of a stream.
He made his way to the path between the dining area and the church
and followed it to the stream. There was a terrible pain building in his
chest. Lacy had taken care of himself for almost thirty years, at least ten
of those living this lifestyle. Thad's worry was overblown, ludicrous.

He sat by the stream and opened the messages anyway.

What're you doing? He typed with shaking fingers and hit send.

Lookin at a big ass church, came the swift reply.

Maybe it was because he was still addled by sleep, maybe it was
because he couldn't take much more of this, he replied: *Seriously.
What are you doing? You can tell me.*

A photo came back. Thad recognised it—it was the Vatican from
the front, the sky streaked pink behind the statues of the apostles.
The setting sun cast them in a glow, made more dramatic by the lights
underneath them, shining against the darkening sky.

I'm seriously looking at a giant fucking church.

Thad rubbed his face and made himself type. *What are you doing
later?*

Dunno. Probably eat something. Drink too much. A laughing emoji.

Before Thad could reply another message popped up.

Shouldn't you be asleep?

Bad dream. Thad replied.

His phone rang in his hand for a video call. Thad startled but hit
answer.

"Hey," Lacy said. He was walking, the phone cradled in his hand
so Thad had a view of him from below—the sharp cut of his jaw, his
lips half-smiling, his eyes darting from the screen to the street to see

where he was going. "You alright? What'd you dream about? Let me find somewhere to sit."

Thad gripped his phone and drank Lacy in. It was stupid to be so relieved—they'd spoken like this every second day in the past week—but he was. Lacy looked good. He took a seat in a wicker chair, the red canopy above him giving the atmosphere a red glow, and his smile was warm as he said, "Peroni, grazie," in a thick Australian accent. He refocused on Thad, the smile turning concerned. Thad roved his eyes over every part of him to make sure he was okay.

"Alright, whaddid ya dream about? Fuck, it's dark there. Where are you?" Lacy asked.

Thad laughed, he didn't know why. "I'm down by the stream. Everyone's asleep."

"Yeah, 'cos it's like midnight over there," he glanced up at the waiter and thanked him as his beer was placed in front of him. His face looked sharper against the black collar of his jacket. It'd be late autumn over there, right on the cusp of winter, the nights presumably cool.

"What'd you dream about?" he asked again and sipped his beer.

"Nothing, it was stupid," Thad dismissed. "You seem to be seeing a lot of churches?"

Lacy rambled about how every step you took there was another church—"You'd love it," he grinned, but it was tinged with sadness and all Thad could say was, "But I'm not Catholic."

"Hmm," Lacy replied and looked away. "You can tell me about your dream, ya know? I won't laugh."

Thad blushed and rubbed the back of his neck. Lacy wasn't looking at him and that made it easier.

"I thought someone was hurting you," he murmured.

"Me? Who the fuck would hurt me?" Lacy asked.

Thad smiled weakly. "It was stupid," he shook his head. "What're you doing later?"

"Well," Lacy replied and stretched. Another beer appeared in front of him. He met Thad's eyes. "I reckon this is a nice establishment, so I'm gonna eat, probably drink more, then watch soccer in my room until I pass out."

Thad tried to smile. He wished Lacy would just tell him. He knew it'd take his concern to another level, but he'd rather know than not know. He knew what Lacy did on these trips.

"You said soccer was boring," Thad said.

"I said soccer is boring as fuck," Lacy winked. "But it's growin' on me. Reckon I've watched like, ten matches since I been here. It's on everywhere."

They talked for a while longer about soccer, about the teams Lacy was getting invested in—"You'd think Real Madrid, right? But I'm lovin' Juventus,"—and Thad sat on the compact dirt, his phone gripped in his hands, elbows resting on his propped-up knees.

"You should get some sleep," Lacy said after an hour. He'd eaten some pizza and drank another beer while talking, his phone leaning against something on the table. "Don't you have like, a hundred kids to take care of or something?"

Thad laughed. "I'm mainly building the school." He didn't want to hang up, but Lacy had a point; he'd be exhausted tomorrow, today, if he didn't sleep. "You sure you're okay?" He asked, his voice more worried than he meant it to be.

"Thad, man, I'm legit fine. It was just a dream," Lacy replied seriously though.

"Good, I know, but," he blew out a breath. "Good."

"Go on, go back to bed," Lacy said, eyes shifting away, flashing with sadness before he shook it off like it'd never been there. "When you get up, you're gonna have a bunch of texts about the game, okay?"

"Can't wait," Thad replied.

"Well, don't get too excited. It's still boring as fuck, but ya know," he huffed a laugh, "it passes the time."

Thad managed to hang up shortly after, their goodbyes lingering in the noise of the jungle around him. Lacy was okay. Lacy was going back to his room to watch soccer. But what about after? And what about the next night? And the next? And the rest of the month?

Thad wasn't sure he could take much more of this.

26

L ACY WASN'T SURE HOW much more of this he could take.
He was lying on his hotel bed, his hand cradling his semi,
the soccer on the screen—Real Madrid versus Las Palmas—the
afternoon shifting to night outside his window, the soft sound of
nightlife gearing up from the street below. It was off peak season,
and on just the right side of busy.

He'd come here to check out the bath house. He'd been wanting to check it out for years—the pictures looked incredible. The
actual bath flowing between columns, the neon lights casting the
place in a glow, a basement with the promise of rooms off to the
side, the nameless, faceless men he'd imagined fucking him until
he could barely stumble back to his hotel room.

But he'd stood out the front on his second night after he'd
slept off the jet lag and couldn't go inside. He'd been frustrated
with himself. He always did this. Got the hell out of Melbourne
and fucked his way across Europe. What the fuck was wrong with
him? Just go through the fucking door, do some coke, take a pill,
get lost in it.

He couldn't do it. It felt wrong. And then it dawned on him;
it felt like *cheating*.

He was frozen on the sidewalk like one of those statues that were all over the place when it hit him. He'd have laughed if it didn't feel so real. But it was real. If he went in there and let some other guy fuck him when Thad wasn't there, it'd be cheating. Him and Thad weren't official, and Thad never said he couldn't do something. But Thad knew damn well what he was coming here to do.

Why hadn't Thad said anything? Did he not care?

He watched some guys around his age going through the door, their faces briefly illuminated by the red glow above the door. They were handsome, slim. They were probably about to get fucked by some burly guy who could really hold them down. Like Lacy was supposed to be doing.

He left and found a bar and watched Bayan Munich beat Barcelona, these conflicted feelings racing around under his skin.

The only thing he was really enjoying, he'd realised a few days into the trip, were Thad's messages and calls. Thad seemed to like the photos of the churches, so Lacy made a concerted effort to visit every church he could. That'd certainly keep him busy.

Now he was lying on his bed, barely able to get himself hard. He wanted to go home. But Thad wouldn't be there either. He cringed when he thought of the messages he'd sent two days ago, *I miss you, I wish you were here*. He'd been drunk. He shouldn't have said it. Thad had replied, *I miss you too, I wish I was there too*.

He groaned and rolled over, rubbed his dick against the mattress to try and get off that way. Anything to get out of his fucking head. He thought about Thad inside him, his big hands cradling Lacy's head, his eyes watching Lacy's face so carefully, studying him between gentle kisses, his hips smacking against Lacy's groin as he fucked him so good.

He was hardening up now—

There was a soft knock on his door.

Lacy rolled onto his back, startled. He hadn't ordered room service. He scrambled to his feet, rearranged his dick so it was less obvious and opened the door.

Thad was standing there, head ducked, his case and carry-on back-pack beside him.

"Hi," Thad said, his smile unsure.

"Thad," Lacy breathed out. He was so shocked, he thought he must be drunk.

But no, Thad was very real in front of him. His clothes rumpled like he'd been sleeping in them, his smile slipping further into uncertainty.

"You wished I was here," he said like he'd been repeating the line.

Lacy threw himself at him and Thad caught him, crushed him against his chest, his arms squeezing him so tight Lacy felt the air wheeze out of him.

"What? How? You're here," Lacy said against his throat.

He pulled back. Thad was smiling down at him. "Can I come in?" he asked.

Lacy laughed, grabbed his hand, his case with the other hand and dragged him into his room.

The door hadn't even clicked shut when Thad's hands were under his shirt, on his hips, spinning him and claiming his mouth. Lacy kissed back like they were being reunited after the war. Thad lifted him and walked them to the bed, knee-walking onto the mattress with Lacy in his arms.

Thad's hands slid under his shirt and pushed it up, followed the path with his lips. Open-mouthed kisses, biting kisses, sucking on his skin like he was reclaiming every inch of him.

Lacy urged his head back up to kiss him more, rocked his dick against the hardness he could feel in Thad's pants. He got his hands between them and undid Thad's fly, slipped his hand inside and gripped him. Thad bucked into the touch with a wounded sound, wriggled around trying to get his pants off. He got them bunched around his thighs, his hands refusing to do more before they had to be back on Lacy's skin, shoving his tracksuit pants down and off one leg.

Lacy scrabbled for the lube on his bedside table. Thad reached up and grabbed it. He got two wet fingers inside, stretched him, wiped the excess on Lacy's inner thigh. His mouth was on Lacy's as he pushed inside.

It was frantic and over quickly, Thad groaning into Lacy's mouth as he came before he jerked Lacy off expertly, drawing his orgasm out as he kissed Lacy's throat, behind his ear.

They lay tangled together afterwards, Thad softening inside him, his kisses never stopping, his hands never ceasing in their caresses.

"Fuck," Lacy breathed out. "It's so fucking good to see you, ya got no idea, eh."

Thad huffed a nervous a laugh against his throat. "That's good, I wasn't sure..." he murmured.

Lacy gripped him by the hair and tugged. Thad lifted his head and rested it against his sternum. Thad's eyes were a beautiful brown, rich and deep and they always looked warm, and they always watched Lacy carefully. Lacy peered into them now, the sated look and the uncertainty looked back at him.

"I'm so fuckin' glad you're here," he said again.

Thad leaned up and kissed him.

Rome finally came alive for him. With Thad by his side, they explored the churches, saw the Trevi Fountain, climbed ancient stairs to the gardens high above the city, meandered around the Colosseum, watched soccer matches in an open-air bar and cheered with the locals. Walked the night streets, the excavations of the old city lit up against the black sky dotted above them. And they went back to Lacy's room after lunch and kissed and sucked and fucked until they fell, tangled together, into an afternoon sleep. They went out for dinner before returning to the room and fucking until they couldn't keep their eyes open.

"So," Thad said, an apprehensive edge to his voice. It'd been a week and Thad had waved away his concerned question about Thad leaving his work in the Philippines and Lacy hadn't pried. Now it sounded like Thad had something to say and Lacy didn't know why that was making him nervous.

"So?" he prompted. He finished buttoning his shirt. They were going to dinner at a restaurant Thad had looked up and gotten excited over.

"How was the bath house?" Thad asked, his eyes on his own shirt. He sounded like a reporter asking a question they'd been told by their editor they had to ask but really didn't want to.

"Yeah, didn't go in," Lacy replied dismissively.

Thad lifted his gaze, his face breaking free of the pinched look. "You didn't?"

Lacy shrugged. He was embarrassed and he didn't know why. "Wasn't feeling it."

Thad moved in front of him. "So, you didn't..."

Lacy looked up. "I didn't go in, no."

"No, but," Thad was looking at him so expectantly, so hopefully, Lacy finally realised what he was asking.

"Nah," he tried to sound cool about it, "wasn't feelin' it without you there."

Thad crushed him in a hug. "That's good," he said. "That's really good."

Lacy laughed and hugged him back. Thad rubbed his back, pressed his face into the crook of Lacy's neck. "You still want to go?" he whispered against his skin. Lacy could feel him stiffening in his pants.

"Yeah," Lacy breathed out.

Thad tightened his arms, mouthed at his skin. He didn't say anything, but then, he didn't need to.

It was different, standing across the street with Thad beside him. He could tell Thad was nervous, but he was putting a confident face on it, meeting Lacy's eyes and smiling reassuringly.

Lacy laughed, giddy, took Thad's hand and dragged him across the street, through the door and into the bath house.

The sound of Thad's phone blaring woke them far too early the next morning.

"Ugh," Lacy groaned. "Who the fuck is calling at this hour?"

Thad pressed a kiss to his shoulder. "Pretty sure it's after lunch," he murmured before rolling over to get it.

Lacy felt the energy shift as Thad scrambled off the bed. He rolled over and watched through slitted eyes as Thad reached for his pants, got them on quickly, took a deep breath, reached for the still blaring phone with wide eyes. Lacy sat up.

"Hello," Thad said and turned to face the window. "I'm fine, sorry, I should've called."

Thad was silent, his hand on his hip, other hand gripping the phone tightly. "No, no everything's fine. A friend needed me, so I had to go. Everyone understood—"

Lacy could make out the tinny voice of a woman on the other end of the line and realised it was Thad's mum.

"Matthew had it covered," Thad said guiltily. Lacy drew his knees up to his chest, the white sheet stretching like a canopy over his legs and waist.

"Alright," Thad said after a while of nothing but the voice. "I promise. I'm sorry." He sounded defeated. "How's Dad?" He lifted his head and gazed out the window.

The call wound up and Thad dropped the phone to his thigh, sighing.

"She didn't want you to come?" Lacy asked.

Thad turned slowly to face him. "It's not that," he replied, "it's—" he stopped abruptly and shrugged, all the joy and heat from the night before gone from him. He looked at his feet. "I shouldn't be here."

Lacy had to calm his hurt; a hurt that felt like sharp anger.

"It's not like I forced you to come," he said and it wasn't what he wanted to say and he didn't want to make this worse.

"I wanted to come," Thad replied simply. "I'd do it again," he shrugged and looked away. "But she's right. I've got an obligation to service. I work all year for myself, the church doesn't ask much—"

Lacy scoffed, he couldn't help it. "You deserve a fucking holiday too."

Thad didn't say anything. He placed his phone on the table under the TV. "I'm going to shower, then maybe we could get breakfast?" He moved for the bathroom.

"Yeah, course."

Thad smiled, small, and disappeared into the bathroom with a soft click of the door. It was the first time he hadn't asked Lacy to join him.

27

ON THE FLIGHT HOME from Barcelona, Thad draped blankets over them, carefully covering their hands so he could hold Lacy's in a loose grip, his thumb rubbing up and down the skin of Lacy's knuckles from Barcelona to Dubai, Dubai to Melbourne.

He knew his mum had expected him to jump the next flight back to the Philippines and she didn't even know he'd been in Italy, had no idea he'd travelled with Lacy to Spain, booked a seat next to him for their flight home. She'd assumed he was in Melbourne and he didn't correct her.

He also knew he should feel bad about that. And he did. But the desire to be near Lacy, to be with him in the bath houses and clubs and bedrooms of other men, to watch him as those men penetrated him, his hand always reaching for Thad's, his eyes searching for Thad's as those men used his body, he wanted that more.

The relief he'd felt when Lacy said he hadn't been with anyone else before Thad got there was so profound, Thad felt it like a revelation. A revelation of what he wasn't sure. He hoped it was the fierce protectiveness he felt for his most cherished friend, but he knew it was something more and it couldn't be.

Lacy smiled over at him, his face lit up by the glow of the little TV screen on the back of the chair in front of him, the edges around him blue in the dim of the cabin. Thad returned the smile and stroked his thumb over Lacy's knuckles.

They both attended the first to fourth years training and Thad was surprised, but probably shouldn't have been, that even after almost two months in Europe, Lacy was best on ground. He'd seen him hit the gym at least five times a week in the hotels they stayed in, worked out with him. But it was still amazing given the amount of other stuff he put into his body. He was rapidly approaching thirty and he put nineteen-year-olds to shame. And he was always laughing. Not meanly, never cruelly. He laughed with the new guys, gave them a hand to their feet, tapped them on the ass and gave them specific pointers. Met Thad's eyes over the newest rookie's head and grinned, winked. Thad felt heat go through him at those looks, could barely wait for the door to close behind them when they got home so he could touch him, kiss him, be inside him.

He went home for Christmas, his parents happy to see him, his mum only chiding him gently a few times for leaving his congregation in the lurch. He stayed for New Year's, secure in Lacy's promise that he'd be going to a party in Frankston, "Not that kinda party," and he'd be at the airport "with bells on" to pick Thad up on the second.

It was February when Thad realised how happy he was. He had this special friendship with Lacy, the physical aspect of which was carefully compartmentalised until he got married, and then he'd leave that part behind. He didn't like to think about that too much and anyway, even though his mum and even his dad were getting more exasperated with him now that he was approaching twenty-six and not married, he knew it'd be fine. It'd happen when it was meant to happen.

In the meantime, he had the perfect life. The season started well, contract in its final year but secure after last season's performance, and with Lacy's help they might keep him in Melbourne for the next three years. He had a routine, a life, with Lacy. It really was perfect.

Until everything went terribly, horribly wrong.

28

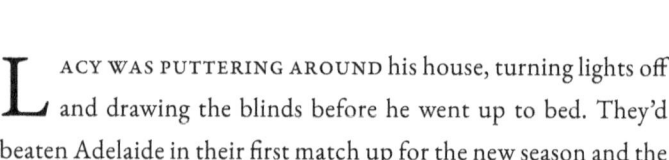

LACY WAS PUTTERING AROUND his house, turning lights off and drawing the blinds before he went up to bed. They'd beaten Adelaide in their first match up for the new season and the thrill was yet to wear off. There was something special brewing with them this season, he could feel it.

He went upstairs, heard the soft murmur of Thad's voice from the guest room. He paused on the landing. Thad normally closed the door, but he'd left it open a crack. Thad always came in once he was done, slipped into bed beside him and touched him. They didn't always fuck, but they did always do something, even if it was just kiss. They'd fucked with charged energy and giddy laughter after the Adelaide win and he was still in the throes of it, thought maybe they could chase the tail end of it tonight.

He crept down the hall to peer in, get a gauge on how long until Thad would be finished and then he could time touching himself.

"Forgive me, Father, for I have sinned..."

Lacy stilled outside the door.

"I've lain with another man," Thad sighed, a rote note to his voice, "again."

Lacy couldn't bring himself to move as he listened to Thad ask for forgiveness for everything he'd done with Lacy in the past twenty-four hours. Worse was his tone, like he'd said all this before, but also like he really was sorry, like he really wished he wasn't doing this, that he would stop doing this, that tomorrow he'd be better, stronger, and "with Your guidance, Lord, I will be delivered from these sins."

Lacy crept back, went into his room and sat on the edge of the bed. There was a careful blankness in his mind, like he'd gone numb, like he couldn't allow thoughts to enter because he wasn't sure he could handle them if they did. He'd felt like this once before, completely unable to grasp the reality in front of him.

"Waiting for me?" Thad said cheerfully as he came into the room.

Lacy looked up. Thad's smile dimmed.

"What's wrong?" Thad came towards him.

"You think what we do is a sin?" Lacy asked.

Thad froze mid-stride. Lacy watched him carefully. Thad dropped his eyes to the floorboards.

"I—" he began and broke off like he couldn't get the words out.

"What do you think we're doing here?" Lacy asked, his tone curious. He was numb.

"We're," Thad waved a hand between them, flicked his eyes up, "being friends."

"Ya reckon I be friends like this with Finn? Tommy? Cary?" Lacy felt the urge to push behind those words; he needed to know what Thad had been thinking about all of this.

Thad's jaw clenched. He didn't say anything.

"You're in there every night asking God to forgive you for fucking me?" Lacy asked.

There was nothing but the sound of Thad breathing, heavier than usual.

Eventually, Thad said "Yes," quietly, realising Lacy was prepared to wait him out. He crossed his arms and wouldn't meet Lacy's eyes.

That 'yes' tore into Lacy's chest and pierced the numbness, a new reality coming to him in painful clarity.

Lacy rubbed his forehead. "What was the plan? Say sorry every day for the rest of our lives?"

"No," Thad replied, "just until—" he stopped abruptly.

Lacy looked up at him again, what Thad was about to say dawning on him with a horrible feeling. "Just until what?"

"Nothing, just until nothing," Thad said quickly.

Lacy stood and Thad took a step back like he was scared. Lacy almost laughed.

"No, tell me, say the words. Just until what," Lacy pushed.

Thad looked past him and out the window beyond the bed. The faint sound of one of the possums starting up came from the trees, a deep hissing sound.

"Until I get married," Thad said, his voice rough like it pained him to say that.

Lacy felt the pain in his chest grow, it radiated outward and shattered the numbness completely. He was too dumbstruck for anger and almost too hurt to speak. Almost.

"So, you're sinning with me until you get married?" he asked, his voice surprisingly steady.

Thad glanced at him. He looked devastated. "Lacy, please."

Lacy couldn't look at him. He went for the ensuite, giving Thad a wide berth. "I reckon you should go."

Thad grabbed his arm. "No, not like this—"

Lacy leapt back. He was shaking. He wasn't sure what he was capable of just then. The thought of hitting Thad was abhorrent to him. But he needed him to go so he could get his fucking shit together.

"Just go home, alright? We'll," he swallowed, "we'll talk tomorrow."

"You promise?" Thad rushed out.

"Yeah, course, man, course," Lacy said, he could hear the words struggling around the lump in his throat. He needed Thad to go away. Or he needed to be away from him.

He went into the bathroom, shut the door, sat on the toilet lid and strained to listen for Thad leaving. It took a while, but eventually he heard his footfalls on the stairs, the front door opening and closing.

Lacy dropped his head into his hands, pressed his palms against his eyes. He could feel the burn behind the orbs. He hadn't cried since his brother died. Hadn't felt this shattering inside himself either, a pain intermittently buttressed by a numb feeling, an incomprehensibility over what had just happened. The unreality and the inability to comprehend it was almost a balm to the reality. But inside was always the knowledge, no matter how small, that reality would come.

Lacy didn't sleep. He'd moved from the bathroom to his bed, lain down on top of the covers and watched the tree shifting outside his window, making out the dark lumps of the possums as they raced up and down the branches, screeching and hissing at one another. The blue of the dawn was coming when his phone pinged. He ignored it. It pinged again as the yellow of the sun took over the blue. And again when the sun was shining fully into the room.

He rolled over.

He almost ignored the messages completely, but the years of muscle memory of opening and reading Thad's texts made him pull the phone over his head and thumb them open.

You awake? The first one said simply. It made the dull ache in Lacy's chest throb.

You still want to go today? The second one asked and Lacy remembered. They were on a break week and they'd booked a place in the Blue Mountains, had a whole week of antiquing carefully curated after months of planning. They were driving up, had booked a place to stay in Sydney on the way there and back. Dinner plans with Finn and George. A proper road trip. Lacy remembered with a pang turning down Finn's offer to stay at their place; Lacy had thought Thad couldn't fuck him if they were in someone else's house.

Let me know. I can pick you up. The final message said.

Lacy felt that heat in his eyes again and typed quickly.

Not feelin it. Sorry.

The reply was instant: *It's okay. When do you want to talk? I can come over.*

Lacy squeezed his eyes closed. He couldn't do this.

Not right now. Text u later.

His phone pinged again but he threw it on the bed and rolled over to stare out the window.

He had to get up eventually. For one thing, he needed to call Finn and tell him they weren't coming. For another, he needed to piss. He took care of that first, then hit Finn's number. They usually video called, but he couldn't do it, he couldn't handle the eye contact.

"Hey, Lace," Finn said when he picked up after a few rings.

"How's my godson?" Lacy asked with excessive enthusiasm.

"You can see for yourself soon, you almost here?" Finn replied, a smile in his voice.

Lacy could hear George in the background, the muffle of his words and the sound of the baby making a small cry.

"Ah, yeah, not gonna make it, eh," Lacy was proud of how steady his voice sounded.

"Really? You alright?" Finn asked.

"Yep, all good, just, ah," he didn't know how to finish the sentence.

"Hang on," Finn said abruptly.

Lacy heard him say something to George and then the sound of his feet on tiles, a door closing.

"'Kay, what's up?" Finn asked.

"Nothin', ya know, just can't make it," Lacy looked out the window, the afternoon light shifting to night. He needed to eat something. He should have thought of an excuse before calling.

"Damn, eh," Finn said easily though, "was really looking forward to you meeting Laine and giving George shit. You should see him," Finn huffed a laugh, "he won't let anyone else hold Laine, it's hilarious."

Lacy huffed a laugh and listened to Finn talk. He'd never wanted what they had. But he'd thought, with Thad... He didn't know what he'd thought.

"You guys sound happy," Lacy said and cursed himself for the melancholy tone.

Finn zeroed in on it. "Are you sure you're good, man? Did something happen?"

Finn knew Lacy had been seeing someone, but none of the particulars.

"I'm good, shit just got fucked up, ya know how it is," Lacy replied, voice going brittle.

"Fuck, Lace, I'm sorry, ya wanna talk about it?"

Lacy swallowed around another lump in his throat. He couldn't speak.

"Want me to fly down and kill him? I can, I totally can. Seriously, George is fully on Dad duty, I could come down," Finn said.

Lacy laughed. Finn could not fight.

"Thanks," he said and it sounded wet so he really had to go.

Finn sucked in a breath. "Shit, Lace—"

"Not right now, 'kay?" Lacy cut him off.

"Okay," Finn said seriously. "But call me back, okay? Call me back. And I can come down."

"Thanks, all good, I'll just, yeah..."

"Shit, Lace," Finn said with feeling.

"I better. I'll call you later."

"Seriously, whenever."

"I know, thanks. Later."

"Later."

Lacy hung up before he broke down. He knew Finn wouldn't tell anyone, not even George. He was embarrassed anyway.

The break was horrible. Lacy's phone pinged with messages, rang out with calls. He ignored it but checked it every night to make sure there was nothing he needed to know. Everyone on the team thought he was away for the week, so there wasn't much on that front other than photos and messages about the other guy's holidays. Messages from Finn checking in, reiterating that he could call whenever. And Thad. Several calls a day. Unopened messages climbing in number as the days wore on. Lacy couldn't bring himself to look at them.

He ordered in. Watched sport—soccer, golf, surfing, Formula One—whatever was on. He drank beer. He worked out. He went through the motions and tried not to think about how in the fuck he was going to face Thad on Monday morning.

And it wasn't until Sunday night that he thought about how Thad never came over. Never tried to force Lacy into talking to him. He should've been relieved. He wasn't.

29

WALKING INTO THE LOCKER room had never been as nerve-wracking for Thad as it was that Monday morning. Not when he was getting scouts looking at him playing in Tassie, not when he finally got a start on the Gold Coast, and not when he started in Melbourne. His heart was absolutely hammering beneath his rib cage, his palms sweaty. His body felt unreal, untethered to the world around him.

Lacy hadn't replied after that first morning, nor answered any of his calls. Thad had picked up his keys, all ready to drive over every single day, only to decide against it each time. Lacy needed space and Thad needed to respect that.

He didn't think he'd ever forget the look on Lacy's face when Thad confirmed he'd been asking for forgiveness for what they did, the careful compartment he'd constructed disintegrating with that look of shock, of disbelief. Lacy had looked winded, like he'd been hit from behind.

Worse was the way he'd shrunk in on himself, trembled, when Thad touched him. The shake in his voice when Thad repeated the plan that'd been drilled into him since he could remember—he'd get married, he'd have kids. But it was so abstract, so far away, yet Lacy had reacted like it was real, like it was about to happen. And Thad hated himself because he couldn't say it was never going to happen.

He braced himself, pushed the door to the locker room open and his eyes went straight to Lacy's locker. Lacy was in front of it, his bare back to the room. Thad heaved a sigh of relief at the sight of him—he was here, he was real, he was alive—and then the nerves returned tenfold. The door clanged shut behind him and he saw Lacy tense, but otherwise not move from squirting Deep Heat on his palm, reach back and rub it into his shoulder, his head down and hair falling around his face.

"Morning," Thad said as he came alongside him. He'd been practicing his greeting all the way in the car. He thought it came out normally.

Lacy made a noise that could've been a hello, but didn't look up.

Before he could ask anything else, Lacy grabbed his shirt, turned so his back was to Thad as he yanked it on and moved away down the hall.

The door clanged open behind him and Thad turned to the beaming face of Les, who began talking immediately about how good his break was, asking where Lacy was and how their trip to the Blue Mountains went.

"Good," Thad replied and turned to get ready.

Lacy didn't reappear until Alanson was in the room, and he stayed at the entrance to the hall, stretching, eyes never leaving Alanson as he gave them a talk. Thad didn't hear a word he said. His heart pounded. He felt completely frozen out. He wondered if Lacy would ever look at him again. If he could survive if he didn't.

They meandered out of the locker room, jogged up the tunnel, Lacy with a couple of the new guys they'd got that season, Thad near the back next to Cary. The configuration stayed that way through the warm-up, through the drills, and once they were split up to run plays, Thad was put in the group on the other end of the ground.

During the cool down Thad watched Lacy stretching opposite him in the circle on the grass, the long line of his back as he bent at the waist and rested his head on his knees. He hoped to catch his eye when he came up, but Lacy never lifted his gaze. He was all business, aside from the odd pointer Thad heard him give one of the rookies. The sound of his voice skittered along Thad's skin.

By the time they were back in the locker room there was no way everyone hadn't noticed the distance between them. But Thad also knew no one would say anything. They'd assume a falling out had happened, leave them to it, wait for it to blow over. Thad hoped to catch Lacy by their lockers, but Lacy was already heading to the showers.

Thad stripped quickly and followed—if he could match Lacy's pace then they'd be getting dressed at the same time and they could talk.

He couldn't make out where Lacy was amidst the steam and line of bodies. Thad faced outwards under the shower, his back to the tiles, and darted his eyes up every time a shower went off and somebody went by. He scrubbed his body, washed his hair, closed his eyes momentarily as he rinsed.

"You planning on drowning yourself in there?" Cary asked with a smile as he turned his shower off beside Thad.

Thad huffed a nervous laugh and got out. When he stepped back in front of his locker, he glanced at Lacy's. It was closed. Thad breathed out slowly.

By the time he was dressed and ready to leave, he was the last person left in the room, the sound of water dripping slowly onto the tiles from the empty shower stalls echoing through the empty room.

He sat on his couch later that night, rolling his silent phone in his hands. He'd texted Lacy so much by this point, he had to concede another one probably wouldn't change anything. Lacy never replied; all of Thad's messages stared back at him, none of them read. It was possible Lacy had turned the read notifications off, but either way, he wasn't replying. He thought about calling, again, but Lacy wouldn't pick up.

But he'd said they would talk, Thad thought desperately; like a man who'd been wrongly convicted and promised an appeal and never got one. If Lacy would just let him explain. Tell him it was just the way it was, he'd never questioned it—you got married, you had children, you emulated the Christian family and worked with your congregation for God. But this was all in some faraway future and it had nothing to do with Lacy, with what he had with Lacy.

And yet, something about it had been bothering him for some time. He couldn't place what it was, but the only consolation he'd felt when his mum asked if he was seeing someone, the hint of insistence and bewilderment in her voice, or when Carol and the other women at the church looked at him like they were waiting for him to ask them something, was that it wasn't the right time yet. He felt that as certainly as he felt the warmth of God in his heart. He knew, from that warmth, he was on the right path. That it wasn't his time yet.

He thought about Lacy not meeting his eyes, not once all day and he had to keep his breathing even. There was no warmth now. All he could feel was a shocked kind of hurt, a pain in his chest.

He went to his room and kneeled in front of his shrine, made the sign of the cross. He spoke his prayers in a soft murmur, rote and empty. He sighed, squeezed his eyes closed.

"If you hear me, if you're with me," he whispered, "please tell me how to make him look at me again."

He clenched his hands tightly and sucked in a breath.

"I'll perform whatever service it takes, I'll be your instrument, just, please…"

He felt nothing, just the same ache in his chest, the complete absence of warmth.

Torture. The week was absolute torture. Lacy wouldn't look at him and when Thad got up the courage to speak to him in the seconds Lacy stood beside him at the locker before he rushed off to be somewhere else, Lacy grunted back unintelligibly and then he was gone.

Going into the game that weekend, Thad worried if he'd be able to play at all. He was so despondent that, for the first time in his life, he didn't feel like doing anything.

What he hadn't anticipated—but who could've?—was how badly Lacy played. The first time he missed a set shot on goal, the collective gasp of shock from the packed stadium ricocheted around them. But he was bound to have a clanger one day.

Except then he fumbled a mark—an easy mark for him, right on the chest from a beautiful drop punt from Cary. Lacy fumbled it and created the turnover, which turned into a goal for Carlton.

Then he booted one out on the full. Under pressure, but still, Lacy lived for being under pressure.

At half time, Thad expected Alanson to come at Lacy with a spray for the ages, only he didn't, it was like he was shocked as well and didn't know what to say.

The second half wasn't much better. Lacy was slow out of the pocket. The defender on him was shoving him and Lacy was stumbling with it. Thad looked at him when they were jogging back for a centre bounce after one of the rookies scored and the steely mask he saw made him miss a step. He saw the flicker of pain in his eyes and he wanted to turn around and go to him. He didn't. He knew if he did it'd make it worse.

They lost, unsurprisingly, and Alanson told them all how shit they were, how embarrassed he was for them and how they better turn up prepared to get their asses handed to them the next week in training.

The following week was much of the same. Lacy barely acknowledged him and played like shit on the weekend. Thad sat and watched Lacy as he walked by him in the rooms after the recovery session the following Monday, his eyes down, shoulders slumped, and Thad saw what he hadn't been able to see before. He'd read Lacy's disengagement as anger, as a rejection steeped in contempt for Thad's religion. But when he watched him walk by, he realised he was in pain. Thad hadn't been so stupid as to think he hadn't hurt him, of course he had, but he'd not realised the extent until that moment. It tore at something inside him. Lacy disappeared into one of the physio rooms and Thad couldn't move.

Everything might be a mess, but he couldn't stand for Lacy to be in pain. He had to fix it. He wasn't sure how, but he had to come up with a way to fix it. God was giving him nothing, but Thad knew he was a man too, a man who could reason himself out of things pretty well. He could reason a way out of this. He would never abandon Lacy in his hour of need, even if the need had arisen because of him.

30

L ACY HAD BEEN SURPRISED, though maybe he shouldn't have been, by how much Thad's presence pained him. When Thad entered the locker room that first morning after the break, Lacy had been so taken aback by the feeling of wanting to turn to him, pull him close and wrap himself in the envelope of his warmth, while simultaneously knowing he could never have that again, that he'd had to get away. He couldn't look at him, he couldn't speak to him. He wanted to, desperately, but he couldn't. It was beyond conscious, it was in his body, his soul if he had one.

After the disaster of a game on the weekend, he'd gone home, braced his hands on the kitchen counter, breathed through the pain and started drinking. He was hammered when he called Finn. Recounted the whole story, finally letting the tears flow. Finn listened, interjected comments, gasped, murmured, "I'm so sorry, Lace. Fuck, I'm just so sorry."

The next week, he was determined to do better. He'd try and be normal around Thad. He hadn't missed the hurt looks that followed him around the room and it killed him, even with everything Thad said about sinning and a fucking wife and kids, even with all of that it killed Lacy to feel Thad hurting because he was freezing him out. Only when Monday morning came, he couldn't do it. All he had to do was say, "Hey," or "Morning" or fucking anything, but he couldn't.

After another shocker of a game, he messaged Colton. He said he had someone holding; he was in Brunswick but he'd drop the gear around shortly. Lacy got changed, met the scrawny kid when he knocked on the door, took the bag and did a few lines with a vodka and soda water at his kitchen counter.

He went out. He drank. Did more lines. An older guy met his eyes and Lacy held the gaze. When the guy followed him into the bathroom and into the stall and crowded up behind him, Lacy panicked. He smothered it. He needed this. He needed to move the fuck on. The guy's beer gut pressed into Lacy's back as he got his hand around him and rubbed the front of Lacy's pants. Lacy wasn't hard and he choked on a breath. The guy started working his pants down, pushing his erection against Lacy's low back.

"No," Lacy said, his voice like steel. He didn't know where it came from, he didn't want to know.

The guy stopped, but stayed close. Lacy could smell the beer on his breath, feel the stubble like pine needles scraping his cheek, the ugly hand still pressing against his crotch.

They breathed together for a moment, balanced on the edge of something. Lacy hated Thad in that moment.

"'M not feelin' it, sorry," Lacy pressed against the guy to get him off. The guy hesitated, a mean smirk flickering on his face when Lacy met his eyes. Lacy met that look and stared right back at him.

The guy huffed but deferred and Lacy went out of the stall, punched the bathroom door on his way out.

His anger simmered and carried him into the locker room on Monday morning. But when he felt Thad enter the room, stand beside him, his soft, "Morning," drifting over Lacy's skin along with his smell, the anger flamed out briefly, replaced by the image of himself in that stall, that bruiser pressing against his low back with a grunt as he tried to get his pants down, the drag of his impersonal, rough touch. He felt like he'd cheated.

He was seething again.

"Right, fuck, morning!" he slammed his locker shut and walked away. He could feel Thad's bewildered hurt behind him and he didn't know how to make that fucking stop on top of everything else.

Wednesday afternoon he was stretching with Cary, Lesley and Les in the locker room, most of the guys gone for the day. They'd ended up lingering, stuck in a stupid conversation about Les' plans to propose to his girlfriend. Thad had already left. Lacy knew because if Thad was in the room, Lacy would know; he'd be tracking his every movement even though he didn't bloody well want to be.

"So you know where you wanna do it?" Cary asked.

Les nodded, smile dreamy. "She's Catholic, so I'm gonna suggest St Patrick's Cathedral, but you know," he shrugged and tried to hide his nerves, "she's gotta say yes first."

"I meant where are you gonna propose," Cary laughed. "But it's cool you're already planning the wedding."

"She's gonna say yes," Lesley said gruffly and bumped him.

"She's religious?" Lacy asked.

"Yeah, went to those all-girls' schools, goes to church and stuff," Les replied.

"No sex before marriage?" Cary asked, smirking.

Les laughed, embarrassed. "Course not," he blushed and looked down at his legs.

Before, Lacy would've teased him, said, 'Get it, Les,' and bumped him. Instead, his mouth was opening and his voice was hard. "Religion's a refuge for the intellectually weak."

There was a sound behind them. Lacy saw all their eyes lift to a point near the door. Lacy turned his head back slowly, but he knew what he was going to see.

"Sorry," Thad mumbled, he dropped his eyes but Lacy didn't miss the flush rising on his cheeks, the flash of shame in his eyes. "Just forgot my..." he trailed off but walked awkwardly to his locker, fumbled with it, the only sound in the room the door opening, the rustle of his things, the clang as he closed it and shuffled by them with his head down.

The door banged closed.

"Fucking hell, Lacy," Cary hissed.

Lacy didn't say anything. He didn't even know where the words had come from—he'd heard them on TV. He'd only paid attention because he'd been affronted on Thad's behalf. Thad wasn't weak and certainly not when it came to his intellect—he thought about all that bible and God shit constantly.

Lacy shrugged and got to his feet. "Just messin' around. Good for you, Les."

"You better tell Thad you were just kidding," Lesley said. "You know he's for real right into all that shit, prays every day. Hanny up in Queensland told me about it, said he never went out or drank, just went to church all the time. Like, every day."

Lacy stared down at Lesley, wondering why he was telling him about Thad like Thad was some fucking stranger he didn't know.

"He goes on Sundays," Lacy said and went to pack his shit up.

"Nah, man, every day. They got these like, whaddya call it," Lesley was directing the question at Les. But it was Cary who answered.

"Bible study or evening service," he said crisply.

"How the fuck you know that?" Lacy asked. He had his bag over his shoulder and he just wanted to get the fuck out of there. He had seen the hurt look on Thad's face and he fucking hated himself.

"I went to Trinity," Cary retorted primly, like it was something to be proud of, attending that prestigious, religious school for *losers* in Kew.

Lacy rolled his eyes and went to leave.

"Hopefully you can catch him in the car park," Cary called as he pushed through the door.

Lacy gave him the middle finger without turning back, but a thrill went through him at the thought of Thad waiting for him in the car park. Which was fucking stupid and he was a moron to still be getting like this.

He stepped into the carpark and his eyes immediately landed on Thad's Toyota. Nerves skittered up and down his limbs and he told himself to fucking stop it. He focused on Thad in the front seat; he was gripping the steering wheel, his head resting on the top of it, eyes closed. Lacy's heart clenched. He wanted to go over there, knock on the passenger's window until Thad startled and looked at him. Lacy would smile. He'd apologise, explain how he didn't mean it, how he was just angry and hurt and fucking frustrated and he missed him and he hated him and he loved him and he didn't know how to be friends again.

He looked away and beelined for his car. He sat behind the wheel and breathed carefully in and out. He was behind Thad, could make out his slumped form just fine. He started his engine and Thad sat up, his eyes darting to his rearview mirror. Lacy met his gaze and tried to smile, but he felt it contort into a grimace, the shock of Thad's eyes on him causing him to lose his nerve.

He eased out of his spot, made his fingers lift off the steering wheel in a small wave and hoped and didn't hope Thad saw the gesture.

Things between him and Thad were more awkward as the week spluttered to an end. They were playing on Sunday, Friday night to themselves, a light training session scheduled for Saturday, just enough to keep them loose, keep them focused.

Lacy was floating in his jacuzzi, a beer beside him. Thad had been dropping his eyes like he was embarrassed every time Lacy was near him the last couple of days and the memory would not let him be. He wanted to be furious at him—how dare he act like the hurt party here?—but he couldn't muster much beyond the occasional flicker of anger. Seeing Thad hurt made him hurt and there wasn't much that would change that. Not Thad's fucking lies, his denial, not the way he'd broken Lacy's heart into a million fucking little pieces.

And there was the anger again.

His doorbell rang.

And who the fuck was that?

He got out, rubbed the towel over his naked body quickly, secured it around his waist and went to the front door. He opened it, ready to tell whoever it was to fuck off, but all words left him.

Thad stood hunched on the landing, his hands stuffed into his pockets, his eyes trying to meet Lacy's defiantly. Lacy stared at him. Thad's eyes flicked to his bare torso before dropping to the ground.

"Sorry," Thad said, his voice cracking.

"What're you doing here?" Lacy asked, his voice horribly quiet.

Thad straightened, met his eyes again. "I, we... need to," he cleared his throat, shook his head at himself. "You said we'd talk."

Lacy frowned. When did he say that? Oh right, he remembered. Right after. The last thing in the fucking world he wanted to do was talk because talking would involve Thad telling him, again, about how what he did with Lacy was a sin and one day he'd get married and God would forgive him and all would be right in his perfect fucking world.

"We don't need to talk," Lacy managed.

Thad's shoulders slumped, that same posture of defeat from the carpark. Lacy nodded like that confirmed things and went to close the door.

"Please," Thad said.

Lacy hesitated. He focused on Thad's shoes—they were a nice pair of boots, Thad liked to wear them when they went out, saving his dress shoes for when they wore their suits. His nicest jeans cuffed the top of them. He was in one of his best shirts too, white with yellow patterns; Lacy always said it made his eyes look warmer. His deodorant smelled fresh on clean skin.

"What is there to say?" Lacy asked Thad's boots and hated the desperate edge that bled into the words.

"Let me explain—"

Lacy held his hand up. "No, I don't," he shook his head. "I can't hear it again, alright? I get it," he didn't, "but I can't hear it again."

"Then tell me what to do," Thad said, his own voice desperate, "tell me how to fix it."

"You can't," Lacy replied.

Thad made a broken sound and looked away. "So we can't even be friends anymore?"

"No, we can," Lacy said even though he damn well knew they couldn't, but what else was he supposed to say with Thad having a nervous breakdown on his doorstep.

"We can?" Thad asked, like he was daring to hope.

"Yeah, man, course," Lacy mumbled.

"Would you like to get dinner?" Thad asked and Lacy knew him well enough to hear how fucking nervous he was. And then he realised Thad had showered and gotten carefully dressed to come and ask him to dinner.

His heart thumped and damn butterflies started up and he was a goddamn fucking moron.

"Umm," he clenched the doorframe.

"I was thinking just the burger place, nothing fancy," Thad said, his voice pitching breathlessly.

"Yeah, alright," Lacy conceded, eyes down. "Lemme get dressed."

He left the door open and heard Thad come in, the sound of it closing softly as he raced up the stairs. This was such a terrible fucking idea. He yanked on boxers, nice jeans, a Louis Vuitton long-sleeved black shirt, styled his hair, put on deodorant and checked his reflection in the mirror. He told himself he was going to tell Thad it was a bad idea and maybe some other time, meaning: maybe fucking never.

But Thad looked up at him as he pounded back down the stairs, a small smile breaking out on his face like he was asking for permission to be happy in Lacy's presence. And Lacy knew he'd never turn him down. Even being in pain around Thad was better than not being around Thad.

"Let's go," Lacy said roughly as he leaned down to pull on his socks and boots.

Thad opened the door and Lacy followed him out.

The car ride was a new kind of torture, the tension between them palpable. But Thad turned the music on, a playlist Lacy had put on Thad's phone, and Lacy tried to relax.

"I think we've got a real chance on Sunday," Thad said.

Lacy couldn't help it, he laughed. Thad met his eyes and smiled like he'd done something right.

"Where you been playing the last two weeks?" Lacy quipped.

Thad's smile dimmed.

"But yeah, I heard Carson's carrying an injury, might even be out, so that's a good equaliser ..." Lacy rambled as Thad drove them to his favourite burger place and like a balloon with a slow leak, he felt the tension easing ever so slightly.

Thad held the door open for him at the burger place, which was packed; the noise of so many people should've accosted him, but instead he was hyperaware of Thad's body coming up behind him, the feel of his breath ghosting over his hair.

"Busy," he said to say something.

"There'll be a table out the back," Thad said and Lacy did not miss the aborted hand movement—Thad had been reaching for his hip, something he'd done all the time before, just a gentle touch when they moved. Lacy had braced for it, then deflated when Thad moved away, gaze shifting in front of him as he led them to the outdoor seating area.

There was an empty table tucked in the corner and Thad slid the "reserved" plaque off it as Lacy slid into the seat that'd give him a view of the place, his back to the wall.

"I'll go and order," Thad said as Lacy said, "Didn't know ya had it in you. What're you gonna do if the people whose table this is come?"

Thad gave him a confused smile, his eyes still downcast like they had been since Wednesday.

"Here," Lacy said instead of looking at that. He reached for his wallet.

"No, it's on me," Thad replied and then he was gone.

Lacy watched him stroll back inside. He was always several inches taller than everyone everywhere they went, his broad shoulders drawing the eye before they inevitably dropped to the muscular shape of his ass against his jeans. He'd put on muscle since coming to Melbourne, but his frame remained that of a lean man and the way he moved, cautiously, apologetically, always made Lacy's dick take interest. If he got hard in Thad's presence now it'd be the saddest fucking boner he'd ever had in his life.

Fuck's sake, why had he come?

Thad reappeared with one of the metal poles with the number 27 on it, a pale ale for Lacy and a bottle of orange juice for himself.

"Sorry, there was a line," he said as he sat down.

"It's all good," Lacy mumbled and took a swig of his beer. "Seriously though, lemme go halves."

"You can get the next one," Thad said and then seemed to realise what he'd said because he got busy opening his orange juice.

Lacy sighed, took another swig of his beer, then another, sat up and planted his elbows on the table.

"Look," he began, which was great because he had no idea what he was about to say. But he needed to say something. "We're always gonna be mates."

That was a good start. Thad nodded nervously at him, no doubt waiting for the impending 'but.'

Lacy finished his beer, placed the empty bottle on the table.

But you broke my fuckin' heart.

He took a deep breath, focused on the pink table cloth, the salt and pepper shakers.

"But ... I'm gonna need a minute," he said inadequately and hoped Thad understood what he meant.

"However long it takes," Thad replied quietly. "I'm not going anywhere."

Right now, Lacy thought viciously, but when he met Thad's eyes, they were so sincere, just damn well pleading with Lacy to let him back in. And fuck it all to hell and back, Lacy was a goner for the religious nutcase.

"But," Thad said after a moment.

Lacy raised his eyebrows.

"But I think it's really important that you're," Thad paused like he was trying to choose the right word. Lacy waited, terrified.

"Happy," Thad said finally on an exhale. "I think you need to be like *you*."

Lacy laughed, humourless. "Yeah, I'll get right on that."

"No, I mean," Thad sat forward. "The last couple of games..."

Lacy felt a part of the life drain out of him. So Thad was only here because he cared about how Lacy was playing?

"I reckon I can handle my own shit on the field, no need to be my *friend* to get me playing better," Lacy said. "I played just fine before you got here. And after," he tacked on the end. So he had two bad games because his heart was fucking broken. Give him a break. Most guys had a few bad games a season and they weren't even dealing with anything.

"That's not what I meant," Thad said.

He was cut off by the arrival of their food. Thad had ordered him his favourite with real chips, not those disgusting sweet potato fries Thad was having and the nutritionist said he should be having as well. The waiter also had another beer, which he slipped out for the empty with a smile before zipping away.

"This looks good," Lacy said because he didn't want to hear what Thad really meant.

"I guess it's your favourite for a reason," Thad replied, eyes on his food. He was frowning, caught back in what they'd been talking about and Lacy really didn't want to hear any more about it and he didn't think he could bring himself to apologise for the insult he'd made in the locker room, so he began nattering about how his soccer team were doing, and Thad loosened up across from him, the bemused smile he wore whenever Lacy talked about soccer making an appearance.

31

Dinner had been good, Thad thought as he drove home, a start. He'd been working himself up to asking all week. They always ate together, it'd be a familiar space for them to return to. He'd popped into the burger place after training on the Monday and asked them to hold the table for him. All he had to do was ask Lacy. Tuesday and Lacy was scowling at everything—Alanson, his locker, the door to the physio room—and Thad lost his nerve. Wednesday saw no opening because Lacy was always enmeshed in a group—the rookies, Cary, Les—but as he was about to leave, he told himself to have courage. To go back in and ask. He knew Lacy hadn't left yet and if he was lucky, he'd catch him alone and get the words out, "Do you want to have dinner on Friday? Nothing fancy, we could get burgers and talk. You said we'd talk." He'd been rehearsing the lines so much he was worried they would come out like he was a bad actor with an awful script.

There were voices inside when he came to the door, his heart sinking at the thought of having to ask Lacy in front of the others. But maybe that would make it more difficult to say no.

"No sex before marriage?" Cary was asking as Thad pushed the door open quietly. He panicked at the question—surely Lacy wasn't talking about him?

But it was Les who answered, "Course not," he was laughing. Cary and Lesley laughed with him.

Lacy's back was to the door, his legs stretched in a V in front of him as he moved gracefully from one side to another, his hair tumbling down his back, the tips skirting the top of his shoulder blades.

"Religion's a refuge for the intellectually weak," Lacy said, a cruel edge to his voice that drew the shocked sound from Thad's throat before he was able to stop it. He flushed with shame. He'd heard variations of this before, of course he had; the general consensus in Australian society was religious people were intellectually inferior, using a crutch, somehow trying to dodge responsibility for their lives by hiding behind a belief in a fantasy. God was the equivalent of Santa Claus and adults were meant to grow out of that. The strength of his faith had always allowed him to shrug it off, bemused, secure in his relationship with God, in his mission to service.

But to hear Lacy say it, to discover that's what Lacy thought of him, cut through the armour he wore, found him naked and cut open with no way to defend himself.

When Lacy turned and looked at him, expressionless, Thad could do nothing but drop his head in shame, mumble about picking up something he'd forgotten. He felt Lacy's eyes on him as he fumbled to grab something—he went with a pair of his training skins because if anyone asked, he could say he needed to wash them, he'd just remembered, and he thought this as if the thought were a line flailing around in the plume of scattered thoughts around him, something to grab onto amidst the shock.

No one said anything and the few seconds felt like an eternity before he was back on the other side of the door, the sound of muffled voices starting up as soon as the door shut behind him.

He'd sat in his car, paralysed by this new knowledge. Lacy thought he was intellectually inferior. Had probably always thought it, looked down on him. But Thad never got that impression. Except the way Lacy said it? It sounded like the truth had finally been ripped out of him.

He dropped his head on the steering wheel. Closed his eyes and asked God what he was supposed to do now. He knew the answer—what did it matter what anyone else thought? He knew his own truth and so did God, what did it matter what Lacy thought?

"It matters," he mumbled into the leather.

A car starting behind him made him jerk upright, his eyes flying to the rearview mirror. Shock washed through him like plunging into an ice bath when he caught Lacy's eyes in the mirror. Lacy didn't break the eye contact and Thad couldn't look away. Lacy watched him and it felt like a long time passed before he eased out of his spot.

Lacy's fingers lifted from the steering wheel in an acknowledging wave. Thad's breath caught in his throat and he mirrored the action even though Lacy wouldn't see it.

He had a new heart soreness, but something in him, something akin to the knowing he had when he was on God's path, told him he still needed to make amends.

He lost his nerve on Thursday at training. Friday presented the perfect opportunity when he passed Lacy coming out of the ice baths, no one else around, but he couldn't make the words come and Lacy nodded an acknowledgement and then he was gone.

Thad went home and showered, dressed carefully for the dinner. He'd built himself up for this all week, had reserved the table for seven. He would go to Lacy's and ask.

The strangest thing was what came to him that afternoon as he got himself ready, what gave him the final push for courage: Lacy would do this for him. If Thad was hurting, regardless of whatever else was going on between them, Lacy would never leave him alone in his pain. Lacy was the best friend he'd ever had for a reason.

When Lacy answered the door in nothing but a towel, Thad's acceptance that he'd never touch him again deteriorated. Water droplets ran over his inked chest, tracing a path down the grooves of the sinew of muscle, slid over the bones of his ribs and trailed an erratic path down the flat planes of his torso, dispersing into the trail of hair below his navel. The arousal he felt at the sight of him roared through him and made it difficult to remember why he was no longer touching him.

Keeping his eyes on the ground seemed like the safest option. He knew he sounded desperate but he didn't care anymore. He realised then he wasn't as noble as he liked to think he was because it wasn't about saving Lacy from his pain, it was about him. He wanted to be around Lacy. Even as fraught with tension and misunderstandings as the dinner was, it was the best couple of hours of Thad's life since everything got ruined.

When he dropped Lacy off, he wanted to turn the engine off and come inside. Wanted to wrap his arms around him as Lacy bent to take his boots off, kiss his nape, slide his hands under his shirt and trace the path the water had made.

But Lacy had hopped out with a "Thanks for dinner," and closed the door on Thad's, "You're welcome."

But it was a start, he repeated to himself as he parked in his driveway. Even though Lacy had taken his words the wrong way—Thad didn't care about Lacy's performance for the sake of football, he cared for the sake of Lacy. Lacy loved to play, came alive on the field. To see him struggling there, of all places, was too much to bear. And Thad was certain restoring their friendship, at a minimum making it okay to look at one another again, would re-centre Lacy.

The thought gave him the courage to message Lacy the next morning.

Thanks for coming last night, he hesitated, unsure how far he should push it. He typed what he wanted to say. *I had a great time*.

He hit send with a panicked breath, which was stupid—Lacy was ignoring his messages.

His phone pinged.

Me too.

Thad smiled, his whole face breaking with radiant relief.

Lacy played one of the greatest games of his career that Sunday.

Jogging back to the centre after Lacy had snapped a goal out of a packed forward line, Thad couldn't stop smiling. He felt a bump at his elbow.

"What're ya grinning about?" Lacy asked him. It wasn't completely unencumbered, Thad heard the bridle holding the words back from being fully what they were before, but it was so close that Thad actually laughed with relief.

"Nothing much," he said as he panted, "just a nice day for a game."

Lacy huffed a laugh before turning back for his position.

And then a minor miracle happened. For two weeks they'd been carefully re-establishing their friendship with polite dinners and lunches at their favourite places, and while Thad ached to pass the evening with Lacy on his couch, to spend the night with him in his bed, he was too grateful for the time he was getting to get caught up over what he wasn't.

It was Tuesday and he was about to leave to coach the junior league he'd set up for troubled kids two years before. The league had blossomed into a team of real contenders, some of the boys and girls who'd started with him going on to play in decent competitions and, more importantly, getting into courses and trades, getting some stability around them. They still came down for the Tuesday training when they could to help the new kids.

"Hey," Lacy said from beside him.

"Hi," Thad replied stupidly.

Lacy snickered, still guarded, but it was something. It was always something.

"You still trainin' those messed up kids on Tuesdays?" he asked.

"I don't know if I'd say the kids are messed up—"

"I know where ya trainin', buddy," Lacy bumped him, "and I ain't judging. I'm just askin' if you're still doin' it?"

"Yes," Thad replied.

Lacy nodded, yanked his bag over his shoulder. He met Thad's eyes, a glint of defiance and a hint of vulnerability there. "Mind if I join you?"

Thad's lips parted. "You want to help?"

"Ah, yeah, I mean, if you need it? I'm not sayin' ya do, but if you did, I could come down," he replied, hoisting his bag higher on his shoulder.

"The kids would love that," Thad breathed out. He could picture their faces when Lacy stepped onto the field and couldn't stop the smile that took over his face.

Something flickered in Lacy's expression, but he grinned, smothering it. "Sweet, let's do it."

Thad didn't know what he'd done right to get Lacy's help, but he wasn't going to ruin it by asking any questions. He followed Lacy out of the room, smiling at the top of his head.

The kids were ecstatic, their little eyes like saucers when Lacy strolled to the centre of the ground where they huddled, ready for warm-ups. Thad couldn't tear his eyes away from how good Lacy was with them. Correcting their form with gentle words tinged with humour, celebrating madly with them when they did well.

"Are you gonna come next week?" one of the older boys, Tyler, asked.

"Yeah, course, if Thad wants me to?" Lacy smiled over at Thad.

"I'd love you to," Thad replied, tossing a ball in the air and catching it to downplay how much he wanted Lacy to come every week.

"Then I'll be here," Lacy said to Tyler.

Tyler smiled gruffly, hiding his happiness in that special way only fourteen-year-old boys could, and put out his fist. Lacy bumped it with a solemn smile of his own. Tyler relaxed. "See ya next week."

The following week, Thad had double the number of kids in attendance and parents in the stands, complete with Esky coolers and beers in hand, but still, they were there, invested, if by proxy, in their kids' activities.

"Reckon we're gonna need a bigger boat," Lacy said to Thad as they got the kids warmed up.

"This is your fault, you better find me a new venue," Thad replied, smiling so much he thought his face would break.

"Have I ever let you down?" Lacy grinned and took off to jog with the kids, playfully asking them if that was the best they could do as he matched their pace.

"No, you haven't," Thad murmured softly, doing his best to pretend 'Religion's for the intellectually weak' wasn't floating through his mind.

32

H E DIDN'T WANT TO push it, but the training with the kids had gone so well, Lacy reckoned it was time he nutted up and asked to join Thad on his Thursday excursions to help the junkies or whatever it was he did.

It'd eaten at him, what he'd said, the look on Thad's face in the locker room—flushed and ashamed—taunted him when he tried to sleep. Lacy might be nursing a bruised heart over Thad's stupid fucking declaration because of his stupid fucking religion—and he really tried not to go there because he could go on a real tirade—but he'd been talking to Finn, shooting the shit about their latest games, when a new thought occurred to him. Finn was playing some beautiful football and Lacy could not let that go by without calling him to give him shit about being one of those guys who got better when they got married and had kids. It was during one of these conversations that he spat out what'd happened in the locker room like he had Tourette's, and Finn had been sympathetic to Thad, but had also said, "Yeah, but c'mon, he kinda used his religion to pretend he was never in a relationship with you."

"Yeah, I dunno," Lacy replied, thinking about it. And he kept thinking about it. He'd been best mates with Thad for two years, been more than that, at least in his mind, for a year, and yet he'd never made any real effort to understand his religious thing. Maybe if he had then Thad would've seen him as his partner.

"I feel like there's something really wrong with that logic," Finn replied. "It's like, the opposite of the reality."

"I dunno what that means, but I reckon I gotta try."

Finn sighed, long-suffering and Lacy chuckled.

"Just watch yourself, alright? I know you said he's a good guy or whatever, but what he did was fucked up," Finn said.

"He doesn't know any better," Lacy mumbled.

"Fuck, man, don't defend him," Finn replied, uncharacteristically animated over it.

"I'm not, look I gotta go, tell George I said he's gayer than a fairy," Lacy said and Finn laughed.

"I'll tell him you love him and said hi," he said.

Lacy cackled and hung up.

But Lacy was certain he was onto something. And the footy with the kids had gone well. He got to spend more time with Thad and he was surprised, though maybe he shouldn't have been given how Thad was with him, that Thad didn't mention God or Jesus at all. He was just there to make their lives better for no other reason Lacy could see than he could.

"Why don't you tell them finding Jesus would fix all their problems?" Lacy asked after training with the kids the following week. Everyone was gone, everything was packed up and they were standing alone in the gravel carpark, the only light coming from the street lights beyond the suburban ground. He couldn't quite believe that'd just tumbled out of his mouth and he did not miss Thad's flinch. Of course he was wary, Lacy had taken a public shit on his belief system.

Thad met his eyes, shrugged. "I don't think that's my place," he replied hesitantly. Lacy could feel how much he didn't want to talk about it, but he had to push it.

"Yeah, but," he leaned his arm on the roof of his car, settling in. "That's like your whole thing, right? Telling people if they just believed in Jesus all their problems would go away."

Thad huffed a laugh, but he wasn't laughing at the question, Lacy knew he was laughing at the idea of it. He rocked back on his heels, tucked his hands in his pockets like he was settling in.

"Going out and preaching the Gospel is part of what we're called to do, yes. But," Thad looked over Lacy's head, his eyes on the road, "but I've never been comfortable with that approach. It's personal," he shrugged and met Lacy's eyes, something wistful in his expression. "I get a bit of hassle for it, but I wouldn't be comfortable doing it, so, I don't."

"Right," Lacy replied. Thad got hassled by people like him.

"The people in my church," Thad said, his voice surer. "My parents. They've hassled me for not doing more witnessing. Or well, any really."

"Oh, right, well, that sucks," Lacy kicked the ground. "So, like, can I come with you to meet the junkies then?"

"You want to help on Thursdays too?" Thad sounded surprised.

"Well, yeah, I mean, I don't reckon you need it, but I'm around, not busy..."

"I'd love you to come," Thad said. "It's not only drug addicts. Homeless people, sex workers, we do coffee, provide a meal, sometimes just doughnuts, have a chat. Stacy usually brings other stuff they might need, sleeping bags, woman stuff."

"Sounds like fun," Lacy said.

Thad laughed and it lit up his face under the blue of the street lights. Lacy laughed with him and it felt good. Even if everything still hurt, it felt good for a second.

"I don't know if fun is the word," Thad said carefully, still smiling. "But it's rewarding to be," he paused like he wanted to get the words right, "someone in the world who isn't judging them. It's one of the things I love about this Melbourne congregation, the outreach isn't about judgement, it's about, well, love and acceptance, which I know sounds corny—"

"No, it doesn't," Lacy said.

But Thad nodded, relieved.

Lacy had the feeling they could stand there all night and talk and while he wouldn't mind that, they had training in the morning and he needed to eat and get away from Thad before he leaned up and kissed him because hearing the words 'love and acceptance' out of his mouth made him remember all the reasons he loved and accepted him.

"Right, well, I better," he said and moved to get into the car.

"Of course, sorry," Thad said and backed up.

"Nothin' to be sorry for."

Thad smiled. "Oh, just a head's up. Glen, he's the guy I organised this with, he'll be witnessing. So, ah, be prepared for that."

"Gotchya," Lacy said. "Be prepared to hear about how Jesus could save me."

"Letting Jesus Christ into your heart as your Lord and saviour will save you," Thad said in a deep voice and then he laughed. He looked young for a second, carefree.

Lacy cracked up and shook his head as he got into his car. He felt like they were a couple of school kids, shooting the shit and laughing about everything they were discovering. Shit, but it was fucking nice.

"Later, Thad," he said.

"Bye, Lacy," Thad replied, smiling shyly.

And Lacy really needed to get out of there.

Carol was there. Lacy thought if Thad was going to give him a heads up about anyone, it should be Carol. She was sitting in one of those camping chairs beside him, talking with her hands, Thad's head bent down to listen to her.

Lacy almost turned around and left. They were in a well-lit carpark, the shiny lights of McDonald's behind them, a few people who looked worse for wear lingering around the end of the van where another guy and woman—Glen and Stacy he presumed—were talking and handing stuff out. He was about to shrink back into the darkness when Thad looked up. His body was out of the chair as his face lit up with a smile.

"Lacy, you came," he said and strolled over to him.

"Course," he replied and tried to sound cheerful. He didn't know why Carol bothered him so much, maybe it was because she was exactly what Thad would marry. The memory of her in the white gown at the Brownlow's didn't help, even though Thad had said when he'd mentioned he was going, she'd offered to be his plus one and he couldn't think of a reason to say no.

Thad looked like he was about to hug him, but then he stopped and they stood there in the awkward aftermath of a hug that never happened, Lacy's whole body braced and tingling for it.

"Come and meet everyone," Thad said.

Glen was a short, compact guy with a big smile and kind eyes. He was what Lacy imagined religious people looked like—plaid shirt under a V-neck, dress pants with boots, a perpetual, uncomplicated smile on his face. He seemed genuinely thrilled to have Lacy there and handed him a booklet and mini prayer book with zero irony as he said hello, shook his hand and asked if he was prepared to take Jesus into his life as his Lord and saviour.

"And this is Stacy," Thad said with a low laugh as he steered Lacy away from that.

"Hi," Stacy said and shook his hand vigorously. She was older than the rest of them, maybe mid-thirties, with wild curly hair, friendly eyes and another big smile. "Excuse me," she said apologetically and turned back to a young woman who was still on the edge of girlhood and looked like she needed more than a hug, maybe a thousand hugs, some food, and a better place to live.

"And you remember Carol," Thad said.

Carol was standing and she was a textbook perfect woman. Long brown hair, almond shaped eyes, brown eyes like Thad's so if they had kids, they'd have nice looking, brown haired, tall kids with warm, kind brown eyes.

Lacy shook her hand and smiled the smile he used when he had to go to sponsor days and meet a bunch of executives working in businesses he did not give a shit about.

"It's so nice to see you again," Carol said enthusiastically. "Thad talks about you all the time," she bumped Thad, "all the time."

Thad laughed good-naturedly, like that wasn't an embarrassing admission, and gestured for Lacy to take a seat. "Carol was just telling me about some drama with the City Church," he sat when Lacy did. "A lot of their young people are leaving to join our congregation because we're, well, more accepting I guess."

"We're more fun," Carol said and winked at Lacy. It was a simple gesture, an invitation into their little world, but it was incongruous with what Lacy understood about church so he just smiled politely and looked around at the empty seats, listened to the soft hum of Stacy's voice as she spoke with some women, Glen's baritone as he asked a guy if he'd like a coffee.

"There are factions in the denomination," Thad said to Lacy, his eyes hesitant like he wasn't sure Lacy wanted to hear this, but keen to make sure he knew what they were talking about. Lacy gave him an encouraging nod as Glen handed him a cup of coffee with a smile and clap on the shoulder.

"Thank you," Lacy said and tried not to feel too out of place.

"Some of the old-school thinking still seeps in, like, we shouldn't be conducting outreach to the fallen. They'd never come out and say it, but, the thinking is more one of judgement," Thad continued.

"And you guys don't judge, eh?" Lacy asked, his smile careful.

"No," Thad replied with a wider smile.

"Because if everyone accepts Jesus then it doesn't matter what they did before?" Lacy asked.

"No," Thad shook his head, glanced down. He had an empty Styrofoam cup next to his boot, a small book bag Lacy had seen in his car, next to his bed at his house. "We accept people anyway, as they are."

"Well," Carol chimed in, her smile and voice smooth. "We certainly prefer it if they give their life to Him." She giggled, her eyes crinkling and Thad huffed a laugh and sat back. "And if they join the church they have to change, but here, it's about outreach, a first step."

They looked like a perfect couple, Thad reclining in his camping chair with his legs outstretched and hands clasped over his flat stomach. Carol leaning forward, her head tilted back to look at him as she smiled.

Lacy took a sip of coffee to cover the rush of jealousy at the picture they presented.

Fortunately, a couple of guys joined their huddle and the conversation moved to them—gambling and booze, losing their families, living on the streets—and Lacy noticed Thad just listened, laughed when they said something funny, asked if they wanted something to eat, but did nothing to make them feel like he wanted something in return. It was Carol who steered the conversation to Jesus and Lacy felt as discomfited as the pair did, the subtle shifting in the seat, the drop of the eyes.

The evening passed with different people coming and going, most of them recognising Lacy and getting star-struck before wilting as if ashamed, and Lacy made sure to shake their hands and help Thad get them something to eat, asked about their day like they'd been at work, laughed when one of them told him he'd spent it doing enough B&Es to get a fix and how was Lacy's fucking day? It broke the tension when Lacy cracked up and the guy laughed back. Thad kept shooting him grateful smiles, his eyes wandering from whoever he was speaking to until Lacy found his own eyes slipping over to meet Thad's. He basked in the warmth of that gaze, felt flushed and unsure under it as much as he felt giddy.

But then Carol would shift, cross her long jean-clad legs, toss her long hair and Thad would look at her and smile and Lacy felt wrong-footed.

By the time they were packing up, he was ready to get out of there.

"I'll walk you to your car," Thad said.

"Nah, I'm good, man. Stay, ya gotta get goin' too," he said as he stretched.

Thad shook his head and walked beside him, careful not to touch him as he began to walk in the direction Lacy had come from, a chorus of "Bye, thank you!" from behind them.

"You were great with them," Thad said as soon as they were on their way.

Lacy snorted. "Not like it's hard to talk to people. And I'm certainly not as good as you at it."

"No, but," Thad slanted his head down and Lacy looked up. "You make people feel so at ease, like you're this big star and yet, you make them feel okay about themselves. Thank you."

Lacy didn't really know what to say to that so he made a sound to acknowledge he'd heard it. They were at his car and Thad stopped, tucked his hands in his pockets. It was dark, the glow of the van and hum of voices of the other three discernible in the distance.

He wanted to ask about Carol, ask what was going on there. He wondered if he could get his voice to ask it in a casual way, just like a guy friend asking their mate.

"See you in the morning," he said instead.

Thad nodded and tightened his hands in his pockets. "Yep, bright and early."

"Yeah," Lacy replied, "thanks, that was fun."

Thad shook his head, his smile rueful. "No, I'm the one should be thanking you. For," he took a deep breath. "For everything."

"Yeah, man, don't mention it," Lacy rushed out because he got the feeling 'everything' meant being mates again and he couldn't talk about that yet. "Later."

"Bye, Lacy," Thad said softly as Lacy got in and closed his door.

Thad was going to marry Carol or someone like her one day. And he needed to accept it. Church boys like Thad didn't come out of the closet and marry cocaine snorting dudes who liked to take it up the ass. He needed to accept it and move on. He needed to rip off the Band-Aid and get laid and start putting down tracks that were moving on.

33

L ACY WAS GETTING OUT of his car the following morning and Thad jumped out of his Toyota, grabbed his bag, and when he looked up, Lacy was waiting for him. He had his hands tucked loosely in the pockets of his tracksuit pants, his hoodie up, but loose, so his face was haloed in black, a smile playing on his lips but his eyes cautious as Thad made his way over to him.

"Morning," Thad said and tried to restrain the cheerfulness. He'd gotten his friend back and while it pained him not to touch Lacy, he consoled himself with the knowledge that it was better this way. He might've successfully compartmentalised what they'd been doing for over a year, but that didn't change the facts—homosexuality was a sin and he couldn't be with a man.

"Morning," Lacy said slowly, his smile growing. "What're you smiling about?"

"Nothing, just happy to be here," Thad replied.

Lacy hoisted his bag up. "Happy to be at training? Ya know we got cardio all morning, right?"

Thad preferred conditioning days to cardio, but he was so happy to be talking to Lacy again, he could've run a marathon if Alanson asked it of him, matching Lacy's pace for the duration.

"Should be good," he said.

Lacy bumped him and the brush of contact made Thad stutter in his step. "Who are you and what have you done with Thaddeus Clay?"

Thad laughed. He glanced down at Lacy's profile. Lacy flicked his eyes up; there was caution there, but it was fading.

Thad rushed ahead and held the door open for him. "It was just so good with you there last night," he said as Lacy brushed by him. "You're a natural."

Lacy looked over his shoulder. He pushed his hoodie down so it sat at his ears, wrapped around his head like a soft scarf, his glossy hair ruffled, his eyes more whiskey-coloured this morning. They were always sharper in colour when Lacy hadn't drunk or taken anything; Thad could read Lacy based on his eyes—they dimmed or flared brighter depending on how much he was partying.

"I dunno if that's a compliment or not," he grinned, but it didn't touch his eyes. "I'm a natural at talkin' to junkies and prostitutes?"

"No," Thad shook his head, "you're a natural at making people feel like they're equals, no matter who they are. We were talking about it after you left. Stacy said you have the gift."

"The gift?" Lacy gave him a sceptical look.

"Yes, the gift for making people feel—"

He cut himself off because saying, 'making people feel loved' felt like the wrong thing to say in this building. It was one thing to talk about God's love and acceptance with his Church friends, but he certainly couldn't talk like that around footy people, even Lacy.

Lacy raised his eyebrows at the aborted comment. They were walking briskly, would be in the room in a matter of seconds.

"Making people feel okay about themselves," he said and it felt inadequate because he'd said that already last night.

Lacy clocked the repetition, Thad could tell from the way he shook his head, but there was disappointment in the movement too, like he knew Thad was going to say something else and didn't.

"I reckon that's called just not bein' an asshole and ya know I know people like that, so, it's whatever, man, happy to do it," Lacy pushed the door open.

Thad followed him in, said good morning to the guys already there, and wondered how he could tell Lacy it wasn't just the people they were helping he was referring to. Lacy was at ease with his church friends and they all commented on it, how his easy manner made anyone who entered his orbit feel completely accepted. "God's love flows through him," Glen had said with an approving nod after Stacy said he had the Gift, and while Thad had to hide his cringe—there's no way Lacy would want to hear that—he knew what Glen meant. And he also knew you could call it whatever you wanted. Universal love, good energy—Lacy had it and if you were lucky enough to step into his orbit, you never wanted to leave it.

He got changed, Lacy quietly doing the same beside him. He was back in Lacy's orbit but he wanted more. And he couldn't have it. Even if he could get past seeing what they did together, sexually, as okay—highly unlikely—Lacy saw him as inferior. He wasn't stupid—Lacy saw him in lots of ways—but the way Lacy delivered those words, there'd been the power of a simple truth behind them, like he'd been thinking that all along.

"Hey," Lacy jerked him out of his thoughts.

Lacy was in his skins and one of his tight cropped singlets, his hands pulling his hair back into a ponytail with quick flicks of his fingers, revealing the freshly shaved sides of his head, the sharp cut of his cheekbones.

"You good?" Lacy asked quietly.

"Great," Thad replied.

"Good, you just," Lacy shook his head and dropped his hands. He bounced on his feet before looking back up. "You just went away for a sec."

"Sorry, thinking," he sat and got his boots on.

"Well, don't break anything," Lacy rubbed his head roughly before taking his hand back too quickly. "See you out there."

He jogged across the room, ruffled Les' hair before slamming out the door, telling everyone they were too slow.

Thad exhaled slowly and focused on tying his laces, his scalp tingling.

A few weeks later and Thad was stuck in two conflicting places with Lacy. He figured he always had been—the part of him who loved Lacy and was constantly desperate to express that physically, and the part of him who prayed for it to stop. Now, he was stuck between profound gratitude at having his friend back—Lacy joined him every Tuesday and Thursday—and wanting to touch him so badly it bordered on obsession.

He watched Lacy's throat when he drank from his water bottle, the bob of his Adam's apple, the sweat dripping down his neck, and he had to hold himself back from brushing his thumb over Lacy's wet bottom lip, cupping his jaw with his palm and kissing him.

Or they'd be on the couch and he'd have to crush his hands between his crossed legs to stop from stretching his arm out to pull Lacy against his side, kissing the top of his head before he moved down to his brow, his cheek, to find his mouth.

Or in the hallway at Lacy's house when they arrived or he was leaving, he had to tell himself that he could not reach for Lacy and haul him against his chest, walk him back against the wall and kiss him and hoist him up, carry him to the bedroom, lay him down, touch him, enter him, cradle his face in his hands while he rocked in and out of his body.

He was watching Lacy so much, of course he saw it immediately. A mark on Lacy's nape, barely visible because of the tattoos, but Thad studied Lacy's skin so much he saw the new mark as if it'd appeared on his own skin. It was red, bruising, mouth-shaped. Thad went hot and blinked rapidly, his composure slipping as his stomach dropped out. He sat down hard on the bench. Lacy spun back at the sudden noise.

"You alright?" he asked, his frown quickly morphing to greater concern as he stepped closer.

"Fine," Thad said shortly. His mind was filled with the image of another man putting that mark on Lacy's skin. He was having trouble breathing.

"Shit, you look sick," Lacy stepped into his space and placed his hand on Thad's forehead.

Thad gasped.

Lacy dropped his hand. "You're not hot," he mumbled, gaze roving over Thad.

Thad's heart pounded, his chest ached. *Stop being a dramatic fool!* But all he could see was another man holding Lacy, his mouth on his skin while he took him from behind.

"Thad, Thad," Lacy was saying.

"I'm alright," he said and implored himself to get under control. "Hot, I might be too hot."

Lacy was squinting at him. It was the middle of winter—the low grey clouds hung all around them, the threat of heavy rain set to burst any minute.

"From the warm-up," he said. "I'm okay, just need to sit down for a second."

Lacy clapped him on the shoulder and Thad closed his eyes. He was losing his mind, he was losing control of himself, but the thought of it, Lacy moving on, sleeping with another man? It crushed him.

"I'm gonna get a trainer," Lacy shook him and Thad wanted to tell him not to, but he couldn't. He dropped his head into his hands when Lacy let him go, the sound of his boots on grass jogging away from him as he called for Carson.

Embarrassed or not, he was glad to be off the ground and away from Lacy so he could compose himself.

"Lacy said you felt hot?" Carson asked as he took his vitals, shined a torch in both eyes like he was checking for a concussion. Thad almost laughed—he did feel like he'd been hit, but it wasn't physical.

"Yes," he mumbled.

"Hmm," Carson looked at the numbers as the cuff around his arm loosened. He grabbed Thad by the wrist and felt his pulse. They lapsed into silence while Carson counted.

"Heart rate's up a bit," he said.

"I think maybe I didn't eat enough this morning," Thad said.

Carson nodded and asked what he ate, reminded him of the importance of following the nutrition plan, a complex carbohydrate and some protein with every meal when Thad lied and said he'd only had a piece of toast with jam.

"Sugar on sugar could be giving you a blood sugar crash," Carson finished. "Hit the showers and get some rest. Don't want you risking it if it's something worse. Call me tonight and let me know how you're going. We can get Nance to run some tests if you're not feeling better."

Thad almost laughed again—he was never going to feel better. He was in hell. He was in love with a man. He'd hurt that man and suffered horribly every time he thought of that night and Lacy's face. And it turned out, the man he loved not only thought he was stupid for being religious, but had also moved on with another man. He didn't think he'd ever feel better.

"Will do," he hopped off the table.

He skipped the shower, grabbed his bag and went home.

U okay?

Thad rubbed his forehead. No, he was not okay, but he needed to be.

Want me to come round? Can bring food.

Thad got the usual thrill at the thought of seeing Lacy, but it was quickly followed by that hot feeling, his heart hammering and a pit opening up in the bottom of his stomach.

Carson said it was probably blood sugar?

Thad sighed. Of course that was a question—Lacy knew how well he ate.

Lemme know. I'm in the car, can be there in twenty.

They had a game tomorrow and he needed to get it together. He'd also rather Lacy not text and drive—he was not a good enough driver for that.

I'm alright. Thank you. See you tomorrow.

The bubble appeared immediately, Lacy typing.

It disappeared, reappeared, disappeared again.

Thad dropped his phone on the counter and braced his hands on the bench, watching the little bubble, barely breathing.

Okay. C u tomorrow.

Thad exhaled. He felt defeated.

He left his phone on the bench and went into his room. He got down on his knees and clasped his hands together, the words he'd been praying for well over a year now ready on the tip of his tongue—begging for this to stop, to make him not attracted to Lacy, to be a good friend to Lacy but not like this.

But for once he couldn't say it. What was the point? It wasn't going away. He thought back to his friendship with Christian and for the first time, he thought about those times when they had sleepovers and watched movies together. Christian would press his leg against Thad's and Thad liked it. Sometimes Christian would push his back against Thad's chest and he liked that too. He remembered Christian's thick hair and long eyelashes, how much he liked looking at him.

He took a deep breath.

"Am I a homosexual?" he whispered.

He felt nothing, his mind like a deserted windy street, his chest still buzzing with nervous energy and pain.

He exhaled roughly. Okay, that was a negative. Maybe.

He took a deep breath, terrified of what he needed to ask next.

"God, if you can hear me, please help me. Please answer me this one question," he said softly.

He thought about Lacy, about his uncomplicated smiles when they were in bed together, his face creased from the pillow, eyes sleepy as his mouth widened into a delighted grin when Thad bracketed himself over him and leaned down to kiss him.

"How I feel about Lacy," he said, trying to keep his voice calm. He closed his eyes. "Is that... is that okay?"

His eyes popped open.

And then, he gasped.

THEY MADE THE FINALS and lost in the semi-final the day before the Brownlow Medal ceremony. Lacy's play found a whole new level after the disaster with Thad, taking the team with him. He was the favourite to win it. He was usually a favourite, but this year was different. He could feel it. He knew his team could too. He knew Finn could. Finn was the other favourite, but he reckoned deep down they both knew how it would turn out.

Lacy was getting ready for the ceremony, his mum ready and waiting downstairs and he thought about Thad. When did he not think about Thad? He shook his head and checked out his reflection. He looked good. The custom Alexander McQueen stretched perfectly over his build, his hair slicked back with too much gel. He'd knocked his tooth out again in a game the week before, the old gap-tooth grin restored. He wished Thad was coming, but he'd begged off, said with a reluctant smile that people would question the presence of a second-rate ruckman at the ceremony, said he'd already booked a flight down to Tasmania. Lacy didn't point out Thad had attended the year before, instead snapped that they could all get fucked and clapped him on the shoulder. Thad flinched and then carefully relaxed. He'd been acting like a spooked horse around Lacy for months and Lacy wanted to ask him about it, but knew he couldn't.

"You wanna go to this thing or not?" his mum called up the stairs.

"Coming!"

He and Thad were friends again. That was the important thing. That was all that mattered. And Thad was back in Launceston, probably courting some church girl, or maybe he'd taken Carol with him. And Lacy would go out after the ceremony, find another guy to hold him down and fuck him and try and fail not to think about how the guy wasn't Thad and without Thad there, the guy was doing a pretty average job pounding into his ass. But he'd get off and it'd be fine. He'd feel hollow afterwards, but everything was fine. He rubbed his chest as he came down the stairs.

"You'll crease the shirt," his mum said, glass of champagne in hand. She was a vision in the golden dress; it draped to her heeled feet and clung to every curve of her body. She was approaching fifty, but still managed to turn heads, though to be fair, they usually snapped back around pretty quick once she glared at them. She'd been like that since his brother died.

And he wasn't thinking about Parks tonight. It'd be the cherry on top of what he was already feeling.

"Are you worried?" his mum asked like it was a ridiculous notion.

"Nope," he replied and took her champagne and drained it. "Let's do it."

He won. Of course he did, he thought with a grin he wasn't feeling as he posed for the photo. He'd underestimated how fucking shit it would feel to have the camera in his face while they went through his 'slump'. The games where he couldn't buy a point. That night with Thad in his room flooded back in and he'd clenched his jaw, made his face like stone. His mum had patted his thigh and he was able to breathe again.

But he'd won and now it was time to party. He'd get pissed, do a few lines; his season was done, no more piss tests to worry about. Not that he'd had to worry, the new masking agent worked a treat.

He was working the room, taking the backslaps and congratulations, sinking into Finn's hug for a moment too long before he extricated himself and asked if they were coming out.

"Nah," Finn grabbed George by the waist and pulled him against his side. "We're heading back to Sydney 'cos someone doesn't want to be away from little man for a whole night."

"Hey, now," George said, but his affronted tone was undermined by the adoring look he was giving Finn, "I'm pretty sure you booked the flights."

"Like I had a choice," Finn snickered.

George pressed a firm kiss to Finn's temple and Finn leaned into it, his hand tightening on George's waist. And Lacy loved them, he really did, but he needed to get away from the vision they presented in their sharply tailored suits, the open affection they'd displayed all night.

He made a hasty exit, but not before Finn could tug him into another tight hug; bloody kid had super instincts for when a man needed a hug, and Lacy gripped him back, knowing Finn would get it.

"Come up to Sydney after the Grand Final," Finn said.

"Yeah, maybe." He got out of there.

He bumped into Sandra as he tried to get out of the ballroom. She was dolled up nicely, standing with Lacy's mum.

"We're going to the after party," his mum said, "you really should make an appearance."

"Yeah, not feelin' it, eh," he replied. He'd hit up a bar where he knew other guys from the parties would be, get laid. He turned to Sandra. "That stuff Colton got worked a treat, eh?"

Sandra frowned at him. "No," she said like he was stupid, "miners gettin' done all over the place."

"What?" he asked. He'd been 'clean' all season according to his samples.

"He didn't tell you?" she asked, her made-up face smoothing out as she realised something.

"Who?"

"That lanky ruckman you're banging," she laughed and drained her glass.

Lacy felt a hot rush at the thought of Thad banging him. Except he wasn't, not anymore. So he needed to get out of there, pick up and get rid of this awful feeling.

"What's Thad got to do with it?"

"He swapped out all your samples," she said, glancing around the room like she was looking for more champagne. She was already pretty pissed, but she'd obviously done some coke because she was buzzing drunk, like where he wanted to be. She looked back at him.

"I think I wasn't supposed to tell you that," she laughed and wandered off.

His mum watched her go. "Hmm."

"I've gotta get out of here. Sorry, Mum," he leaned up, kissed her cheek and she patted him on the shoulder.

"You do what you gotta do," she squeezed his bicep. "Congratulations. Don't let whatever this business is ruin your night."

"Yeah, no, course," he strode away from her.

Clearly, she didn't get it. He pushed through the huge door and strolled across the carpeted foyer, nodded to the few people mingling, drinking.

Lacy stopped at the top of the stairs.

Thad turned from where he'd been leaning against the rail at the bottom of the steps. He was dressed in a nice suit, nothing fancy, black and fitted, a white shirt and tie, his hands tucked loosely in his pockets as he smiled up at Lacy.

"What're you doin' here?" Lacy asked.

"I was watching at home and when it was clear you were going to win it, I changed and came down," he shrugged like it was no big deal. "Wanted to say congratulations."

"But... you're in Tasmania."

Thad smiled bashfully and ducked his head, his hair falling in his eyes. "No, I'm here."

"Why?" Lacy asked. He was frozen at the top of the steps, the medal heavy around his neck.

"Umm," Thad met his eyes, friendly enough but hesitant too. "I guess I didn't feel like going home yet."

Because he's probably dating fucking Carol.

"Are you going to celebrate?" Thad asked warmly.

"Yeah, I dunno, wasn't really feelin' it," he ran a hand through his hair, but it was sticky with gel. He dropped his hand.

"Oh, well, you should, I mean, watching and re-living all those games?" Thad prompted. "You were incredible this year."

"Eh, same old shit," Lacy quipped because he never felt comfortable harping on it. "Are you gonna head to the after party?"

Thad seemed surprised by the question. "Well, I'd rather go where ever you're going, but if you're not up to celebrating then I guess I'll go home too." He smiled, perfectly fine with returning home after getting changed and coming out only to see Lacy for a few minutes.

"Nah, you should go to the party, it's always a blast, especially when you're not in the final, you can really cut loose," he didn't know what he was on about—Thad didn't drink, how would any of that be a bonus for him?

But Thad simply smiled, nodded his head. "Well, I better," he waved at the doors. They hadn't moved to get closer and he was still at the bottom of the stairs while Lacy stood above him. "Can I drop you home? Or somewhere?"

"Wanna get a coffee?" Lacy asked.

"I'd love to," Thad responded quickly.

Lacy exhaled. "There's this place in Docklands, quiet."

"Sounds perfect," Thad smiled, disarming in its sincerity.

Lacy trotted down the steps, Thad's smell wafting over him as he got closer—his deodorant on clean skin—and he had to stop himself from leaning in, tucking his head into Thad's throat to breathe it in. He knew if he pressed himself against Thad like that, Thad's arms would come around his back immediately and hold him close. Or, they would have before. He didn't know what Thad would do now, probably push him off gently with an apology.

"Let's do it," he said, maintaining a careful space between them as they headed out the massive glass doors.

It was cold. They perched on the edge of a wall overlooking the black water of the bay, the apartments and high-rise buildings of Docklands sterile behind them, the little van that served coffee a squat box of warmth in a sea of concrete.

Lacy blew on his coffee and looked out over the water, Thad a warm line beside him, close but not touching.

"Congratulations again, it really was something else, re-living those rounds," Thad said.

"Yeah," Lacy replied. He wondered if Thad re-lived the slump the way he did. Or if he remembered those weeks with relief—he'd finally gotten his prayers answered, gotten free from his sin.

"That game up in Brisbane," Thad shook his head with wonder. "It was like you had the wind at your back when there was no wind at all."

Lacy laughed. That had been a good game. The old feelings for the game had come back—footy had always been the one place where he'd come fully alive, like nothing else mattered and no one could touch him. Footy had rescued him like that once before.

"I never did tell you about Parks did I," Lacy said, eyes on the water, the lights reflecting and rippling below them. "My brother."

"No," Thad said after a moment, his tone careful like he knew this wasn't a good story. It was obviously not a good story—if someone has a brother that no one's ever seen or heard about, that's not a good story is it? Lacy wasn't sure why he wanted to tell the story now, but thinking about those games, about what Parks gave him, in a roundabout fucked up way, he just wanted to say it. The Brownlow around his neck was a culmination of the player he'd become because of that horrific day.

"I was always a good player, right?" he glanced at Thad. Thad was watching him, expression open and curious, but careful too. "I don't mean in a bragging way, but ya know what I mean," he huffed. "When you're good, you're fuckin' good. And I worked hard and all that, even with the piss and pot back home. I worked hard."

Thad made a noise of acknowledgement, of course he knew.

"But I went next level after Parks died," he finished quietly.

He didn't know how to put the next part into words because it wasn't for good reasons. It wasn't to honour his memory or any of that bullshit. Parks and him had been thick as thieves. They had different Dads—Parks was the kid his mum had from the brief marriage to Mr Parker. Another poor kid with a horrendous soapie name, Thorne Brandon Parker, so everyone called him Parks from the start to save him from that horror. He was like Lacy's little shadow. Lacy was three years older, but he couldn't remember Parks not being there. They did everything together except sports. Parks was tall and he would've grown into a muscular beast if he had grown up beyond sixteen at all. He'd played basketball, done martial arts. He'd been funny and kind once you got to know him, but he had a chip on his shoulder too. Mr Parker had walked out and never looked back before Parks could even talk. But it was all garden variety shit—Parks could be sullen, but then he'd come out and hit the piss and do funny shit like take his pants off and wave his dick around, draw with permanent marker on Tommy's face when he was passed out, giggling-drunk and high—there was never anything to show there was something wrong. To this day, no one knew why he did what he did.

"He killed himself," Lacy said and heard Thad's intake of breath. "Yeah," Lacy breathed out. "It was fucked up." He could still see it—opening the bathroom door and seeing Parks hanging there, his face so purple, bloated, he couldn't recognise him and yet he was trying to lift him and he must've been yelling for help but he didn't remember making the noise, just the sound of his mum behind him, the screaming.

"But anyway," he said, swallowing a few times. "After the start bit, ya know, the grief, it was like, he set me free, ya know?"

Lacy looked over at Thad. Thad was waiting for him, a question in his eyes.

"Like, I saw death. I saw it and I knew any second I could be gone too and I just, I felt free after that, felt like I'd found another gear," he fingered the medal around his neck. "And I reckon I got Parks to thank for that."

"I'm so sorry, Lacy," Thad said and Lacy knew he really meant it.

"It's in the past, eh? Almost ten years ago," Lacy shrugged. "But Tommy, he reckons I'm an asshole for never goin' to the memorial each year. It's just a piss up, but see, I reckon I remember Parks whenever I play. And I don't wanna remember him like they do. Gettin' pissed and cryin' by the end of the night, thinkin' only of him as this dead guy. He's not just some dead guy to me, he was really fuckin' alive."

"I can't even imagine it," Thad said. "But I think it's good you remember him the way you do, because he wasn't only his death."

"Right?" Lacy said. "The part that sucks is it was like a part of me died too. I know people say that, but I don't reckon they mean it right. Like, actual stuff died. All the names we called each other, that shorthand and shit. The way we'd rip into Mum, just for fun, it all died too. Anyway," he drained his coffee, "I don't like to think about him except to remember what he showed me about comin' alive. And I come alive when I play."

He didn't mention that when Thad had entered his life, he'd come alive then too.

"So," he held up the medal, pointing it out at the ocean. "Thanks, Parks, wherever you are, ya useless cunt," he laughed wetly.

Thad wrapped his arm around his shoulders.

Lacy sank into it. There was nothing sexual about it, but it was exactly what he needed.

35

THAD WAS IN THE box for the Grand Final the following Saturday, Lacy by his side for the whole game, sipping his beers, commentating, cheering for Sydney, gutted for Finn when Sydney lost.

Thad was only half watching the game. He was more focused on Lacy beside him. He hadn't lied—he really had booked a flight back to Tasmania—but at the last minute, he knew he couldn't go. He had to stay on the mainland, he had to stay close to Lacy.

As they left the ground and headed for Lacy's place, Thad asked when Lacy was heading off on a trip. He'd been reluctant to ask because he didn't want to know. But he knew Lacy had a flight booked for the next day, somewhere in Europe, somewhere Thad could no longer go.

"Nah, probably gonna hang around Melbourne for a bit," Lacy said.

"Really?" Thad glanced at him in the passenger's seat. Lacy was slumped, hands tapping the beat on his knees.

"Really," Lacy smiled over at him. "How 'bout you? Did you book another flight?"

"Umm, no, not yet," Thad focused on the road. "I'm thinking I might hang around in Melbourne for a bit too."

"No shit?" Lacy asked, the smile in his voice. "Well, if you want some company."

Thad met his eyes. "I want some company."

And the summer was looking a whole lot brighter. He might never have the courage to tell Lacy how he felt, his plan to say something after the Brownlow firmly relegated to the backburner when Lacy told him about his brother, which was obviously more important. But Thad had lost his nerve before they'd even made it to Docklands. Looking at Lacy in his designer suit, slicked back hair, his radiant face, all of his resolve had fled. Thad didn't feel worthy of Lacy on a good day, never mind when he was standing above him in all his masculine glory, the medal resting on his chest a physical manifestation of what everyone already knew—Lacy was the best man amongst them. And Thad knew that went way beyond who he was as a player.

"So," Lacy said. "What's on the agenda? Building homeless shelters? Rescuing kittens? Starting a tennis club for heroin addicts?" Lacy snickered. "Can you imagine people on smack tryin' to play tennis?"

"I think that would be a very slow game."

Lacy cracked up. "Do you play tennis?"

"I do, yes. Do you?" Thad glanced at him.

"Yeah, I'm a bit of a loose cannon with it, but yeah," Lacy said. "We should have a game."

"I'd love to," Thad beamed and felt emboldened to ask Lacy if he wanted to do something else.

"There's a church social this weekend," he tapped his fingers on the steering wheel as he made his way down Lacy's street. "But other than that, not much on other than the usual," he answered Lacy's original question. He took a deep breath and asked. "Do you want to come to the social?"

He parked. Lacy hadn't answered.

"You want me to come to your church social?"

Thad felt embarrassed. Of course Lacy didn't want to go to something like that. "Please don't feel obliged, it's just, well, you know Glen and Stacy and Carol and they ask about you, so..."

"Yeah, no, ah, sounds lit," Lacy replied, so much effort in his tone, Thad had to laugh.

"I don't know about lit, but there's always good food."

"Do you bring food?"

"I always bring a plate, yes."

"Then I'm in," Lacy said with more enthusiasm.

"Good, great, alright," he tapped the steering wheel.

"You wanna come in? Watch the highlights. Actually, no, I don't wanna see Finn crying again. But we could watch Juventus?"

"I'd love to," Thad replied.

He settled in next to Lacy on his couch, their feet kicked up onto the coffee table. Every now and then Lacy's barefoot would tap against his and rest there. Thad would work up to it, but then he'd rub his foot up and down the side of Lacy's. Lacy always pushed back into the touch.

36

"ALL OF THE WOMEN here have tried it on," the pretty woman Lacy was talking to said, her eyes drifting to where Thad was talking to Carol near the DJ booth. She inclined her head at Carol. "Age appropriate," and then to a group of older women, "and not."

It was a joke and Lacy forced himself to laugh. It sounded like a crow dying, but the woman—Cathy, he was sure she introduced herself as Cathy—giggled and focused on him.

"We thought maybe he already had someone back home?"

Lacy took a bite of the quiche and placed it back on the paper plate. He chewed and hated how good it tasted. These church fuckers could really cook. He heard Thad's laughter over the eighties ballad the DJ had snuck in between the Christian rock, *Icehouse* blaring "Electric Blue" not loud enough to drown out the hum of chatter, the burst of Thad's laugh. Carol was saying something, her smile stretching her beautiful, smooth face under the blue and pink fairy lights strung up around the hall.

He looked back to Cathy and realised she was waiting for an answer. Lacy had no idea. Did Thad have someone back home? Did this religion do some purity ring bullshit and that was why he hadn't formally started up with Carol? It seemed nutty enough if Thad's virginity and celibacy were anything to go by. Lacy almost cracked it thinking how epically Thad had failed at that because of him. But then he thought it wasn't funny at all.

"I dunno," he said honestly.

"Hmm," Cathy said. "Carol doesn't think so either."

"Thad talked to Carol about it?" he asked before he could stop himself. He sounded like a high schooler trying to gauge who his fucking crush liked.

"Oh, I don't know? But they're friends," she shrugged, it made her perfect tits move enticingly under her cream jumper. She was as pretty as Carol, but in a womanlier way, with a tiny waist and an obvious ass. Lacy knew she was the kind of chick guys would try to fuck—small with a lot to grab onto.

"I think Carol wants more, but—"

"Footy's really important to Thad," Lacy cut in. "Not much time for the other business." He shoved the rest of the quiche into his mouth to stop himself from talking.

"Oh, of course," she nodded, smiled politely. She was probably thinking about all the players with wives and kids. Hell, Finn and George had a kid and this religion might be anti-gay but it's not like they wouldn't be aware that a player and an assistant coach were married with a kid.

Lacy swallowed. "Maybe after," he said to try and soften the blow. "Excuse me."

"Of course," she smiled warmly. "Hopefully we'll see you on Sunday."

"Uh, yeah."

He needed to leave. There was probably a tram he could catch. He could get a car, but then he'd have to wait around. Surely there was a tram. If Carol wanted more, it was only a matter of time before Thad realised what was right in front of him, if he hadn't already.

The cool of the evening around him helped him breathe as he headed for the road. He heard the door whoosh open behind him, footsteps on the asphalt.

"Lacy," Thad called.

"I'm heading out," Lacy called back, raising his hand. He didn't want to look at Thad right now, he was too angry at himself—what had he been thinking? That he'd show Thad he could be interested in his religion and Thad would what? Deign to fuck him again? Stop seeing what they did as some fucked up sin?

Thad jogged alongside him. "You should've said."

"I'm good, you go back in. I'll just get the ah," he looked at the dark, suburban street, stopped, pulled out his phone and opened maps. "I'll get a tram."

"What? But we're having dinner," Thad said.

"I already ate," Lacy said.

"Social food is not a proper meal," Thad said warmly. He was either oblivious to Lacy's freak-out or ignoring it. "Come on. I've had the slow cooker going all day."

Lacy was staring down at his maps. Thad hovered beside him. Thad was here now with him, not with Carol, he was willing and happy to take Lacy home, spend the evening together. Lacy was never going to have the ability to say no to him.

"Yeah, alright," he said.

Thad breathed out, relieved.

"You coming?" Thad was leaning back into the car, the cool air of the night rushing over Lacy where he sat.

"Ah, yeah, I dunno," he mumbled.

"Are you feeling okay?" Thad asked. Lacy was staring ahead out the windscreen, but he could hear the concern in Thad's voice.

"Yeah," Lacy replied, really dragging it out. "I might just go home."

Thad didn't say anything. Lacy could hear him breathing quietly beside him.

"Okay," he said finally and got back into the car.

"Nah, man, I'll get a car," Lacy unclipped his seatbelt. "You go in, eat."

Thad clapped him on the thigh and Lacy froze. "You're not getting a car," he said quietly. "I can drive you."

"Okay," Lacy replied because he couldn't say anything else with Thad's hand on him, radiating warmth all through his body.

The drive to his place was silent. He kept trying to think of something to say and came up empty and the longer they both went saying nothing, the more awkward it would feel to say something.

Thad parked and turned the engine off.

"Thanks," Lacy said.

"Can I come in for a sec?" Thad asked.

"Yeah, sure," Lacy replied because why the fuck not at this point? It's not like things could get any more strained.

Thad stood in his kitchen, a glass of water in hand, untouched, his gaze going to Lacy before shifting away again.

Lacy stood there, tapping the bench. He couldn't even bring himself to drink a beer. He watched his hand and thought about the couples at the social, their kids running around in fancy dresses and nice pants with proper button up shirts, balloons and streamers in their hands as they shrieked and played to the music. He thought about Thad and Carol together in some future, together at church, and God help him, Thad would probably invite him to his wedding. Thad would probably expect him to come to another social and see how his kids were doing.

"Guess that's gonna be you one day, eh?" he said, eyes on his hand.

"What's going to be me?" Thad asked.

"Getting married, having kids," Lacy replied.

Thad made a surprised noise. He placed his glass of water on the counter with a loud clink. Lacy couldn't look at him.

"I know," Thad began nervously, "I know I'm not good enough for you—"

Lacy's head snapped up. "Not good enough for me?"

Thad's eyes were skittish, but he was straightening like he really had something to say. "Religion's for the intellectually weak, remember?"

"I shouldn't have said that—"

"And I get it, I really do. I've heard it before," Thad finished.

"I didn't fuckin' mean it."

Thad looked away like he didn't believe him. "It doesn't matter."

"Yes it does," Lacy straightened up too. "I'm really fuckin' sorry, okay? I shouldn't have said it. I was just mad 'cos you were acting like you weren't gay."

"I'm not gay," Thad replied.

Lacy deflated. If Thad wasn't even prepared to fight the first round, what chance did they have? He almost laughed—they never stood a chance.

"I reckon your dick up my ass would beg to differ, but alright," he muttered.

Thad blushed, but he didn't drop his gaze. "Well, it's inconclusive. But, look, don't laugh at me, okay?"

"I'm not gonna laugh at you," Lacy said.

Thad gave him a sceptical look, but it was Thad so it was tinged with kindness, which made it worse.

"I'd never laugh at you," Lacy said.

Thad nodded like he believed him. He took a deep breath. "I prayed on it."

Lacy wasn't laughing. He knew what Thad prayed about.

"And I asked if I was gay," Thad said.

"And you're not. So, good for you, praise Jesus," Lacy said.

"No, I'm not, I don't know," Thad rambled, but his eyes wouldn't leave Lacy's face, like he really wanted him to hear this. "But then I asked about how I feel about you."

Lacy tensed.

"I prayed on it and—"

Lacy really didn't want to hear this. "How do you know you're not just hearin' what you wanna hear when you do that?"

Thad smiled, it was small and it touched his eyes. "It's called faith."

"Right, well, lucky you, ya dodged this bullet—"

Thad stepped closer. "Can you let me finish? I really need to say this. Then I can go, but I need to say this."

Lacy looked up at him. He took a deep breath. "Shoot," he said on the exhale.

"I asked if what I felt for you was okay," he took a deep breath, his eyes never leaving Lacy's, "and it is. What I feel for you is okay."

"What do you feel for me?" Lacy asked, his fingers twitching on the bench.

"I love you," Thad said simply.

Lacy clenched his hand into a fist. "Like in a best friend's way. Yeah, man, me too—"

Thad shook his head and inched closer. "No, in a lover's way. In a partner's way."

"What about Carol?" Lacy asked because he could not believe Thad was saying lover's and partner's in his direction and he was so close it was making Lacy's heart race.

"Carol?" Thad asked like she was an alien he'd never met.

"Yeah. Carol. Aren't you gonna marry her?" He tried to sound normal, even bitter would be better than the hurt colouring the question.

"No," Thad said slowly, baffled.

"Oh, well, maybe let her know that," he mumbled.

"I've never, not once, done anything to indicate to Carol or anyone else that I was available or interested," Thad said.

"Yeah, but, you are," Lacy said.

Thad sighed. His hand, when he placed it beside Lacy's on the bench, trembled. "I know, or I knew, telling you... you wouldn't want to hear it. But I had to say it, because I was wrong."

"Hold up," Lacy said. "I don't wanna hear it? Why would you think that?"

"Come on, Lacy, I know you've moved on. And you think I'm weak, mentally, for believing in God—"

Lacy held up his hand. "Moved on?"

Thad waved his hand at Lacy's throat and then dropped his gaze, his jaw clenching.

Lacy touched his neck. Guys left marks. He'd fucked other guys since he broke up with Thad. But moved on? Those were perfunctory fucks to get off. What he did with Thad? Whole other ball game.

He grabbed Thad's hand.

"I don't think you're mentally weak for being religious, alright? I was mad. I thought we were something and you were praying that away every fucking night," he squeezed Thad's hand. Thad squeezed him back.

"And yeah, I let some other guys fuck me—"

"How many?" Thad said.

Lacy had to pause. "I dunno, a few."

Thad scoffed. "Did you go to one of those parties?"

"No," Lacy said. He got invited. He couldn't go. Thad had ruined it.

Thad crushed his hand. "How many's a few?"

"It doesn't matter. I thought you were gonna marry Carol, so what did it matter?"

"It matters to me," Thad said. "How many? Did you like them?"

"Like them? I wouldn't even be able to identify them in a line up."

"Did they make you feel good? Did you, you know," Thad waved the hand that wasn't crushing Lacy's at Lacy's dick.

"Well, yeah."

Thad made a pained sound.

"Thad, man, you were prayin' the gay away," Lacy said.

"I was wrong."

"How do you know you're right now?"

Thad met his eyes and he looked so sure. "I know."

"Yeah, but—"

"You know what it felt like when I asked about you?"

"What?"

"Warm, like everything was finally right, it felt right," he shrugged, casual. "I got my answer."

Lacy swallowed. Surely Thad wasn't serious. "So, now that God says it's all cool, then what, we can be together?"

"Yes," Thad said.

Lacy was about to object, but Thad cut him off. "It's not God, it's me. It's the Holy Spirit communicating through me. Like, that's how I speak with God because it's part of me. I've never had something feel so right. Never. I know. So, now it's just, well," he shrugged, his warm brown eyes flitting nervously on Lacy's again. "Well, it's your call. If you want to be with me."

Lacy extricated his hand and panic flitted across Thad's face, but Lacy gripped him by the hips and dropped his head against his chest.

"Lacy?" Thad asked, his palms coming to rest on Lacy's back tentatively.

"Give me a sec," Lacy said, his voice choked.

Thad's hands moved up and down his back gently, Lacy's head moving with his even breaths.

Lacy cleared his throat, pushing down the lump tightening around his voice box. He looked up. "Do I wanna be with you? Are you fuckin' kidding me?"

"No?" Thad replied.

Lacy leaned up and kissed him.

Thad wrapped his arms around his back and kissed him back so fiercely, Lacy was crushed against the edge of the counter.

Thad broke the kiss. "Is that a yes?"

Lacy laughed. "It's a hell yes."

Thad snickered. "Lacy."

"Sorry, it's a fuck yes," Lacy said and deepened the kiss.

Thad sat naked on the edge of Lacy's bed, reaching for him with a warm smile. Things had gotten heated fast in the kitchen, months of pent-up sexual frustration spilling over. It was still there, in the way Thad was looking at him, but as Lacy straddled his waist and Thad kissed him, he felt the restraint in Thad's movements.

"Like this," Thad said against Lacy's lips.

He was cradled in Thad's lap, Thad's feet planted on the floor, his arms holding Lacy close. Lacy lifted his hips and lined himself up with Thad's erection, his hole hastily prepared with Thad's tongue and fingers when things went warp-speed in the kitchen.

As he sank down, Thad tugged him closer, rested his forehead against Lacy's as he panted softly.

Lacy rolled his hips and Thad thrust up, inching his head back so he could see Lacy's face. Lacy knew their fucking had always been heavy on the eye contact, but this was something else. On the edge of his bed, face to face, the lights bright, watching each other, mapping every little sound, clocking the spot that made Thad feel good and clenching his ass muscles to do it again.

Thad cracked a smile, a puff of air. "Missed you."

"Yeah? Miss this ass, baby?" Lacy asked. Thad laughed and groaned at the same time.

"Missed all of you," Thad said, rolling his hips up. Lacy was a fan of the core strength this position demanded—he dropped his gaze and traced his fingers over Thad's abs, touched the grooves and lines of his muscles, panted against his collar bones.

"I won't last," Thad said apologetically.

"Yeah?" Lacy looked up and met his eyes, spoke against his lips. "You haven't come since the last time we did it?"

"No, I," Thad planted his feet and really started to give it to him. "I masturbated, thought of you."

"Oh, yeah, fuck yeah, you did, me too, me too," Lacy replied. Thad was absolutely nailing him; he grabbed his dick and started to jerk off roughly.

"Same time?" Thad panted, his forehead dropped to Lacy's, his gaze on Lacy's dick. Lacy felt him wet his lips.

"Yeah," Lacy breathed.

"I'm going to—"

"Give me a sec," Lacy bit out and increased the pressure on his dick, increased the pace.

Thad held himself back, panted against Lacy's cheek.

"Now," Lacy said as he felt it rushing up.

Thad crushed him against his chest as he let go, his hips pounding in. Lacy felt deliciously wet as Thad filled him with his come.

His own orgasm was a second later, shooting all over Thad's chest, catching on his nipple.

Thad cradled him and Lacy slumped into his chest, semen and sweat slick between them. Thad rubbed his scalp, kissed the side of his head, ran a firm hand up and down his back.

"I missed you so much," he whispered against Lacy's hair. "Do you know how hard it's been not to touch you?"

"Yeah," Lacy breathed. "I've got a bit of an idea. I thought you were gonna marry Carol."

Thad tightened his arm around him. "Never," he kissed the side of Lacy's throat. His soft laugh was a puff of air against Lacy's skin. "Carol."

"What?" Lacy said and inched back. Thad's dick was still inside him. Lacy lifted to stretch his legs around Thad's waist, crossing his ankles at his lower back. He loved this position, he felt held. "She's fuckin' hot, man. And she's so into you."

Thad rolled his eyes. Lacy had never seen him do that before. He laughed. Thad smiled like he'd done something right. "How could I marry Carol when I'm in love with you? I can't even kiss anyone but you."

Lacy grinned, but it was thin with bravado. Thad was in love with him. Thad wasn't going to marry Carol. He still didn't know if he had permission to believe it.

"I reckon a lotta gay church boys marry women," he said.

Thad stroked his back. "You're probably right, but I think," he lifted Lacy and shuffled back, bringing them down to lay together on the bed, Lacy sprawled on his chest. He tucked Lacy's hair behind his ear, stroked a finger down his cheek. "I couldn't get you out of my heart, I couldn't marry someone else. I'd always be thinking of you."

Lacy turned to kiss his hand.

Thad smiled. His hair was fanning out on the white bedspread, his smooth skin flushed, eyes warm and all for Lacy.

"What about the other stuff?" Lacy leaned down and kissed Thad's chest, teased his nipple with his tongue. Thad arched into it. "The parties and stuff."

Thad tightened his arms around Lacy's back.

"You wanna be exclusive?" Lacy asked.

"I," Thad swallowed. "I don't ever want another man to touch you if I'm not there."

"And if you are there?" Lacy kissed between his pecs.

"I," Thad rolled his hips up, his laugh was a whoosh of breath. "I can't even pray on it, it's so…"

Lacy rested his chin on Thad's chest and looked up. Thad met his eyes. "Maybe we can keep this one between us, leave the big man out of it."

"Yes," Thad said, smiling, his gaze all heat.

"Fuck, ya love it, don't you?" Lacy said, grinning.

Thad groaned and buried his face in Lacy's throat. "I love you. I love making you happy."

"Yeah? It doesn't make you happy? Ordering some other guy around on how best to fuck me?" Lacy asked. He loved it, but he didn't need it. But he reckoned Thad loved it even more than he did.

Thad pressed his face against Lacy's cheek and breathed his answer against his skin. "It makes me so jealous. It makes me feel so," he mouthed at his skin, "aroused."

"Yeah," Lacy turned his face, whispered his answer against Thad's lips, "'cos ya know ya gonna fuck me after, ya know I'm all yours."

Thad turned the conversation into a kiss, a kiss that lasted until they were hard again and Thad rolled him underneath his body, fucked him missionary with more of that crazy eye contact, and as Lacy arched and gasped into it, he couldn't believe it was real.

37

"**S**HIT," LACY PUSHED OUT of the hold Thad on him.

"What is it?" Thad asked, his heart rate picking up. He knew Lacy had agreed to take him back far too quickly.

"You've got the slow cooker on," Lacy said.

"It's set to warm," Thad replied, relief bubbling up to dampen the fear. "I set it to warm before the social."

"Thank, fuck," Lacy slumped back into the pillow, "just had a horrible thought of all that food burning."

Thad laughed and ran his hand up Lacy's chest. "Are you hungry? You want me to go get us some food?"

"You don't gotta do that," Lacy smiled up at him. He was gorgeous, his eyes finally shedding the darkness that'd been flanking them for months. The sadness Thad had put there. He was going to spend his life making it up to him.

"If you're hungry, I do," he leaned down to kiss him, then moved to get out of bed.

Lacy slid his arms around his waist to hold him back. "Don't be ridiculous, babe."

Thad's heart skipped a beat at the endearment.

"I'll come with you," Lacy shuffled forward.

Thad grabbed his hand before he could get out of bed.

Lacy glanced back, his smile a question. Thad squeezed his hand. Lacy returned it and searched Thad's expression.

"All good?" he asked.

"Yes," Thad breathed out and stood.

Lacy put a hand on his chest to stop him. Thad looked down. Lacy's lips quirked up, but his eyes were nervous.

"Ya know I love you too, right?"

Thad felt his heart bloom with that warmth again. How could he ever question the rightness of this feeling? How could loving Lacy ever be a sin?

"I had hoped so," he replied stilted around the feeling.

"Ain't no need to hope, babe," Lacy said, the words sure but he was nervous, Thad could tell.

"Well then," Thad cradled his face in his hands and leaned down, "we love each other," he grinned, giddy, the kiss a fumble of lips as they laughed.

They'd been together for a week when Thad brought up what he wanted to do next. He was driving them home from the tennis club because they'd actually gone and played a game. Lacy hadn't been kidding—'loose with it' was one way to put his style of play. He was like a maniac on the court, rushing the net and smacking volleys so hard the ball shot into the sky and flew up for so long they both stopped to watch it. He danced on the line and ran at Thad's serves, cracking them back with compact speed, skidding the lines of being in every time in ways that seemed to defy the laws of physics. And a good rally wasn't the nice, clean shots Thad had been used to learning and playing at the Launceston tennis club; they involved Lacy racing back and smacking the ball over his head with a no-look hit, before charging the net to crack the ball back into Thad's chest on the return.

He won in three sets.

"Where'd you learn to play like that?" Thad asked when they were done. He was watching Lacy wipe the sweat off his face and throat, his hands twitching at his sides because he wanted to reach over and stroke Lacy's hip, his ass, lean down and kiss his panting lips. But people were playing on other courts, people had recognised them.

"We had to do tennis in PE," Lacy said easily. He smirked as he went on. "But we used to play on Sundays at the Frankston Tennis Club. Get loaded on piss and dexies and scare all the oldies. Summer, ya know? No footy."

Thad huffed a laugh imagining it. "No cricket?" Summer was either cricket or tennis. He didn't know why he'd never wondered which one Lacy did—most players were cricket. But now he thought about it, he couldn't imagine Lacy playing cricket. And Thad himself had always loved tennis, even though he was a decent cricket player, a solid opening batsman.

Lacy placed his towel around his neck with a sharp tug and grinned. "I played one game, coach asked me never to come back."

"What'd you do?" Thad asked. He wanted to kiss the beaming smile off Lacy's face; he was loving the return of the gap-toothed grin.

"Bodyline," Lacy said and winked. "Those Melbourne private fuckin' school boys asked for it."

Thad cracked up. Bodyline was the infamous play the English cricket team brought to shut down Don Bradman—the GOAT of cricket—in 1932. It involved bowling the ball into the opponent's body rather than aiming for the wicket. He could only imagine Lacy's interpretation against a private school team. And with his speed and agility, he'd have been a killer fast bowler.

"So, yeah, tennis," Lacy finished with a shrug. "How 'bout you?"

"Both," Thad smiled. "But I prefer tennis."

"Sweet, so, same time next week?"

"It's a date," Thad replied. It took all his willpower not to take Lacy's hand as they left the court.

Lacy bumped him, let his body linger against Thad's side as they walked like he wanted to take Thad's hand too. "Tennis, sex, dinner, more sex, drinks, then more sex?"

Thad snorted a laugh. He felt a blush rising, but he answered with a simple, "Yes."

He knew what he wanted to do next. Or maybe not right next, but after that. It was time. He needed to ask.

They were sprawled on Lacy's couch after they got home, sweaty and naked, the litany of Lacy's words about how horny Thad got him with the way he played—Thad thought he played pretty boringly compared to Lacy's display—about how hard it was to play with his dick getting hard—and they were catching their breaths, gazes held as they chuckled softly at how frantically they'd just sucked each other off when Thad asked.

"Come to Tassie and meet my parents?"

"I've met your parents," Lacy replied. "Several times."

This was true, Lacy came over for dinner whenever they played in Launceston. He hadn't come this year after Thad hurt him, but he did the year before.

"I mean," he reached for Lacy's hand, "meet them as my boyfriend."

Lacy was still sucking in pulls of air, had been smiling. The smile vanished. "You sure? Won't they be like, disappointed?"

Thad took an extra deep breath. "They love me. And I love you," he ran his fingers over Lacy's knuckles. "I don't want to hide you from them."

Lacy let his eyes slip closed and nodded. There was a little frown between his eyes. "I love you too. Shit, so much," he exhaled and rolled his head on the couch to look at Thad. "I don't want you gettin' hurt."

"They'd never hurt me," Thad smiled reassuringly.

"If you're sure," Lacy rolled closer and hooked his leg over Thad's waist, sat up and straddled him. Thad rested his hands on his hips. "'Cos, like, yeah, I'm super fuckin' down to be introduced as your boyfriend, but like, I can't say I'd be okay with anyone hurtin' you. But if you're sure..."

"I'm sure," Thad said. He was excited.

Lacy smiled down at him and Thad had to kiss him.

They kissed until it was dark and dinner and a shower became imperative, and all Thad could think as he felt Lacy's lips against his, touched his skin, was how lucky he was to have found this, how could anyone he loved not be happy for him?

He wasn't naïve, he knew the church would not be okay with it and he'd manage that bridge when he came to it. His parents though? He wanted to share it with them.

The clock on the wall in his parents' dining room ticked loudly. Thad knew the clock well; he didn't remember it ever feeling like it consumed the room. His parents had been thrilled when he said he was coming down, though he heard the subdued confusion when he said he'd be bringing Lacy to stay for a few weeks and they'd rented a house halfway between the farm and Launceston.

"Why?" his mum had asked.

"Well, we're on a break, so we're probably going to be going out, getting in late. We'd rather not disturb you," he explained and wondered if she could already tell all the parts he was leaving out. He wasn't sure if he hoped she could or not—it'd certainly make it easier if she had an inkling of what he and Lacy were to each other.

"You could never disturb us," she said, still baffled.

"No, I know, it's just a," he tried to think of a word, "a holiday."

She didn't say anything and Thad took the opportunity to end the call.

They'd rented a hire car at the airport, dropped their bags at the house they'd rented. A gorgeous cottage on a little farm. Thad wrapped his arms around Lacy in the bedroom, the cast iron four-poster bed a promise. But he needed to see his parents first. He was buzzing with nervous excitement and he needed to get it done. Then they could come home and celebrate.

He told Lacy as much.

"Sounds like a plan," Lacy said and took his hand. He gave Thad a reassuring smile. He'd been in this mode since they woke up—it was the same way he got when they had a big game and he was reassuring the whole team with a solid presence. Thad didn't know how to tell him it wasn't necessary—his parents loved Lacy.

Sitting at the dining table, his mum across from them, his dad at the head of the table, steaming cups of coffee in front of them, a plate of freshly baked scones, he felt that warmth again, that feeling of rightness.

"So what have you boys got planned for the holiday?" his dad asked and sipped his coffee. "You have to take Lacy up to Cataract Gorge. And the tennis club. Thad says you've been playing?" he directed at Lacy.

"Actually," Thad said before Lacy could answer. "There's some news I want to share."

The energy in the room shifted, his parents snapping to attention, a brusque expectancy from his dad in the way he straightened, his mum's lips curling up at the corners. He took Lacy's hand and brought their clasped palms to rest on the table.

"Lacy and I are together," he took a deep breath. "We're in love. We're together."

The clock ticked steadily. His mum's eyes darted to their joined hands. His dad's brow creased.

Thad glanced at Lacy. Lacy nodded his head, squeezed his hand.

"We'd love your blessing," Thad said and looked from his mum to his dad.

"You boys are..." his dad trailed off.

His mum said nothing. Thad looked at her.

She'd gone from shocked to tight around the eyes.

"Thaddeus, you're not..." she trailed off like she couldn't say the word.

"I'm in love with Lacy," he said.

"And I'm in love with your son," Lacy said firmly. And by God, Thad loved him. To look at, Lacy was a party boy; a tattoo-covered, scrappy-looking wild man. But he was serious when it mattered, the kind of guy you wanted at your back in a war—he'd fight beside you and patch up your wounds afterwards.

"Sorry, boys, I think you need to explain this," his dad said, a note of fragility behind the gruffness. "Thaddeus, are you saying you're a homosexual?"

"Don't say that," his mum said quietly, her tone sharp. All eyes looked at her. "You're not," she said firmly, her warm features like stone.

Thad faltered. Her look was so foreign. "I am with Lacy," he said and he could hear the wavering of his certainty. "I'm going to spend my life with him."

"No," she stood. "No, you're not. I can't," she dropped her eyes, her head shaking. "We can't accept this."

She left the room, the sound of her little feet clipping down the hallway, her bedroom door closing with a soft click.

The clock ticked and Thad watched the space where she disappeared. A pain he couldn't believe spread through his chest.

"Thaddeus," his dad said.

Thad looked at him through the haze of shock.

His dad swallowed and lowered his voice. "You sure you just haven't met the right girl yet?"

Thad gripped Lacy's hand so tightly, he was crunching the bones. Lacy gripped him back. He could hear Lacy breathing beside him, steady, but Thad could feel how much he was holding himself back.

"I'm never going to meet a girl," he said, probably more affronted than he needed to be. "I'm in love with Lacy."

"You boys spend a lot of time together," his dad said, his tone reasonable. "You could be confused." He gave Thad a look and Thad knew he was implying Christian, his friend from school.

"I," Thad opened his mouth, closed it.

"He's not confused," Lacy said, his voice quiet but firm. "We ain't neither of us confused."

His dad sat up, his head shaking. "The church will never accept this," he said like he was speaking to himself.

"I know," Thad said, his heart breaking. "But I thought you would."

His dad rubbed his face and sighed. He stood and Thad and Lacy automatically stood with him, the chairs scraping on the floorboards.

Thad didn't know what was going to happen next. He felt like he'd been transported into a parallel universe. He didn't expect his dad to look past him and at Lacy.

"You're a great player, Lacy," his dad said and Thad almost laughed. "But we're not going to be able to accept this."

"Dad," Thad said pleadingly. He couldn't believe what he was hearing.

"I think you better go," his dad met his eyes briefly. It hurt him to say that, Thad could see it.

Lacy linked their fingers together.

"Dad, please," Thad said, his voice cracking.

"I need to check on your mother," he wouldn't meet Thad's eyes. As he walked out of the room all Thad could think was, he didn't mean that, of course he didn't mean that.

"C'mon," Lacy whispered.

Thad looked down at him. "But," he was lost.

"Hey," Lacy tugged on his hand, his gaze and voice never wavering. "We live to fight another day, alright? Let 'em let it sink in, we'll try again later, alright? It ain't over, they love you."

Thad nodded. "Okay, you're right. Okay."

He followed Lacy out of the house, the sunshine a shock to his eyes after the dim of his home. He felt like he wasn't in his body as he got in the passenger's seat and Lacy drove them out of there, the farmhouse shrinking in the distance in a puff of gravel.

38

SILENCE PERMEATED THEIR CAR as Lacy drove them back to the cottage, interspersed only by the clinical woman's voice on the GPS telling him where to go. He wound down the highway, the straw-coloured rolling hills dotted with sheep, flanked with the bush whipping by them as Thad shifted from complete stillness to bursts of movement like he was about to speak but then didn't. Lacy knew he needed a moment to gather himself. He'd had a bad feeling about it, but figured Thad knew his parents, figured he was just being paranoid.

His mind flashed with the look Thad' mum had given him—her warm features, so much like Thad's, turning so cold—and he'd thought, *Thad would never look at anyone like that, no matter what they were, no matter what they said.*

It'd taken a level of self-restraint to sit there and let them talk to Thad like that. But he knew telling them they were a fucking insult to the shit they preached would not have helped Thad, would have hurt him worse than he was already hurting, his big body hunched in the seat beside him, the sunlight and shadows whipping over his huddled form, his breathing loud.

"Come on," Lacy said once he'd turned the engine off. "It's gonna be alright."

Thad didn't say anything, which was when Lacy knew it was really bad.

They got inside and Lacy didn't know what to do. The door closed behind him with a thud and he wanted to reach out but he wasn't sure it'd be welcome.

It was Thad who turned and grabbed him in a fierce hug. Lacy clutched him back, his breathing going rough to match Thad's.

"I'm so sorry," Thad said, heartfelt.

"You've got nothin' to be sorry for," Lacy said vehemently into the skin of his neck. Thad was bending down to hold him. He lifted him and Lacy wrapped his legs around his waist. He always found it so fucking hot when Thad did that, and that was there now, but it was the unbelievable comfort it brought him that was more pronounced. He didn't realise until then that he'd been scared Thad wouldn't want him anymore. A nascent thought that hadn't fully bloomed, but he saw it'd been planted when he felt how much Thad still wanted him in the way he held him now, carried him into the bedroom.

Thad sat on the edge of the bed, tipped them back, shuffling up until they were wrapped around each other on their sides.

"I do," Thad said into his neck, "to put you through that, I should've known—"

"You shoulda known the people you love most in the world were goin' to act like that?"

Thad breathed into Lacy's neck and when he spoke, it was resigned. "You knew."

Lacy sighed, kissed Thad's throat. "I didn't know. I just wasn't sure. But I am sure they'll get over it."

Thad was already shaking his head. Lacy knew what he was picturing—that look his mum gave him.

"Do you want to go home?" Thad asked.

"I wanna do what you wanna do," Lacy replied. He pulled his head back and was surprised he felt afraid to look at Thad.

He shouldn't have been. Thad was waiting for him, his brown eyes sad, but fully there, the same look he'd been giving Lacy since they met still residing steadily in his gaze.

"Let's eat, sleep, regroup," Lacy said.

Thad brushed Lacy's hair behind his ear, traced his forefinger down his cheekbone. Lacy turned his face and pressed a kiss to his hand.

"Sex?" Thad asked with a faint smile.

Lacy huffed, nervous. "I'm always down to fuck," he said. "But are you sure?"

Thad pushed up onto his elbow, his hand coming to rest on Lacy's hip. "I'm sure about us. I know I'm right."

"Yeah, but, after all that—"

Thad shook him. "It doesn't change anything about us."

Lacy nodded, slipped his hand under Thad's shirt and stroked his stomach.

"Did you think I'd leave you if my parents didn't approve?" Thad asked.

It sounded like such an insane sentence. Who gave a shit about their parents' approval? Where he came from people like his mum got pregnant at sixteen and had an antagonistic relationship with her parents over it, but no one got to approve or disapprove. Everyone fucked up and got on with it.

But it mattered to people like Thad, which meant it mattered to Lacy.

"No," Lacy said slowly, unconvincingly. "I dunno."

Thad gripped his hip. Lacy wet his lips, his mouth suddenly too dry with Thad staring at him so intensely. The room was thick with their breathing, the sounds of nothing but nature chirping and bustling for miles outside. Lacy was relieved when Thad dropped his eyes to his hand, his face softening, rueful almost.

"I never want to be apart from you, not ever," he flicked his eyes up. "I can't ever imagine leaving you."

"Yeah, but," Lacy started, he needed to get these words out. "You mighta just lost your parents over it."

Thad's face flickered with pain, but he smiled anyway. "Thought we were gonna live to fight another day?" he parroted back in an imitation of his drawl and Lacy laughed.

Thad smiled and God, Lacy loved him. Even in the midst of his world falling apart, he wanted to make sure Lacy was okay. But Lacy wasn't going to let Thad not be okay. He resumed caressing under his shirt.

"I think they're just in shock, like," Lacy said, "they were so expectin' you to say you'd met a chick."

Thad frowned. "I just don't see how everyone thinks that. Where is this mysterious woman I'm supposed to be dating? I spend all my time with you."

Lacy rolled onto his side, cradled his head in his palm, dragged his other hand up Thad's side. "Don't take this the wrong way, but I don't reckon people in your world see the gay. They got like, gay blindness.

Even though you're not like," he made himself say it, "totally gay or whatever."

Thad quirked a smile. "I might be kind of gay for you."

Lacy chuckled. "Yeah, I'm gettin' that."

Thad sobered and Lacy braced for it. The reprieve couldn't last.

"I think, actually," Thad looked at his hand again, "I am homosexual."

Lacy exhaled slowly. Thad was squeezing and releasing his hand on Lacy's hip, his eyes distant.

"I just thought I was really good at celibacy," he said after a moment, "because I was never tempted by a woman. But umm," he met Lacy's eyes.

"But ya liked looking at guys?"

Thad blushed and Lacy hoped he never stopped doing that—no matter how many times they fucked, no matter how many times Thad watched him get fucked by other guys, he hoped Thad still got shy.

"Yes," he whispered. "And I had this friend…"

And Lacy listened as Thad told him about Christian, how he liked it when they sat pressed together, how they'd press their bodies together under the sleeping bag when they went camping, how he'd watch him get changed, how he'd explained it away to himself as admiring the male form, God's perfection.

"But I always wanted to do more," he finished wistfully. He re-focused on Lacy. "How about you?"

"Well, I ain't totally gay," Lacy said and leaned over to kiss him because the whole Christian story was getting him worked up.

Thad pulled back. "You're not?"

"Nah, bisexual, but like, ninety percent dudes," he shrugged, ran his hand up Thad's flat chest. "I've banged chicks, don't really like the typical thing. You know, pretty with big tits? But I can and have slept with 'em. But sometimes a real athletic woman or like, a butch chick?" he said and Thad nodded. "Yeah, I could be into that."

"I don't feel anything for any women," Thad said.

"Well, like I said, I'm way more into dudes. I'd always pick a dude over a woman," Lacy rolled Thad's nipple between his thumb and forefinger.

"One dude," Thad smiled and rolled Lacy under him, slotting his thighs over Lacy's so he could feel his hard on.

Lacy quirked his lips. "Yeah. I've only ever loved one dude."

Thad responded with a sure smile, rolled his hips down, his thigh rubbing Lacy's stiff cock.

"Me too," Thad said.

They kissed and rubbed off on each other until they came, a fragile feeling at the centre of something so very sure.

Lacy watched with simmering anger when Thad tried to call his parents and his mum hung up on him. That anger morphed into Thad's pain. He wished there was something he could do, but there wasn't.

They stayed in the cottage for two days, eating, taking a stroll around the property, fucking. Fucking with an edge of desperation that'd culminate in a sharp kind of intimacy—Thad holding him so close as Lacy came, kissing his throat, his ear, his collar bone, whispering into his skin how much he loved him, how beautiful he was. And Lacy would clench his ass muscles around Thad's dick, tell him how much he loved him too, how he loved to feel him inside, filthy and sappy shit he never thought he'd say. But as he bit it out against Thad's lips, felt Thad's choking breaths, he meant every word.

On the third day, Thad pulled him into his chest under the covers and said, "I want to go home."

"We can do that," Lacy said, sleepy. He reached for his phone to change their flight.

Back in Melbourne, Lacy stepped into the cool lines of his home and felt his shoulders loosen. He'd felt the tension easing from the moment the plane's wheels touched down on the runway.

"Lacy," Thad said from behind him.

Lacy turned. Thad was standing in the entryway, the enormous door still open behind him. His hand gripped and released on his case.

"Thad?"

"I can't go home."

"Not right now, maybe, but—"

"No," Thad shook his head, "my house, it's my family's house. I can't," he took a deep breath, "I can't live there anymore."

"Oh," Lacy said and wanted to scream at Thad's parents, but at least there was an easy solution. "Ya can just live here."

"I can't impose on you like that," Thad said.

And Lacy rolled his eyes and sauntered over to him. He slid his arms around his waist and looked up. Thad's arm came around his shoulders.

"Not really imposin' if you're my boyfriend, is it?"

Thad's eyes lit up. "I guess not." But there was sadness there too. He'd lost his parents and now he was losing his home.

There was no point dwelling on it though. "You wanna get your stuff now?"

"I better let my parents know..." he trailed off, lost. Because his parents wouldn't answer his calls. He leaned down and kissed Lacy on the forehead and extricated himself. "I'll just leave a message and then we can do it tomorrow. I think I need to," he waved a hand upstairs and Lacy figured he meant he needed to sleep or shower or fuck and Lacy was down for all three, so he said, "'Kay, I'll make some room in the closet," and he jogged upstairs to give Thad some privacy to leave his message. He couldn't make Thad's parents see what a colossal mistake they were making, but he could welcome Thad into his home with open arms and a wide-open bed.

In fact, he was fucking pumped about it. He was living with his boyfriend. He had a boyfriend. He smiled to himself as he started moving half his clothes into the wardrobe in the spare room.

39

THAD WAS STANDING IN his kitchen the following evening and debating whether or not he could take the slow cooker. The whole venture had been marked by similar questions. Technically nothing in the home was his and yet everything had always been his because it was theirs. His family's. But now he wasn't a member of the family. The thought carried too much to comprehend. He knew they'd get over it. How could they not get over it? They loved each other.

He decided to leave it and buy a new one. In the end, he only had two suitcases, his travel backpack with his bible and notebooks, his weights and yoga mat, and the framed picture of Jesus his grandfather had given him and he'd brought with him from home when he first went up to Queensland.

He'd declined Lacy's offer to help. He needed Lacy there like he needed to breathe, but he knew he needed to make himself do this part alone. And now he realised why—he was saying goodbye.

He stood in the quiet living room, remembering himself as a boy in here with his parents, his mum softly directing him how to assemble the Noah's Arc toy his grandfather had bought him as she'd chided her father for getting him gifts. But she'd smiled at him as he played, her face filled with joy.

His chest ached at the memory.

A key was turning in the front door. Thad moved into the hallway at the same time as his dad appeared, haloed by the last of the day's sunshine.

"Dad?" he asked. He couldn't hide his surprise, but he could hide the fear that washed over him.

"Thaddeus," his dad said and shut the door behind him.

Thad tensed as his dad walked down the hallway towards him. His dad stopped in front of him. They were the same height and it was easy to see how tired his dad's eyes looked, but his lips were curled up at the corners, a barely-there smile in an otherwise troubled face.

"I've got all my stuff. I'll leave the key in the meter box," he said.

"I got your message," his dad said because that was about the gist of the message. "There's no need to move out of the house."

Before Thad could object, his dad said, "Come on, let's have a cuppa."

He went by him and clapped Thad on the shoulder. Thad startled. He had thought his dad would never touch him again. He followed him into the kitchen and watched his dad move fluidly around the space, turning on the stove, filling the kettle, pulling out the mugs and the coffee. He opened the fridge.

"You've got no milk," he said.

"I've been at Lacy's," Thad replied.

His dad twitched at the name, but didn't say anything more than, "Hmm."

He went into the pantry and pulled out the lifelong milk Thad knew he hated.

They sat at the dining table, cups of coffee in front of them, the house cool and quiet around them save for the distant hum of the occasional car.

"Your mother doesn't know I'm here," he said, his rough voice so sudden in the room, it made Thad flinch. "She thinks I'm helping the Landos in Hobart."

The Landos were one of their oldest family friends. They had seven children, with Thad the same age as their eldest, Mary. Thad had once thought Mrs Lando heavily pregnant and surrounded by children would upset his mum since she only had one, but it never seemed to—his mum adored those kids, spent hours talking to Mrs Lando in their respective kitchens, then on the phone after the visit.

"What will you say when she finds out you weren't?" Thad asked.

"I'll deal with that then," his dad said and sipped his coffee. He winced. "Awful stuff."

"Sorry," Thad replied.

His dad sighed and set his mug on the table. "You don't need to move out of the house."

Thad looked at his coffee, the white bits floating on the top. "I think I do."

"Well, I'm telling you, you don't," he shifted in his seat. "It's your house too."

"Is it?" Thad met his eyes. "Does mum not want me to move out?"

His dad shifted again and looked away. "I'm saying you don't have to."

Thad couldn't hide how that hit him—he glanced away and had to blink a few times.

"It's fine, I can live with Lacy," he said reassuringly.

His dad blew out a breath. "Lacy's a good man," he said after a moment of nothing but their breathing filling the space. Thad knew he meant it even if it was now tinged with caution. "But it's important you have your own place. You can't be indebted to another man like that."

Thad looked at him again. So he knew Thad moving out meant moving in with Lacy.

"Is that why you've come? You don't want me living with him?" he asked.

"No," his dad said swiftly. "I want you to know this is your home, that we can give you a home."

"You," Thad said, "you want to give me her father's home. She doesn't."

His dad sat up and shook his head. "Semantics," he replied gruffly. "And that's not the only reason I came, I can see you thinking it. It's not. You're still my son."

"Am I hers?" he asked.

His dad hesitated and that pause contained all the pain Thad could possibly feel about it.

"Your mother is a pious woman," his dad said. "And I can't speak on her behalf. But I'm saying you're still my son. Besides, this is probably just a phase, boys get close, things get confused."

Thad laughed. He couldn't help it. His dad frowned at him.

Thad sobered. "I'm not confused."

He held eye contact and his dad studied him. His dad looked away first with a grunt that meant the conversation was over but not resolved.

Then something occurred to Thad. "It was her, wasn't it? When Aunt Celia came down, when I was born."

His dad raised both eyebrows like he didn't know Thad knew about that. He drank his coffee, shifted in his seat. Finally, he said, "She never would've forgiven me."

Thad thought about all those years of Aunt Celia despising his dad for choosing his religion over his wife's life when he refused lifesaving treatment that would also render his mum infertile. His dad bore her hatred stoically and never said a word. He also bore the way their congregation held him in such high esteem for that choice. But it hadn't been his choice. And looking at him now, he knew he would've saved her in a heartbeat.

"It doesn't matter now," his dad said. "What matters is this is your home and I would prefer it if you stayed here."

"And if I don't?"

His dad smiled and it was lighter than anything on his face since he walked through the door. "Then you don't," he shrugged, finished his coffee. "I just needed you to know this is still your home if you want it."

Thad tapped his forefinger on his mug. "I don't want to live here if she doesn't want me to."

His dad sighed like he was back there, stuck between a rock and a hard place. So Thad decided to tell him the whole truth.

"And I'd rather live with him," he focused on the table. "He's my boyfriend. I want to live with him."

His dad didn't say anything and Thad was scared to look up. It felt like an eternity when his dad stood. Thad looked up at him. He was smiling, an honest expression on his handsome face. He was only forty-five and the years had been kind to him, no doubt aided by not drinking, working a physical job.

"Keep the keys," he said, "sometimes you might need your own space. Space is good for," he faltered and flicked his eyes away, but his face remained happy, "partners." He said the word like he'd only just learned it. Thad had an image of him looking it up, in between thinking Thad might just be confused, he could picture him thinking maybe he wasn't, and he'd want to know the right words, what it meant to be a homosexual couple.

"Thank you," Thad said.

His dad met his eyes again. He leaned forward and Thad didn't flinch this time. His dad clapped him on the shoulder gave him a good shake.

He took his hand back and took his mug into the kitchen.

Thad was standing when he came back in.

"I better get going," he said. "Don't be a stranger."

Thad nodded because he didn't know what to say.

His dad left and Thad stood there, a small part of the pain in his chest dissolving.

Lacy was cradled between his thighs in the jacuzzi, his naked back resting on Thad's chest and stomach, hair fanning out on top of the water. He'd given Thad the biggest hug when he told him about his dad. "I'm so fuckin' glad, babe," he said over and over again, like he was as relieved as Thad was. It wasn't perfect, but it was something. His mum might never speak to him again, but his dad flying up and back, prepared to endure her wrath for it, well, it was something. It really was something.

"I'm going to have to leave the church," he murmured to Lacy now. He was running his hands up and down Lacy's chest under the water, pausing to rub his nipples between his thumb and forefinger before sliding down again and teasing the delicate skin of his groin.

Lacy looked over his shoulder. "Why? You love that shit."

Thad huffed a laugh. He was miserable over it, but Lacy always made everything lighter.

He kissed him, a brief press of lips. "Because," he said when he pulled back, "it's going to come out. Not the details, but it'll be apparent something has happened when I don't come home for Christmas, for New Year's, for," he shrugged, "everything."

"So? What's that got to do with the church you go to here?" Lacy turned in his hold and went to push away to the other side.

Thad snaked his arm around him and hauled him into his lap. Lacy wrapped his legs around him.

"My mum will tell the leaders," he said, and it pained him to imagine her calling the meeting. But she would. She'd insist his dad do it actually and she'd insist they both go. "She'll inform them that I've fallen," he shrugged like it didn't matter and he was trying hard to hold onto the part of himself that wanted to resent them for it—a life of service and he would be cast out for loving another man. "And that will be reported to my congregation here. It's better if I leave quietly on my own. Otherwise, they'll call me in, and I'm not telling them my business."

Lacy's eyes were whiskey-clear as they flicked back and forth on Thad's, propped higher with Thad's hands cupping his ass.

"That's fucked up. That's like, seriously fucked up," Lacy said. "What the fuck is wrong with them? Ya didn't do anything wrong."

"I know," Thad said. "I really know that now. But they won't see it that way. And if I leave of my own accord then they won't have any reason to find out the truth."

Lacy dropped his eyes to Thad's collar bones. "I feel like I've ruined your life."

Thad clenched his hands on Lacy's ass. "No, this is who I am."

"Yeah, but—"

"No, I was always this, you just gave me a reason, the best reason, to be honest about it," Thad loosened his hold and caressed Lacy's skin.

"Yeah, but, you love goin' to church," Lacy said.

"Do you remember what you said when we were at the bath house in Rome?" Thad asked.

"I reckon I said a lotta shit at the bath house in Rome," Lacy snickered.

Thad smiled and kissed him. Lacy had, indeed, said a lot of shit in the bath house in Rome. It had been intense, beautiful, making love to Lacy on the benches beside ancient columns, the water lapping nearby, the neon lights adding a modern club vibe to the medieval space. He'd shared Lacy with men that night, watched him writhe in ecstasy, his eyes never leaving Thad's as slick bodies took him roughly from behind before Thad drew him away and into the water, held him as he went lax, came down and babbled, "This is my church," with a slurred laugh.

Thad had brushed his hair back and kissed his forehead. He knew Lacy was making the joke with reference to the Vatican not a stone's throw away. Had heard Lacy make a similar joke on the football field. Hordes of screaming fans shouting his name, he'd raise his arms and wink at Thad as he delivered the line. There was no mockery in it, he was just making a point about worship. Thad had thought about it again since he left his family home and he'd known, even then, what it meant, that he could never put his parents through a public coming out, a public shaming in the church.

What did it mean to worship? Because Lacy was right, he did love church. Felt at peace there, felt it was the place he could be closest to God, to honour him by stopping what else he was doing and simply be in His presence.

"You said," he smiled up at Lacy, "this is my church."

Lacy grinned. "I reckon I was just messin' around."

"I know, but, maybe it doesn't have to be a building, a place that would throw me out for loving you," Thad said.

Lacy shook his head. "I'm just so fuckin' sorry."

"I'm not," Thad smiled and he felt free. "Loving you? Any place that says that's not okay is not my church."

"Maybe we can build our own church," Lacy said.

Thad chuckled. "Let's not get too carried away."

"What? It could be a gay church with like, orgies and stuff."

Thad dropped his head on Lacy's chest to hide his laughter.

Lacy carded his hand through his hair. "For what it's worth? I reckon this is my church."

"What is?" Thad said against his skin.

"You and me," Lacy murmured.

"Pretty small congregation," Thad replied.

"Eh, we can have some hotties come in every now and then."

Thad tightened his arms, felt his dick pulse. He knew Lacy felt it too.

"Ya know, for a church boy," Lacy tugged on his hair. Thad looked up. "You're about the filthiest dude I ever met."

Thad blushed, but he leaned up and whispered his reply against Lacy's lips. "I am, but just for you."

Epilogue

♥

L ACY GRABBED THE MAIL as he headed in from training, the new place in Prahran he'd bought with Thad over the summer glowing with all the lights on in front of him. After two years in the Fitzroy place and with the club deciding not to renew Thad's contract at the end of the last season, they'd decided to move, get a bit more privacy and a place with a garage for Thad's work ute.

He'd almost fallen over when Thad told him he was a carpenter.

"How in the fuck? How did I not know this?" Lacy asked.

"How did you think I was building those schools?" Thad replied, bemused.

"Oh my God, Thad," Lacy grabbed his arm. "Did you become a carpenter because Jesus was?"

"How do you know Jesus was a carpenter?" Thad replied and rubbed the back of his neck. "And, yes, maybe. Did the apprenticeship out of school before I got drafted."

Lacy howled with laughter while Thad smiled down at him losing it, his blush rising.

"Fuck, that's hot though. Do you have like, a tradie outfit you're gonna wear?" Lacy could picture it—Thad coming home from work in nothing but overalls, his bare chest under the straps all sweaty.

"Umm, yes?" Thad replied, bewildered.

Lacy was planning on having a lot of fun with that. He'd been heartbroken, more even than Thad, when they didn't renew. Thad got an offer from Port Adelaide, a pretty shitty offer, but it was still an offer. Lacy did his best to be the supportive boyfriend, "It's still the league, you'd still get to play," he'd said, smothering the ache in his chest at the thought of Thad moving to fucking Adelaide.

But Thad simply raised both eyebrows, baffled by what Lacy was saying. "I'm not leaving you," he'd said simply. "I can get a job, start a business here."

"Business? What kinda business?"

"A carpentry business," Thad said. "I'm a carpenter."

Which led to Lacy losing it, though to be fair, part of his hysterics was probably down to sheer relief.

"Hey, babe!" he called out as he came inside.

"In the kitchen," Thad called back.

Lacy kicked his shoes off, strolled down the passageway and found Thad in front of the bench, chopping tomatoes, his face lighting up with a smile under the fall of his hair in his eyes as he looked up.

"Hi," he said. "How was training?"

"Same old shit," Lacy replied and came around the bench, leaned up as Thad bent to kiss him. He smelled so good—Lacy's eucalyptus soap, deodorant on clean skin that still lingered with the sweat from work—and he looked great in his after-work clothes, faded jeans, a white shirt and bare feet, and his mouth tasted minty.

Lacy rested his hand on his low back, rubbed circles there before breaking the kiss to see what Thad was cooking.

"Italian?"

"I will master it," Thad said.

Lacy grinned. "I reckon it already tastes pretty fuckin' great, but I ain't objecting to more research."

They'd made a thing of it, going to all the Italian restaurants in Melbourne so Thad could study the flavours and try to replicate with recipes in their kitchen. He had his business, the cooking, he'd started going to an Anglican service on Sundays, still ran the youth footy and did the outreach with Stacy and Glen. Carol never turned up again, which Lacy was sorry about for Thad's sake, but Thad merely shrugged. "It's better to know who your real friends are."

His projection for how it would go—"Thaddeus Clay has fallen" doing the rounds in the congregation—were accurate, and while Lacy's heart broke for him, Thad bore it stoically until one night he sat up on the couch back in the Fitzroy place, grabbed Lacy's hand and started apologising.

"What've you got to be sorry for?" Lacy had asked, taken aback. He'd been in a post-orgasm glow, enjoying Thad's hand running up and down his spine while he cursed Juventus' inability to score.

"We can't come out," he'd said, crestfallen. "At least not until—"

That got Lacy to sit right up, yanking his trackies back up his thighs and over his ass as he moved. He felt like he needed his dick back in his pants for this conversation. "Come out? You wanna come out as gay?"

"Don't you?"

"Uh, no," Lacy replied.

"But, George and Finn, they had a wedding, they have a kid, they can be together in public. But I can't, I can't put my parents through that and I didn't think about you. I've only been thinking about me," Thad said.

"Thad, babe," Lacy squeezed his hand and tugged him back down. "Ya reckon I wanna go public given what else we get up to? If we go shining the spotlight on ourselves, well, people could think it's alright to talk. Besides," he moved Thad's hand back to his spine as he sprawled over his lap, "I ain't as much of an attention-whore as those two. Contrary to popular opinion. You're good, we're good."

Thad resumed stroking his back. "If you're sure," Thad said. "But if you ever change your mind or it comes out, then I'll... It'll be okay."

Lacy was pretty sure it'd become an open secret at this point—how many dudes lived together, bought a house together, had a weekly tennis date together, did absolutely everything together, never had a woman even remotely in the picture and could still be considered 're-ally good friends'? But until someone straight up asked, they weren't telling. It was nobody else's business.

Lacy went around the bench and perched on a stool, flicked through the mail.

There was a letter for Thad with nice hand-writing.

"For you," he held it up.

Thad looked up and froze. He placed the knife down, wiped his hands carefully on the tea towel tucked into his jeans and reached for it.

"That's my mum's hand writing," he said.

"Oh," Lacy felt hope rise in his chest. He knew Thad missed her, knew it was a hole in his life nothing could ever fill.

Thad took it like it was something precious and stared at it.

Lacy hoped to a God he'd never believe in it was a nice letter.

Thad opened it with a gentle slide of his little finger under the back and pulled out what looked like a pamphlet. His eyes scanned it quickly, then he pulled out a white folded note and slid the pamphlet under it. He smiled, a very small curl of his lips and met Lacy's eyes.

"She got in touch," he said.

"What is it?" Lacy asked, exhaling.

Thad handed him the pamphlet.

Lacy read it and the more he read, the more he frowned. It was all about repenting and turning back to God, there was still time, you could be saved. The only relief he found once he finished reading was that it wasn't anti-gay, specifically.

He looked up.

"She said she's praying for me," Thad handed him the note. He was still smiling.

Lacy read the note and that was all it said, signed off, "Yours, Mum."

He handed it back. He wasn't sure there was much to rejoice about, she couldn't have said more? She couldn't have mentioned how her son was the greatest fucking guy in the world and she was lucky to have created him?

But Thad looked so touched, he couldn't bring himself to say any of that.

"She got in touch," he said again and nodded, smiled brightly at Lacy. "It's a step."

"It is, yeah," Lacy returned the smile. "She'll get there," he said because he wasn't sure what else to say.

"She really might," Thad replied and went back to cooking, humming to the playlist he had strumming through the house's speakers.

He saw his dad every month or so. Lacy had welcomed him into the Fitzroy place on several occasions, heard how he was at odds with his wife over these visits. But Thad's dad had said, "She's going to have to deal with this one." And it made Thad so happy every time he came, which made Lacy happy because Thad was happy. Plus, he was an alright bloke, Thad's dad, dry sense of humour, quietly supportive of his boy, and so proud of him it confused Lacy when he saw how much he tried to tamp it down.

Nevertheless, Thad put up with Lacy's mum, so he wasn't about to get all judgemental on Thad's family. When Lacy informed her Thad was his boyfriend, his mum put Lacy's misery together pretty quickly and straight up froze Thad out. They had dinner and his mum didn't even speak to him, not once. Until Lacy cornered her in the kitchen and told her, "If you don't stop it, I ain't ever comin' round again."

"He deserves a bit of it," she said and lit a cigarette. "And you'll be comin', don't be ridiculous."

"I won't," he stared her down. "I'm not even fuckin' kiddin', be nice to him or I'm out."

She twisted her lips to the side and studied him. "I reckon I just figured out which one your dad was."

Lacy rolled his eyes. She played this game whenever he held a certain look. Or when she didn't want to deal with what was right in front of her.

"Are ya gonna cut it out?" he asked her.

She took a drag, blew the smoke to the side away from him. "You're that serious about him," she said like it was funny, her eyes canting to the side, mocking him.

He continued to stare at her.

She shot out an annoyed breath. "Alright, alright, I was just messin' him around for messin' you around."

"I can handle my shit. What I can't handle is anyone fuckin' with my boyfriend," he said.

She turned on the tap, ran it over the top of the cigarette. "Understood," she glanced at him, her smile amused. "I knew you'd be a loyal one."

Lacy jerked his chin and returned to Thad on the patio. Thad was copping it from his own family and Lacy was not going to allow him to cop it anywhere else.

"Everything alright?" Thad asked, his eyes unsure. How he'd managed to remain polite was beyond Lacy. He would've left.

"Thad, would you like dessert? Coffee?" his mum asked from the kitchen door in a grand voice.

Thad looked surprised that she'd addressed him. "Yes, please, thank you. I can help," he went to stand.

"No, no, I'll get it, you just sit there and look pretty," she said with an exaggerated smile and went back inside.

Thad sat and looked at Lacy as he did, still uncertain.

"It's gonna be one of those hideous sponge cakes," Lacy said. "Ya don't have to eat it."

"I'm sure it'll be great," Thad replied, smiling a little breathlessly.

The evening was quiet around them, the ocean breaking on the cliffs a dull sound from below where they were perched on the decking. His mum might've refused to leave Frankston when Lacy offered to buy her a house, but she had insisted on getting out of East Frankston, selecting an ocean-facing property that she could parade in front of her friends. It was a small place, one of the older joints, but the price tag was down to the location and the sight of Melbourne across the bay, twinkling with its city lights.

Lacy snorted, took Thad's hand and squeezed. "It won't, but I appreciate you tryin' here. She's gonna drop it," he finished, voice low.

"I deserve it," Thad said quickly like he'd been waiting all night to say it.

"No," Lacy said firmly. "Ya don't."

Thad smiled his easy-going smile, his brown eyes fond on Lacy's face. "I deserve some punishment for what I did," he squeezed Lacy's hand, "it's fine."

Lacy didn't get to answer, his mum reappearing with a store-bought sponge cake and cups of coffee on a tray that looked precarious in her half-drunk hands. Thad stood to help her and she waved him off, gritted through exaggerated pleasantries and politeness for the remainder of the night.

Thad had barely gotten out of her driveway when Lacy pounced. "I don't want you goin' through the rest of our lives thinkin' I'm still mad about all that shit."

The steering wheel spun smoothly against Thad's hand as he straightened the car, but he jerked slightly at Lacy's words. He flicked his eyes to the rearview mirror to check the dark winding road for an oncoming set of lights before accelerating onto the road. Lacy watched his chest rise and fall.

"I don't think you're mad," he said once they stopped at a red light.

"Good," Lacy said.

"But I did hurt you. And I wish," he glanced at Lacy, the light changing to green washed over Thad's face, made his cheeks look sharper, the sockets of his eyes deeper, "I wish I had been braver sooner, spared you that."

"Yeah, well, then I went and hurt ya back, so we're all good, eh?"

"Eye for an eye?" Thad smiled over at him, the road empty in front of them as he navigated them back to the highway.

"Exactly."

"Makes the whole world blind," Thad said. "So, I'm sorry."

"Me too," Lacy replied and snagged Thad's hand on the console. He didn't reckon he'd ever get tired of being able to touch Thad, reach for him, feel the soft part of his palm against his own.

"Does mutual forgiveness make the whole world see?" he asked after they'd been driving down the highway for a while, the pleasant hum of the tyres sliding on the bitumen lulling the inside of the car into contented quiet.

Thad chuckled, glanced over, his brown eyes twinkling. "Are you sure you're not religious?"

"Get ya hand off it," Lacy laughed.

His mum was fine after that. She just had to throw her weight around like a statement, a way to let Thad know he was being watched, he'd hurt her boy and she wouldn't forget. It was as much an act for her sake as for Lacy's—her inconsistent care for what him and Parks got up to, got hurt by, when they were kids, made this kind of behaviour impossible to see as anything but for her own benefit, but Lacy believed she wanted to care about it, which was something. Problem was, they'd done without it as kids, so it was pointless her pretending now he was an adult. And he'd never let anyone disrespect Thad, he didn't care who they were.

"Ya sure you're all good?" he asked later that night after they'd eaten Thad's Sicilian-style grilled tuna steaks, Sicilian cauliflower salad and Sicilian anchovy pasta (Naples was next on the agenda, Thad explained over dinner).

Thad looked down from his book. Lacy was sprawled on his chest, scrolling through his phone while Thad read another tome on homosexuality and Christianity.

"I'm great," Thad smiled. "Are you?"

"Perfect, I just meant 'cos of your mum," Lacy replied.

Thad set the book down. "I'm really happy she reached out."

Lacy nodded. "Alright, well, so long as you're good."

Thad carded his fingers through Lacy's hair. "I am," he murmured.

Lacy nodded, returned his head down to nuzzle his face into the material at Thad's groin.

"There was another letter," he said as he blew a hot breath over Thad's dick.

Thad clenched his hand in Lacy's hair. "What letter?"

Lacy mouthed around the outline of Thad's dick. "A party."

Thad groaned and rolled his hips up.

"You wanna go?" Lacy flicked his eyes up, kept pressing his mouth against his length.

"Definitely," Thad breathed out.

Lacy laughed, but before he could get Thad's dick out, Thad was hauling him up, kissing him and rolling him under his body, pawing at his clothes to get to his skin.

"Why are you wearing clothes?" he asked as he shoved his shirt up and kissed his chest.

"Because I ain't a heathen," Lacy replied, his hands running through Thad's hair. "Party's this weekend."

Thad groaned and tugged Lacy's pants off.

"Yeah? That gettin' you hot, babe? Thinkin' about all the guys you're gonna share me with?" Lacy teased as he rolled his hips up to help.

Thad stroked both hands between Lacy's bare thighs to spread his legs.

"What gets me hot," he said as he caressed him, kissed him, broke away to speak. "Is knowing you'll always be with me after."

"Yeah, babe, I will," Lacy said. He never could've pictured himself as one of these guys—these guys who said sappy shit and lost their train of thought when their guy looked at them.

"It still makes me jealous," Thad said quietly between kisses as his fingers teased Lacy's hole, "but it'd be worse if you went home with one of them, let them cook for you, kiss you, sleep beside you."

He pushed a dry finger inside and Lacy arched. "Never gonna let anyone else cook for me."

"Good," Thad said and kissed him.

As Thad fumbled for the lube on the bedside table, Lacy pondered whether or not to call Colton beforehand. He'd finished preseason training, the summer stretching before them, freedom from the drug tests on the horizon. He'd quit using during the season after Thad moved in.

"It's not 'cos I'm worried about my health," he'd explained to Thad after training one day, though the comedowns were getting worse.

"And it's not 'cos of the tests," he went on, which wasn't entirely true either—he didn't want to keep putting Thad in that position. "Well, it's kinda 'cos of you and the tests," he clarified.

"I don't—"

"No, I know ya don't mind," Lacy continued, letting his pinkie finger link with Thad's as they walked into the carpark at the stadium. "But like, I don't reckon I need it as much anymore."

And that was the whole truth. Since Thad had moved in, since they got on the same page, his need to unwind by losing consciousness in a haze of booze and sex had diminished. Thad knew everything about him, Thad was always there—happy and available to talk, to let Lacy lose himself under Thad's touch for as long he needed.

"And well," Lacy looked up. Thad met his gaze, his brown eyes warm. "I kinda regret not remembering that first time."

Thad's eyes widened, a blush crept up his neck and his mouth opened but he didn't say anything.

They got in Thad's car and Lacy regretted saying it. It was probably a harrowing memory for Thad, losing his virginity at a gangbang, Lacy out of his mind—

His thoughts crashed to a halt when Thad's hand snaked behind his head and he kissed him; a quick, punishing kiss right there in the stadium carpark. He pulled back just as suddenly, leaving only his hand on Lacy's nape.

He was flushed, but his voice was steady when he spoke. "Would you like me to show you what happened?"

"You mean like, re-enact it?" Lacy asked, breathless.

Thad squeezed his fingers lightly on Lacy's neck. "Yes."

"Yeah, yeah," Lacy nodded. "Fuck yeah."

Lacy remembered that night now as Thad worked him open with slick fingers, kissed his throat, under his ear, his hard dick sliding against Lacy's, remembered the explicit details and the nervous lilt to Thad's voice as he narrated how special it'd been to kiss Lacy for the first time.

Lacy moaned and found Thad's mouth, his kisses frantic as Thad pushed inside.

After, Lacy was face down on the bed, panting, Thad's come dribbling down his thighs, Thad's hand rubbing up and down his back.

"It's got a costume theme," Lacy slurred.

"The party?" Thad asked.

"Yeah, masks and shit," Lacy replied. "I was thinkin' of goin' as the devil."

Thad chuckled. "I guess I better go as a saint then."

Lacy rolled his head to the side. Thad was smiling, pleased with himself.

"After what ya just did to my ass?" Lacy grinned. "You ain't no saint."

Thad blushed. "And you're no devil."

Lacy smiled and let his eyes slip closed. Thad kissed the top of his spine and Lacy listened to him moving around the bathroom, getting a wash cloth, coming back and cleaning Lacy up with gentle hands as Lacy drifted off to the feel of Thad's fingers on his skin, his mind toying with masks and costumes, Thad in a white suit, bare chested, Lacy beside him in red hot pants. He smiled. It was going to be a great party.

Acknowledgements

First and foremost, my Street Team! Their generosity and our bi-weekly chats made me feel so excited for this book; I truly hope it lives up to their energy. To the handful of readers on my mailing list who emailed their thoughts—thank you, these messages are often inspiring and frequently hilarious. And to my Beta Team: Ana, Donatella, KP, and DF—these four read my work in record time, take the job seriously and offer cogent insights that make every book better, and this one was no exception. I must also acknowledge Anthony Venn-Brown's memoir, *A Life of Unlearning: A Preacher's Struggle With His Homosexuality, Church and Faith*. This book provided significant insight into the specificities of the conflicts, both internal and external, a religious man must endure if he is gay. As always, my editor, Kath, for a thorough edit, and Maria at Steamy Designs for the beautiful cover. Finally, my precious galah, my best little mate, Monster. This one's for you little man.

About Author

Sasha Avice is the author of nine novels (and counting!) and one PhD (which is enough). She lives with a changing cast of birds and a dog. When she's not writing or teaching, she's fostering birds. She loves hearing from readers! Email direct at sasha@sashaavice.com or join her mailing list at sashaavice.com for regular updates.

Also By

Contested Possession

"... possession is achieved as a result of winning a contest." *Australian rules football*.

Each book features a football player whose possession of the guy he wants is... contested.

Shop now at Amazon.com for current books and future releases in this series.
Bonus Scenes available at sashaavice.com

His Boyfriend's Rookie

A Contested Possession Novel

How far would you go to keep your boyfriend?

This is the debut season of the second greatest rookie of all time: Finnegan Flynn.

This is the season the greatest rookie of all time, George Creed, takes his position in history as the youngest person ever to coach a league team.

And this is the season Head of Stadium Security, Joaquin Nord, watches his boyfriend, the deeply closeted coach, fall in love with his superstar rookie...

Joaquin watches this mutual attraction unfold with patient horror, certain his boyfriend will get over his crush. But a moment of aching intimacy caught on camera forces him to intervene.

Will his desperate act of sabotage be enough? Or will it cement George and Finn as the first in Australian Football history at something else?

Available at Amazon.com

Because He's My Guy

A Contested Possession Novel

He's been in an open relationship for twelve years
He's never touched another guy...
Until him.

George Creed will soon debut as the youngest coach in Australian
Football history.
He's excited, he's nervous.
He's more obsessed with meeting his new rookie.

Finnegan Flynn is finally joining the team after being sidelined with
injury for two seasons. As the number one draft pick, he's got a lot to
prove.
He's more obsessed with meeting his new coach—his footy idol and
teenage crush.

When George invites Finn over for dinner, Finn suspects they're about
to take their budding attraction to the next level. Until he meets
George's boyfriend, Joaquin.

Finn is crushed, but George explains he's in an open relationship.
Except George doesn't do open, he's a one man kind of guy.

Finn is utterly confused: if George doesn't do open, why tell him?

Because George isn't open, until he meets Finn.

But if George is a one man kind of guy, then whose guy is he?

The second novel in the *Contested Possession* series, *Because He's My Guy* is *His Boyfriend's Rookie* according to George and Finn. Each novel stands alone.

Available at Amazon.com

Perimeter

Set in Western Australia at the turn of the millennium, each book is a standalone featuring guys who don't want love, don't seek it.

They drift, they work... and then some guy turns up and the dull isolation goes bright, blinds them like a splinter of sun caught in the eyes.

Shop now at Amazon.com for current books and future releases in this series.

A snippet from the Sasha Avice newsletter...

An interview with Lacy & Thad:

Me: Lacy, your book is releasing today and so far people have really liked it, do you have any idea why?

Lacy: What book? A footy book? Thad!

[Footsteps approaching]

Thad: Lacy? Is everything alright?

Lacy: Do you know anything about a book I did?

Thad: Did you write a footy book?

Me: No, it's a romance. About you two. Well, there's some footy in there, but it's mainly about how you two met, became friends, became... more than friends.

[Thad sits down heavily on the couch next to Lacy]

Thad: Is it a sex book?

Lacy: *[scoffs]* Of course it's not a sex book, I got NDAs all over the place. It's not a sex book, right?

Me: Umm, well, you two do have sex...

Thad: *[crossing himself]* Dear God...

Lacy: *[grabbing Thad's hand]* Just us with each other though, right?

Me: Well, no... But it's all very romantic.

Thad: *[laughing hysterically]* I'm sure the romance will make it much better for my parents to stomach.

Lacy: Shit, babe—

Thad: But *[sobering, looking at Lacy]* if it's me and Lacy, what's there to be ashamed about?

Lacy: *[squeezes Thad's hand]*: But you don't want people to know about...

Thad: If everyone finds out how much I love you? How could that ever be a bad thing?

sashaavice.com